He was with the Asantehene for five years, by which time he had reached the Civil Service retirement age of sixty. He then decided that enough was enough. He left to devote the rest of his life to reading, writing and gardening. He has four other unpublished works.

I0647212

THOUGHTS OF A CLUELESS MIND

JOSEPH OWUSU-ANSAH

Published 2008 by arima publishing

www.arimapublishing.com

ISBN 978 1 84549 327 1

Printed and bound in the United Kingdom

Typeset in Garamond 11/14

Swirl is an imprint of arima publishing.

arima publishing
ASK House, Northgate Avenue
Bury St Edmunds, Suffolk IP32 6BB
t: (+44) 01284 700321
www.arimapublishing.com

CONTENTS

FOREWORD
By Dr Stephen N. Gyamfi
(Seidersdorf Research Centre, Vienna, Austria)

This is a novel that deserves to be read not only by black men everywhere, but also by men and women of every race, based as it is on a theme of universal interest – the theme of racial denigration, which we may simply refer to as Racism.

All throughout the history of man, racism has been the bane of this world. Whenever one nation has succeeded in acquiring material superiority over others, whether by war or by partial triumph over natural forces, that nation has tended to consider itself superior in every way and to look down upon, and treat with contempt, those they now consider as inferior.

This has always led to resentment and hatred which has often erupted into conflict. The ancient Greeks did this when they succeeded in gaining material advantage over the nations around them, calling everyone else a "barbarian". The Romans did the same when they also gained ascendancy over parts of Europe and the Mediterranean region by means of military superiority.

In our own generation, the Germans, having attained to a very high degree of scientific and technological proficiency especially in the art of war, claimed to be the superior race, forgetting that many years ago their ancestors were among the fierce savages from the North who invaded Rome and over-threw the Roman Empire. Fortunately for the rest of mankind the Americans cannot claim to be the superior race, since they do not form a racial group, otherwise, having been the first to tread on the moon they would have said that they are the only ones whose heads are filled with brains, the rest of mankind having only hollow skulls. How ridiculous can human beings be in claiming intelligence for themselves and empty heads for others whenever they have succeeded in achieving material superiority through inventions.

In our own times the inhuman phenomenon of slavery and subsequent colonialism, which retarded the Blackman material progress and reduced him to a position of material inferiority, while further promoting western material superiority, known as "Western Civilisation", have deprived the Blackmans of respect and esteem in the eyes of the rest of mankind, so that no matter how great his abilities and intrinsic qualities he is underestimated by the rest of the world. The adverse image of the Blackman has, no doubt, been exacerbated by the often lurid and fictitious accounts of grim conditions on the African continent brought home by white travellers for the entertainment and ready consumption of their untravelled compatriots.

In this connection Dr Wiseman's apology is as it should be.

The author is commended for bringing into the open for dispassionate discussion this century – old phenomenon of racism. He has managed to do this without acrimony and without offence by wrapping it all up in a story replete with humour.

The story has no readily noticeable flaws. The highly sophisticated language in which Kotodro, the hero of the story, sometimes expresses himself in spite of his tender age and illiteracy; the very adult and mature sentiments which often characterise his conversation, the rather unimaginative way in which the over-intelligent Dr Wiseman frequently behaves, and the deliberate exaggerations that often characterise the accounts of incidents, may all be said to over-stretch our credulity somewhat. But these traits could have been considered flaws only in a book of factual information, not in a fiction, the primary purpose of which is to entertain and possibly generate discussion, but not to instruct. If anything, these exaggerations only heighten, not diminish our enjoyment of the story.

As a novel the book is replete with humour, wit, philosophy and beauty of expression – not always found in a story produced from one's imagination. The author has definitely written a first-class novel. It is very interesting all the way. You cannot put it down until you have finished reading it.

INTRODUCTION

This is a satirical novel, the characters in which are purely imaginary, so that any resemblance to any person of group of persons living or dead is purely accidental.

Its main aim is to make fun of the Whiteman's misconceptions about the Blackman while not entirely sparing the latter. It was provoked by a speaker on the BBC African Service (presumably white) who pronounced with an amazing degree of confidence that of all the "races" of this world the Black African "Race" is the least intelligent.

This bold assertion at once brought back to my mind the things that were said of the Blackman by the white colonialists in the days of Africa's colonial dependence. It was said, for example, that the Blackman was not only unintelligent but also dirty, smelly, lazy, dishonest, cowardly, childish, superstitious, ignorant and everything that was anything but complimentary.

Such assertions were freely and openly bandied about by the colonialists and even appeared in their books on Geography, Sociology, Economics and other branches of learning. Nay, a certain autobiographer even went to the extent of declaring that the Blackman was sub-human!

After Africa's independence, however, these derogatory remarks ceased to be made openly. Obviously it would have been diplomatically, if not politically and even economically indiscreet to have continued to make such assertions about people who were now free and able to react effectively to such insults.

It came as a surprise to me, therefore, when I heard this assertion repeated in this day and age, when the Blackman had demonstrated in all spheres of human life and endeavour that he is no different from any other "race".

I decided therefore to write a rejoinder. But on reflection it occurred to me that any such rejoinder might not be read; or, even if read, might not make any impact. So I decided to write instead a story in which an African boy would be made to demonstrate that he (and by extension his "race") was as good as any other "race"; and that the material achievements from which others claim superiority could not provide adequate grounds for their claim.

It was not expected, of course, that the story would, by itself, prove or disprove anything. Nevertheless it is hoped that, based as it is on real human situations, it will not only provide some entertainment to the reader, but it will also draw attention to the age-old misconception of "races".

To me there is only one race – the Human Race. It is multi-coloured; and, like the rainbow, none of its colours can be said to be superior or inferior in any way to the others.

The Author

CHAPTER ONE
KOTOKRO GOES TO LONDON

Dr. John Alexander Scantiberry Wiseman was a very learned man, not only in his own conceit but also by universal acclaim. It was said that he knew almost everything, from the number of stars in the sky to the psychology of a louse, and that what he did not know was not worth knowing. His special field, however, was anthropology, that branch of science which, in theory, is supposed to be concerned with the study of all mankind, but which in practice is devoted almost exclusively to research into the lives and cultures of "primitive" people.

He had set up an Anthropological Research Centre at No. 13 Baron street, London, N.W.6, with endowments from the Dick Robinson and other foundations. There he carried on his research into the origins, growth and development of the Negro Race. It was a large three-storied building, the top floor of which consisted of four large apartments, occupied by the Doctor himself and his family, as well as by his three Research Assistants, namely Dr. Springfield, Mr. Balmer and Mr. Suppercot. The remaining three of his six research Assistants occupied the second floor, together with Mrs. Casely, Dr. Wiseman's house-keeper, and Mr. Oblong, the handyman.

The ground floor was divided into a library, a museum, a research laboratory, a Conference hall, Dr. Wiseman's Office and a Reception Room. In the library could be found almost every book or document that had ever been written on the subject of anthropology, not only in English, but also in French, German, Portuguese, Spanish and Dutch. Dr. Wiseman could read them all, for he was a great polyglot as well.

The museum contained all sorts of "primitive" artefacts, including "grotesque" carvings and "bizarre" painting, as well as crude utensils, instruments and implements and replicas of barbaric dwellings, all of which were said to have come from Africa.

One evening, in July 1969, Dr. Wiseman sat in his study overlooking the street below. He watched the long procession of motor vehicles plying up and down like endless columns of soldiers-ants conveying fodder from a distant field into an underground cellar. From where he sat he could also see the railway line at a distance, along which a train came speeding from time to time, meandering its way like a giant millipede. As he watched these with interest his attention was now and again distracted by a deep rumbling in the sky like the sound of thunder. Then he would look up and see an aeroplane gliding overhead like a monstrous eagle circling over an unwary prey.

All these scenes of activity produced by man-made machines produced a most exhilarating effect upon the mind of Dr. Wiseman. He felt very happy and proud of his country's achievements, of the achievements of his race. "What a great and wonderful people we are" he said to himself.

Suddenly Dr. Wiseman heard his wife calling him. He answered, but it seemed as if Mrs. Wiseman did not hear, for she continued to call. "Where are you, John, where are you?" She repeated again and again.

Dr. Wiseman quickly made for the television room from where his wife's voice was issuing.

"Why what's the matter?", he asked as soon as he entered and saw her sitting there with eyes glued to the Television.

"Look, John, look" was all she said, pointing to the pictures on the screen.

Dr. Wiseman looked. He saw what was going on, but could not immediately comprehend what it was all about.

"What is it?", he asked.

"It's the Americans", she replied. "Neil Armstrong and his crew mate, Edwin Aldrin, in the Apollo II have touched down on the moon with their space-craft."

Dr. Wiseman looked with amazement. He saw Edwin Aldrin climbing down the ladder from the lunar module. When he touched down he seemed to be hovering close to the ground as he tried to walk. It was a breath-taking spectacle.

"Great! Capital! Superb achievement", exclaimed Dr. Wiseman, scarcely able to contain himself with excitement. "This is the beginning of our conquest of space."

"What does that mean, daddy?" asked Dr. Wiseman's five year old son, Tommy, who had been squatting on the carpet cross-legged, quite close to the TV and was gazing intently upon the scenes that were being enacted on the screen but was unable to understand what it was all about.

"It means that we shall henceforth be able to explore the stars and the solar systems and unravel all the secrets of nature", he explained.

"Is that so, mummy?" asked Tommy, turning to his mother for confirmation.

"Yes dear", she confirmed.

"Then you and daddy won't die and we shall all live happily for ever?" asked Tommy again.

"No, not that", replied his father.

"But what", Tommy persisted.

"It's something more than that."

"What is it?"

"You won't understand now. You will understand when you grow up", he assured him.

"Ah, I wish I could grow up now", said Tommy with a sigh. Then turning to his father he asked again: "Daddy, will unravelling the secrets of nature make children grow up quickly, so that they will understand everything?"

"Possibly", he replied.

"So that they will understand everything immediately they are born?"

"No, no, not so", he replied hurriedly.

"Ah, well, I do not understand what it is all about then", commented Tommy sulkily.

"You will understand when you grow up, as your father has said" intervened Mrs. Wiseman who had been listening with amusement to the dialogue between husband and son and was not at all sure herself whether this achievement would make any difference to man's life and happiness here on earth or anywhere else in space to which he might decide to migrate.

By now little Tommy had begun to feel sleepy, so he rested contented with his father's assurance that he would understand everything when he grew up. Getting up he said good night to his parents and went to bed.

Dr. Wiseman and his wife continued to watch the television. He felt immensely proud of the American exploit. It was true that it was the Americans who had done it; but who were the American? They were not just a hotchpotch of all the races - Europeans, Chinese, Indians, Negroes and people from all the four corners of the globe - as someone had said. They were predominantly European. It was Europeans who had originally settled on that continent, bringing their civilization and culture with them, and they were still the dominant racial group in that hemisphere. Their achievement was the achievement of the white man, and the entire Caucasian Race shared in the glory that it brought.

At last the transmission ended and Dr. Wiseman and his wife retired for the night.

After breakfast next morning Dr. Wiseman went to his office to continue a dissertation he was writing on the Intelligence Quotients of the different races. The previous night's experience had reinforced his conviction that the white race was by far superior, and the black race by far inferior, to all the other races. "While we travel in machines over the surface of the earth and under it, beneath the sea and on top of it, in and above the air, and have now even trod on the moon, they are still crawling on the ground" he wrote. "This conclusively proves that their Intelligence Quotient is almost nil, as compared with that of the white man. This comparative deficiency of intelligence in the Negro accounts for his intellectual, moral, spiritual and Economic under-development."

Dr. Wiseman went on to speculate on the reasons for the Negro' s lack of intelligence, saying that they were either hereditary or environmental or both. He took the whole day writing on the subject.

Just before he closed for the day he summoned Dr. Springfield to his office and asked him to see what he had written and tell him what he thought of it. The latter read carefully through it and handed it back to him.

"Well, what do you think ?" asked Dr. Wiseman.

"It is well written", pronounced Dr. Springfield. "But I do not see what purpose it is supposed to serve."

"I want the whole world to know why the whites are so far ahead of all the other races in scientific and technological achievement, and the blacks so far behind." he explained.

"And if the whole world knew that, what would be the benefit to anyone?" Dr. Springfield asked again.

"My dear fellow", replied Dr. Wiseman, "you as a scientist should know that every knowledge is useful, even if it leads to no practical result."

"But this is bound to lead to some practical result", said Dr. Springfield. "It is bound to offend all Negroes, if it does nothing else."

"And what does it matter if it offends all Negroes? Must scientific truth be suppressed simply because it will offend the sensibilities of some people?"

"But why do you consider your personal opinions about the Negroes to be scientific truths when they are merely based on personal prejudice'?"

"On personal prejudice!", exclaimed Dr. Wiseman in a tone of surprise.

"Yes, on personal prejudice", Dr. Springfield repeated, "If you want them to be accepted as scientific truth then you should take steps to investigate them scientifically."

"In what way? Have I not arrived at my conclusions deductively?"

"You have, but from a false major premise."

"How?"

"You have assumed, what is not proven, that high scientific and technological achievement is an indication of high intelligence. If you want your conclusion to be accepted as scientific then you should conduct intelligence tests."

"All right, I shall do as you say. You will see that the result will amply confirm my conclusion which you consider as unscientific", agreed Dr. Wiseman. "Can I have your assistance then?"

"What do you want me to do? " asked Dr. Springfield.

"What I want you to do for me is this: I would like you to go to China and bring me a seven-year old boy for an intelligence Test. Similarly I would like Mr. Balmer and Mr. Suppercot to go to India and Italy respectively and bring me two boys of that age. I myself will go to Africa and bring a seven year old boy from the deep jungles of the Republic of Gamberia. I shall test them on their comparative intelligence."

Dr. Springfield agreed to help and immediately set about getting ready for the journey. Then Dr. Wiseman summoned his two other Senior Research Assistants and put the suggestion to them also. They agreed to co-operate. A week later they all set out.

"Be sure you bring, as much as possible, a boy untouched by modern civilisation", he said to them just before they departed.

Having agreed to do as he had instructed they immediately went to take planes for their respective destinations. Dr. Wiseman also got ready for his journey to Africa. He bought travellers cheques, booked a plane to Gamberia and telephoned the British High Commissioner in Blaft, the capital of Gamberia, to say that he would arrive there the next day. He briefly explained the purpose of his visit and requested him to find an educated Gamberian who would lead him into the interior of the country for the purpose he had in mind. His Excellency, Mr. Alexander Cowfoot, who was a great friend of the doctor's, agreed to help.

Saying good-bye to his wife and Mrs. Casely the next day Dr. Wiseman boarded a plane for Gamberia.

The direct flight from London to Blaft took only six hours and he arrived the same day to find the High Commissioner waiting for him at the airport. Having acquainted His Excellency with more details of his project, Dr. Wiseman asked if he had secured him a guide as he had requested.

"Oh yes", he replied. "One of my locally-recruited staff will go with you. His name is Jimfa - Fiko Jimfa. He studied in Britain, at the University of Reading. He comes from one of the most backward tribes in the country, the Gonjani tribe, which also happens to be the dominant tribe."

"What was his field of study?" asked Dr. Wiseman. "Anthropology", replied his Excellency.

"Good. You have hit upon the right person", said Dr. Wiseman with relief. I hope you have explained everything to him and he is keen to accompany me?"

"I have, and he is quite excited about it", replied the High Commissioner. "As a student of anthropology he has, of course, already heard much about you and he is eagerly looking forward to meeting you."

They proceeded to town, where Dr. Wiseman lodged in the Independence Hotel. The next morning he went to see the High Commissioner in his office. There he met Fiko Jimfa, who was definitely pleased to meet the distinguished Doctor and was highly excited at the prospect of acting as his guide and interpreter on his journey to his homeland.

"I learn you come from the Gonjani tribe", Dr. Wiseman said in discussing the project.

"That is correct", he replied.

"And that you are willing to take me to one of the remotest villages in the hinterland of Gonjani-land?"

"That is correct too", he confirmed.

"How far is it?"

"About ten hours journey, by canoe and foot."

"We are going by river and foot-paths then?"

"That too is correct."

Dr. Wiseman was nothing daunted, for he was already used to travelling in wild and hazardous places. So the next day they set out. Jimfa had said that the village he had in mind as their destination was called Kantoma, and was situated about twenty miles from Tonko, a village at the confluence of River Dimpo and River Mamba, two of the largest rivers in Gamberia, which joined to form the River Mambadimpo, on the estuary of which stood the Gamberian capital, Blaft. Tonko was about two hundred miles from Blaft; which meant that a journey of 220 miles or so lay ahead of them.

Jimfa carried no luggage, save a plastic band-bag containing his toilet articles and sleeping-cloth. Dr. Wiseman was also travelling light, for all he had was a small suit-case containing his pyjamas and toilet articles, as well as a few things which he intended to distribute as presents. But he had plenty of cash, having changed two hundred pounds sterling into the local currency, the Cupras at the rate of 1,000 Cupras to one pound. Before the devaluation of the Cupra, which occurred on the recommendation of the International Monetary Fund as a condition for granting loans to the Government of Gamberia, the Cupra was the equivalent of one pound sterling. The people of Gamberia blamed their Government for agreeing to this drastic debasement of their national currency, but the Government retorted by saying that they, being beggars, had no choice. They either had to do as they were told or the people would starve. And which of them would have been prepared to starve?

It was about 8 a.m. when they set out in a hired canoe, there being no motorable road from Blaft to any part of the hinter-land. It cost 6,000 Cupras, and the Canoe man was to row them to the village of Tonko, where he was to wait for them until they returned from Kantoma, at an extra charge of 200 Cupras for every night he spent at the village.

The voyage up the River Mambadimpo proved to be more difficult than any of the three occupants of the canoe had imagined. The canoe man, Tompiri by name, who had gone up to Tonko several times before, had not underestimated the difficulties of the journey. He knew that there were major rapids which they had to cross by carrying the canoe round them overland, and there were also several boulders jutting out from the river bed which they had to avoid, some of them standing so close together that passing between them required the highest skill of boatmanship. But he was so used to them by his frequent journeys up and down the river that he was confident they would arrive at their destination without much difficulty. Jimfa too, although he had performed the journey only once, it being the occasion when he went with his uncle to Kantoma to a medicine-man when the uncle was sick, had not anticipated any difficulties, for his first and only voyage on that river had not been unpleasant, despite the difficulties connected with the rapids. As for Dr. Wiseman he had formed his idea of the journey from the accounts which both Nampiri and Jimfa had given him, and these were not at all daunting.

Almost from the start of the journey; however, they ran into difficulties. The Canoe sprang a leak when they had done barely ten miles upstream and they had to drag it ashore. It took more than two hours before the canoe-man succeeded in caulking it with "sapo" fibres and latex from the "FUNTUMIA" tree.

They had hardly resumed their journey when the sky darkened and a thunder-storm erupted. The winds seized the canoe and spun it like a top, bringing them close to the danger of being dashed to pieces against the many jutting rocks. The rain which soon began to descend in a fierce downpour, drenched them mercilessly, there being no awning or any other form of protection over their heads. Then the river began to swell in volume and rush with unwonted speed over the precipices, producing deafening roars at the waterfalls.

It was fortunate for them that they were journey upstream, or their canoe would have been carried irresistibly along and dashed into pieces at the first waterfall they encountered. As it was, their main difficulty lay in having to struggle hard against the adverse current, which so retarded their progress that it was already dark when they arrived at Tonko and put to shore.

By now it was too late for them to proceed on their overland journey to Kantoma, so they spent the night at Tonko under the thatched roof of Chief Wansama, head of the village.

Leaving behind the canoe-man to wait for their return Dr. Wiseman and Jimfa set out on their journey to Kantoma early next morning. They travelled by narrow bush-paths, meandering their way underneath the canopy of the giant trees that darkened the virgin forest. The only human dwellings they came across were hunters' camps, consisting of single thatched huts in little clearings.

Now and again they lost their way, straying along hunter's trails until they reached the end of them and had to turn back.

At last they heard the crow of a cock. It was the first time they had heard a cock crow since they set out on their journey from the village of Tonko.

"We are about to arrive at our destination", said Jimfa to Dr. Wiseman.

The Doctor felt greatly relieved. The journey had taken much longer than he had expected, owing to their constantly straying off the right path. It was now more than fifteen years since Jimfa last went to Kantoma with his uncle. It was no wonder then that he found his way to the place with difficulty.

They soon came to a brook, through which they waded. It was from here that the villagers fetched their water for all domestic uses, but there was not a soul in sight, from which Jimfa concluded that the people had not yet returned from their farms. He told Dr. Wiseman. The latter looked at his watch. It was 4 p.m.

"I hope we shall not have to wait for long before they come", replied Dr. Wiseman.

They proceeded on their way and soon afterwards they issued from the darkness of the forest into broad daylight like one arriving at the end of the long tunnel. They had arrived at the village of Kantoma.

It was a medium-sized village of about forty houses and three hundred inhabitants. The houses, all of which were round huts with thatched roofs, were of various sizes, from small ones capable of accommodating not more than three or four people, to quite large structures that could contain from ten to twenty inmates.

In the centre of the village about half-a-dozen children were at play, who, as soon as they saw the two strangers approaching, ran to meet them. They were particularly attracted by the sight of a white man. Although there were two albinos in the village they were quite different. Their skins were not as smooth as that of Dr. Wiseman, nor were their eyes so clear and sparkling. Apart from the whiteness of their skins they retained all the features of a Negro. One could therefore tell at a glance that this was a white man, of whom they had heard so much.

11

Jimfa asked for the Chief's palace, and they all pointed to a round hut only a few yards away. It was like any other hut around, not bigger or finer in any way. As they made their way there the children followed them talking and arguing excitedly.

Chief Brongo had just returned from his farm and was relaxing in the open shed in front of his palace when they arrived. He was surprised to see the two strangers, particularly the white man.

This was the second time Chief Brongo had ever set eyes upon a white man in all his sixty years. The first was when Father Borringer, a German Missionary, arrived in the village some fifty-six years before. He remembered him only dimly, for he was but a little boy of about four at the time. Father Borringer came talking about God and telling people that unless they offered prayers to Him every day and also met together to pray and sing in praise of Him every Sunday they would not go to Heaven when they died. He said that Heaven was the place were God lived.

Father Borringer obtained a piece of land from Chief Brongo's father, Chief Lampronu, who was then reigning, and built a bamboo shed which he called a "church". Only about half-a-dozen of the people of Kantoma ever met in Father Borringer's "church" to sing and praise God; for most of them preferred to be with their ancestors when they departed this life and did not care much about going to any other place.

In time Father Borringer set up a school to teach the children to read and write, so that they could read for themselves what the Bible said. But he was able to enrol no more than four pupils, for most of the parents were of the opinion that knowledge about the land's cultivation was more important. He had been in Kantoma for only one year when the first World War threatened to break out and he had to flee back to his country. He would have preferred to remain in this remote corner and carry on with his work, but for fear of being apprehended and imprisoned by the British who were then ruling Gamberia. Apparently the British would have considered him a wolf in a sheep's skin; that is to say, a spy in the guise of a Missionary.

By the time Father Borringer was leaving he had been able to teach his four pupils the Alphabet and the numerals up to forty. But after his departure his school came to an end; and by the time Dr. Wiseman and Jimfa arrived in the village only one of his four pupils, old Rakito, was still alive.

Besides being one of the pupils in the school, old Rakito had also been a "mission boy" whom Father Borringer had once taken to Blaft. They had spent two weeks there before returning to Kantoma. Young Rakito (for he was then only eight years old) came back with a glowing account of all the wonderful things he had seen in the city, which he was never tired of recounting. Up to the time Dr. Wiseman and Jimfa arrived in Kantoma he was the only one in the whole village who had ever been to Blaft.

Everyone regarded old Rakito as a great scholar, since in addition to his journey to Blaft he was the only one who could recite the Alphabet and count the numerals up to forty in the white man's tongue. Most of the youngsters in the village were eager to learn from him; and he, not being averse to showing off his knowledge, readily obliged them. Counting on his fingers he said that the numerals were "one, two, six, seven, four, three, five, nine, eight, ten." As for the letters of the Alphabet he mixed them up even more hopelessly. But since no one in the village knew any better, his authority went unchallenged. And so the youngsters went about reciting the numerals and the Alphabet in the way he had taught them.

The sight of Dr. Wiseman made Chief Brongo remember Father Borringer at once. He began to wonder if another white man had come to tell them about God and to set up another school to teach the children about Him and His ways.

Having offered seats to the two strangers, Chief Brongo welcomed them with handshakes and immediately summoned his elders, old Rakito being among them. When they were assembled he enquired through his linguist what had brought the two strangers.

Jimfa briefly introduced Dr. Wiseman and explained the purpose of their visit. After that Dr. Wiseman, who had been following the proceedings through the interpretation of Jimfa, got up and spoke in greater detail.

"Tell the Chief", he said to Jimfa with an indulgent smile, "that what I am looking for is a seven year old boy, of average intelligence. l am conducting some experiment in my country with boys of that age and I would like him to take part in it. He will be away for about a year, after which period of time I shall return him in person to his parents. He will not come to any harm, and I shall reward both the boy and his parents handsomely for their co-operation." With that he sat down again and waited for the response.

Jimfa translated what the Doctor had said into the Gonjani language.

It was old Rakito who first spoke in reply.

"Is this a revival of the Slave Trade in another guise?" he asked, amid laughter from the by-standers.

Jimfa hesitated to interpret to Dr. Wiseman what he had said.

"What did he say?" asked the Doctor, looking expectantly into Jimfa's face.

"He wants to know what sort of experiment you are conducting", he replied. "I hesitated because I do not quite know how to explain it to him."

"Simply tell him that I want to find out how soon boys of this age can learn the English language", instructed the Doctor.

"The white man says that the Slave Trade was abolished in his country many years ago and that everyone under the sun is now free and independent", he interpreted.

Old Rakito was about to say something again when Chief Brongo interrupted.

"Tell your white friend", he said, "that at present only a few people have returned from their farms, as he can see. He will have to wait a bit until many more people come, when I shall cause a gong-gong to be beaten to summon all parents. He could then put his request to them."

Jimfa interpreted it to Dr. Wiseman.

"All, right, I hope it won't be long before they return", he said.

"The sun has begun to cast long shadows", Jimfa explained. "In about thirty minutes most of the people would have returned from their farms."

Jimfa was right. Not long after Old Rakito and the other elders had dispersed, the village, which had seemed almost deserted except for the few children and elders, began to be thronged with people once more. The news having already gone round that two strangers, one black and the other white, had arrived and were in the chief's house, large crowds, moved by curiosity, soon began to gather at the palace.

Then Chief Brongo caused a gong-gong to be beaten, summoning all parents to the palace. Soon the place was swarming with men, women and children, all eager to know what was afoot.

When Chief Brongo saw that a sufficiently large number of people had gathered together, including all his elders, he asked Dr. Wiseman to repeat his request. He did so through Jimfa.

The Doctor's words were greeted with giggles and murmur by all present. For some time no one would say anything. As before, it was old Rakito who first spoke:

"And which parent does the white man think will be willing to give his son to a stranger to take away to a strange country?" he asked. "If he means well let him stay here and continue the work which Father Borringer started but left unfinished. Let him rebuild his school which has long fallen into ruins and teach our children to read and write. Then when they have learned sufficiently from him and are grown enough to be able to stand on their own feet he may be able to persuade one of them to accompany him to his country for the purpose he has in mind."

His words were greeted with approval by all present. But when it was interpreted to Dr. Wiseman he replied that the project he had in mind could not wait for more than a month at the most and that, in any case, the assistance he required must come from a boy of seven who had never learnt anything from the white man.

Old Rakito was about to raise an objection again when he was interrupted by the voice of a boy of about seven who stood among the crowd and was towering above everyone.

"I want to go with the white man"; he said.

Old Rakito looked fiercely in his direction.

"Hey, you, come here at once!" he ordered, catching sight of the boy.

Everyone turned to look at the youngster as he made his way forward.

Soon he stood in the middle of the crowd, still towering above everyone. "Come down at once" old Rakito ordered again.

The boy unloosened from his legs the stilts on which he had been standing and stood down. He was about four feet tall.

"Now, tell me", ordered old Rakito for the third time. "what on earth did you say?" And he strained his ears to make sure that he would hear correct what the boy said.

"I said I want to go with the white man", he repeated.

"You want to go with whom?" asked old Rakito in a tone of great surprise before Jimfa could interpret to Dr. Wiseman what the boy had said.

"I want to go with the white man", the boy repeated for the third time.

"What! are you out of your mind?" exclaimed old Rakito again. "Get away at once!"

"I want to go with the white man", he said again.

"What is going on?", asked Dr. Wiseman of Jimfa who had not as yet said anything to him but had stood listening with interest to the exchanges between the boy and old Rakito.

"The boy says he wants to go with you", replied Jimfa.

"Good. But I must make sure that he is the sort of boy I want for my project", said Dr. Wiseman. "Ask him what is his name".

Jimfa did so, after calling for silence from the crowd which had been finding the boy's insistent replies a source of great mirth.

"I have no name", replied the boy.

The crowd giggled and laughed.

"You have no name?" asked Dr. Wiseman in astonishment when the reply was interpreted to him.

"No, I have no name", he replied again.

"But what are you called?"

"I am called Kotokrotintomaguri," he replied.

"But that is your name?" asked Dr. Wiseman again.

"No, it is not my name", he insisted. "It is the name of my great grandfather. It was borrowed for me by my father when I was born, and he has always asked me to bear it carefully and not allow it to get tarnished in any way, because it belongs to my great grandfather."

Dr. Wiseman was not sure whether the boy's reply was intelligent or silly, but he saw that it set the crowd laughing, some quite hilariously. Even old Rakito, whom the infirmities of old age had almost deprived of a highly risible disposition, could not help slightly opening his toothless mouth in a short titter.

"It is too long a name", said Dr. Wiseman. "I shall call you Kotokro for short."

"Well, you may do so if you like", he agreed. "Many people here do so too. But is it longer than your own name?"

"Yes it is."

"What is your own name?" he asked.

"Wiseman - Dr. Wiseman."

"Is that all?"

"No my full name is John Alexander Scantiberry Wiseman."

"Johnalexanderscantiberrywiseman?" he asked in surprise. "Why, it is much longer than my own!"

"Well, they call me Wiseman - Dr. Wiseman - for short."

"Oh, I see. Then you may also call me Kotokro for short."

"How old are you?" Dr. Wiseman asked again through his interpreter.

"My father says I am seven years old."

"But what do you yourself say?" asked Dr. Wiseman, who had by now begun to find the boy's replies rather amusing, but was not sure whether they betrayed intelligence or stupidity.

"I do not know", he replied, pulling at the tangled growth of crinkled hair that capped his head. "But I think my father must be right, for he knew when I was being born, but I did not."

"You did not know when you were being born?" asked Dr. Wiseman.

"No, I did not. Did you, in your own case?"

"No, no, of course not", Dr. Wiseman replied hurriedly. "But who are your parents?"

"My father is Papa Asuboni and my mother is Mamma Alimana."

"Are they here?"

"I believe not", he replied, casting searching glances through the crowd. "If they were they would have spoken out by now. I think they have not yet returned from the farm."

"This boy must be very stupid"; Dr. Wiseman said to himself. "His answers to simple questions are so silly. He is certainly typical of this race."

Before he could open his mouth to say anything, however, Chief Brongo interrupted. Addressing Jimfa he said:

"Tell the white man that if the boy wishes to go with him, I have nothing to say. But he must wait for his parents to return from the farm. If they approve of his going it will, of course, be their business. But I don' t believe that any parent here present will agree to let him take away his son."

"Quite so!" shouted the crowd in agreement.

After they had all dispersed Chief Brongo said that as it was already getting late he would advise the two strangers to spend the night in the village and go away the next day. It would afford them the opportunity to discuss the matter fully with the boy's parents on their return from the farm. They readily agreed to his suggestion, for they were already very tired and hungry and could not have returned the same day even if their mission had been accomplished there and then.

Chief Brongo provided them with accommodation in his palace, which consisted of four round huts with thatched roofs, joined together by low walls and forming a circular compound about twelve feet in diameter.

Meanwhile young Kotokrotintomaguri (whom, following Dr. Wiseman's suggestion we shall henceforth call Kotokro for short) had gone back home. There he found that his parents had returned from the farm and his father had just finished taking a bath.

"There are two strangers in Chief's house, one black and the other white", he informed them. "The white man says he wants a boy of my age to go with him to his country and I have offered to accompany him."

"You have offered to accompany whom to where?" asked Mamma Alimana in a tone of disbelief.

"I have offered to accompany the white man to his country", he repeated.

"Do you know what you are talking about? You must be out of your mind!" she shouted.

"I want to go and see his country. He says he will bring me back in a year's time."

"You shall not take one step from this village with anyone, white or black, you fool", shouted his mother again.

"Leave the boy alone", Papa Asuboni intervened. "If he has the opportunity to go and see the white man's country I don't see why he shouldn't go. See the respect which everyone gives to old Rakito, simply because he accompanied Father Borringer to Blaft for only two weeks and is able to count in the white man's tongue."

"And so what?" asked Mamma Alimana.

"And so we must not try to stop the boy from going to the white man's country. I myself would have been eager to go if the whiteman would take me."

"You are welcome to go. It would be good riddance. But my son shall not go to that far-off country from where he may never come back.

"He will come back. He is a smart boy and nothing can prevent him from returning to us. So if only it is true that the white man wishes to take him away we must not try to stop him."

"It is true, papa", Kotokro replied at once. "The white man is in Chief's house, as I have said. You can go and ask him."

Papa Asuboni immediately put on his cloth and followed the boy to Chief Brongo's palace.

The Chief was the first to see them coming, and he told Jimfa, who also told Dr. Wiseman. The latter had just re-emerged from the room which had been prepared for them for the night, wondering whether his journey to that village would not prove to be in vain. Both old Rakito and Chief Brongo had said that no parent in Kantoma would be willing to let his son go with him, and this opinion seemed to have been endorsed by the crowd. It was unlikely then that the parents of that boy would let him go with him. It was with a faltering hope that he received the news of their coming.

Soon they reached the palace and greeted. Chief Brongo returned the greetings and motioned Papa Asuboni to a seat while Kotokro remained standing. Then he asked the boy's father what had brought him to the palace. Not that he did not know, but it was the demand of custom.

"My son tells me that this white stranger wishes to take a boy of seven to his country from this village, and that he has offered to go with him. I have come to find out if this is true."

17

"It is true", Chief Brongo confirmed. "This white man and his black companion arrived here this afternoon while you were in the farm and said that he wished to take away with him to his country a boy of seven. He would like him to take part in some experiment which he is conducting and would bring him back in a year's time. Of course, none of the parents present would hear of such a thing, but your boy offered to go with him. If you will permit him to take your son away it is up to you."

"You say the white man promises to bring him back in a year's time; What guarantee is there that he will, in fact, do so?" .

"Well, ask him and hear what he says", replied Chief Brongo.

"You need not entertain any fear about his bringing the boy back", intervened Jimfa without first putting the question to Dr. Wiseman. "The white man is well known all over the world. I personally had long heard of him even before I met him in Blaft two days ago. I can guarantee that he will bring him back. Besides, he is a great friend of the British High Commissioner in Blaft, His Excellency Mr. Alexander Cowfoot, who is my employer. He can always be traced through him. His excellency is himself a very important person in his own country, who can always be contacted through his Government wherever he may be. So you should have no fear on that score."

"Well, I do not doubt your assurance; for he seems to me to be an honest man, although he appears somewhat contemptuous of our way of life due to ignorance, as I can discern from his countenance and demeanour. Let him go with the boy and bring him back in a year's time as he has promised. I am sure Kotokro will be able to teach him a thing or two."

Turning to Dr. Wiseman who had remained in ignorance of all that was being said, Jimfa informed him that the boy's father had agreed to let him go. The Doctor was greatly relieved to hear this and immediately pulled out six thousand Cupras which he offered to Papa Asuboni.

"No, no," refused the latter. "I do not want any money. He is my only child. l am not selling him."

"I know you are not selling him, and there is no suggestion that I want to buy him", replied Dr. Wiseman. "This is only a gift from me, in appreciation of your co-operation."

"Thank you, but I do not want it", Papa Asuboni said firmly.

"Please take it", intervened Jimfa. "He does not mean to buy the boy. As he says, this is only a gift."

"If you say so I cannot refuse it", replied Papa Asuboni.

He accepted it. And Dr. Wiseman then added two clothes and two head-kerchiefs for his wife, which Papa Asuboni also received with pleasure, for he knew these would go a long way to mollify her opposition to the boy's departure. And so they did, when Papa Asuboni brought them to her.

Next morning Dr. Wiseman and Jimfa set out on their return to Blaft, taking Kotokro with them.

When they arrived at Tonko they found the canoe-man waiting for them. The journey back to Blaft was fast and smooth, as they were now going downstream and were aided by the current.

It was about 4 p.m. when they arrived at Blaft. There young Kotokro saw for the first time many things about which old Rakito had spoken - magnificent houses, very wide streets with motor vehicles plying up and down, shops bulging with divers articles of merchandise of which he had seen only a few before; and above all, the sea. When he saw the sea he thought it was part of the sky that had curved down to meet the earth. Only the waves convinced him that it was spread on the surface of this earth.

"Whither does it flow?" he asked Jimfa.

"It does not flow", he replied.

"Really? I have never seen a river that does not flow", he said.

"Well, this is not a river. It is stagnant water."

"How strange. So who lives on the other side?"

"The white man."

"I see. No wonder he is so different from us."

After Dr. Wiseman had paid off the canoe-man all three of them went into a shop to buy clothes for Kotokro. They found many suits, sewn in different fashions, of which Dr. Wiseman bought three for the boy, for Kotokro had arrived clad in an ill-fitting shirt and trousers which the Doctor had given him in the village. When he put on one of them he looked so changed that not even his parents would have easily recognised him. He was filled with delight when he saw himself in the mirror.

The next morning Dr. Wiseman and Kotokro said good-bye to the High Commissioner and Jimfa and boarded the plane for London.

As the plane took off Kotokro's heart was filled with joy. He was not afraid at all. The swift ascent into the sky was like swinging on a rope from one tree to another, a game which he frequently played while wandering alone in the forest. But when the plane had at last steadied on a level flight and was sailing smoothly through the empty sky he thought he was dreaming, for he could not believe that he was physically suspended in midair.

He was still more amazed when he saw some of the passengers walking up and down the plane without falling. They must have some special skill for doing it successfully, he thought. Then he noticed that they were all going to the tail end of the plane and back. By signs he asked Dr. Wiseman what was afoot.

"They have been going to the toilet", he explained.

"Do they actually attend nature's call there?" he asked again.

"Yes some do, but others only go there to wash their faces and hands.

"I want to go there to attend nature's call", he said. "but I am afraid to get up, lest I should fall."

"Well, come with me", said Dr. Wiseman. "I shall take you there."

So saying he held Kotokro by the hand and helped him to rise up. They went down the aisle until they came to a door. Dr. Wiseman looked up at the door and said that someone was inside the room, so they must wait until he came out. They waited for a long time but no one came out.

"There is no one inside there", said Kotokro.

"There is", disagreed Dr. Wiseman.

"Why has he kept so long then? Maybe he has fallen asleep. Let us bang on the door to wake him up."

"Be patient", advised Dr. Wiseman. "He will come out soon."

They continued to wait and wait. Kotokro was about to say something again when the door opened and a man came out. He immediately closed it behind him. Then Dr. Wiseman opened it again and told Kotokro that he could enter. He did so and closed the door behind him.

He looked round. There was no sign that anyone had answered nature's call there. The whole place looked very neat and clean, unlike the bush immediately behind his father's house in Kantoma. There you did not have to look twice to know where to squat to do your business immediately you arrived there. The grounds there were abundantly marked with conspicuous signs of business done. Here it was not easy to know whether to do it on the floor, or in the bowl with a seat on it, or in the receptacle containing crumpled soft tissue-paper, or in the basin with soap at its side.

At last he decided not to make a nuisance of himself by letting go at the wrong place, particularly as he was not hard pressed. Perhaps the place was not meant for nature's call after all, as the Doctor had said, but for temporary rest. That would account for that man's long stay there.

Having thus made up his mind he opened the door again and came out. He found Dr. Wiseman waiting for him.

"Have you finished so soon?" asked the Doctor.

"I did not know where to do it", he replied. "But never mind; I am not hard pressed."

"Let me go and show you", suggested Dr. Wiseman.

"No, that will not be necessary. I don't feel it any more."

Not long after they had returned to their seats the air hostess came round asking people what they would like to drink. When she came to Kotokro Dr. Wiseman interpreted to him by signs what she had said.

"I don't want anything to drink", he replied. "I am not thirsty."

"It is not for thirst", explained Dr. Wiseman. "We are going to have a meal soon. It is for appetite."

"I have appetite all right", he replied. "I am very hungry." Dr. Wiseman told the air hostess. He himself asked for whisky and soda.

Soon afterwards lunch was brought. Kotokro immediately attacked his plate with avidity. But no sooner had he put the first morsel into his mouth than he took it out again and pushed his plate aside, making a wry face.

"Why, don't you want it?" asked Dr. Wiseman, observing him.

"I want something to drink first", he replied.

"I thought you said you didn't want anything to drink?"

"I want something to drink for appetite", he explained. "I have no appetite for this food. It was not cooked with salt and pepper. It has no taste."

"What would you have to drink then?"

"Palm wine".

"There is no palm wine here."

"Well, the kind of drink you took for appetite."

Dr. Wiseman summoned the air hostess and told her that the boy wanted something to drink after all.

"What does he want?" she asked.

"Bring him something strong", he recommended.

Concluding that Kotokro was not feeling well she brought him brandy.

He accepted it with a smile and gulped it down. After a while he drew the plate towards him again and started eating with as much relish as he had seen Dr. Wiseman eat his portion.

"Does the food have taste now?" the Doctor asked.

"I think not. But I have appetite now."

After he had finished eating, Kotokro licked his fingers clean, leaned back in his seat and was soon fast asleep.

He began to dream of home. First, he saw himself wandering alone in the forest. Then he climbed a tree and tied a rope to one of its branches. He held the end of the rope and began to swing on it. It was so delightful, swinging in the air like that. He laughed and laughed, breaking the silence in the plane. Many passengers turned to look. Dr. Wiseman nudged him in the ribs and woke him up.

"Stop disturbing", he said to him.

"What did I do?" he asked, rubbing his eyes.

"You were laughing".

"Oh yes, it was so delightful, wasn't it?"

"What was delightful?"

"Swinging on that rope."

"Swinging on which rope?"

He rubbed his eyes again and looked round.

"Oh, I see", he said with a smile. " I was dreaming."

Dr. Wiseman shook his head. This boy could not be in possession of average intelligence, he thought. He must be a dunce. Everything he did or said seemed so silly.

Not long afterwards the air hostess announced that they had arrived in London. She asked everyone on board to fasten his seat-belt for landing. Dr. Wiseman did so and helped Kotokro to do likewise. The boy looked down through the window. He could see nothing but a wide spread of fog, looking exactly like the sea.

"Where is London?" he asked Dr. Wiseman.

"What you see is fog. London is underneath it", he explained.

"Is that so? The way they describe it, I always thought London was in the sky."

"It is a city. How can it be in the sky?" asked Dr. Wiseman.

"Are you sure there are no cities in the sky?"

"We hope to build some in the sky one day; but right now all the cities we know of are on earth."

"You and who hope to build?"

"We, the white race."

"Why, will you be happier living in the sky?"

"Possibly."

"Ah, I wouldn't like to take the risk of living in a city in the sky. Why, I might fall down to earth and land in several pieces." he said.

The plane had begun to descend as they spoke, now inclining to the left, now to the right. At last it dived beneath the fog and London was immediately revealed to view. There it was, an endless stretch of buildings, streets, parks, gardens and empty spaces, with a river running through them all.

Kotokro watched and watched as the plane circled and circled. He began to see the buildings, the streets, the parks, the gardens and the river more clearly. Then it came over a long and wide open space and began to descend even more rapidly. At last it bumped lightly on the ground and began to speed along. The speed gradually diminished. Then it turned round and proceeded slowly until it came to a dead stop.

The door opened and the passengers began to descend in a queue. Dr. Wiseman got up, held his hand and they both joined the queue. At last they issued out of the plane and climbed down the ladder. Kotokro had stepped on London soil.

"This is not gold, is it?" he asked Dr. Wiseman, stamping on the tarmac.

"No, it isn't. It is the tarmac. It is made of asphalt."

"Oh, I thought it was gold. They said London is paved with gold. They didn't know it is just paved with asphalt."

"It is not paved with asphalt", corrected Dr. Wiseman. "It is only where the planes land that are paved with asphalt."

"What is the rest of the city paved with?" he asked.

"You will find out presently."

They followed the other passengers to a large building and soon arrived in a room where there was hustle and bustle as people searched for and retrieved their luggage. Dr. Wiseman had no difficulty in finding his suit-case. He took it, and they went through the building until they emerged into a street where many motor vehicles were lined up in a queue. They boarded one and were soon speeding through the city on a wide road full of many other vehicles. Houses stood to the right and the left, with gardens in front and open grounds between. Some of the grounds were covered with weeds, others were bare earth with black soil.

"So London is not all paved with gold or asphalt but has weedy grounds and black soil just as in Kantoma?" Kotokro asked with surprise.

"Of course not", replied Dr. Wiseman.

"Then the people here also cannot be different from the people in Kantoma, except in the colour of their skin?"

"Well, you may say so. After all, all human beings are human beings."

"I see. I always thought that people here were different kinds of human beings."

"Well, now you know better," said Dr. Wiseman.

"I do, indeed. And I am glad I came, or I would never have known."

The car had been speeding with them as they talked. It was not long before they arrived in the middle of town. Many huge buildings, some seeming to touch the sky, stood right and left. A stream of white humanity was flowing on either side of the street. Now and again they came to a cross road and the car stopped for a while. There was a red light ahead and people were crossing from one side to the other. Then the red light changed to amber and to green, and their car started moving once more. Kotokro had never seen or dreamt of anything like this before. It was all so thrilling. He hardly knew how he would be able to describe it to anyone in Kantoma when he returned home. At last the car stopped in front of a large building and Dr. Wiseman told him that they had arrived at their final destination.

CHAPTER TWO
THE INTELLIGENCE TEST

When Dr. Wiseman returned from Gamberia with Kotokro he found that his three senior Research Assistants had arrived back some days earlier. The first to return was Dr. Springfield. He came back from China with a plump golden boy of about seven whose name was Tsung Tsuang Tseng. Tseng had a medium-sized head, with a face as round as the full moon, and a bright pair of slanting eyes. His hair was straight and jet-black and covered his head like thatch. He looked rather serious for a boy of his age, but he was not unfriendly. He spoke little himself but he was a good listener and could laugh moderately if the joke was really funny.

The second to come back was Mr. Balmer. He returned from India with a boy of seven called Raj Khandari. He was brown-skinned with a big head and a long narrow face. His forehead, which protruded above his small nose, almost blotted his eyes from view. When you looked at him you would think that he was not seeing you, but he had a keen sight and could take in many details at a glance. He too had straight and dark hair.

Mr. Suppercot came back from Italy only three days before Dr. Wiseman returned from Gamberia. Although his journey was the shortest he had the greatest difficulty in finding his quest. He travelled to many remote parts of the country, but no place was remote enough to be outside the influence of modern civilisation. Everywhere he went he found that almost every child of seven was already in school, where he had learned enough to give him advantage in any intelligence test in the way it was conducted. Even those who were not in school had already acquired much knowledge from their material environments, which could stand them in good stead. So he continued to go from place to place until at last he came to a very remote farming village in the Alps, called Calsivo, close to the border with Switzerland. There he found a peasant boy of seven who had never been to school and was not very much acquainted with modern civilisation and civilised life. His name was Venito Scalini. His skin was as white as snow. Like Tseng he had a medium-sized head, but his face was slightly oval, with pointed chin. His nose, which was long and narrow, rose from his face at an angle of eighty degrees and overhung a small mouth. His golden hair flowed down his shoulders in wavy curls.

When Kotokro joined the three of them a more diverse assortment of boys you never saw in your life. In point of size and cranial capacity Khandari had the largest head, followed by Scalini. Tseng's was only slightly bigger than Kotokro's. In point of height and bodily stature Scalini was the tallest and stoutest, and Tseng was the shortest and smallest. Kotokro was only a little taller and bigger than Khandari. Kotokro was also the most active, followed by Khandari and Scalini and Tseng, in that order. However, all four had at least two things in common: common age and common humanity. They could talk and laugh at identical situations, although Kotokro often laughed the longest and

Tseng the shortest. They also knew, to varying degrees, how to reason and to judge if the reasoning was correct or faulty. All four shared in these peculiarly human attributes and in other attributes in which many other creatures also participated.

At first they were unable to communicate in words and had to use signs to make themselves understood by one another. But they were very friendly and ate and played and slept together. Kotokro and Scalini slept in one room and Khandari and Tseng in another.

Mrs. Casely loved them all with a motherly love, and often took them out to see interesting places in London and other cities, even though none of them could understand the English Language. She did this on the instruction of Dr. Wiseman, who wanted to know how soon the boys could acquire the language for themselves without formal instruction. It was part of the Intelligence Test. It was not long, however, before they began to supplement the use of signs with spoken words. Then gradually, as their vocabulary increased, their use of signs decreased until they were able to dispense with signs altogether.

At first Mrs. Casely did not like Kotokro much. Not only did his colour and physical appearance offend against her acquired aesthetic taste, but he was always doing things which annoyed her. He particularly angered her on the first day of his arrival. She had gone out of her way to prepare for the boys a special dinner, a very appetizing meal according to her taste. When it was set before them Scalini ate his portion with great relish; Tseng and Khandari ate theirs with some degrees of appreciation; but Kotokro pushed his plate aside at the first taste of it and made Mrs. Casely know by signs, supplemented with a wry face, that the food was tasteless, because it was not cooked with salt and pepper.

"I want something to drink first, for appetite." he added.

Mrs. Casely replied that there was nothing to drink, whether for appetite nor for anything else, and that in any case boys were not supposed to take alcohol, the only thing that could be drunk for appetite.

"But they gave me something to drink for appetite when we were coming on the plane", he argued.

"Well, we are not on the plane now", replied Mrs. Casely, "And in any case it is not good for you."

"Why did they give me then?"

"I don't know. But I wouldn't have given you, and I wouldn't give you now even if we had any in the house."

Kotokro concluded that Mrs. Casely did not like him. He refused to eat the food and went to bed hungry.

The next morning Mrs Casely had the greatest difficulty in persuading him to get out of bed when she came to tidy their rooms. Kotokro curled up and refused to budge, saying that the place was too cold. He got up only after he had drank hot tea which Mrs. Casely hastily prepared for him.

Again the first and only time he accompanied Mrs. Casely and the other boys to the Zoo he made them cut short their visit and return to the house before they had seen many animals, much to the annoyance of Mrs. Casely and the disappointment of his companions. After they had seen the monkeys and other land animals Kotokro suddenly asked:

"Why were they brought here for imprisonment? Did they destroy crops?"

"They weren't brought here because they destroyed any crops", replied Mrs Casely.

"But why were they brought here for imprisonment?"

"They were brought here so that people who had not seen any of them before might have the opportunity of doing so" explained Mrs Casely.

"And if those people saw them, then what?"

"Then they would be happy."

"Would they be happy all their lives because of having seen them?"

"No, not all their lives, but they would be happy at the moment of seeing them, because they would have satisfied their curiosity."

"I see. For how long will each of the animals be imprisoned then?"

"For as long as it lives." replied Mrs. Casely.

"What!" he exclaimed. "Is each animal to serve life sentence just for the purpose of giving momentary happiness to some people?"

"Yes. But they are animals. They don't mind."

"So if you open the cages they will still prefer to stay?"

"Of course not. They would escape instantly."

"Let us go back home", he said. "I don't want to see more."

When Mrs. Casely asked why, he replied that all the animals he had seen looked sad. Most of them seemed to be appealing to the visitors to rescue them from their captivity. And as it was not in his power to oblige them he thought the best thing to do was to go away from there. Mrs. Casely laughed at the idea, saying that he was only imagining things; but Kotokro insisted that he was not imagining anything. What he saw was real. Did she not see the monkey with the lugubrious face looking at them with hands clasped in supplication, and the tears that were welling up in the gazelle's eyes as it gazed expectantly at them with raised head?

"Well, we can't cut short our visit just because you don't want to go any further", said Mrs. Casely.

"I shall sit under that tree and wait for you", he said, indicating a fir tree that stood a few yards away.

"All right. You may do that if you wish", said Mrs. Casely, and immediately motioned to the other boys to come along. They went from enclosure to enclosure, and everywhere they went the boys gazed at the animals with great interest and amusement.

But they had not gone far when Mrs. Casely began to get worried over Kotokro. The boy had said that he was going to wait for them under the fir tree. But suppose he had changed his mind and had tried to follow them after they were gone, would he not get lost in that seething crowd of visitors and in that labyrinth of cages and enclosures? If that happened and she returned home without him Dr. Wiseman would certainly not forgive her. No sooner had the thought occurred to her than she decided to go back to Kotokro.

"Come, boys, let's go back home", she said to them.

"Please, we want to see more" pleaded Scalini on their behalf. "It is very interesting."

"You have seen enough for the day. We shall come again another day", she promised.

She led the way back to where Kotokro was waiting for them under the fir tree. They found him still sitting there, fast asleep.

"Get up", she said, tapping him on the shoulder. "Let's go back home."

Kotokro sprang to his feet at once. On their way back home he said to Mrs. Casely:

"I think if it is necessary to imprison those animals for the purpose of making some people momentarily happy, then they should be imprisoned for only short periods and others be brought to take their places. They should not be imprisoned all their lives, especially when they have done no wrong."

When they returned to the house Mrs. Casely told Dr. Wiseman what Kotokro had said and done. The Doctor had instructed her to report back to him everything of interest that the boys did or said during their outings.

"Well, it is hardly surprising", he commented. "As I have always told you, the boy has little or no intelligence. His questions, remarks, and suggestions are always ridiculous and silly in the extreme. He thinks it is very easy to get animals for the Zoo. He has no idea how much it costs to bring in even one animal. As for his sympathy for them it is typical of his race. They have close affinity with animals with whom they dwell in the jungle, hence his concern for them."

Mrs. Casely did not feel that the Doctor's comments and conclusions were entirely justified.

"But even in this country there are many whites who also show concern for those animals in the Zoo", she pointed out. "Does it mean they too have little or no intelligence, or that they have close affinity with the animals?"

"Of course not", replied Dr. Wiseman. "Those are mawkish sentimentalists. Even though they may be highly intelligent they are emotionally unstable."

"Then the feeling of concern for animals in captivity does not spring from affinity with them, nor is it necessarily an indication of lack of intelligence?" asked Mrs Casely.

"Among the whites it is not; but in blacks, take it from me, it certainly is", he assured her.

Mrs. Casely remained unconvinced, but not wanting to argue further with the learned Doctor she held her peace. Then Dr. Wiseman added, as if to appease her and set her mind at rest;

"Please bear with him, for I shall be taking him back immediately after the intelligence test."

But far from finding the boy a nuisance Mrs. Casely had actually begun to like him; for all at once Kotokro had begun to make himself useful in the house. It seemed that he was now getting used to the food and climate. He would get up in the morning and make his bed while his room mate, Scalini, lay cuddled up. And when Mrs. Casely came to clean their room he helped her with the sweeping and dusting. Sometimes too, when the other boys went out for a walk or window-shopping he would stay behind and help in the kitchen, washing plates and assisting in other chores. "The boy is helpful at least, even if he has little or no intelligence", Mrs Casely said to herself.

But even on the question of intelligence it was not long before she began to have some doubt about the Doctor's conclusions. Kotokro was always asking questions that seemed silly at first, but not all that silly when you thought deeply about them.

The first time this conviction fully dawned upon her was when she took all four boys to see a boxing match. Mohamed Hussein, the world's heavy weight champion, was defending his title against Reginald Busher of the Azores. They had not been there for long when Mohammed Hussein entered the ring, beating his chest and angrily threatening to finish Reginald Busher with one blow. He was soon followed by Reginald Busher who also began to shake his fists in the air in great fury, saying that he would knock the nonsense out of Mohammed Hussein's head. Soon the fight began. The large crowd of spectators in the stadium, where it was being held, yelled and chanted as the two angry men slugged at each other without mercy.

"What brought about the quarrel?" Kotokro asked Mrs. Casely after watching the fight for a while.

"Quarrel? They have no quarrel", replied Mrs. Casely.

"No quarrel? Why are they fighting then?"

They are fighting for money", she explained.

"Who is going to give them the money?"

"The spectators who are gathered here. I paid for the four of you before entering."

"And who is keeping the money?"

"The people who are ensuring that there is a fair fight."

"Then why don't they place it in one place and ask the two men to race for it instead, so that the one who gets to it first would take it?"

"No, that wouldn't do. Those who paid to enter want value for their money. They want to be entertained," she explained.

"But they would have even greater entertainment from watching the two men race for the money. You can imagine the energy with which they would run. That would be a more humane form of entertainment than seeing these two men, who have no quarrel, pounding each other so cruelly just for money."

He had hardly finished delivering his opinion when Reginald Busher suddenly delivered a blow that sent Mohammed Hussein sprawling on the canvass. He lay prostrate and motionless. People rushed to the stage and bore him away.

"Does it always end like this?" asked Kotokro, turning to Mrs Casely.

"No. Sometimes it ends in a draw, and then the decision is given on points. That is to say, the one who delivers the greater number of correct blows is declared the winner."

"I see. But that man they have just carried away: Is he dead?"

"I don't think he is dead", replied Mrs Casely.

"But do people sometimes die during these fights?"

"Yes, occasionally."

"Oh dear! Then it is not a good form of entertainment at all, and no one should encourage it by paying money to come and see it."

When Mrs. Casely narrated all this to Dr. Wiseman on their return home he said:

"You see, I told you the boy is very stupid. He is always drawing wrong conclusions from false premises",

"How?" asked Mrs Casely.

"He assumes that people fight only when they have a quarrel. So when he saw those two boxers fighting he concluded that they have been quarrelling. In the same way, he thought that it is only when one commits a crime that one suffers imprisonment. So when he saw those animals in the Zoo he at once jumped to the conclusion that they must have committed some crime. It is all a mark of stupidity."

"But is it not true that people are imprisoned only when they commit a crime?" asked Mrs. Casely, not at all in agreement with the learned doctor's conclusion.

"Well, that is true of human beings. But why should anyone think that animals too should be confined in a zoo only when they have committed some crime? No, only a white psychopath or a person with little or no intelligence will think that animals too should be treated in the same way as humans."

Mrs. Casely could not agree that Kotokro's remarks and suggestions on this occasion, as on the others, showed stupidly. It seemed to her that there was some sense in them. But since the learned Doctor had pronounced them stupid, who was she to argue, especially as her own education was so limited as compared with his? So she returned to her apartment in silence, although she still believed that the Doctor's opinion about the boy must be wrong.

To Dr. Wiseman, however, everything the boy said or did served to confirm his conviction that he had little or no intelligence. This conviction was further strengthened by what Mrs. Casely told him on her return with the boys from a football match a week later.

It was one Saturday afternoon, exactly five months after Dr. Wiseman had returned from Gamberia with Kotokro. There was to be an international football match between the Mighty Giants of Spain and The Great Wizards of Peru. Dr. Wiseman bought gate tickets for Mrs. Casely and the boys, so that they could go out and see the match. They had by now mastered the English language sufficiently and could express themselves without much difficulty, but the Doctor had decided that since they were not being given any formal instruction it was necessary for them to go out as often as possible, as this would afford them the opportunity of increasing their command of the language.

There was an unusually large crowd of fans when they arrived at the stadium. But since they already held tickets they had no difficulty in entering. Soon the place was packed full with spectators. There was hardly any room to sit or stand in.

Kotokro felt very uncomfortable, for he had never before been among so large a crowd in all his life. His discomfort was exacerbated by the behaviour of a huge giant of a man, more than six feet tall, who sat to his left. He pressed hard against him and stepped on his foot every now and again with his large and clumsy shoe. Sometimes too, he dug his elbow into the boy's ribs inadvertently when he took out a cigarette to smoke. Kotokro winced and moaned, but the man took no notice. The boy became very restless.

"When will they start the game?" he asked Mrs Casely. "I want them to start and finish quickly. This place is too uncomfortable."

"It is not time yet", replied Mrs. Casely "We must wait a little more."

"Then why did we have to come so early? We should have waited until they were about to start."

"If we hadn't come early we wouldn't have had any place to sit" Mrs. Casely explained.

"But we already have this paper", he pointed out. "Does it not say that we must be given a place to sit?"

"Yes, it does. But it says so for all the people here too, so if we hadn't come early we wouldn't have had any place to sit.

"Maybe it would have been better than coming early, only to receive harassment before the game starts", he said sulkily.

Mrs. Casely was about to ask who was harassing him when she was cut short by a loud applause which rose up as the Mighty Giants suddenly entered the field. They were followed soon afterwards by The Great Wizards. Everyone cheered and cheered. Then there was silence and at the blow of a whistle, the game started.

It soon became clear to Kotokro that some of the spectators favoured one side, others the other. He himself was indifferent as to which side would win. But even among his three companions Scalini seemed to favour the Mighty Giants of Spain, while Tseng and Khandari appeared to be on the side of the Great Wizards of Peru. This was evident from the way they either cheered or held their peace when one side or the other appeared to play the better game. Even Mrs. Casely was not neutral. She cheered and cheered when the Mighty Giants appeared to be gaining the upper hand, but remained silent when the Great Wizards seemed to be on top.

As for the man sitting to the left of Kotokro he could not contain himself at all. He made it very obvious to everyone that he was on the side of the Great Wizards of Peru. Whenever any of their players had the ball and was running with it he rose up and yelled and cheered, flinging his hefty arms about and shooting his foot, sometimes forward, sometimes sideways; in doing which he struck Kotokro repeatedly. The boy's groans and protests went unheeded. At last as he flung his arm again he hit Kotokro full in the face, making several stars dart from his eyes.

"Hey! see what you have done to me!" shouted Kotokro, rubbing his eyes and pulling his assailant by his trousers.

"What did I do?" asked the man angrily, turning round.

"Don't you know what you have done? You struck me in the face."

"Is that so? Sorry", was all he said, and at once turned round and began to yell and cheer and fling his arms about as before. Suddenly he shot out his arm again in the direction of Kotokro and struck the boy hard in the stomach. This was more than Kotokro could stomach. Greatly enraged, he immediately applied his teeth to the man's right buttock and bit hard. He bit so hard that had the man not been protected by his thick woollen trousers and heavy underpants his flesh would certainly have been badly bruised. As it was, the points of his teeth just missed piercing his skin. He screamed and turned round to look at his attacker.

"Hey, you! Why did you do that?", he asked angrily.

"What did I do?", Kotokro asked in turn.

"Don't you know what you did? You bit my buttock!"

"Is that so? Sorry," replied Kotokro casually.

"Foolish boy!" said the man, and immediately turned round again to watch the game.

The boy had taught him a lesson, however, and thenceforth he became more restrained in his reaction to the trend of the game.

As the game progressed it soon became clear to everyone that The Great Wizards were by far the better players. Again and again they sent the ball into the goal of the Mighty Giants. But repeatedly it failed to penetrate it, for the goalkeeper invariably caught and sent it back. There was no doubt that he was a very competent goalkeeper. As for his counter-part, the goalkeeper of the Great Wizards, he might as well have gone to sleep in the goal, for that would have made no difference to his side, in fact he began to dose as he idly stood in the goal. The Mighty Giants were so incompetent that they never succeeded in bringing the ball anywhere near his goal, with the result that he was never faced with the situation of having to catch it.

The first half ended without either side scoring a goal. And when the whistle blew at the end of the second half there was still no score.

"Is the game over?" asked Kotokro.

"Not yet", replied Mrs Casely "It has been a goal-less drawn game and they have to settle the issue through penalties."

"What does that mean?"

"You will see presently."

Soon all the players withdrew from the field, leaving behind only the two goal keepers and one player from either side. Then the Mighty Giants' goalkeeper stood in the goal and the Great Wizards' player placed the ball some distance away and stood ready to kick it. At the sound of the whistle he kicked it with all his might. The goal-keeper immediately caught it.

A loud applause rent the air. Next, the Great Wizards' goal-keeper also stood in the goal and the Mighty Giants' player got ready to kick the ball. At the sound of the whistle he too administered a kick to the ball, but not half as hard as the other had done. The goal-keeper was unable to catch it, however, and it went rolling into the goal. They repeated the performance with the same result, so that the Mighty Giants were declared the winners, by two goals to nil. About half the people in the stadium rushed into the field, yelling and dancing with joy.

"The Great Wizards were by far the better players. Why were they the losers?" Kotokro asked Mrs. Casely.

"They lost on penalties", replied Mrs. Casely. "Their goal-keeper could not catch the ball."

"But if the purpose was to discover which goal-keeper could catch the ball, then why did they make all the other players waste their time and energy in playing?"

"No, that was not the purpose", replied Mrs. Casely. "The purpose was to find out which side had the better players."

"In that case they should have either made both sides play without goal-keepers; or they should have continued to play until one side scored a goal; or they should have decided the result on points, just as you said they sometimes do in boxing.

"I agree it is not really fair, as it is", conceded Mrs. Casely. "But that is the rule of the game, and they have to go by it."

"They have to go by the rule of the game that is not fair?" Kotokro asked in a tone of surprise.

Mrs. Casely was about to answer when pandemonium broke loose at the stadium. All at once the crowd that had surged on to the field had begun to engage in a scuffle. Soon the scuffle degenerated into a pitched battle. People punched and kicked and laid about them with whatever weapon came to hand, breaking their opponents' limbs and inflicting grievous wounds upon one another. Kotokro had never seen the like before.

"Come, let's get out of here quickly", said Mrs. Casely to the boys.

They got up and made for the exit. The place was choked with people frantically trying to get out. They struggled and jostled and kicked and hustled and stamped and fell and rose. Those who could not rise up quickly were trampled to death.

Suddenly Mrs. Casely fell. As Kotokro bent over to help her up to her feet again he felt himself lifted up by two powerful hands with the force of a crane. He was set aside, and the same powerful hands immediately lifted up Mrs. Casely too before any harm could come to her. They both turned to look at the owner of those hands that had been their saviour. He was no other than the man who had received a bite from Kotokro.

"Follow closely behind me, all four of you", he said to them, and immediately began elbowing his way through the crowd.

The man was so strong that his progress was irresistible. The crowd fell to his right and left as he made his way forward. Mrs. Casely and the boys followed closely behind as he had instructed, with Kotokro at the rear. After what seemed a long time they emerged into the ground outside the stadium. They all heaved sighs of relief.

"Thank you very much", they said to the man.

Then Kotokro added: "And I am sorry to have bitten your buttock. Please forgive me."

"That's all right, muchacho", replied the man, and immediately strode off.

Kotokro felt that it was a good thing he bit the man's buttock, for it made him take particular notice of them and led to their rescue; but he kept his opinion to himself.

When they arrived back in the house Mrs. Casely went up to Dr. Wiseman as usual and told him all that had happened, dwelling more particularly upon Kotokro's remarks and behaviour.

"Well, I am sure you are now thoroughly convinced that the boy has no intelligence", pronounced Dr. Wiseman.

"I am not so sure, Doctor", replied Mrs. Casely. "It seems to me that some of the things he said are rather sensible, particularly about the result of the football match."

"In other words you mean he has more sense than the officials of the World Football Federation who fixed the rules?"

"Not that, but......"

"But what?"

"I thought   there was something in what he said."

"My dear lady, take it from me, there was nothing in what he said, any more than there was something in what he did, namely so wickedly biting the buttock of that gentleman."

"I agree he acted rather foolishly; but he must have been sorely provoked."

"Well, he was lucky the man took it all so calmly. He could have boxed his ear and put some sense into his empty skull."

Mrs. Casely was very much taken aback by the severity with which the Doctor criticised the boy, but she prudently refrained from saying anything more. It seemed to her that the more the boy displayed some degree of intelligence the angrier the Doctor became, because it contradicted a firmly held opinion. Anyhow, he had said that there was only one week to go and he would conduct the Intelligence Test which would scientifically establish the boy's mental capacity. She was sure the result would prove the Doctor wrong.

That one week came sooner than Mrs. Casely had anticipated. Dr. Wiseman had told her that immediately after the test he would return to Africa with the boy. And as she had grown to like him the days passed by rather too quickly for her.

It was on Monday, and early in the morning Dr. Wiseman told the boys that they were to begin the tests for which they had been brought there.

The tests were to be on their sense of direction, linguistic ability, resourcefulness, power of observation, mathematical aptitude, power of recollection, and other mental attributes.

The first to be tested was Scalini. On Dr. Wiseman's instruction Mr. Suppercot took him on foot to Marble Arch, a distance of some two miles from where they lived. From there he asked the boy to find his way back. Having noted the time the boy set out on his return journey, he himself returned home by a taxi. About thirty minutes from the time the boy set out he arrived back in the house.

The next to be tested was Tseng. He was taken to the same place by Mr. Balmer and asked to find his way back. He took thirty-five minutes in doing so.

Then came Khandari, who also took exactly forty minutes in finding his way back.

And now it was the turn of Kotokro. As he accompanied Dr. Springfield to the place he looked right and left, carefully observing the houses and shops they passed by on their way. At last they arrived at Marble Arch.

Leaving him there Dr. Springfield asked him to find his way back to the house. Meanwhile he himself took a taxi and quickly disappeared from sight.

Kotokro set off immediately. He walked very briskly, for he was able to identify the houses and the shops he had seen on their way.

He had covered more than three-quarters of the journey back when he suddenly came upon an old woman in tears following hard upon the heels of a young man of about twenty-four. The latter was carrying on his left arm a lady's handbag and held a jack-knife in his right.

"He has my bag, stop him" the old woman cried again and again.

But although there was a seething crowd in the street no one attempted to stop the robber. Apparently they were all afraid of what he might do to them if they dared to intervene. So the young man continued to make his way through the crowd, brandishing his jack-knife in the most menacing manner, while the woman followed him crying in vain for help.

What had happened was that this woman, a sixty year old widow, had gone into one of London's most prestigious shops, Harrods, and had just re-emerged from the shop when the young man, a worthless scamp of no trade or fixed address, thinking that she must be very rich to have gone into this expensive shop, pounced at once upon her handbag and began to make away with it. He walked very briskly without resort to outright flight, so as not to give the impression of being a thief.

Kotokro took in the situation at once. Going up to the old woman, who, in spite of her age, was managing to keep pace with the young brigand and was following closely behind him, he asked:

"Is it your hand-bag he is carrying away?"

"Yes, he snatched it from my hand", she confirmed. "He is a thief. Please stop him."

"You wait exactly on this spot for me", he said to her, and immediately turned round and began to follow the young man, keeping him at a discreet distance. He followed him for about half-a-mile in a direction quite off his course.

At last the robber, no longer seeing his victim in pursuit, stopped at a bus stop, ready to board a bus for his destination. Kotokro came up and stood behind him as if waiting for a bus too. Three buses came and took off without the young man boarding any of them.

At last a double-decker came and pulled up. The thief immediately entered it and ran upstairs. Kotokro quickly followed him. Arrived up there the thug folded his jack-knife and slid it into his pocket. Seeing an empty seat he ensconced himself in it and placed the hang-bag on his lap. Kotokro approached as if to sit by him; but before the latter could realise what was happening the boy snatched the bag from him and ran with it downstairs. He sprang down the bus just as it was taking off. The thief gave a chase, but by the time he arrived downstairs too the bus was in full motion. He quickly jumped down, but alas! it was too late for him to land on his feet. He fell heavily on his belly and was dragged forward for some distance by the propulsion of the fast-moving vehicle. His clothes tore and his belly and hands were badly bruised. It was quite some time before he could rise up to his feet again. And when he did so he forgot all about the hand-bag, his sole concern now being about his life, for he was so dazed that he thought he was on the point of death.

Meanwhile Kotokro was quickly making his way back to the spot where he had told the old woman to wait for him. He found her still waiting there. There was something in the boy's manner that had assured her that if anyone was to retrieve her bag for her it was that black urchin with the unusual features.

"Here is your hand-bag," said Kotokro, coming up to her.

"Thank you, thank you. May God bless you", cried the old woman.

Then she opened the bag and took out two Pound notes which she offered to Kotokro.

"Here, take this", she said.

"Oh no", refused the latter. "I don't want it. Thank you." And with that he turned round and soon disappeared among the crowd, being in a hurry to return to the house.

But now arose the difficulty of finding his way back. He had strayed so far from the route by which Dr. Springfield had brought him that he could not identify any of the houses or shops that he then saw. All the buildings now looked the same to him. He wandered from street to street, straying further and further away from his proper destination until he felt completely lost. Then panic seized him and he began to ask the way to his house. But no one could tell him, because he was unable to say exactly from which part of London he had come.

Meanwhile Dr. Wiseman had been waiting and waiting in vain for his return. By 5 o'clock in the evening he had still not turned up, having been away for seven hours. Dr. Wiseman became worried, for it was now obvious to him that the boy was lost. What was he to do? He could not go through London looking for him. It would have been like looking for a needle in a hay-stack, even though by reason of his colour alone Kotokro was conspicuous enough among any white crowd.

At last he decided to contact London Police Headquarters and report the boy's loss. He did so and gave a description of Kotokro and the spot in London from where they might begin a search for him. He did not, of course, tell them that the boy had been taken there and asked to find his way back. The police would not have been too pleased to hear that.

The hours passed slowly by and Kotokro had not returned, nor had any word of him come from the police. Dr. Wiseman became greatly worried. If anything happened to him and he did not return, how would he be able to go back to Africa and tell his parents that he was missing? They would not believe him. They would think he had either sold him into slavery or he was keeping him as a slave.

It was true they could do nothing to him, but he would at least have marred his reputation. The news was sure to spread, and thenceforth he would find no help in his anthropological researches on that continent. It was not at all a pleasant prospect.

The clock in the sitting room struck eleven. It was time for him to go to bed. He got up and made for his bedroom, not at all sure that he could have a peaceful sleep with this situation weighing heavily on his mind.

Just as he was about to close the door of the sitting room the telephone rang. He ran quickly and took up the receiver and listened. The call came from the Police Headquarters and he was being asked to hold on and speak to the Inspector in charge of the Kensington Police Station. His heart beat fast. It must surely be about Kotokro, he thought. Had he been found alive or dead?

"Hello, is that Dr. Wiseman?" a voice came through the phone after he had held on for sometime.

"It is", he replied with a heart that had begun to race even faster within him.

"This is Inspector Ivy speaking from the Kensington Police Station"

"Yes?"

"We have found a black boy who calls himself Koto ... something."

"Kotokro?"

"Yes, Kotokro . . . something. "

"Kotokrotintin?"

"Yes, Kotokrotintin . . . something."

"Never mind the something. Is he all right, and where is he?"

"He is sitting right here in my office and seems more than all right. He asks so many questions. Right now, however, he has fallen asleep. I believe he is the boy you reported missing. You may come for him."

"Thank you. I will be there right away."

Putting the receiver back on the telephone box with a mind disburdened of its load, Dr. Wiseman rushed to his bedroom and changed from the pyjamas he was wearing into a lounge suit. Then he woke up Mrs. Wiseman, who was by now fast asleep, and told her Kotokro had been found and he was going for him.

"Where was he found?", asked Mrs. Wiseman with eyes still heavy with sleep.

"In Kensington, I should imagine; the telephone call came from the Kensington Police Station."

"What?" exclaimed Mrs. Wiseman "How was he able to stray so far, a distance of some twenty miles or so from here?"

"He must have kept walking the whole day. You see what a stupid boy he is."

"Very stupid. He could have asked any policeman the way back to this place."

"Well, I am going for him. Keep the door locked, and open for me when I come back."

So saying Dr. Wiseman descended into the garage where he kept his car. He sparked it and was soon on the way to Kensington. There was hardly any traffic on the streets, and he arrived at his destination just before midnight. He found Kotokro sitting in an armchair which the Inspector had provided for him, fast asleep. After covering such a long distance he was thoroughly exhausted and could not help falling asleep immediately he installed himself in that cosy seat.

Dr. Wiseman introduced himself to the inspector, who sat behind a table, and said that he had come for Kotokro.

"Well, there he is. You can wake him up and take him away", said Inspector Ivy.

"Where was he found?" asked Dr. Wiseman.

"He was found by one of my men on the beat, about an hour ago, near the Kensington Tube Station. He was asking passers-by to show him the way back to your house; but, of course, no one could help him, as he could not give your address."

"Thank you, Inspector," said Dr. Wiseman. "He is a very stupid boy. But that, of course, is not surprising. He comes from Gamberia."

"And where is that?", asked the Inspector.

"In Africa, of course. You can see that he is an African."

"Oh yes", replied Inspector Ivy, not sure that all blacks came from Africa. He had always thought that some came from America too - and Russia. "He asks many questions and makes interesting remarks."

"He does. He does not understand anything" said Dr. Wiseman.

"The first question he asked me, immediately he arrived here, was whether I knew Dr. Wiseman. When I replied that I did not, he said that he was surprised that a man who was said to be well-known all over the world should apparently be unknown in his own country. All the people he had asked didn't seem to know you."

"Well, you see how stupid he is. He supposes that in a city with such a large population everyone should be known to everyone else."

"That's exactly what I told him. I said that it was impossible for people to know one another in such a large population as this. And do you know the suggestion he made? He said that in that case we should make some machine to record the names, addresses and photographs of everybody who dwells in this city. Similar machines should be made for all the other cities in the country."

"Preposterous" opined Dr. Wiseman.

"Well, I think he has said something which ought to engage the attention of computer scientists", said Inspector Ivy with a smile.

"I am sure they wouldn't have the time for that."

"He is really an interesting lad", continued the Inspector. "When he saw these guns here he asked if we were hunters. When I said no, he asked what were the guns used for then I replied that they were for keeping law and order."

"In what way?", he asked.

"By shooting those who would violate them", I replied.

"Are law and order so much more important than human lives that you should kill those who would violate them?" he asked. "He is really an interesting fellow."

Dr. Wiseman, who could not agree with the Inspector's assessment, even though it hardly contradicted his own, simply shook Kotokro and told him to get up. The boy stood up, rubbed his eyes and looked around him. His face lighted up with joy when he recognised Dr. Wiseman standing before him.

"Come, let's be going" he said, leading the boy by the hand.

Thanking the Inspector again he brought Kotokro to the car and helped him to get inside. Although he was very angry with the boy for causing him so much trouble, he said nothing to him all the way back to the house. Kotokro too said nothing, although by now he was wide awake.

Mrs. Wiseman was still up and opened the door immediately she heard the sound of the Doctor's car in the garage. He entered, followed by Kotokro.

"What does he say happened?", she asked immediately she saw them.

"Well, ask him" replied her husband. "I have not asked him anything yet. The police say they found him near Kensington Tube Station."

"What happened, my boy", asked Mrs. Wiseman, addressing Kotokro.

"I was coming back to the house when I saw an old woman following a man with a jack-knife who had snatched her hand-bag from her. She was crying for help, but no one would help her to get it back. They all looked on as if it was nobody's concern. So I followed the man and snatched it from him when I had the chance. I brought it back to the woman; but I had strayed too far from the places I could recognise, and so I could not find my way back. That is how I got lost."

"You see, I have always told you that this boy has little or no intelligence", said Dr. Wiseman to his wife when Kotokro had finished explaining. "What business had he to follow the thief when he knew that he might easily get lost? Besides, he could easily have been stabbed by him?"

"But I think he is a brave and kind-hearted boy" she replied.

"I don't dispute that. But bravery and kind-heartedness have nothing to do with intelligence. They are usually the attributes of the lower breed, such as the lion and the terrier. Their intelligence is not to be compared with that of human beings. For one thing, they cannot solve problems or behave in a rational manner."

Mrs. Wiseman did not contradict, being anxious to get back to bed; so she said good night. When Kotokro returned to his apartment he found Mrs. Casely still up. She had been anxious all day when Kotokro failed to turn up for lunch and dinner and was still unable to sleep.

She was greatly relieved when she saw the boy back. She got up at once to serve him his meal, for she knew that Kotokro must be very hungry, not having eaten all day except for the light breakfast in the morning.

"What happened to you?", she asked as soon as she had set his food on the table.

Kotokro narrated the story exactly as he had told it to Mrs. Wiseman and the Doctor.

"The Doctor must be very mad with you", suggested Mrs. Casely when he had finished.

"Yes, he is very angry". he replied. "He said I am very stupid. I have no intelligence."

"Did he say so, indeed?"

"He did. But Mrs. Wiseman also said that I was brave and kind-hearted."

"She said that, did she?"

"Yes, that is what she said."

"Well, I agree with her. But come, eat your meal and go to bed."

Kotokro came to the table and started eating.

"Mrs. Casely", he called after taking a few mouthfuls.

"Yes, dear?"

"What is intelligence?"

"Intelligence is . . . eh . . well, intelligence is when you are able to do the right thing at the right time."

"Not when you are able to solve problems or behave in a rational manner?"

"Well, it includes those too."

"But I was able to solve the problem of getting that old woman's hand-bag back for her? Was that not the right thing done at the right time, and was it not rational behaviour?"

"Well, some people would only call that bravery."

"But what do you think?"

"I think they are right. Some people would even call it fool-hardiness. You exposed yourself to danger."

"How?"

"The thief could easily have stabbed you, as the Doctor said."

"Why didn't he stab me then?"

"Because you were too quick for him."

"Then he couldn't have stabbed me, because I was too quick for him?"

"Yes, but you could have been too slow."

"Why was I not too slow then?"

"Because you were too quick."

"Then he couldn't have stabbed me, because I was too quick?"

"Look hero, let's stop arguing round and round in a circle", said Mrs. Casely with some exasperation, for she wanted to get back quickly to bed. "The Doctor says that you are stupid, and he should know. It is his business to study human intelligence."

Immediately after breakfast next morning Dr. Wiseman called the boys and told them that he was going to test them in mental Arithmetic. They should go to the library from where he would call them to his office one by one to answer questions.

Kotokro was excited. No one had taught them to count since he arrived in London, but he had learned to do so even before he left Kantoma, thanks to old Rakito. He was sure all the other boys did not know how to count as much as he did. He would surprise Dr. Wiseman who had always said that he was stupid. He was sure that a stupid person could not do well in mental Arithmetic.

The first to be called to Dr. Wiseman's office was Scalini. He and Tseng and Khandari had learned to count up to fifty without anyone teaching them. They had picked it up in the course of their visits to the Zoo, where the zoo-keeper always told them how many animals were in each cage. Sometimes there was only one animal, such as the giant panther from Sumatra; or two, such as the two yellow pythons from Angola; or three, such as the three white elephants from India, and so on. As Kotokro never went with them again after their first visit, he had not learnt to count in the same way.

"Now, tell me" began Dr. Wiseman when Scalini stood before him, "what is four plus six minus three?" And he looked at his stop watch to see how long the boy would take over the answer. Scalini counted four of his fingers, then counted further six and removed three.

"Seven", he replied.

Dr. Wiseman's stop-watch indicated that he had taken exactly thirty seconds to return the answer.

"Correct", said the Doctor. "Go away and call me Khandari."

It was not long before Khandari entered his office and stood before him.

"What is four plus six minus three?" asked Dr. Wiseman.

Khandari counted four of his fingers, then he counted further six and removed three.

"Seven", he replied.

Dr. Wiseman looked at his stop-watch. The boy had taken exactly forty seconds.

"Correct", he said. "You may go away. But call me Tseng." Tseng soon stood before him. He asked him the same question.

Tseng said the answer was six. "Wrong", said Dr. Wiseman "Try again."

He repeated the question, and after a while the boy said that the answer was seven. Dr. Wiseman looked at his stop-watch. He had taken fifty seconds in answering the repeated question. Dr. Wiseman asked him to go away and call Kotokro.

It was not long before Kotokro confidently stood before him. Dr. Wiseman looked at him and smiled wryly. He was sure the boy was going to return some ridiculous answer.

"Tell me, what is four plus six minus three?" he asked.

Kotokro quickly counted on his fingers the numerals in the way old Rakito had taught him: One, two, six, seven, four. He got five fingers. Then he counted one, two, six. He got three fingers. He added both and counting them again on his fingers, got nine. Then he again counted one, two, six, seven, four, three. He got six fingers. Then he said "nine fingers take away six fingers equal six."

"The answer is six", he replied at once. He had taken twenty-five seconds.

"Stupid! Stupid!" shouted Dr. Wiseman "Try again." Then he repeated the question and began to look at his stop-watch again. In less than twenty seconds Kotokro returned the same answer.

"It is six, sir", he said.

"Nonsense! It is not six", the Doctor contradicted angrily. "The answer is seven. Ask all the other boys, and they will tell you that it is seven. I put the same question to them and they all got the same answer, seven. That is the correct answer."

"They were all wrong, Sir," argued Kotokro. "The correct answer is six, as old Rakito would confirm if he were here."

"Who is old Rakito?" asked Dr. Wiseman.

"Why, don't you remember the old man at Kantoma who asked whether you had come there to revive the Slave Trade in another guise?"

Dr. Wiseman scratched his head. He did not remember; for of course, Jimfa had not translated that to him.

"Did he say that, indeed?" he asked doubtfully.

"Yes, he did. And he also said that no parent in our village would be willing to give his son to a stranger to take away to a strange country."

Dr. Wiseman now remembered the old black crow with the gnarled face and a mouth like pontoon who had nearly ruined his plan by his negative suggestion. He wondered if the man himself could count up to ten, even in his own language.

"Oh yes, I remember him all right" replied Dr. Wiseman. "And I am sure he would say exactly as you have said, or even something worse still."

"So the correct answer is not six?" asked Kotokro incredulously.

"It is as six as zero plus zero is six!"

"But that is two zero's?

"It is zero, only one zero, my clever block-head! A thousand zeros are but one zero!"

Kotokro could not understand how a thousand zeros could be only one zero, but he did not argue, for fear of making the Doctor more angry. Anyhow, as far as his answer was concerned, he was sure he was right. However, if the Doctor said that he was wrong there was nothing he could do about it.

"Can I go away, Sir?" was all he said.

"You may go", he replied. "But call me Khandari. You are all going to begin another test."

With a heavy heart Kotokro left the office. He found the other boys waiting for him in the library. They became curious to know what had happened when they saw him re-emerging from the Doctor's office with a despondent face. It was Tseng who first asked him.

"He tested me in very easy mental Arithmetic and I got it correct in no time, but he said that I was wrong." he replied.

"What was the question?" asked Scalini.

"He asked what was four plus six minus three."

"Well, he asked us the same question. And what answer did you give?"

"I said six."

"Then you were wrong", they all said. "The answer is seven."

"You were all wrong. The answer is not seven. It is six. Old Rakito would confirm it if he were here."

"Who is he?" they asked.

"He is a learned old man in our village. He taught me to count in English."

"Then he didn't teach you to count correctly", said Khandari.

"All right, I won't argue. All I know is that I am right and you are all wrong", he replied firmly. Then he added:

"The Doctor says we are going to begin another test and he wants you to come, Khandari."

Khandari went at once and stood before the Doctor.

"Kotokro says you want to see me, sir", he said to him.

"Yes, you are going to have another test, a very simple one." the Doctor confirmed.

"Yes, Sir. I am ready", said the boy.

"Well, here we go: A is taller than B, and B is shorter than C. So between A and C who is taller?"

Khandari scratched his head for some time. He did not know what to say.

"Will you repeat the question, Sir?" he said.

Dr. Wiseman did so. Khandari scratched and scratched his head again. He found the question baffling. At last he said:

"I don't know, Sir."

Dr. Wiseman had been gazing at his stop-watch from the time he put the first question. It had taken exactly two minutes for the boy to give an answer.

"Correct", he said with a smile.

Khandari's face lighted up with pleasure. He had not anticipated that this could be the correct answer.

"Did you say my answer was correct, Sir?" he asked incredulously.

"Yes, that is the correct answer", replied Dr. Wiseman. "you may go away, but call me Tseng."

The boy left the office in high spirits. He found Tseng and Scalini and Kotokro still arguing about the answer to the mental Arithmetic, although before he left to go and see the Doctor, Kotokro had said that he wouldn't argue any more. He soon discovered the reason. The other two boys had been teasing Kotokro over his answer, saying that it showed that he had no idea at all about numbers.

"Stop this argument", said Khandari, who was, by nature, not at all fond of any talk that engendered ill-feeling. "The Doctor says he wants Tseng to come."

Tseng lost no time in presenting himself before Dr. Wiseman. The Doctor asked if he knew what he had been summoned for. He replied in the affirmative.

"Tell me then", he began, "A is taller than B and B is shorter than C. So between A and C who is taller?"

Tseng thought for a moment.

"I don't know, Sir", he replied.

Dr. Wiseman looked at his stop-watch. He had taken exactly ten seconds.

"Why do you say you don't know?" he asked.

"Because I don't know by how much A is taller than B or B is shorter than C." he replied.

"Correct", said the Doctor "You may go away; but call me Scalini."

It was not long before Scalini stood before him.

"A is taller than B and B is shorter than C. So, between A and C who is taller?" the Doctor asked him.

Scalini thought and thought. He did not understand the question. He asked the Doctor to repeat it. He did so. He thought and thought again. It seemed to him there must be a catch somewhere, for the question seemed so tricky. At last he gave up trying to figure it out and said:

"I don't know the answer, because you have not told me by how much A is taller than B, or B is shorter than C."

Dr. Wiseman looked at his stop-watch. The boy had taken twenty seconds in returning an answer after the repeated question.

"Correct", he said. "You may go away, but call me Kotokro."

Kotokro's heart began to beat fast as soon as he saw Scalini re-emerge. He knew that it was now his turn. Would he be able to pass the test this time? Even though he was always right the Doctor was always saying that he was wrong. Well, he hoped that things would be different this time.

He started for the Doctor's office even before Scalini told him he wanted to see him, and soon he stood before the formidable examiner with apprehension.

"Tell me", began Dr. Wiseman after silently surveying him up and down for a few seconds; "A is taller than B and B is shorter than C. So between A and C who is taller

"I cannot tell you until you tell me by how much A is taller than B, and also by how much B is shorter than C," he replied at once.

"I shall not tell you. You must use your common-sense if you have any!" replied Dr. Wiseman angrily.

"Well, if this is a riddle then I would say that A is taller, because he is the only one who is said to be taller."

"Nonsense! Nonsense!" shouted Dr. Wiseman, "Very stupid. Go away!"

Kotokro left the office in a dejected mood. He thought he had answered correctly, but as always, the Doctor said that he was wrong. He did not at all understand why. He made his way back to the Library where he joined the other three boys. He found them discussing the question the Doctor had asked them and their answers.

"Did you get it correct?" asked Tseng as soon as he appeared.

"I got it correct, but the Doctor said I was wrong"

"What did you say?" all three asked simultaneously, for they were eager to know what made Kotokro think he was right when the Doctor had said that he was wrong.

"I said that if this was a riddle then I would say that A was taller because he was the only one concerning whom the word taller was used.

"Then you were truly wrong", they all pronounced. "You should have said that you didn't know, because you did not know by how much A was taller than B, or B was shorter than C."

"Was that the answer and explanation you gave?" he asked

"Yes", replied Tseng and Scalini.

"I simply said that I did not know", said Khandari. "But that was the reason why I said so."

"What reason?"

"Because the Doctor did not tell me by how much A was taller than B, or B was shorter than C.

"Then all of you were wrong", said Kotokro.

"What!" they exclaimed. "But the Doctor said we were right?"

"He did not listen carefully to the reason you gave for your replies. If he had done so he would have said that you were wrong."

"But you simply said that A was taller than C, which is definitely wrong", remarked Khandari.

"Well, my first reply was that I could not tell whether A or C was taller until the Doctor told me by how much A was taller than B, and also by how much B was shorter than C. He replied that he would not tell me and that I must use my commonsense. I gave the second answer because I began to think that this was a riddle depending upon the use of the words "taller" and "shorter."

"Then there was no difference between your first reply and ours. Why then did the Doctor say that you were wrong?"

"There was some slight but very important difference", he replied. "And, by the way, he did not say that my first reply was right or wrong. He only refused to tell me by how much A was taller than B, and by how much B was also shorter than C. But he was definitely wrong to say that your answer, depending upon the reason you gave, was correct."

"Hey, do you mean to tell us that you know more than the Doctor?" they asked in astonishment.

"No, I have said that he was not paying sufficient attention to the explanation you gave for your answer."

All right, Mr. Know-all", said Scalini sarcastically, "you are right and we are all wrong, including the Doctor. Tell him so, when he comes out of his office."

Kotokro did not reply but remained sullen and silent. He felt that he would never be able to convince anyone that he was right.

And it was a lucky thing he shut his mouth just in time. For just at this moment Dr. Wiseman issued out of his office and came towards them. Had he overheard what Kotokro was saying he would undoubtedly have been very angry. Even as it was, his anger over the boy's reply had hardly cooled down. He had been so angry that he had forgotten to ask him to tell the boys that another test was to begin, hence he had to bring the information himself.

"All right, boys", he said. "We have just one more test for today. It is going to be the repetition of nonsense rhymes. You must come to my office again one by one, beginning with Scalini, followed by Tseng, Khandari and Kotokro in that order. Now you, Scalini, follow me." And with that Dr. Wiseman re-entered his office, followed by Scalini.

Arrived at his office Dr. Wiseman sat down and pulled out a paper from a drawer.

"Listen carefully", he said to Scalini, looking on the paper. "I am going to read to you this nonsense rhyme, which I want you to repeat correctly. Here it is:

"Speed amber zebra go,
"Steed antler ambler so;
"Tarmac tar propels aisle
"Thundering crowd deserts file."
"Now repeat."

Scalini repeated the first and the last two lines correctly. Then Dr. Wiseman asked him to go away and call Tseng. He did so, and soon Tseng stood before him. He read out the lines and asked him to repeat. He did so, getting only the first two lines correct. He was next followed by Khandari who got only the second line correct.

And now it was the turn of Kotokro. The Doctor read out the lines to him twice and asked him to repeat.

"Speedy zebra antlers go,

45

Steeds repel deserts so.
Too much tear peppers eye,
Thundering cloud dries fine",

he repeated.

"Wrong! All wrong!" shouted Dr. Wiseman when he had finished. "Why, you could not get even one line correct. Even my parrot could have done much better."

It was true. Dr. Wiseman's parrot, Jacko, was a truly remarkable bird. He could recite long passages from many authors, both ancient and modern, from Aristotle to Shakespeare and Byron and many of the modern authors. It was particularly delightful to hear him recite by heart the whole of the Gospel according to St. Matthew, Chapter 1: "... And Abraham begat Isaac; and Isaac begat Jacob; and Jacob begat Judas and his brethren; and Judas begat Phares and Zera of Themar; and Phares begat Esrom; and Esrom begat Aram.."

In spite of his extraordinary power of memory and his unrivalled eloquence, however, Jacko was classified as a dumb creature, with the implication that he was unable to think at all.

Not relishing the comparison therefore, Kotokro turned round and began to retreat even before Dr. Wiseman could order him to go away. The Doctor looked on until he had disappeared through the door. He arrived in the Library looking very morose.

"How many lines did you get correct?" asked Scalini observing him.

"None. The Doctor said I did not get even one line correct." he replied.

"The lines were really difficult", said Khandari. "Only one made some sense to me: the one about steed and antler, of whom we have many in my village.

Kotokro said nothing. Tseng was about to endorse Khandari's verdict when he was cut short by the appearance of the Doctor. He had put on his hat and overcoat and was obviously on the point of going out.

"Well, boys", he said. "The tests are over for today. We shall continue tomorrow with practicals. So you can go away now."

The boys were glad to have finished for the day and they hurried upstairs to their apartments. Mrs. Casely had just finished preparing their lunch. When they sat down to eat she noticed that Kotokro was rather morose and did not seem to be enjoying the food, although by now he had learned to enjoy English meals which he had at first found tasteless and unappetizing. Kotokro himself was surprised to see how quickly his palate had succeeded in adapting itself to it.

"Why, what's wrong with you?", Mrs. Casely asked him.

"Nothing," he replied.

"He failed in the tests. He got all his answers wrong" Scalini informed her.

"And have you completed all the tests?" asked Mrs. Casely.

"No, the Doctor says it remains the practicals tomorrow", replied Scalini.

"Well, cheer up", she encouraged. "I am sure you will do better in the practicals."

Kotokro did not reply. He continued to eat his meal with a lump in his throat. After they had eaten he helped Mrs. Casely to clear the table and wash up as usual. Still he said nothing. And when Mrs. Casely tried to cheer him up by saying funny things he only smiled, although in normal circumstances he was a hearty laugher. His father had always said that laughter cleanses the teeth and purifies the heart; and in his few years of existence he had found this to be true. People who did not laugh did not have good teeth or good hearts.

Immediately after the work in the kitchen was over he retired to his room and lay in bed, thinking of home. Dr. Wiseman had said that the tests would end the next day. This meant he would soon be going back to Kantoma. If he had known that this was what the Doctor was bringing him for, he wouldn't have volunteered to come. Anyway he did not altogether regret it. He had seen and learnt many things which even old Rakito had never seen or known. He had seen the white man's country, his inventions and how he lived. He would have a long story to tell when he went back home. First of all, there was the aeroplane. He remembered what his father said about the day when one flew over Kantoma. The villagers, who had never seen any before, were frightened beyond measure. All those at home fled in panic to the bush, while those in the bush rushed home in great alarm, everyone imagining that some dreadful monster was descending from the sky, from which they ought to run for dear life. None had flown again over the village since he was born and he had never been able to imagine what it was really like. But now, not only had he seen one plainly, but he had actually sat in it. He was sure no matter how he described his experience he would never be able to make anyone in Kantoma understand exactly what it was like. Next, there was the train, that monstrous machine that wormed its way through the earth's bowels or meandered above the ground like a giant millipede, carrying multitudes of people in its segmented belly; the motor vehicles that flowed in endless streams in opposite directions, stopping occasionally at colour-changing traffic lights; the huge monstrous buildings that invaded the sky and had to be ascended or descended in mobile cages; The shops that bulged, almost to the point of bursting, with many man-made goods; the electric lights that burst forth at the touch of a button, instantly sweeping away the surrounding darkness; the telephone by which you could speak to someone at the other end of the world as if he stood before you; the Zoo with its disconsolate inmates, many of whom he had only seen for the first time, even though they were said to have come from his own country; the boxing match in which two contestants pounded each other mercilessly for the money and entertainment of others even though they had no quarrel; the football game that galvanized sane men into behaving like lunatics; the possibility of an open attack by a street ruffian in broad daylight without anyone from the milling crowd intervening; all the virtues and vices of the white man's inventions, of his economic and social life, of his outward behaviour and inner character. He was sure it would take him several years to finish in recounting them, even without repeating and repeating as old Rakito did. Suddenly he had fallen asleep and was dreaming again of home.

Immediately after breakfast the next morning Dr. Wiseman summoned the boys to the Library for the practical tests, as he had promised the previous day. This time there was no need to call them into his office one by one. The tests were to consist of problems that were to be solved in silence. He wished to find out how quickly each could solve them.

The first test was the unravelling of a jig-saw puzzle. The Doctor made the boys sit around a large table in the centre of the Library. Then he placed before each a board on which had been heaped several small pieces of painted and plain card-boards, all cut up into odd shapes and different sizes.

"What you see is a jib-saw puzzle", he explained." Correctly arranged they will present the picture of a well known scene. What I want you to do is to arrange them in such a way that this scene, which has been cut up, will emerge again. I shall give you a clue by saying that it is the picture of two creatures doing something. You are to start as soon as I give you the signal. We shall see which of you can finish first."

After he had spoken he asked if they had understood. If anyone had not, let him ask for repetition. They all replied that they had understood.

"Good. Then get ready", he said, raising his hand. "Start!" And he brought his hand down again.

The boys set to work at once. In less than five minutes Kotokro had put together a picture that looked like a man with a bulging front holding a woman with thighs set wide apart. They were both very scantily clad, almost to the point of nakedness. "Oh no," he said to himself, "this cannot be it. If the Doctor sees this he will be very angry with me. He does not like to see the picture of naked or semi-naked people, since it is very indecent. I must try once more." So he mixed it all up and started all over again. He put them together and got the same result. "Oh no, I must try a third time." In the end he succeeded in producing something that looked like two crocodiles fighting, although the pieces did not quite fit together. He raised up his hand at once.

"Have you finished?", asked Dr. Wiseman.

"Yes, I have." he replied.

"All right, keep it. I shall come round and look at it." said the Doctor.

Kotokro was followed immediately after by Scalini, who also said that he had finished. The Doctor told him to keep it for inspection later on. Tseng came next, followed by Khandari.

And now Dr. Wiseman started going round, looking at their pictures one by one, beginning first with the last; that is to say, with Khandari. The boy had produced the picture of a man dragging a bull by the horn, in the way one often saw in India.

"Wrong" said Dr. Wiseman

He next went to Tseng. He looked at his picture. It showed a man and a woman fighting judo.

"Wrong!" pronounced Dr. Wiseman.

He went on to examine the picture which Scalini had produced. It was that of two ballet dancers, a man holding the raised foot of a woman who had entwined her right arm around his neck and had the left hand raised above her head. They were both so scantily clad that they appeared almost naked.

"Correct" pronounced Dr. Wiseman.

And now it was Kotokro's turn. The Doctor looked and looked at his picture.

"What" he exclaimed, "Two fighting crocodiles? This really beats my imagination."

"Is it wrong?", asked Kotokro.

"It is wrong; and not only wrong but silly in the extreme. It bears no resemblance whatsoever to the correct picture."

"What is the correct picture?", asked Kotokro, greatly disappointed.

"Scalini, get up and show them your picture", he said by way of a reply to Kotokro's question.

Scalini got up and showed them.

"But I got that picture!" said Kotokro.

"Do you mean to say that your picture of two fighting crocodiles is the same as that picture of two ballet dancers?" Dr. Wiseman asked incredulously.

"No, but I got that picture the first time that I put my pieces together."

"Then what happened?", asked Dr. Wiseman, trying hard to keep his temper which was almost stretched beyond endurance. The boy was always arguing even when he was manifestly wrong.

"Then I mixed it all up and began all over again", he replied.

"Why did you mix it all up?"

"Because I thought that you would be angry with me if you saw it. It showed semi-naked people. It was indecent."

"Don't you have naked people in Africa?"

"We have, but not pictures of naked or semi-naked people."

"Which are more indecent - naked people or pictures of naked people?"

"Pictures of naked people."

"Why?"

"Because where people go naked they don't take any interest in one another's nakedness. But where people don't go naked many take interest in the pictures of naked or semi-naked people. So nakedness is not indecent among naked people; but pictures of naked or semi-naked people are indecent among people who don't go naked."

"Absolute nonsense", shouted Dr. Wiseman "It is because your naked people are all so very stupid. If they had any intelligence they wouldn't go naked, in the first place."

Kotokro said nothing. He saw that the Doctor was very angry and he would make matters worse by any further argument. It was plain that nothing he could say would convince him that he had really got the picture right at the first attempt. He wished he had stopped trying again and had presented the first picture he got. Then he would have finished by far the first. But how could he have known that the Doctor would not be angry to see it, that the Doctor was one of the many people in his country who liked to see the pictures of naked people?

"All right, boys, you are going to begin the second test, so get ready", said Dr. Wiseman, after he had taken some time cooling off the anger which Kotokro's unnecessary argument had aroused in him.

"We are ready." all three boys said in unison. Kotokro remained silent.

Dr. Wiseman went into his office and was soon back with four tins of corned beef, together with four keys for opening them, four tin-cutters and four knives. He placed a set of one corned beef, one key, one tin-cutter and one knife before each boy.

"Now listen carefully", he said to them. "What I want you to do is to open the corned beef before you at a given signal. I want to see which of you will be able to open his corned beef first. Ready?"

"Ready", they replied.

He raised up his hand.

"Start!" he said, bringing his hand down again, as he had done for the jig-saw puzzle.

Scalini seized the key and started to open. Tseng plunged the tin-cutter into the top of the rectangular tin and began to turn it round with difficulty. Khandari took hold of the knife and began cutting his. Kotokro seized the projection from the tin with his strong teeth and immediately ripped it open.

"I have finished, Sir!" he shouted triumphantly.

The Doctor looked at the three instruments lying untouched on the table before the boy. He was puzzled.

"With what did you open it?" he asked.

"With my teeth", replied Kotokro

"With your teeth!" the Doctor exclaimed in astonishment.

"Yes, Sir. That's the way we do it in Kantoma."

"Jesus Christ of Nazareth!" exclaimed Dr. Wiseman. "This is incredible. You mean you open a tin of corned beef with your teeth?"

"Yes, sir. We do so when we are in a hurry."

"Well, you were in a hurry all right. But what do you think those instruments were for?"

"You did not tell us to use them, Sir. You only said you wanted to see who would be able to open his tin of corned beef first."

"Stupid! Nonsense! Did I have to tell you that you should use one of those instruments?"

Kotokro did not utter another word. He saw that the Doctor was angry again.

"I have finished, Sir", said Scalini, raising up his hand.

Some minutes later Tseng also said that he had finished. Khandari was still struggling with his. He had already cut his right thumb with the knife and was trying to open it with the left. It was some time before he succeeded in doing so.

"My dear boy", said Dr. Wiseman to Kotokro, seeing him looking very quiet and despondent, "you should never try to open a tin of corned beef or sardine, or indeed any tin of canned food, with your teeth. Not only is it very uncivilised but it is also highly dangerous. Why, you could easily have cut your lips or your tongue."

Kotokro had wanted to say: "Why did I not cut my lips or my tongue then?" And if the Doctor had replied that it was because he was careful, he would have said that he couldn't have cut his lips or his tongue then, because he was careful. He realised, however, that any such argument would only inflame the Doctor the more. So he only said: "Yes, Sir."

The Doctor said that the intelligence test was all over now. He would tell them the results presently. With that he rose up and went again into his office. He soon re-emerged holding a paper.

"Listen to the results", he told them "Scalini came first, with 90 out of 100 marks. Tseng came second with 75 marks; Khandari is third, with 65 marks. Kotokro took the last position, with only 2 marks out of 100. Therefore Scalini has the highest intelligence, and Kotokro the lowest. In fact, as you can all see, Kotokro's intelligence is so low that we can hardly say he has any at all. Well, you can all go away now."

As they got up to go Kotokro looked almost as if he would cry. It was with great difficulty that he could hold back the tears that gathered in his eyes.

"Cheer up" Scalini said to him, noticing his mood. "I am sure if the Doctor had asked us things about the jungle you could have scored more marks."

Kotokro did not reply. He felt that even if it had all been about trees and monkeys Dr. Wiseman would have pronounced all his answers wrong. Well, whatever the Doctor might think of him he would soon be back among his own people. There no one thought that he was stupid. Intelligence he might not have, whatever it was. But he was certainly not stupid. Even old Rakito knew that. He was among those who took two days in learning from him how to count in the white man's tongue, while others took, some three days, others even four.

When the boys arrived at their apartment Mrs. Casely noticed that Kotokro still looked downcast.

"What is wrong with you?", she asked.

He did not answer.

"He failed in the test again" explained Scalini "So that he got only 2 marks out of 100 for consolation. The Doctor said he was very stupid and that his Intelligence Quotient was almost nil."

"In what did he test you, this time?" asked Mrs Casely.

"He tested us in jig-saw puzzle and in the opening of a tin of corned beef", Tseng replied.

"And he couldn't open a tin of corned beef?"

"He could, but he used his teeth."

"Dear me !" exclaimed Mrs. Casely, turning to Kotokro, "did you use your teeth indeed in opening a tin of corned beef?"

"I did", he replied.

"Why? Did the Doctor not give you something for opening it?"

"He did."

"And yet you used your teeth in opening it"

"He did not tell us to use anything in particular. He only said he wanted to see who would open his tin first."

"And so you used your teeth?"

"And so I used my teeth and finished first."

"Well, I guess you were right to use any means to open it, if the Doctor did not tell you with what to open it," conceded Mrs. Casely. "But you must never again use your teeth in opening a tin of any canned food. Why, it could easily have cut your tongue or lips"

"That's exactly what the Doctor told him", Khandari cut in.

Kotokro said nothing. The usual reply came into his mind again but he gave no utterance to it. He did not want Mrs. Casely to say again that he was arguing round and round in a circle.

In the evening Dr. Wiseman summoned Mrs. Casely and his three Senior Research Assistants and told them that he had finished testing the boys. The results had been exactly as he had expected. It had indicated that Scalini had the highest Intelligence Quotient, with a score of 90 per cent, followed by Tseng with 75 per cent and Khandari with 65 per cent. Kotokro was the last, with a score of only 2 percent, which was, in fact, only a consolation mark, for his actual score was 0.

"So you see that I was right, after all, in concluding even before this test, that the African has the lowest Intelligence", he said, turning to Dr. Springfield. "Conclusions based upon actual observations are always valid. If the Intelligence Tests had proved that Kotokro's Intelligence was higher than that of Scalini, for example, then we would have been hard put to it to find an explanation for the fact that the latter's race is superior to the formers in all fields of human endeavour."

Dr. Springfield did not reply. It was he who had suggested the Intelligence Tests to Dr. Wiseman, and now that the latter had carried them out he could find no objection to the result. Mrs. Casely, however, was not satisfied with the Doctor's information.

"I am rather surprised to learn that your tests have established conclusively that Kotokro has little or no intelligence", she remarked "I have been closely acquainted with all four boys since their arrival here, and I am convinced that even though Kotokro often asks silly questions and makes ridiculous remarks it would be rather unfair to say that he has little or no intelligence. Indeed it seems to me that his silly questions and ridiculous remarks often exhibit a high degree of commonsense and practical wisdom."

"My dear lady", replied Dr. Wiseman "believe me, the boy has no intelligence in any shape of form. My scientific tests have established beyond every reasonable doubt that his Intelligence is almost nil, which means that all his thoughts and actions are merely instinctive, so that the sense and wisdom which you seem to detect in his actions and utterances are like the sense and wisdom which one discerns in the actions of the lower breed, such as the ant and the parrot. I said this before and my tests have now proved conclusively that I was right."

"But", persisted Mrs Casely, not prepared to give in so easily "he has at least done well in learning the English language in so short a time. When he first arrived he had not a word of English. And yet within this space of one year he has learnt to express himself as well as the other boys, indeed even better than Scalini, I would say."

"Did he find it easy at the beginning?", asked Dr. Wiseman.

"No, he didn't. For the first four weeks or so it seemed he would never be able to learn the language. But after that he made rapid progress and quickly overtook the others and was able to express himself as well as any of them. Right now I think he understands the language better than any of them. Is that not an indication of some intelligence?"

"Did he say why he found it difficult at the beginning?"

"He said that the language was very unlike his own. We have too many words standing for the same thing, where as in his own language one word often stands for many things. He said that, for example, instead of using the word dwelling to denote the living place of any creature, we use the words house, den, coop, burrow, nest, sty etc. for the dwelling of a human being, a lion, a chicken, a rabbit, a bird, a pig, etc. respectively. Again instead of saying that lions, cocks, horses, elephants, cats, bulls, pigs etc cry, we say they roar, crow, neigh, trumpet, mew, low, and grunt respectively. He found it difficult to learn so many words that denote the same object or the same activity."

"Well, is that not a further proof of his lack of intelligence?" asked Dr. Wiseman. "How can you use one word to denote objects or sounds that are dissimilar? If you say, for example, that a horse or a bull cries, how would one know what sounds they actually emit? No, take it from me, the boy's lack of intelligence is hereditary. He comes from a race whose cranial capacity is so small that it cannot contain even a tenth of the words in our dictionary."

"But does neigh or bark or low or trumpet or any of those words tell us the exact sound that the particular animal ....."

Before she could finish the sentence the telephone rang.

"Excuse me", said Dr. Wiseman, getting up.

He went to the telephone and picked it up. He listened and in turn spoke for about five minutes before putting down the receiver. Then he returned and resumed his seat.

"Yes, what were you saying?" he asked Mrs. Casely.

Dr. Wiseman's three Research Assistants had sat quietly listening to the exchanges between the Doctor and Mrs. Casely. Not a word had they interposed in defence of the boy. They all looked upon Dr. Wiseman not only as a distinguished anthropologist, but also as the final authority on encephalology, a branch of science which the learned Doctor defined as the study of the nature and functioning of the brain, particularly of the Negro brain. They therefore never opened their mouths whenever the learned Doctor was talking about Intelligence Quotients and the like. Mrs. Casely, therefore, not receiving any support from the three gentlemen, whom she regarded as more educated than herself, decided to say no more on the matter but to change the subject.

"I was saying that the boy has, at least, a high sense of humour", she replied. "He seems to discern instantly the humour in every situation. Is that not an indication of some degree of intelligence?"

"My dear lady", said Dr. Wiseman gravely "that excessive sense of humour which cannot even distinguish between the tragic and the comic is characteristic of the boy's race. The Negro will laugh at anything. Slap him and he will respond with a smile. Box his ear and he will burst out into outright laughter. Is that a sign of the possession of some intelligence?"

"Well, .. eh ..", Mrs. Casely began with some hesitation. "Certainly not", continued Dr. Wiseman, cutting her short. "It is an indication of their utter lack of maturity. And, as you know, an immature person is, like a baby, without much intelligence."

"But the boy does not laugh always." Mrs Casely pointed out. "In fact, since yesterday he has been very morose and even sad, as though he would cry."

"What has made him morose and sad?"

"His failure in the Intelligence Tests."

"Ah, there you are!" exclaimed Dr. Wiseman with the air of one who had now proved his point beyond every reasonable doubt "Why should he be morose to the point of wanting to cry? You see, the Negro not only laughs readily but he also cries readily, just as little children do. He is extremely emotional. You should see even grown-ups, including toothless old men and women hardly able to stand on their legs on the last leg of their journey through this world, wailing like babies at the death of a relative!"

Mrs. Casely was hearing for the first time that old Negroes could wail like babies. She said to herself that if that was true then it was really astonishing. She was not sure, however, that it was a conclusive proof that they lacked intelligence. Even in Britain people felt grief when they lost a dear one, except that they took care not to betray their feelings, because it was considered undignified. Perhaps the difference between intelligence and the lack of it was the difference between not crying aloud and letting yourself go. If so the learned Doctor was perhaps right, and it would be presumptuous of her to argue further.

"I see; that is really abnormal, to say the least" she replied simply.

"All that is by the way, however", Dr. Wiseman resumed. "The real purpose of my summoning you here this evening is to inform you that I have decided to let the boys return to their respective countries the day after tomorrow. But there are one or two things we have to do for them before their departure. We cannot let them go back empty-handed, for they deserve some reward for their participation in the test. I want you, therefore, to ask them what each would like to take home as a present. Each can ask for things up to the value of One Thousand Pounds."

"Do you mean we should each ask the boy we brought here?" asked Dr. Springfield.

"Exactly" replied Dr. Wiseman. "That is to say you, Dr. Springfield, should ask Tseng, Mr. Balmer should ask Khandari and Mr. Suppercot should ask Scalini. As for Kotokro I think Mrs. Casely would be the best person to ask him. She seems to be the only one who understands the boy's queer ways. When they have told you what they want let me know, so that I give you money to make the necessary purchases for them."

They agreed to find out immediately and come back to inform him. In less than a quarter of an hour they were all back with the answers. Tseng had asked for two pairs of shoes, two shirts, two pairs of trousers, a broad-brimmed hat and a bicycle. Khandari wanted two pairs of trousers, two shirts, twelve yards of suiting, a pair of shoes and a guitar. Scalini preferred a football, a transistor radio, a pair of ski; a wrist-watch and a violin.

"And what was Kotokro's choice", Dr. Wiseman asked Mrs. Casely before she could open her mouth.

"He said he wanted a pen-knife for himself, a tin of corned beef for his mother, a cutlass for his father, and two half-pieces of cloth for both parents."

"What! Is it only a pen-knife he wants for himself?" asked Dr. Wiseman incredulously.

"Yes. He said he didn't want anything else. I suggested to him that he could also have a bicycle or a football or a wrist-watch or in fact all three together. He said no to everything I named. With regard to a bicycle he said that when going to his father's farm he had to cross rivers and fallen trees. If he went on a bicycle he would end carrying it more than being carried by it. Concerning a football he explained that if he introduced its play into his village it would only bring quarrels and frequent exchanges of blows. He did not want that. He and his companions would rather play draughts and run races on stilts and compete in the climbing of trees, which were great fun and brought no quarrels. As for a wrist-watch it was unreliable, as it could stop at any time or show the wrong hour even if it was working. In any case he did not need it, as he could tell the time without it."

Dr. Wiseman shook his head.

"So all he wants for himself is a pen-knife?" he asked, scarcely able to believe it.

"Yes; but remember that he also wants something for his parents", replied Mrs Casely "It shows he is devoted to them."

"Quite", agreed Dr. Wiseman "That shows, of course, that he is also sentimental, another indication of his intellectual deficiency."

Dr. Wiseman' s words revived in Mrs. Casely a latent fear for the future. Her husband died when she was forty-seven and she was now in her mid-fifties, with old age beginning to stare her hard in the face. She lived with her eldest son and his wife and contributed to the family budget by working. But it was likely that in a few years time she might not be able to earn a living and would have to depend entirely upon her son for maintenance. What would happen then? Suppose death did not take her away in time and she had to live up to about eighty or even beyond, for how long would her son be prepared to look after her? Like most white parents who lived too long for their children's comfort, she might be bundled into an old people's home, where she would spend the rest of her life without love and affection, being considered only as a nuisance by those who would be in charge of her. It was this thought that made her shudder at the Doctor' s words. She had heard that in Africa parents did not have to worry about what would happen to them in their old age, for their children would automatically take good care of them until death claimed them at any age. If this was what sentimentality enabled the children to do, then it was a good thing, and it ought to be preferred to intelligence if a choice had to be made between the two. There was no need, however, to argue it out with the Doctor. Personal experience would make him see things differently if he lived to a very ripe but penurious old age.

"Well, if that is all that he wants for himself we should let him have it", continued Dr. Wiseman, when there was no contradiction from any quarter, after a long pause. "As for his parents I meant to give them money on my return with the boy. But we can also buy for them the things he has asked for. Let us buy four cutlasses for his father, a dozen tins of corned beef for his mother and four pieces of cloth for both parents."

Having said this Dr. Wiseman issued cheques to his three Senior Research Assistants and Mrs. Casely and asked them to collect the money from the bank the next day and do the purchases. They should get everything ready, so that they could all depart the day after the morrow. He added that he himself would be very busy the next day, as he had a great deal to write up about the Intelligence Tests before his departure. He would be away for about a month, for he meant to conduct further research in Africa after returning the boy to his parents. Having established conclusively that the Negro was by far inferior to all the other races in intelligence, his next step was to seek to discover the reason or reasons for this inferiority. This would call for further research on the African continent.

All the four boys were excited about the prospect of going back home, Kotokro being the most so. He was particularly happy because Mrs. Casely had said that the Doctor had not only acceded to his request but that he had also said that he could have as many as four cutlasses for his father, twelve tins of corned beef for his mother and four pieces of cloth for both parents. His father would be very pleased with the cutlasses and his mother with the corned beef. It was true that cutlasses were manufactured in Gamberia, but everyone preferred the one coming from the white man's country. It was stronger and more durable. Corned beef was also produced in his country, but the meat was tough and not as tasty as the one he had been eating here in London. As for his own pen-knife, there were many things he could do with it - cutting ropes, peeling fruits and tubers, weaving baskets and doing a thousand and one little jobs with it. He had always wanted one ever since old Rakito's grandson, Tipeka, showed him an old rusty one, quite an apology for a pen-knife, which his grandfather had given him as a present. Father Borringer had bought it for him when they went to Blaft.

The boys had supper early and sat watching the television until about 10 p.m. when they got up and went to bed. Kotokro was very fond of watching the television, and it was the only thing he regretted having to leave behind. The first time he watched one he had marvelled and marvelled. He could not understand how pictures of human beings and animals were able to move and yet remain impalpable on the screen. How he wished he could have taken one to Kantoma, but he had long understood from Mrs. Casely that it would not work in his village. It seemed the pictures would only appear where there was electricity and there was none in Kantoma.

He lay tossing and tossing in bed, waiting anxiously for the day to dawn once more, when he would have all the things the Doctor had instructed Mrs. Casely to buy for him.

Suddenly he felt a sharp pain in his stomach. It was on the right side in the vicinity of his groin. He tried hard to sleep but could not. The pain grew sharper and sharper until he could no longer bear it. He groaned and groaned. He did not want to disturb anyone at that late hour, but he could not help it. The pain was so excruciating. His groans became louder and louder until they woke up Scalini who had fallen fast asleep as soon as he went to bed.

"What's wrong with you?" Scalini asked, switching on the electric light.

"My stomach ! Oh my stomach:", he cried.

"Wait, let me call Mrs. Casely", said Scalini, rising up. She may be able to give you some medicine that will bring you relief."

So saying he went and knocked at Mrs. Casely's door.

She got up at once and came and opened it.

"What is it?" she asked anxiously upon seeing Scalini.

"Kotokro is in great pain. He says he has severe stomach ache", he informed her.

Mrs. Casely quickly put on her night gown and came to Kotokro. He was doubled up with pain, turning this way and that on his bed. She bent down and examined him. There was no doubt that the boy was in great agony.

"I must send for the Doctor at once", she said, and immediately went to the telephone which was in the sitting room and began to dial. Kotokro could hear her talking to the Doctor. In less than five minutes she put back the receiver and returned to Kotokro who was still writhing with pain.

"You will be all right", she said to him encouragingly. "I have summoned the Doctor. He will be here soon."

Kotokro tried hard not to groan. He thought it was Dr. Wiseman who was coming to see him, and he did not want to give him the impression that in addition to being unintelligent he was also a coward who could not bear pain.

They waited and waited. For more than ten minutes the Doctor had not appeared. Kotokro wondered why the Doctor was taking so long to come when he was only on the next floor.

"Is he still angry with me?" he asked Mrs. Casely.

"Who?"

"Dr. Wiseman,"

"I don't think so."

"Why has he delayed so long in coming to see me then?"

"He is not the one who is coming to see you. It is Dr. Stockdale a medical Doctor."

"Why is Dr. Wiseman not coming to see me if he is not angry with me?"

Mrs Casely smiled.

"He can't come and see you, because he is not a medical Doctor. He knows nothing about curing people when they are sick."

"Why is he called a Doctor then?"

"He is a doctor of Philosophy in Anthropology", she explained.

"What does that mean?"

"It means he knows all there is to know about primitive people."

"Is that all? Then he is of no use to me or anybody else who is in pain?"

"Well, you may say so."

Nearly twenty minutes elapsed before there was a knock at the door. Mrs. Casely went to open it, and in came a be- spectacled elderly gentleman with stooping shoulders carrying a heavy handbag that seemed to weigh him down further.

"This is Dr. Stockdale", Mrs. Casely introduced him. "He will examine you and make sure that you get well."

The kindly old gentleman smiled at Kotokro, opened his hand-bag and pulled out some queer contraption consisting of rubber tubes joined together in a strange way. Kotokro wondered what it was for. The Doctor applied two arms of it to his ears and a third and longer arm to the chest of Kotokro, then to Kotokro's stomach and to his back, listening at each stage. Then he folded and put the queer contraption back into the handbag. After that he turned to Mrs. Casely and said:

"He has acute appendicitis. I am surprised that he is bearing it so bravely. He is a courageous lad. We must take him at once to my clinic for operation. Is there anyone here to help him downstairs into my car?"

"Yes," replied Mrs. Casely. "There is the handy-man Oblong. I shall get him right away."

Mrs. Casely went away to fetch Oblong. Meanwhile Dr. Stockdale brought out from his hand-bag some liquid in a bottle which he asked Kotokro to drink. He did so and soon began to feel some relief. Not long afterwards Mrs. Casely returned, followed by Oblong.

"Please assist him to get into my car downstairs", Dr. Stockdale said to Oblong.

Oblong at once lifted Kotokro up and placed him on his back. He carried him into the lift and descended with him downstairs. Dr. Stockdale's car was waiting on the street quite close to the entrance and he deposited the boy in it. Meanwhile, Mrs. Casely who had run up to inform Dr. Wiseman about what was happening, soon came down too and sat beside Kotokro in the car. Dr. Wiseman had told her to accompany the boy to Dr. Stockdale's clinic and report back his condition later.

By now the medicine which Dr. Stockdale had given Kotokro to drink had begun to take full effect and he felt no pain. He was surprised to see how powerful the medicine was.

"I am quite well now", he informed Mrs. Casely "There is no need to take me anywhere. I don't feel pain any more."

"The pain will come back", replied Mrs. Casely. "You need an operation as the Doctor has said."

"Then it won't come back?"

"Then it won't come back", Mrs. Casely assured him. "You will be free from any such pain for the rest of your life."

"And what is this operation?" he asked anxiously.

"The Doctor will remove from your stomach the sickness that is causing you the pain."

"Then he is going to cut my stomach open?" he asked again with a shudder.

"I don't think so", replied Mrs. Casely, not wishing to frighten the boy. "I think he has a way of removing it without cutting your stomach open."

"I hope so. If he cuts my stomach open then I shall die."

Mrs. Casely assured him that even if the Doctor had to cut his stomach open he wouldn't die and wouldn't even feel any pain. Kotokro thought and thought. He didn't see how anyone could remove sickness from one's stomach without cutting it open, and how one wouldn't die or even feel pain if one's stomach was cut open. He felt re-assured however, by Mrs. Casely's words, for he had heard it said that the white man could do almost anything.

When they arrived at Dr. Stockdale's clinic he was put on a mobile bed which he later learnt was called a 'Stretcher." Then Dr. Stockdale ordered that he should be taken to the theatre. This was done, and he soon found himself in a room with a bed in the centre and several bright lights all around. He was transferred to this bed, and when he turned sideways and tried to go to sleep the Doctor said that he should remain on his back. He did so and saw what appeared like a big bowl hanging from the ceiling. It almost touched his nose. Then the Doctor and two young women who were assisting him covered their mouths and nostrils with bandages. Kotokro wondered why they did so. "They don't want to smell the food when my stomach is cut open", he said to himself.

Standing near the bed and bending over him Dr. Stockdale asked Kotokro to count the numerals in English. He needed no second bidding.

"One, two, Six, seven..." he began.

Mrs. Browneck, the more senior of the two nurses who were assisting in the operation, wanted to stop him, but Dr. Stockdale said it was all right. She should allow him to count on, even though he was mixing the numbers up. What was important was that he should continue to say something until he lost consciousness. So Kotokro continued to count on.

"... four, three, five, nine, eight ..."

Before he could reach ten he began to hear noises in his ears. This lasted only a few seconds. Then he was conscious of nothing, neither here nor there.

When he opened his eyes again in what appeared to be a few seconds he found himself lying on another bed in quite a different room. Mrs. Casely was sitting by his side, looking anxiously into his face. When he tried to get up he felt acute pain down the right side of his stomach. He touched the spot with his right hand and discovered that it was tightly covered with plaster.

"Don't try to get up, dear", said Mrs. Casely tenderly, stroking his hair, "You must keep lying quietly on your back. You will be all right in a day or two."

Kotokro was greatly disappointed.

"Then it means the Doctor won't take me back to Kantoma tomorrow Friday?" he asked.

"No, you are too weak to travel now" she replied. "And, by the way, tomorrow is not Friday. It is Sunday. You have been asleep for three days."

"It can't be true it must be closer to three minutes."

"You remained unconscious for three days after the operation. We all became very anxious. You should have come round again within a matter of three or four hours."

"I see. Then I died?"

"Well, you can say so."

"Was it the sickness or the Doctor that killed me?"

"You can say it was the Doctor. He gave you some medicine, and so you became unconscious."

"What does that mean?"

"It means you remained alive but did not know."

"You mean I did not know that I was alive?"

"Yes."

"Is that what happens when one dies? I mean when one dies one remains dead but does not know that one is dead?"

"No, no. When one dies proper death then one knows that one is dead."

"Ah, I don't understand", said Kotokro.

"There is no need to try to", said Mrs. Casely, who was not sure if she herself understood what she was saying. "The Doctor says that you must not bother your head about anything. You should lie quietly in your bed, and you will be well again in a week or two."

Kotokro shut up and closed his eyes, pretending to go to sleep. But although, according to Mrs. Casely, the Doctor had said that he should not bother his head about anything, he felt he could not allow it to rest. In any case the Doctor could not know what was going on inside his head unless he was a wizard. He began to think and think, all about death. He remembered the day his grandmother died, his grandmother whom he loved so dearly. He had cried and cried, wishing in vain that she would come back. If only someone like Dr. Stockdale had been around before the sickness killed her she might have been still alive; for the Doctor would then have made her unconscious and taken out the sickness from her head - it was her head that had the sickness - and made her come back to life. How he wished Papa Mankani, the medicine man in Kantoma, possessed the powers of Dr. Stockdale! Then hardly anyone would die in Kantoma. He wondered if his grandmother who had been dead for about two years now, knew that she was dead. Perhaps she did, as Mrs. Casely had said. Why then did she not come back? Was it because she couldn't or didn't want to?

Mrs. Casely, who sat by his bed watching him, had seen his eyelids twitching all the while and knew that the boy had not yet fallen asleep. After a while, however, his eye-lids ceased twitching, his lips slightly parted and his breathing became heavier. Kotokro was fast asleep. She got up, covered him properly with the blanket and tiptoed out of the room.

Kotokro took only three days in recovering, to the surprise of Dr. Stockdale. None of his appendicitis patients had ever recovered from an operation in so short a time. When Mrs. Casely told him that Kotokro was to have returned home to Africa just the day after his illness and that he had been quite excited about it, the Doctor said that it must have been the happy prospect of his return home that had occasioned his rapid recovery.

Upon his return to the house after his recovery Kotokro discovered, to his great delight, that Mrs. Casely had already purchased for him all the things Dr. Wiseman had asked her to buy, namely four pieces of cloth, four cutlasses, twelve tins of corned beef and a pen-knife. They were all packed neatly in an iron trunk. He took out the pen-knife and examined it. It was the most beautiful pen-knife he had ever seen - with a sharp shining blade and an ivory handle. He decided not to put it back into the iron trunk but to keep it in his pocket on the journey home.

He asked after his three companions. Mrs. Casely told him that they had all gone back home the day after he was taken to Dr. Stockdale's clinic. Kotokro was sorry to learn that they had gone away without even coming to say good-bye, but he concluded that it was not their fault. Their departure had already been fixed for the following day, and so they would not have had time to come to the hospital.

The delay in setting out for Africa, occasioned by Kotokro's illness, had given Dr. Wiseman ample time to write up his thesis on the Intelligence Quotients of the Races, so that within one week from the time of the boy's discharge from Dr. Stockdale's clinic he had completed the main body of his work. It only remained for him to put in a few finishing touches. Then he would be ready to embark on research into the reasons for the comparatively low Intelligence of the Negro, as he had planned, as soon as he arrived in Africa.

Exactly two weeks to the day when Kotokro fell sick Dr. Wiseman set out with the boy. They boarded a plane from Heathrow Airport on a direct flight to Tremu, Blaft's International airport, 8 miles away from the centre of the city.

Mrs. Casely had come to see them off, and when their flight was announced she embraced Kotokro and said:

"My dear, I shall miss you greatly. Do come back to visit us one day when you are older. Perhaps I may still be alive. I would be very happy to see you once more."

"You bet, I will" replied Kotokro, his eyes moistening; for although he was glad to go back home he somehow felt sad at leaving the kindly old lady behind. He wished she could have come with him to Africa, but he realised at once that that was but a vain wish. She would not be able to live in Kantoma for even one week without wanting to return home, for she would not have any of the amenities she was used to - no splendid house, no rich food and treated water, no clean toilet facilities, no telephone, no television, no electricity, none of those luxuries into which she was born and in which she had lived all her life. She would fall sick in no time and only Papa Mankani, the medicine man, would be there to treat her. And she might end as his own grandmother had ended in his hands.

CHAPTER THREE
THE PLANE CRASH

When they arrived on board Kotokro discovered that, as on the occasion when he was coming to London with Dr. Wiseman he was the only black among the passengers. All the others were either Europeans or Asia tics, or Americans, although Kotokro couldn't tell the difference. All non-black faces looked the same to him, whether they were American or Chinese or, indeed, Red Indian. Some were tourists going to Africa for the first time. Others, like Dr. Wiseman, had been there before and were going back on business or research or on resumption of duty after leave of absence.

Dr. Wiseman had brought with him on board his brief-case containing the papers he was writing on Intelligence Quotients, together with some money in Bank Notes, as well as his toilets articles and heart tablets, for he was prone to heart attack. As for Kotokro all he had brought with him on the plane was his pen-knife which he had slid into his coat pocket. His iron trunk and the things it contained were in the plane's luggage compartment like everyone else's heavy luggage.

"I want to sit close to the window", he said to Dr. Wiseman when they were shown their seats, "for I want to be able to see what is happening on the ground as we fly past."

Dr. Wiseman did not care one way or the other, for he had flown so often in a plane that he found nothing particularly exciting about the slow procession of towns, rivers, jungles and mountains that filed past in miniature as one gazed down through the window. So he suffered Kotokro to sit near the window while he himself sat near the aisle. However, he folded his raincoat and put it on the rack immediately above the boy's head. As for his brief-case he held to it as though it contained all his dearest possessions.

Soon after everyone was seated they were told to fasten their seat-belts for the take-off. Dr. Wiseman did so and assisted Kotokro to do likewise. Then the engines began to roar. The plane moved slowly forward, turned round, stopped, roared again to a deafening shriek, darted forward at a maddening speed, and soon they were air-borne.

Kotokro looked through the window. The sun was just rising slowing from the East, shooting its rays of gold through the mixed white and blue clouds. Far away, below the plane, London was fast disappearing from sight. Only the tops of sky-scrapers dotted here and there were now visible. Gradually, even these began to fade away. And now appeared the level stretch of the boundless ocean with clusters of white clouds dotted on its surface like huge bubbles of soap. They had ascended high above the clouds.

The air hostess began to pass the breakfast. It consisted of bread and butter, bacon, eggs and sausages, corn flakes, sugar, milk and tea.

Kotokro ate his portion with great relish. During his one year's stay in London he had acquired a taste for the white man's food, although he still yearned occasionally for his native diet with its admixture of pepper and salt and other spices and condiments. He particularly liked the English breakfast, because he found it more fortifying than his native breakfast of roasted plantain without anything to go with it. He knew this was the last time he was going to have this kind of meal to eat in the morning, so he decided to call for more, as what he ate were in such small quantities that they whetted his appetite rather than satisfied it.

"Please, can I have another plate?" he asked the air hostess when she came to take away his empty plate.

She looked at him and smiled. He was not entitled to another plate, but he obviously didn't know, she thought. Without a word she took away the tray and was soon back with another tray loaded with an even bigger share than before. Many of the passengers were already suffering from air sickness and had not been able to touch their food, so that there was plenty of surplus. Dr. Wiseman too had found the breakfast very appetizing and would have liked to ask for more, but he dared not. Not that the air hostess would not have obliged him, but he was inhibited by the demands of social convention. And so he let her take away his empty plate, with a half-hearted mumble of "thank you".

He looked at Kotokro and smiled. The boy had no inhibition. It was not because he was still young, but it was the inherited characteristic of his race. The untutored Negro behaved exactly as he felt, without any restraint imposed by social norms, another indication of his lack of intelligence.

After Kotokro had cleared his repeat he adjusted his seat, threw back his head and was soon fast asleep. Dr. Wiseman looked at him and shook his head. The boy could so easily fall asleep, another evidence of the lack of activity in his head.

They must have been in the air for about three hours when suddenly the plane began to shake violently. Kotokro opened his eyes and looked through the window. The sun was buried in dark clouds and a fierce storm was raging. The plane tossed to the right, then to the left, then to the right again quite uncontrollably. Hand luggage packed on top of the rack began tumbling to the floor. Plates and cutlery waiting to be cleared were also flung to the floor, the former smashing into bits. Many of the passengers, unable to cling to their seats, were swept clean off their feet and tossed about, bumping violently into one another. Children screamed and old women sobbed. Among the others the believers prayed in the way each one's faith directed; the unbelievers, including the pagans and atheists, shut their minds in helpless resignation.

The plane tossed and tossed as the violence of the storm increased with every passing minute, and with it the din on board. Suddenly the plane dived, shooting down from the sky like a meteorite. Some of the passengers were lifted up their feet and they bumped their heads against the roof. This was more than most could endure. People began to throw up all the breakfast they had just eaten.

While all this was happening Kotokro sat smiling broadly, with his eyes closed and clinging hard to his seat. He was enjoying it all, for to him it was just like swinging on a rope from the branch of a tall tree in the jungle. He felt only slightly inconvenienced by Dr. Wiseman, who held fast to him instead of to his part of the seat, as though he considered him a firmer support than that immovable rest screwed to the floor.

Suddenly, just as it seemed about to touch the ground, the plane shut up again into the sky. Kotokro gazed at Dr. Wiseman's face. It looked very ashy, all the blood seeming to have departed from it.

"Why, aren't you enjoying it, Doctor?" he asked "It is a very nice swing, you know. You may never again have it so good."

"Stupid! Stupid!", Dr. Wiseman said in his heart, for the alarming situation deprived him of the ability to give utterance to his thoughts. "He is so unintelligent that he does not even know when he is in mortal danger."

Just at this juncture Dr. Wiseman's brief-case, to which he had tightly clung hitherto, was wrenched from his hand and went rolling towards the tail-end of the plane. Not deeming it safe to rise and run after it he looked helplessly on as it continued on its career. Sensing the situation, Kotokro, who was ever ready to lend a helping hand to anyone in adversity, rose up at once and dashed after it with the object of retrieving it for the Doctor.

As if by some decree of fate, no sooner had he left his seat than the emergency exit, close to which he had been sitting, suddenly flew open. Dr. Wiseman was snatched from his seat as if by some unseen hand; and before he knew what was happening he was sucked out of the plane and was flying through the air earthbound.

By now Kotokro had caught up with the brief-case which had already rolled out of the passengers' compartment and reached the very tail end of the plane close to the door of the toilet. As he stopped to pick it up there was a blinding flash and a deafening thunder exploded in the air. As if with some mighty axe wielded from the heavens the part of the plane in which he found himself was severed at once from the main body. It came swooping down with Kotokro alone inside it. Descending like a glider it hit the top of a tall tree, flinging him far away.

Kotokro landed in a tangle of undergrowths. Greatly shaken but otherwise none the worse for the fall, he immediately picked himself up and gradually descended to the ground.

Meantime what was left of the plane continued on its course with a steep descent. On and on it went. At last it struck the top of a tree, then plunged through a dense forest and burst into flames.

Most of the passengers and their luggage were scattered over a wide area, even before it touched the ground. A few who had remained in it up to the last moment were so stunned with the impact that they were already either dead or unconscious when the plane caught fire. They were all burnt to ashes.

Kotokro looked about him. He could not see any part of the plane anywhere, nor any of his fellow passengers. But soon a crackling sound, as one hears when the bush is on fire, assailed his ears. It grew louder and louder.

Then he saw, some distance away, inky smoke ascending into the sky. It immediately occurred to him that where there is fire there is likely to be a human dwelling, so he directed his steps towards it.

It was with great difficulty that he could make any progress, for he was in a thick dark forest with dense undergrowths which impeded his advance.

As he approached the fire he suddenly espied what appeared to be a severed human leg lying a few yards in front of him. It was that of a white man. Cold shudder ran through his frame. Summoning courage, however, he quickly ran past it. But he had not advanced more than a few steps when he saw several corpses with ghastly bruises lying about. This was more than he could stand. Thoroughly scared he wheeled round and ran as fast as the undergrowths would allow. It was not long before he regained the spot where he had landed when he fell from the plane.

He continued to advance and soon came to an open glade. Tired and breathless he sat down to rest and to plan his next move. He had no doubt that the dead men and severed human leg which he had seen were the corpses and limbs of some of the passengers on the plane, and that the fire itself came from the burning machine. The planes cargo must, therefore also be scattered all over the place. He must pluck up courage, then, and return to search for his own iron trunk and its contents, as well as anything else he might find useful.

Having thus made up his mind he rose up and retraced his steps. He soon came to the severed leg again and the scattered corpses. He quickly went past them and began to search through the forest. Here and there lay all sorts of articles, mingled with more severed limbs and mutilated corpses. He saw torn hand-bags, empty suit-cases, tattered clothes, bank notes, wrist watches, jewellery and shattered radio sets, some in good condition, but most utterly ruined. None of these were of any use to him, so he went past them all.

He next came to the spot where the plane had blazed a trail as it ploughed through the forest. He saw more bodies and more articles, but again he could find nothing suited to his need. He continued to advance until he found himself completely out of the zone of wreckage, for now there were no more articles or corpses or severed limbs to be seen but undisturbed virgin forest.

Suddenly he heard what appeared to be the sound of waterfall in the distance. He made towards it.

He had not taken many steps when, as he looked to the right, he saw something that looked like a brief-case suspended on a tree branch quite close to the ground. Approaching he discovered that it was no other than the brief-case of Dr. Wiseman. He immediately unhooked it from the branch and examined it. It had not opened or been damaged in any way when it fell, for the lock was still intact. Holding it he continued to advance towards the sound of waterfall. It occurred to him that, like all the others, Dr. Wiseman was also dead and that he himself was the only survivor, thanks to his having been in the severed tail-end of the plane when it crashed.

He had not gone very far when he came upon an iron trunk lying open and badly battered in a clump of trees. He picked it up and discovered, to his delight, that it was the iron trunk which Dr. Wiseman had made Mrs. Casely buy for him.

He did not have to look far before he saw some of its contents lying about. First, he saw two of the four cloths lying together. As he looked about for the other two he saw two tins of corned beef. He collected them but could not find the remaining ten. He also found two of the four cutlasses after a long search. He was able to collect, in all, two cloths, two cutlasses and two tins of corned beef.

He put them all inside the iron trunk again, except one cutlass which he decided to keep for cutting his way through the dense undergrowths he might encounter from time to time. In order not to handle too many things at the same time he also put Dr. Wiseman's brief-case inside the trunk. Then, carrying the trunk on his head and holding the cutlass he continued his way towards the waterfall.

After advancing for some distance he arrived at an area of open glades with giant trees overhung with all sorts of climbers. Among them was a special type of climber which was highly valued in Kantoma. The Gonjani called it "Krampana". It was a vine with very supple but strong stem which the villagers used as rope. They used it for building houses, constructing bridges over rivers and doing all sorts of jobs for which a strong rope was indispensable. It was so extensively used in Kantoma that it had become very scarce in the forest there. But here it grew in great abundance.

Kotokro was excited when he saw them. He wished he could cut and carry away about a dozen of them for his father. As he did not know where he was, however, and how soon he would be able to find his way back to Kantoma, he passed them all by.

Hardly had he traversed this area, a distance of some four hundred yards, when he suddenly found himself at the brink of a deep ravine. A river, about sixty feet wide, was flowing in it. It was this river that, issuing out of the ravine on to a flat plane, had formed the waterfall as it descended precipitously over a rocky bed into a gorge down below.

Looking towards the further shore he saw two huge rocks standing side by side above the surface of the water.

As he stood and peered down the side of the ravine he espied a man walking briskly on a narrow strand which bordered it. He was making towards the waterfall. Kotokro was greatly relieved to see a fellow human being once more, even though for a moment he could not see how he would be able to contact him.

It was obvious that if the man continued on his course he would soon arrive at the waterfall, where the narrow strand ended. Then he would either have to turn back or advance further at his peril, for his next step would inevitably land him in the water, from where he would be borne off by the swift current. On the other hand if he turned back he would be advancing into the narrower part of the ravine which was filled with deep water and had no strand.

As Kotokro looked on the man took to his heels. At first he thought he had seen him; but he soon discovered the reason for his flight. The water was rising swiftly and would soon invade the strand and leave him no ground to stand on. If he remained there for long, therefore, he would soon find himself carried away by the rising flood into the waterfall and dashed down the precipice.

The man came nearer and nearer. Straining his eyes to look Kotokro perceived that he was a white man. He wondered what a white man would be doing down there in such a perilous situation. It seemed he was trapped beyond rescue.

Suddenly it occurred to him that this must be one of the passengers in the plane who had fallen into the ravine when it crashed. He was soon proved right; for, the next moment, he saw that it was no other than Dr. Wiseman. His heart leapt with joy at the sight of him; so looking down the ravine he called as loudly as he could:

"Is that you, Doctor?"

Dr. Wiseman lifted up his head for the first time and gazed at Kotokro. He recognised the boy at once and was greatly surprised to see that he had survived the crash. He was glad to see another human being around, even if it was only a dunce, who could be of no use at all to him in his present predicament. Indeed, in the situation in which he found himself he could not see how any man, even if he were a genius, could bring him salvation.

"Yes, Kotokro, it is me." he replied in a trembling voice.

Kotokro put down the load he was carrying. He surveyed again the other side of the ravine. There was no place where the Doctor could land in safety even if he could swim across. It was sheer precipice. There were only the two rocks which rose up so steeply that no human could scale them. The safest place was where he already found himself. And even this place would soon be submerged in water, as the flood kept rising. Suddenly an idea occurred to him.

"Wait for me Doctor", he said, "I shall be back soon."

"No, no, you rather must wait", Dr. Wiseman shouted back as Kotokro was about to turn round. "I want you to take a message."

"What is it?" asked Kotokro impatiently.

"Listen carefully. It is this", began Dr. Wiseman, "It is obvious that I am going to die here. There is no way I can get out of this place. I want you, therefore, to take this message to my wife in case you are able to find your way back to Gamberia. Tell her that I keep my will in my office safe. The key to the safe is hidden in a hole at the bottom of one of the four legs of my writing desk in the study upstairs. I use a combination lock and the number is 164420. Can you remember that? It is 164420. Have you got the message?"

"I cannot go back to London even if I am able to escape from here", replied Kotokro "so you will have to deliver that message yourself."

"You don't have to go back to London" pleaded Dr. Wiseman. "Do please tell the British High commissioner in Blaft. You know him. He will send the message to my wife."

"There is no need", replied Kotokro. "You will deliver it yourself. And, by the way, next time you would do well to tell your wife all your secrets before you set out on a journey like this."

So saying he wheeled round and disappeared before Dr. Wiseman could say another word.

The Doctor's heart grew as heavy as lead. That stupid boy would not oblige him even in his last hour. It was true that he had not shown much patience with him ever since he took him to London. It was not his fault. He could not stand stupid people, no matter how hard he tried. And the boy was unaccountably stupid, like most members of his race. However, anyone with a modicum of human feeling would not have thought of thus paying him back as the boy was obviously doing, in this his darkest hour. He had gone, leaving him to die there, after refusing to take the message to his wife.

With these thoughts still rankling in his brain he turned back to look at the rushing flood. It was obvious that there had been a heavy storm upstream. Trunks of trees torn from their roots and all sorts of debris came floating by. He looked again. He saw something else. He was not sure what they were. They looked like several pieces of wood floating together, but they seemed to be coming much faster than any of the other debris. All at once they became clearer. They were a shoal of crocodiles moving fast towards him.

Utter panic seized Dr. Wiseman. He did not know whether to stand there and be devoured by those savage reptiles or to rush into the waterfall with the certainty of being dashed to pieces.

"Hey, Doctor", he heard a voice say.

He looked up. There was that stupid boy again. He was letting down a rope. A ray of hope kindled at once in the Doctor's breast.

"I have tied the other end of this rope to the trunk of a tree", continued Kotokro. "It is strong enough to bear your weight. So catch hold of it and climb out at once."

Dr. Wiseman needed no second bidding. With shaking knees and a grateful heart he caught hold of the rope at once and began to ascend, planting his feet firmly against the wall of the ravine and rapidly working himself upwards.

Before he could reach midway, however, Kotokro noticed the crocodiles. They were making fast towards the rope. It occurred to him that they might seize it and try to pull the Doctor down before he could gain the upper ground.

So he quickly tied another rope round the trunk of the tree and let down one end of it. It was a shorter one, reaching only half-way down the ravine.

"Quick, Doctor", he called to him. "Try and reach this second rope and transfer yourself to it, for I see crocodiles coming to pull you back into the water."

Dr. Wiseman knew at once that the boy was right; for he himself had, of course, seen the crocodiles making towards him before he began to ascend. With strength borne of fear he began to haul himself up like an expert mountaineer. Before he could reach the second rope, however, the crocodiles arrived at where the end of the first rope was dangling on the surface of the water. They seized it with their teeth and began to pull. Kotokro saw that the Doctor was in mortal danger.

"Quick, Doctor quick!" he cried. "The crocodiles are pulling at the rope."

Dr. Wiseman summoned the last ounce of strength left in him. He clambered like a frightened monkey. Soon he had reached the second rope. No sooner had he let go the first and transferred himself to it than the former snapped at the base where it had been tied to the tree and came crashing down into the ravine. The crocodiles had succeeded in pulling it down. Had he still been on it he would thus have ended in the jaws of those carnivorous amphibians.

Being now out of their reach he took his time to climb up. He had to be careful lest this second rope was not very strong and might snap on its own accord and so send him back into danger.

Eventually he found himself out of the ravine and on firm ground once more.

"Thank you, my boy", he said to Kotokro. "I see you possess a certain amount of resourcefulness. How did you do it?"

"Simple", replied Kotokro, beaming with smiles; for this was the first time he had heard any word of compliment from the Doctor. "Just before I came upon the ravine I happened to pass through an area where the "Krampana" grows in abundance. We use this as a rope in Kantoma. It is very strong and flexible. In fact I had wanted to cut some and take away for my father, but as I did not know where I was I decided not to. So when I came and saw you in the ravine it occurred to me that the only way of getting you out was through those ropes."

"I ran back, therefore, and cut two of them, one of which I tied to the base of that tree and let down one end to you. You know the rest."

"It was rather clever of you" Dr. Wiseman said again when he had finished explaining.

"Then I am not stupid?" asked Kotokro.

"Not all that stupid. It seems you possess a little bit of intelligence." he conceded.

"How did you come to be in the ravine?" asked Kotokro, in turn.

Dr. Wiseman told him. He said that immediately Kotokro rose up to go after his brief-case the emergency exit suddenly opened and he was sucked out from the plane. By that time the plane was flying quite close to the ground and over the ravine. So he just fell into the middle of the river. Being unharmed he quickly swam ashore to the only side of the ravine where there was a narrow strip of land. He walked along this strip seeking a way out. The strip grew broader and broader as he advanced downstream. Then all at once he noticed that the ravine had begun to fill up from flood water coming from upstream. It was at this juncture that Kotokro had providentially arrived on the scene.

"I must congratulate you on your lucky escape, Doctor" said Kotokro "for if you had remained in the plane, instead of being sucked out you would by now be dead like all the others."

"Did they all die, and are you the only survivor apart from me?" asked Dr. Wiseman.

"I believe so" replied Kotokro, "for I have seen only dead bodies and severed limbs at the scene of the crash, but no living person. I believe all the others are dead."

Kotokro went on to narrate how he was the only one in the tail-end of the plane when it was severed by the lightning; how it came down and hit the top of a tree; how he fell into a tangle of undergrowths and was able to get dawn unscathed; how he walked through the bush until he came to the scene of the crash; how he saw corpses and severed limbs lying about and the plane's cargo scattered all over the place, and how he eventually discovered his iron trunk and some of its contents.

"Accept my warmest congratulations too, my boy, on your own miraculous escape" said Dr. Wiseman when he had finished.

"Thank you, Doctor", replied Kotokro. "We have both been lucky so far. Let us hope that we shall continue to be lucky, so that we eventually return home in safety."

After this Dr. Wiseman said that he was very tired and needed rest. After he had regained his strength they were to search for his brief-case. It contained not only his money and travel documents, but also his valuable papers on the research he was conducting.

Kotokro laughed.

"What are you laughing at?" Dr. Wiseman, asked, beginning once more to feel the distaste which he always had for the frivolous disposition which the boy had inherited from his race.

"There is no need to go and look for it", Kotokro replied.

"Why?" asked Dr. Wiseman with a frown.

Without answering, Kotokro slowly and deliberately opened his iron trunk and pulled out Dr. Wiseman's brief-case.

"Because here it is", he said, handing it to him.

Dr. Wiseman was delighted.

"How did you come by it?" he asked. "Did you land with it from the plane?"

"No, I was just about to pick it up when the plane broke up into two and I came down in one half of it. I found it by chance suspended on the branch of a tree when I was looking for my iron trunk."

Dr. Wiseman thanked Kotokro once more. Then he took out the key of the brief-case from his pocket and opened it. He began to examine its contents. There were his Passport, his papers on the Intelligence Tests and the sum of sixteen pounds in cash. His travellers cheques however amounting to One Thousand Pounds, were missing.

"Where are my travellers cheques?", he asked Kotokro angrily.

"I don't know", he replied with surprise. "What are they?

"They are papers entitling me to collect money from any bank", he explained. "You won't have any use for them, because they do not bear your name; so give them back to me at once."

"I have not taken anything from your brief-case" denied Kotokro. "In fact it was not opened when I gave it to you, as you could see. You opened it yourself with the key, which was in your pocket."

Dr. Wiseman found it difficult to believe that Kotokro had not stolen his travellers cheques. He had heard that most Negroes were liars and first class thieves who could open and close locks without any key. At the same time it seemed odd to him that Kotokro should have preferred to take the travellers cheques for which he would have no use, while leaving in the brief-case the cash of sixteen pounds for which he would have some use. Then suddenly he remembered that he had left them behind in the chest of drawers in his bedroom. He had kept them there the previous day, as soon as he collected them from the bank, intending to put them into his brief-case the next morning when he would be leaving, but had forgotten about them when the time came for his departure. He felt sorry that he had accused the boy falsely, but how could he belittle himself by apologising to him?

"Well, never mind. It doesn't really matter", was all he said.

"So you are now satisfied that I could not have taken them?" asked Kotokro.

"I don't know. But let us leave it at that", was all the Doctor was prepared to say.

Kotokro felt deeply hurt. Anything that cast doubt on his honesty made him feel very unhappy. However if the Doctor was not persisting in his accusation there was no need for him to press the matter any further. The truth would eventually come out. His father had always said that truth could never be buried.

"All right, Doctor", he said. "Let us plan our next move then."

"Right now I am too tired to plan anything or make any move", he replied. "So let us have some rest first."

So saying he deposited his brief-case on the ground and stretched himself under the cool shade of the tree, lying on his back. He was not normally an easy sleeper. But the unwonted exertion through which he had just gone and the unbroken sound of the continuous waterfall which was close at hand combined to have a soporific effect upon his mind and body and he was soon dissolved in sleep.

By now Kotokro was also feeling tired, what with the terrible plane accident from which he had escaped unscathed, his difficult journey through the bush and the excitement over Dr. Wiseman's peril. So he also sat down, propped his head against the trunk of the tree and was soon fast asleep.

CHAPTER FOUR
THE FIRST DAY

Dr. Wiseman was the first to wake up. He looked at his wrist-watch and found that it was showing 11 a.m. The last time he looked at the watch was on the plane, and the time then was 10.45 a.m. That was only a short time before he fell from the plane. He looked hard at the watch again. The hands were not moving. He put it to his ear and listened. There was no sound in it. It had stopped. It was obvious that either water had gone into it when he fell into the river, or the impact with the water as it struck its surface had damaged the mechanism.

Dr. Wiseman became very worried. Unless he was able to get a good watch within the next two days, his life would be in danger. This was because he had heart-trouble and his Doctor had provided him with tablets which he had to take every other day, between 3 p.m. and 3.10 p.m., not earlier and not later, or he would instantly die of heart attack. He had taken the tablets just before they left London and he was to take them again the day after the morrow. It was necessary for him, therefore, to get correct time before that hour. This was the cause of his worry.

His only hope was that they would either discover a good working watch from the scene of the crash, or fall in with some of the survivors who had a good watch, or find their way to a town or village where someone had it. He woke up Kotokro who was still fast asleep.

"Did you say there was no other survivor apart from yourself?" he asked anxiously.

"I believe not", he replied, rubbing his eyes.

"Did you take the trouble to search for foot prints?"

"No, I did not. I only searched for my iron trunk and its contents and for anything else that might come in handy."

"Ah", sighed Dr. Wiseman, checking himself only just in time from saying that this showed conclusively that Kotokro had no intelligence, whatever else he might possess. "Is that not the first thing you should have done? You should have scoured the area to see if you could find any foot-prints; for if you had found any, then you would have known that there were other survivors besides yourself. And you would have been able to track them and join their company instead of wandering alone in the bush."

"Well, I did not think of that", replied Kotokro "But consider what would have been your fate if I had. By now the crocodiles would have been taking a nap with your limbs safe inside their bellies."

"What a foolish thing to say" said Dr. Wiseman with a shudder. "But never mind. Let us go back to the scene of the crash. There are three things I want to look for there. The first is a good watch. My life or death within the next forty-eight hours will depend upon finding one. The next is some food. Unless we are able to arrive at some human habitation soon and have some food we cannot survive in this jungle. We must therefore go and search at the place where the plane fell for some provisions. The third things we must look for are foot-prints. If we are able to find any foot-prints they will be a sign that some of the victims of the crash have survived besides ourselves. We shall follow them and, if we are lucky we may fall in with them and so join their company. So let us go right away."

"Yes, Sir", replied Kotokro, and immediately bent down to set the iron trunk upon his head once more.

"Wait first", said Dr. Wiseman, interrupting him. "Open that iron trunk and give me the other cutlass. I shall need it."

Kotokro did as he was told and handed him the second cutlass. Then setting the trunk upon his head and taking up the cutlass which he had already been using, he led the way back to the scene of the crash.

Kotokro had already blazed a trail when he was coming to the ravine; so they had no difficulty in finding their way back to their immediate destination. They first came to the spot where Kotokro had found his iron trunk after the crash. He pointed out to Dr. Wiseman the clump of trees in which it lay. Not long afterwards they arrived at the place where he had found Dr. Wiseman's brief-case suspended from the branch of a tree. He pointed out this also to the Doctor.

After this they advanced for some distance without coming across anything else. Then all of a sudden they stumbled upon the severed hand of a woman with a lady's wrist-watch and a wedding ring upon the finger. Kotokro was not afraid of it, being now used to seeing such gruesome sights. Besides, he was no longer alone in the dark forest. Dr. Wiseman, however, could not look at it. He turned his eyes away at the first sight and was about to walk on when Kotokro said:

"Doctor, I thought you said you were coming to look for a watch. Here   is one on that lady's wrist. Let us see if it is ticking."

With that he picked up the hand and applied the watch to his ear. He listened for some seconds and found that no sound was coming from it.

"There is no sound in it, Doctor", he said. "But hold it, put it to your ear and listen . Maybe I am not hearing well." So saying he stretched out the hand to Dr. Wiseman.

"Throw it away! Throw it away at once!" shouted the Doctor, greatly horrified.

Kotokro threw it away. But he found the Doctor's reaction so amusing that he burst out laughing. He had always thought that no white man feared such things, particularly one who was a Doctor, even if all his knowledge was about primitive people. As for Dr. Wiseman, Kotokro's handling of the severed hand awoke in him the strongest feeling of revulsion. How could the boy handle such a gruesome object and go to the extent of applying it to his ear? He must be a true savage like most of his race. Why, he could even be a cannibal.

All the stories he had heard about those man-eating people in Africa came rushing back into his mind. This boy must be one of them. Such people not only had no intelligence but they were also highly dangerous. They could eat you as a delicacy, even when not particularly hungry. If you happened to be in their company when they were on the verge of starvation then you had to consider yourself gone. If he was to survive in the company of this boy then they had to find food quickly or else come upon some human dwelling where they would not starve, or at least they should fall in with some survivors of the crash in whose company he would be safe; for even though Kotokro was only a boy yet with a cutlass in his hand he could hardly be safe from him at an unguarded moment, especially when he would be fast asleep.

"Look, Doctor", said Kotokro, cutting his thoughts short and pointing to some object lying on the ground a few feet away to his right. "That looks like a watch."

Dr. Wiseman looked in the direction of the boy's pointing finger. He saw the object. It looked like a table clock. His heart beat fast with expectation.

"Yes, that must be a Table clock", he said. Go and get it for me at once."

Kotokro put down the trunk he was carrying, crawled through the tangled undergrowth and fetched the watch. Dr. Wiseman examined it. It was indicating 2 p.m. He put it to his ear and found it was ticking.

"It is working", he said.

Dr. Wiseman was greatly relieved. He took it, wound it and gave to Kotokro to put into his trunk.

They continued their search for provisions and anything else that they might need for their survival in case they had to spend some days in the jungle, as well as for foot-prints. They saw nothing but corpses and severed limbs and several damaged articles strewn all over the place. At last, just as they were about to abandon their search, Kotokro saw what appeared to be foot-prints leading away towards a more open part of the jungle.

"Look, Doctor", he said, "Here are foot-prints."

Dr. Wiseman quickly walked up to him. Examining the ground he discovered that there were, in fact, several foot-prints. They could be the foot-prints of three or four people. He became excited, for it confirmed his conviction that there must be other survivors besides themselves and strengthened his hope of eventual escape from the jungle.

They abandoned further search for things from the plane and followed the trail. As this part of the jungle had many open glades and fewer tangled undergrowths they were able to proceed more rapidly than before. Now and again they came to a spot where the people had sat down to rest. These were not far between, from which they inferred that either all or some of them moved with difficulty, having received injuries from the crash.

They must have proceeded for about two miles when suddenly Kotokro, who was leading, saw a man fully stretched on the ground some yards in front of him.

"There is a man lying down over there, Doctor," he said pointing.

"Let me see", said Dr. Wiseman, going past him. Advancing up to the man, who was lying on his face he turned him over and saw that he was an elderly gentleman of about sixty. The Doctor was no longer afraid of dead bodies, having by now got used to seeing so many corpses lying about at the scene of the crash. Indeed he was surprised at himself that he could so easily get used to such sights. The man must have been dead for some hours, for his body was stiff. His open-necked shirt was soaked with blood from a gash on his forehead. It was a wound he must have received when he fell from the plane. He wore a pair of spectacles and was tightly clutching an old cap in his right hand.

Dr. Wiseman contemplated him without any emotion.

"Come, let's go", he said to Kotokro.

There were more foot- prints leading away from the man, from which it was evident that there were still other survivors who had continued to make their way through the jungle.

They advanced for about an hour and came to another spot where the people had obviously rested for some time to have a meal. Crumbs of bread and three empty tins of sardines lay about. It looked as if only two people were now left, a man and a woman, as could be inferred from the prints left by their shoes.

"Let us follow them, Doctor", suggested Kotokro, "They cannot be far off."

The Doctor agreed. They set up a shout to call attention; but although they continued shouting for a long time no one answered back. Only the echoes of their voices came bouncing back to them from the deep recesses of the jungle.

They began to wonder what had happened to the two survivors. Were they also now dead or had they discreetly refrained from answering back for fear of falling into evil hands?

"We are eventually bound to catch up with them if they are still alive" said Kotokro "So let us continue to follow their trail."

But by now Dr. Wiseman was feeling very tired. He was not accustomed to walking on foot, even in town where there were no obstacles. He had always travelled in a car, train or other vehicle. So, here in the jungle where he had to journey on a narrow trail with obstructing undergrowths he found the going very arduous.

"Let us rest here for a while", he said to Kotokro. "I can hardly lift my feet now."

They rested for about half-an-hour, after which Dr. Wiseman said that they should now continue their advance as he had recovered his strength somewhat. They must catch up with the survivors as soon as possible.

They advanced for another half-an-hour and arrived at a spot where the two survivors had apparently rested again. In fact one of them seemed to have lain on the ground while the other sat with his legs outstretched. All that was easy to infer from the marks they had left on the ground. But when they examined the continuation of the trail they found, to their surprise, that the foot-prints of only one person were now visible. Dr. Wiseman was greatly perplexed. He wondered what had happened. He carefully examined the ground for the foot-prints of the woman, but there were none. As he stood trying to puzzle it out Kotokro said:

"The woman is sick, Doctor."

"What woman is sick?", asked Dr. Wiseman, turning to him.

"The woman who has been going with the man. When they reached here she was too sick to walk, so the man carried her."

"If the man carried her, does it necessarily mean she was sick? She could have been only too tired to walk."

"No; if she was only tired then they would have rested here until she regained her strength, as you have been doing. She was sick, so they had to press on with the hope of getting aid."

It occurred to Dr. Wiseman that the boy must be right, so he did not argue. It raised his hope that they would soon catch up with them, for with the man carrying such a burden he could not have gone far.

"I think you are right", he said to Kotokro. "Let us follow the trail then."

They followed the trail for about two miles, when they suddenly came upon a sight that dampened Dr. Wiseman's spirits. Lying on her back on the ground was a woman with her face covered with a man's coat, while sitting down with his back propped against the trunk of a tree was a man in his forties. He had a hand-bag beside him.

Approaching, Dr. Wiseman removed the coat from the woman's face and found that she was stone dead. He next went up to the man and examined him. As he did so the fellow opened his eyes. He was not yet dead.

"The name is Johnson", he said with difficulty, "Peter Johnson. I come from the town of Darnhill in Wales. That woman is my wife. We are survivors from a plane crash. Please tell........tell............"

"Yes, what shall I tell?" asked Dr. Wiseman, looking anxiously into the man's face as he uttered the words with great effort. It was obvious that he was on the point of death.

"Tell. .tell. . tell. . . " was all he could say. Then his head dropped on his chest and he was dead.

Dr. Wiseman gently laid him on the ground and looked round for something with which to cover his face. He could find nothing suitable. He went back to where the woman lay and removed the coat covering her face and was about to tear it into two when Kotokro said:

"Don't, Doctor. There is no need. There are plenty of leaves around. Let us cut some and cover his face with them, if you think that that is necessary."

"It is necessary", replied Dr. Wiseman "We can't go away and leave him lying here like that with his face uncovered."

"But you did not cover the face of that elderly gentleman whose dead body we first came across, even when it had a gash on it. Why do you think it is necessary to cover this man's face?" asked Kotokro.

"I did not think of it", replied Dr. Wiseman. "It is the coat covering this woman's face that reminded me of it."

"I see. So intelligent people too sometimes forget to do what is necessary?" asked Kotokro.

"Yes, of course."

"Well, let us cover up the man's face then."

With that Kotokro immediately began to cut leafy branches from the trees standing by. Meantime, Dr. Wiseman opened and examined the man's hand-bag. It contained two loaves of bread, a torch-light and a few other articles. He took the bread and torch-light.

Having cut several branches Kotokro covered not only the man's face but also his whole body. He then proceeded to the woman and performed on her the same ritual.

"They are now as good as buried" he said when he had finished. "Let's go. The wild dwellers of this jungle will do the rest."

"Do you mean the cannibals?"

"I mean the carnivora, or is that not how you call flesh-eating animals?"

"You seem to know a lot of words in the English language. I am surprised that you could have learnt so much within a space of one year." remarked Dr. Wiseman.

"Is that a sign of stupidity?" asked Kotokro.

"No, it shows some slight intelligence."

Kotokro was delighted. This was the second time the Doctor had credited him with any degree of intelligence, the first being when he rescued him from the ravine.

"Well, let's be going", he said simply.

Dr. Wiseman gave him the bread and torch-light to put in the iron trunk, and they resumed their journey. There was now no trail to follow and they had to make their way as best as they could, going in the same direction. Sometimes they had to cut their way through thick undergrowths, sometimes they traversed spongy grounds, at other times they had to climb over or go under the trunks of fallen trees.

At last they emerged into a clearing, which appeared to be an abandoned hunters' camp. Three bamboo huts, each capable of accommodating about four people, stood in ruins. They had been demolished by white ants, with very little of their walls left and hardly any roofs at all. They must have been abandoned for a very long time, for they were all half-swallowed up by high weeds.

About six palm trees were growing in the camp. All of them had fruits on them, but none was ripe. Behind one of the huts stood a clump of banana trees also. Two of them had fruits on them, but again none was ripe. Kotokro examined them and cut one that appeared quite mature and almost on the point of ripening.

"What are you going to do with green bananas?" asked Dr. Wiseman "We have no means of cooking or roasting them?"

"They will be ripe by tomorrow", replied Kotokro.

"How do you know?"

"I shall make them ripen", he replied.

"How?"

"By burying them in the ground."

Dr. Wiseman had never heard that bananas could be made to ripen by being buried in the ground, but he was by now prepared to believe almost anything the boy said about jungle life.

"Well, meantime what I need is some water to drink", he said. "I am very thirsty, and if we don't find water within the next hour or so I can hardly continue walking."

"There must be water very near here", said Kotokro.

"Are you sure? How do you know?"

"These rotten bamboo huts are a sign that there are bamboos near-by. But bamboos mostly grow only where there is water, so there is likely to be a stream not far from here."

"Let us look for it then", said Dr. Wiseman.

There was no visible track leading out of the hunters' camp. What track there might have been, had been obliterated by the growth of weeds after such a long disuse; but Kotokro said that as the land sloped to the left of the direction from which they had come they must turn that way in search of water. Dr. Wiseman agreed, and they were soon in the thick of the forest again, under the dark canopy of giant trees.

They had not gone more than forty yards when they suddenly burst upon a stream.

It was about ten feet wide and was flowing over a white sandy bed. The water was cool and clear. Dr. Wiseman ran to the brink and, putting his head into it, drank his fill. After that he said that he was feeling even more tired and hungry and that, as the night was already fast approaching, they should rest there until the next morning, because they might not find a better spot than that before nightfall.

Kotokro agreed, and they cast about for a spot where they could conveniently lie down to rest. They found it under the nearest tree quite close to the stream.

After burying the bananas in the ground Kotokro returned to the hunters' camp and brought plenty of banana fibre which he spread on the ground for a mattress. Then he covered it with one of the cloths meant for his parents, thus forming a comfortable bed. He folded the other cloth and put it at the head for a pillow.

"There is your bed, Doctor", he said to Dr. Wiseman. "Stretch yourself on it and see if it is comfortable."

The Doctor did as he was asked and said that it was more comfortable than the bed in his bedroom in London.

Kotokro laughed.

"That is because you are very tired now" he pointed out. "My father says that a tired body can find rest on a rock, just as a starved palate will find the most tasteless food delicious."

"But where is your own bed?" asked Dr. Wiseman, ignoring the boy's remarks. There seemed to be some sense in it, but it was his father who had said it.

"I don't need a bed", he replied. "Anywhere on the ground here will suit me fine."

"Is that so? You mean you can sleep on the bare ground?"

"Better than you ever did on your soft bed in London." he replied.

Dr. Wiseman did not doubt it. He had seen the boy fall asleep at odd times and places. He was truly the hardened and unspoiled child of nature, coming from a race that lived close to the earth.

"All right. If you can sleep anywhere on the ground then all we now have to think of is what to eat. I suggest we eat some of the bread. I am very hungry."

"Yes, and some corned beef too", agreed Kotokro.

So saying he opened the iron trunk and brought out one loaf and one tin of corned beef. He handed both to the Doctor. The latter broke the bread and gave one half to Kotokro.

"No, your stomach is bigger than mine, Doctor", he said. "You must therefore have a bigger portion." And with that he broke a piece from his own share and handed it back to the Doctor.

The Doctor would have refused it, but he saw that there was something in what the boy had said. Besides, he was truly very hungry and he did not see that half a loaf of bread was likely to make much difference, so he accepted it.

And now he asked for the key to open the tin of corned beef.

"Unfortunately Mrs. Casely packed all the keys separately and they were lost in the crash", Kotokro explained. "I looked for them in vain."

Dr. Wiseman was greatly disappointed. He found Mrs. Casely's action very annoying. "She should have attached a key to each tin instead of bundling them all together and parking them thus in the trunk", he said.

"It did not occur to her that we might need them on the way", Kotokro defended.

"Do you still have your pen-knife?" Dr. Wiseman asked.

"Yes, here it is", replied Kotokro, producing it from his pocket.

"Good" said Dr. Wiseman as he laid hold of it. Still sitting down on the bed of banana fibre the Doctor began to open the tin with the knife, just as Khandari had done during the intelligence test. But he had hardly covered a space of half-an-inch on the tin when his thumb suddenly slipped over the sharp edge of the knife, resulting in a deep gash. He flung away the knife at once and pressed the wound tight with his left thumb to prevent it from bleeding. Kotokro laughed.

"You should never try to open a tin of corned beef with a knife, Doctor". he said. "Remember what happened to Khandari."

Dr. Wiseman was too annoyed to make any reply.

"Maybe you want to try with the cutlass", suggested Kotokro when the Doctor continued to nurse his wound in silence.

"Nonsense!" Dr. Wiseman managed to reply at last. "How can you open a tin of corned beef with a cutlass? We shall have to eat the bread without the corned beef."

"Then after we have eaten all the bread we shall have nothing else to eat, because we cannot open any of the tins of corned beef?."

Dr. Wiseman shrugged his shoulders.

"There is nothing we can do about that", he said.

"I can do something about that" replied Kotokro.

With that he seized the tin of corned beef and before the Doctor could suspect what he was up to, he had ripped it open with his strong teeth, just as he had done in the failed intelligence test.

Dr. Wiseman did not know what to say. He remembered what he had said on the occasion: "You should never try to open a tin of corned beef or sardine or indeed, any canned food, with your teeth. Not only is it very uncivilised but it is also highly dangerous. Why, you could easily have cut your lips or tongue." Kotokro remembered it too, as well as Mrs. Casely's subsequent advice in almost identical words: "You must never again use your teeth in opening a tin of any canned food. Why, it could easily have cut your tongue or your lips."

Neither of them however, said anything. They quietly ate some of the corned beef with their bread, leaving about half of it in the tin for subsequent meals. The Doctor said that they should husband everything they had, in order to avoid eventual starvation.

By the time they had finished eating, darkness had set in and the forest was ink-black. It was fortunate that they had the torch-light, for with it they were able to prepare to go to bed. Dr. Wiseman took off his coat and shoes and hung them on a branch, and Kotokro did the same. Then the latter placed the tin of half corned beef on top of the iron trunk and, having cleared a little spot with his cutlass, lay down on the bare ground to sleep. Dr. Wiseman also stretched himself on his more comfortable bed for his nightly ritual. Soon both were fast asleep.

CHAPTER FIVE
THE HOUSE IN THE TREES

They must have slept for about four hours, when Dr. Wiseman suddenly woke up with very sharp pains all over his body. It seemed he was being bitten by several insects. He quickly switched on the torch-light and discovered, to his horror, that the whole place was swarming with soldier ants. They had invaded his bed and the iron trunk and were creeping over Kotokro who was still fast asleep.

"Kotokro, wake up at once", he said, shaking the boy vigorously by the shoulder.

Kotokro woke up and saw, by the light of the torch-light, a large swarm of those vicious insects.

"They are soldier ants, Doctor!" he exclaimed. "Let us run at once into the stream."

"No, no, not into the stream" replied Dr. Wiseman. "There are crocodiles. Let us rather find some spot free of the ants."

With that the Doctor began to run to the hunters' camp, thinking that that place would be safe. But the ants were swarming all along the way there; and when he arrived at the camp they were there also. He rushed back into the forest and tried to climb a tree. Meantime scores of the wicked creatures had begun to ascend by his legs until they arrived at the point between his two thighs. There some halted and set to work, burying their sharp teeth deep into his delicate parts.

Unable to bear the pain the Doctor fell to the ground again and began to take off his trousers. Alas! the zip got stuck and he could not pull it down. Then he left it and attempted to take off his shirt, for they were biting him most vindictively all over his back and belly too.

In his agitation he could not undo the front buttons, so he desisted from this also. But he had already pulled up the shirt from the trousers, thus giving easier access to his spine and shoulder blades, of which more of the irascible termites quickly took advantage. The Doctor hardly knew what to do next.

Meantime, Kotokro who had been standing in the stream, had been calling to him to come into the water, as it was the only safe place for miles around. He had not paid any heed, not because he did not believe the boy, but because he feared the possibility of ending in the belly of a crocodile. But when he discovered that there was no other way of escaping from those little, wicked arthropods, he decided that it would be preferable to die at once in the jaws of a crocodile, if need be, than endure such unbearable torture from the tiny jaws of those little termites. So he quickly made for the stream and flung himself into it, clothed as he was. The ants fell at once from his body and attire and were carried away by the current.

By now dawn was approaching, but Dr. Wiseman did not cherish the idea of standing in the water until the savage insects departed, which Kotokro said they would, as soon as it was daybreak. He there-fore suggested that they should wade to the other side, saying that it was bound to be free from them, since those little things could not cross streams.

"No, Doctor", contradicted Kotokro, "they are bound to be there too, for they can cross streams and even rivers."

"How?" asked Dr. Wiseman.

"In the same way as humans do; that is to say, by means of bridges?"

"What!", exclaimed Dr. Wiseman "Can ants too build bridges?"

"They can't build. But they can cross by means of trees and climbers that span them."

"Oh, I see. Well, let us see if they are on the other side."

So saying he switched on the torch-light, which he still held in his hand in spite of his ordeal, and examined the grounds on the other side. To his surprise he saw the place covered with even thicker swarms of those bustling insects than the ones from which they had fled. Kotokro saw them too and said:

"You see, Doctor, I told you they were there too. Those little creatures are wiser than elephants, in spite of their tiny heads and puny cranial capacities."

"Wisdom does not depend upon the size of the head alone" explained Dr. Wiseman "It depends upon the size of the head in relation to the size of the body. The elephant's head is big, but its body is many times bigger, whereas the ant's head is nearly as big as the rest of its body. That is why he is wiser."

"I see. Then the midget I saw in London must be wiser than everyone else in that city. His head was almost as big as the rest of his body." replied Kotokro.

"Nonsense! He can't be wiser than anybody. He is deformed."

"What does that mean?"

"His head and body are not normal."

Kotokro said nothing. The midget he saw did not behave abnormally, despite the Doctor's pronouncement about the condition of his head and body.

They continued to stand in the water until daybreak. Then the ants formed into one long single file and began to retreat in the direction from which Dr. Wiseman and Kotokro had come. It was a long time before they disappeared.

After they were gone Dr. Wiseman and Kotokro returned to the spot where they had lain down to sleep, to find that the remainder of the corned beef was all gone. The greedy insects had licked the tin clean. Everything in the iron trunk, however, was untouched, for the ants had not been able to enter it.

"It is obvious that we shall have to look for a safer place to sleep for the night if we are not able to find our way out of this jungle today", said Kotokro.

"We can't find a better spot than this" Dr. Wiseman replied. "It is open and quite close to a stream. However, we cannot sleep on the ground again. We shall have to build a house in the trees, so that we shall be free from ants and all other harmful creatures.

"Build a house in the trees!" exclaimed Kotokro "Whoever heard of a house being built in the trees? Why, even the monkeys don't do that!"

"Well, it can be done, and it is the safest thing to do when you are lost in the jungle. Mr. Robinson did that when he and his family were shipwrecked on a jungle island."

"Who is Mr. Robinson ?" asked Kotokro.

"He is the hero of a book entitled "Swiss Family Robinson"

"He is not a real person then?"

"No, but he could have been real."

"What prevented him from being real?"

"Nonsense, nonsense!" shouted Dr. Wiseman. "Persons in a fiction are not supposed to be real persons."

"Then his house in the trees was not a real house?"

"Of course not. But the one we are going to build will be a real house."

"And we shall be safe from soldier ants?"

"Yes, and from all other harmful creature, as I have already said."

"All right, Doctor. Let us build it then. How do we begin?"

"It is going to be a difficult task, so let us have some breakfast first."

Kotokro opened the iron trunk and brought out the remaining loaf of bread and a tin of corned beef. He handed the corned beef to Dr. Wiseman and gave him his pen-knife.

"You may open the corned beef, Doctor", he said.

"You know I can't open it, with my right thumb cut" Doctor Wiseman pointed out.

"You can do so with your left. Khandari did so in the intelligence test." he reminded him.

"Nonsense!" said Dr. Wiseman "Open it with your teeth. It is quicker and safer that way."

Kotokro smiled. Seizing the tin he immediately ripped it open with his teeth. Then they sat down, cut off half of the loaf of bread and shared it between them. After they had eaten they went into the stream and drank. And now Dr. Wiseman said that it was time to build the house.

"First of all we must look for four trees so conveniently placed as to form the posts supporting the house", he explained. "After that we shall cut stout ropes with which to build the structure."

They did not have to go far before Dr. Wiseman discovered four trees suited to his purpose. They were so placed as to form a rectangular base measuring eight feet by six feet.

Then they looked for stout and pliant climbers which could be used as ropes. The "Krampana" vine would have been the best, but none grew in this area. However, they were able to secure some other climbers that were almost as good.

And now they set to work. Dr. Wiseman asked Kotokro to climb one of the trees and tie one end of one of the ropes to the nearest branch and let the other end down, just as he had done in rescuing him from the ravine. He himself would then do the rest.

Using one of the "Krampana" ropes which he had brought with him, Kotokro quickly ascended the tree and tied one end of it to the nearest branch and let the other end down as instructed. With one of the stout ropes tied to his

middle and using the rope which Kotokro had let down from the branch, Dr. Wiseman ascended the tree. He untied the stout rope from his waist and tied one end of it firmly round the trunk of the tree, about twenty feet above the ground. Having untied Kotokro's rope he descended.

He again asked Kotokro to ascend the second tree which stood eight feet away in line with the first, and tie his rope to the nearest branch, so as to enable him to ascend it himself as before. Kotokro did so and when he descended again Dr . Wiseman climbed that tree too with the other end of the stout rope and a second rope . Arrived in the branch he unloosened the end of the first rope from his body and tied it firmly and tautly to the trunk of the second tree, about twenty feet from the ground. He then tied the second rope also to the trunk of the same tree at the same height of twenty feet from the ground. After that he untied Kotokro's rope and descended by the second stout rope.

Next, Kotokro ascended the third tree which stood six feet away from the second and performed the same operation as before. Dr. Wiseman again went up and tied the other end of the second rope firmly and tautly to the trunk of the third tree. They did the same to the fourth- tree, until they had obtained for the house a base made up of ropes, measuring eight feet long by six feet wide.

Then Dr. Wiseman set to work again, weaving a sort of wicker-work at the bottom to form a floor. When he had finished he also constructed a wall about four feet high, all round it, again using some of the ropes. He, however , left one end of the wall open to serve as an entrance. Then with more of the ropes he also made a movable ladder by which to ascend and descend from the house.

After that Kotokro brought banana fibres and spread them on the floor and so made it soft and comfortable.

It was a very difficult task, and by the time they had finished, the sun had begun to set.

They ate their last piece of bread and the remainder of the corned beef in the second tin. They now had two empty corned beef tins, which they henceforth used as cups for drinking water. Then they climbed up with their luggage to go to bed. For Kotokro this consisted of the iron trunk into which he had packed all his things, and his cutlass. As for Dr. Wiseman he had only the torch-light, his brief-case, the table watch and the cutlass which Kotokro had handed him.

Arrived up there Kotokro spread one of the cloths on the floor, thus making it comfortable for them to lie down. They were both so tired that they slept deep and did not wake up until well after sunrise.

Dr. Wiseman was the first to wake up. He opened his eyes and looked round. It promised to be a very fine day. Already the cool shady forest was fully illuminated with the light descending from a blue cloudless sky. Here and there the golden rays of the morning sun were penetrating through the leafy canopy of the giant trees, bringing vital warmth to the little shrubs below.

He looked for his brief-case. It was nowhere to be seen. His heart jumped in his chest and began to race. His tongue warmed up in his mouth. Why, what had happened? He quickly shook Kotokro who was still fast asleep.

"Hey, you, wake up at once!" he said.

Kotokro opened his eyes but still continued to lie down. Sleep had not yet deserted his limbs.

"What is it, Doctor?" he asked.

"Where is my brief-case?" he answered.

"Your brief-case? I have not seen it."

"You have not seen my brief-case? Then where is it?"

"I do not know."

Dr. Wiseman did not believe him. All the stories he had read from the accounts of white travellers in Africa concerning the thievish ways of the Negro and his lying propensity rushed back into his mind. Among other things, it was said, in a pun, that the Negro would lie about what he had stolen even while lying on it.

"Get up at once and let me see", he said to Kotokro.

Kotokro rose and sat up.

"Stand up completely", ordered Dr. Wiseman, suspecting that the boy was sitting on the brief-case.

Kotokro rose to his feet. Dr. Wiseman rummaged through the dry banana fibres where Kotokro had lain but found nothing.

"Now my brief-case is missing, " he said to him. "There are only the two of us here. It is obvious that I could not have stolen my own brief-case, so that leaves only you. Don't tell me then that you have not stolen it."

"I swear I have not stolen your brief-case", protested Kotokro.

"But you saw me bringing it here when we came up to sleep?"

"Of course I did. You placed it close to your head."

"Ah, you see, you know all about it, - Where is it then?"

"I have sworn that I know nothing about it."

"Try and tell a better lie, my boy; for who else could have stolen it?" persisted Dr. Wiseman.

"So you still don't believe me even when I have sworn?"

"What do you swear by?"

"I swear by Kramoko"

"And who is Kramoko? "

"He is the god in our village. He punishes all who swear by him falsely."

"Can he hear you from here?"

"Yes, he is everywhere."

"Why don't you ask him then to show us the way back home?"

"He doesn't help people. He only punishes them when they lie or do wrong."

"That's another lie, my boy. You know fully well that your Kramoko doesn't exist. So stop trying to fool me and let me have the brief-case at once."

"Don't you think it has probably dropped to the ground?" asked Kotokro, this possibility having suddenly crossed his mind.

"How could it have dropped to the ground when there is a wall of wicker-work all around?"

"I could feel the house rocking as I slept. It probably rolled to the entrance and dropped down. Let us descend and look for it on the ground." said Kotokro.

"All right, go down then. I shall come after you. The thief knows best where the stolen article lies hidden."

Kotokro said nothing, for he realised that the more he tried to deny theft of the brief-case the less he was able to convince the Doctor of his innocence. Seizing his cutlass he descended, followed by Dr. Wiseman. They examined the ground over a wide area, but there was no trace of the brief-case. Then Kotokro said:

"It is very strange, Doctor, that your brief-case should have disappeared just like that."

"It would be strange if it took wings and flew away like a bird or grew a tail and scampered off like a monkey" replied Dr. Wiseman sarcastically. "But I do not believe in miracles."

This remark at once suggested an idea to Kotokro. "I think I know where your brief-case is, Doctor" he said.

"Of course you do", replied Dr. Wiseman triumphantly, "I knew that all along. Come, let me have it at once."

"I suspect a monkey must have taken it while we slept." He explained.

"That's a clever proposition" said Dr. Wiseman "But you have to prove it."

"Let us search for him then."

"You take the lead."

Kotokro did so and Dr. Wiseman followed half-heartedly, for he still suspected that the boy had stolen his brief-case and that all this was mere pretence.

As they went along Kotokro kept looking up into the trees, but Dr. Wiseman, who believed that all this was just monkey business on the part of the boy, kept gazing hard upon the ground, expecting to find it concealed in some bush.

They had not gone very far when Kotokro suddenly said: "Look, Doctor, that's the thief up there. He is holding your brief-case."

Dr. Wiseman looked in the direction to which Kotokro was pointing. He saw a huge baboon squatting upon the branch of a tree and holding the brief-case in his right hand while trying to open it with the left.

"So it is you who stole my brief-case, you abominable thief!" he shouted. "Throw it down to me at once, or it will be all the worse for you."

The baboon, however, paid no heed to his insult or threat. He only temporarily suspended his attempt to open the brief-case and glowered contemptuously at the Doctor. Then he struck the brief-case several times with his palm as if to say "I dare you to do your worst." This defiant attitude made the Doctor all the more angry, but he hardly knew what to do next.

Then he said to Kotokro: "Climb up there at once and snatch it from him, with a box on his ear."

"No Doctor. That will not do", he replied.

"What will not do?"

"He will scamper away with it before I am half-way up the tree. He will not wait for my arrival."

"Is that so? All right. Then I know how to deal with him." So saying he cast about for a sapling. Finding one close at hand he immediately cut and chopped it into pieces, each about a foot long. Then going up again to the tree upon which the impudent creature still sat, he addressed it once more:

"Now, I am asking you for the last time to surrender to me my brief-case to which you have no title. If you don't you won't like what is coming to you."

Again the recalcitrant creature stared hard at the Doctor, twisted its lips derisively and started striking the brief-case once more as if to say "You are only wasting your time."

This further act of provocation exasperated Dr. Wiseman beyond endurance. Without further resort to words he started to put his threats into action. He began aiming the sticks at the monkey with all his might.

"Take this ! And that! And that also!", he cried as he aimed each stick at the unrepentant miscreant.

But before even the first stick could reach its target the agile creature had started to scamper off, jumping from tree to tree with the brief-case held tightly in its right hand. It was soon out of sight. They spent another hour or so looking for it. it was Kotokro who first saw it again sitting on the branch of a tree, and pointed it out to the Doctor. The Doctor immediately prepared to despatch another stick after it, but as before Kotokro stopped him.

"Don't, Doctor", he said, restraining his hand "It will scuttle off again with the brief-case and make sure that this time it will be very difficult for us to find it."

"Must it have my brief-case then?"

"No, it won't have it" replied Kotokro. "Just wait here for me. I shall be back soon." And with that he wheeled round and was soon out of sight.

Dr. Wiseman stood there watching the baboon as it tried in vain to open the brief-case. Again and again he was tempted to aim another stick at the impudent creature who paid no heed to him at all as it proceeded with his bootless operation. At last the Doctor saw Kotokro returning with something which he was hiding behind him. He wondered what it could be. He must be bringing stones he thought. If so in what way would they be more effective than the sticks he had been aiming at the heedless quadruped? Soon the boy came up.

"Look, Doctor, this is the best weapon", he said, revealing a cluster of ripe bananas. "You see, that thriftless fellow has no use for your brief-case. It only took it because it thought it contained food, and that is why it is trying hard to open it. But if it sees these bananas, you will at once see that it prefers the food in sight to the one it merely anticipates. So just watch."

With that Kotokro held up the cluster of bananas.

"Hey, you", he said to the baboon, "look at that."

The creature, who had been so busy trying to open the brief-case that it had not noticed what was happening on the ground, now raised its head and looked. At the sight of the bananas it became excited all at once.

"Cheh ! Cheh ! Cheh !" it cried, displaying a powerful row of teeth.

"Do you prefer these bananas, or would you rather have that brief-case?" Kotokro asked.

"Cheh ! Cheh ! Cheh !"   replied the monkey.

"I see; you prefer the bananas, eh? Then catch!"

With that he threw one of the bananas to the hungry creature. It went straight to where it sat, almost hitting it on the jaw. At once the deft anthropoid let go the brief-case and caught the banana instead. Kotokro, who was directly under the tree, caught the brief-case as it fell.

"Here is your brief-case, Doctor", he said, restoring it to Dr. Wiseman.

"You are very resourceful, my boy", said Dr. Wiseman, seizing it with relief.

"Then I have intelligence?" asked Kotokro, highly pleased with the compliment.

"A little bit", replied Dr. Wiseman.

"This is the third time you have said that I have a little bit of intelligence, Doctor", reminded Kotokro   "The first was when I rescued you from the ravine.   The second was when you discovered, by my use of the word "carnivore", that I had acquired a rather large vocabulary in your language within the short space of one year. And this is the third time. It means then that I have a bit of intelligence?"

"A little bit is always a little bit, no matter how many times it is repeated." replied Dr. Wiseman.

Kotokro was disappointed. It seemed that no matter what he did the Doctor would never credit him with a bit of intelligence, not to speak of some.

"All right, never mind, Doctor", he said. "Neither you nor I can survive on intelligence in any degree. What we need right now is some food to eat. So let us return to the house and have some bananas for breakfast. They are all ripe."

Dr. Wiseman, who was also fond of bananas, welcomed the suggestion, especially as there was nothing else to eat. So they proceeded to the house where Kotokro had left the rest of the bananas after he had dug them up from the ground. They were all ripe and golden. Sitting down they each ate his fill. Then they went to the stream and drank water.

"And now, Doctor", said Kotokro after they had rested for a while "I suggest we plan our activities for the rest of the day. We must, first of all, search through the forest for some food. These bananas will not last for more than two days.

And after that we shall be faced with starvation unless we can find something else to live on."

Dr. Wiseman agreed, and they set out to find food, the Doctor taking one direction and Kotokro another. They decided that each should return to the base before sunset whether by then he had found food or not.

Dr. Wiseman did not go far before he came upon a tree loaded with ripe fruits. It was about ten feet high, but its branches were weighed down almost to the ground with clusters of golden fruits, each as big as an orange. He did not know what fruits they were, but they looked good to eat. Many of them were strewn on the ground. He plucked one and sniffed at it. It had a very pleasant smell. He tasted it. It was most delicious.   Dr. Wiseman had heard that many tribes in Africa lived by gathering fruits from the forest. They knew nothing about farming. He concluded that he had chanced upon a source of food-supply that would last them for a long time if they had to remain in the jungle for many days.

He plucked some from the tree and collected some also from the ground. Then sitting down he adjusted his belt and fell to. He ate and ate until he could eat no more. Then he took off his coat and collected a large amount of it into it. Slinging it behind him he made his way back to their base in high spirits.

When he arrived he found that Kotokro had not yet returned from his search. So he sat down and waited for him. When he did not return by lunch time he again ate some of the fruits, together with three fingers of bananas. Then he propped his head against the trunk of a tree to take a nap.

Just as his eyes were closing he was brought back to full consciousness by a rustling sound. He opened his eyes and saw Kotokro approaching. He was carrying something tied up in a bundle. He wondered what the boy was bringing. Soon Kotokro came up.

"I have brought wild yam tubers", said he, putting down his load.

"Let's see", said the Dr. rising up.

Kotokro undid the bundle and pulled out several tubers of wild yam.

"What!" exclaimed Dr. Wiseman at the sight of them. "Do you mean we can eat these raw roots which even the monkeys don't want?"

"Yes, we can eat them roasted", replied Kotokro

"Well, let me show you something that we can eat unroasted" said Dr. Wiseman. And with that he revealed the fruits he had brought.

Kotokro took one and smelt it. He found the scent very pleasant, but he did not taste it.

"Were there many on the tree?", he asked.

"Oh yes. There must be hundreds, all ripe. Several were even strewn on the ground."

"Hum, Doctor", said Kotokro with the air of one who sensed danger, "do not eat them. They are not good."

"Nonsense! I have already eaten several for lunch and I feel fine. Why do you think they are not good?"

"You see, there are monkeys in this jungle, as we have already found out. If those fruits were good to eat you wouldn't have found any on the tree, especially as they are all ripe as you say. The monkeys would have eaten them all."

"They could not have seen them as yet." suggested Dr. Wiseman.

"No, no good fruit in this place can escape the notice of the monkeys. These fruits have been ripe for a long time, since you say several are strewn under the tree. If they were good to eat the monkeys wouldn't have left a single ripe one on the tree, not to speak of those strewn on the ground."

"Well, I have eaten what I brought and I am prepared to take the consequence. You may eat yours, if you think it is more edible, and take the consequence too."

"We must keep these roots for tomorrow", replied Kotokro. "I can do with some bananas for today."

"As you wish", said Dr. Wiseman with a shrug of the shoulders.

Kotokro sat down and ate some of the bananas. Then he went to the stream and drank water. After that they got ready to convey the rest of the bananas and all the food they had brought from the forest into their house in the trees.

In order that the monkeys might not steal Dr. Wiseman's brief-case again while they slept, Kotokro suggested that they should hang some of the bananas at the entrance to the house, so that those thievish creature might take them away when they came. In this way they would not bother to look for the brief-case.

"No, no", disagreed Dr. Wiseman. "Let us rather put the brief-case into your trunk where it will be quite safe. We cannot spare the bananas."

"If they come and find neither food nor your brief-case they will tote the trunk away" Kotokro pointed out.

"Ridiculous!" exclaimed the Doctor. "How can they tote a whole iron trunk away? They couldn't do that even if it were empty. With all the things packed into it, it would require the strength of more than a dozen of them to drag it even on the ground. And as for toting it from tree-top to tree-top, not even an army of them could do that."

Kotokro did not see any need to argue. He had learnt by experience that when once the Doctor had made up his mind about anything he could never be swayed by words. So he packed everything into the trunk, except the cutlasses, the torch-light and the wild yam tubers which he had brought. Dr. Wiseman's fruits had to go into the trunk too, because the latter said that if the monkeys came and found them, not only would they devour all but they would be prompted to search for the source, and when they had found it they would leave not a single fruit on the tree.

After that they tied a rope to the iron trunk and hauled it upstairs. By now darkness had set in, so being very tired with the day's work, they lay down to sleep.

It was not long before Dr. Wiseman began to dream. He saw a violent storm raging. Lightning began to flash in the sky, followed by the deep rumbling of thunder. This went on for a long time. Suddenly there was a blinding flash, followed almost immediately by a loud explosion, and he was struck by a thunder bolt right in the stomach.

He rose up, thinking he was dead. Then he realised it was only a dream. But there was rumbling with griping pain in his stomach. He was hard-pressed to go to toilet. He got up and took the torch light. It was very dark and silent in the forest, save the intermittent hooting of an owl that came from the distance. He was so hard-pressed that he could hardly hold on. He did not know what to do.

He switched on the torch-light and pointed it to the ground. The light fell upon the two shining eyes of some animal below. He did not know what animal it was. It might be some dangerous creature, such as a lion or a tiger, he thought. He could not take the risk of descending from the tree. What was he to do then? He could, of course, stand at the entrance and let go what was pressing down in his stomach. But if he did that, how could he look Kotokro in the face again the next morning? Unintelligent even though the boy was, he would instantly know that it was he who had done it. He would not associate it with any monkey.

At last he had an idea. He broke a twig from an overhanging branch and hurled it down in the direction of the two shining eyes. There was a sudden rustle and the creature, whatever it was, could be heard bolting away at top speed.

Dr. Wiseman's heart settled down within him. He switched on the torch-light again and examined the ground in all directions. There was no further sign of any animal. Quietly he let down the ladder. Then taking the cutlass in his right hand and holding the torch-light in his left, he descended cautiously to the ground. He went a few yards away from under the house and dug a hole in the ground, into which he quickly discharged what was rumbling in his stomach. It was obvious that this was no other than the fruits which he had eaten, as he could easily tell by the smell, which was even now not altogether unpleasant, having failed to digest.

Casting anxious glances around he quickly ascended into the house again feeling greatly relieved. But even before he could close his eyes again in sleep the rumbling resumed in his stomach, and he was hard-pressed to go to toilet once more. Having somewhat got over his initial fear he quickly descended again, dug another hole in the ground and, for the second time, let go. Then he quickly climbed into the house once more.

He had hardly lain down to sleep when he was hard-pressed once more to go to the toilet. He lost no time in doing so. He kept ascending and descending, all for the purpose of going to the toilet, until he began to feel very tired and thirsty.

He decided to go to the stream and quench his thirst, having by now got over all fear of meeting with harm. Besides, he felt so sick that he was rather indifferent as to what might happen to him in his attempt to do the only thing that he thought might save his life. So holding the cutlass and guided by the torch-light, he descended again and proceeded to the stream.

He had hardly covered half the distance when Kotokro woke up. What with the fear of waking up the next morning to find the iron trunk gone he had not been sleeping well. However, Dr. Wiseman had always gone up and down so stealthily that he had not disturbed his sleep. The whole place was so dark that Kotokro could see nothing. He felt about for the iron trunk and found, to his relief, that it was safe.

Gradually, his eyes got accustomed to the darkness. He looked to see if Dr. Wiseman was still fast asleep. He found his bed empty. His heart began to beat fast. What could have happened to the Doctor? he wondered. Had the monkeys carried him away instead of the iron trunk? That could not be. Monkeys were not carnivorous and would have no use for a human being. If he had been carried away, then it must be the work of a leopard, for that flesh-eating creature could climb a tree. Panic seized him.

Suddenly, he noticed a glow far away in the jungle in the direction of the stream. Was it a witch on its nocturnal sally? He had heard of witches going out at night to drink water after feeding on the spirits of their human victims. He looked again. No, it could not be a witch. The glow of light was not emitting sparks as a witch's glow was supposed to do. This definitely came from a torchlight, and it was the Doctor who was holding it. But what was he going to the stream to do at this hour of night and in such darkness? He decided to find out.

He found the ladder hanging down, which confirmed his conclusion that the Doctor had gone down by himself. Cautiously he descended to the ground. He was in two minds whether to call to the Doctor or walk up to him. He concluded that it would be better to do the latter, if he was to find out exactly what the Doctor was up to. Besides, if he was mistaken in thinking that it was the Doctor, he might put his own life in danger by thus calling attention to himself. Having made up his mind he followed the Doctor stealthily. As the latter kept pointing the torch-light in front of him all the time, Kotokro could not clearly see his profile.

Dr. Wiseman soon reached the stream, and bending down, began to drink greedily. In doing this he had put down the lighted torch-light, so that Kotokro was now able to see him more clearly through its illumination. His back was turned towards him.

He drank the water again and again, pausing for breath at intervals. Then he sat down and propped his head upon his knees. Kotokro became frightened. There must be something seriously wrong with the Doctor, he thought, so going up to him he tapped him gently on the shoulder.

"Doctor, what is …….. "

Before he could finish the sentence Dr. Wiseman had jumped to his feet with a scream and plunged headlong into the stream, where he lay quivering with fright. Kotokro regretted having taken this course of action. He had not anticipated that this would be the result.

"It's only me Doctor", he said, to re-assure him.

"Is it you, Kotokro?" Dr. Wiseman asked in a feeble voice.

"Yes, it's me. Please come out of the water."

With difficulty Dr. Wiseman waded back to the shore, the fear of being eaten by a crocodile having now succeeded the original fear of death at the hands of some savage land creature.

On their way back to the house Dr. Wiseman told Kotokro how his stomach had been running to the extent that all the water in him had run dry, resulting in a desperate thirst. He had accordingly gone to the stream to drink, and that was how he came to find him there.

When they arrived at the house Kotokro suggested that Dr. Wiseman should climb up first, since, as the Doctor was weak, it was necessary for him to hold the ladder for him while he ascended. The Doctor agreed to this suggestion and began to ascend while Kotokro kept the ladder steady by holding fast to it. When the Doctor had reached the top he himself began to climb. He had hardly reached half way when Dr. Wiseman exclaimed:

"Hey! Kotokro where is the iron trunk?"

"The iron trunk? It's up there", he replied.

"Up where?"

"Where we put it."

"Come and show me."

Kotokro quickly ascended and was soon in the house. He asked Dr. Wiseman to switch on the torch light. The latter did so without a word. Kotokro looked. There was no iron trunk.

"Well, where is the iron trunk?" Dr. Wiseman asked again with rising temper.

"Oh Doctor, the monkeys must have taken it away! It was here when I was coming down after you."

"Thief and liar!" shouted Dr. Wiseman. "How could the monkeys have taken away that heavy iron trunk within this short space of time that we have been away? You must have carried it down and hidden it somewhere."

Kotokro was taken aback.

"What would I do that for, Doctor?" he asked. "After all the iron trunk is mine and contains my things as well as yours."

"But it contains my brief-case and precious papers on the intelligence test, as well as other valuables which, together, are worth many times more than your iron trunk and all you have in it."

"Well, I can assure you that I have not taken it" , said Kotokro. "All your precious possessions in it are not worth anything to me. And, in any case, if I took it where could I hide it without your finding out? Surely I could not go away from here with the iron trunk without your knowledge?"

"You could do that. You could stealthily disappear from here with it. So let me hear no more denials. You must produce it at once."

"I cannot produce what I do not have" , replied Kotokro. "Just let us wait until daybreak, when I am sure we shall discover who truly took the iron trunk."

"All right", agreed Dr. Wiseman "provided you won't descend again and run away with it while I sleep."

"Let us re-arrange your bed then, so that you could lie on the ladder. In that way I would have no means of descending without your knowledge." suggested Kotokro.

"No, that will not do", disagreed Dr. Wiseman. "You could jump down and run away. You are as agile as a monkey."

"Let us tie my hand to yours then; so that if I rise up it will pull and arouse you from sleep."

"That was what I was going to suggested", replied Dr. Wiseman.

Having agreed upon this device Dr. Wiseman took a string and tied his hand with one end of it. With the other end he firmly tied both hands of Kotokro. He tied them so tightly that it would be impossible for the boy to untie them without assistance. After that they both lay down again to sleep and did not wake up until the next morning.

It was broad daylight when they got up. Dr. Wiseman untied the hands of Kotokro. The Doctor was still feeling weak, but otherwise not very much the worse for the night's ordeal. His stomach had ceased running and was ready for replenishment. As for Kotokro he felt as active as ever, despite the previous day's hard search for food and the interruption of his night's rest.

Before they embarked upon the day's labour Kotokro suggested that they should first have breakfast.

"What will you have, Doctor?", he asked. "There are more of the bananas in the hole, and there are also the roots I brought. Which of the two do you prefer? Or would you rather show me where you picked those fruits, so that I go for more for you?"

Dr. Wiseman replied that the menu presented by Kotokro hardly offered a wide choice. He could not eat any more of those harmful fruits, seeing what they had done to his stomach during the night. As for the roots, how could he, a civilised man, eat uncooked food like that? Let Kotokro bring the bananas then, for those were the only edible food left.

The Doctor having thus made his choice of meal, Kotokro immediately went and brought the rest of the bananas, consisting of two clusters of sixteen fingers each.

After they had eaten they set out to find the missing trunk. As before, while Kotokro kept looking up the trees Dr. Wiseman fixed his gaze upon the ground. He was still not persuaded that Kotokro had not taken and hidden it. He expected to find it either concealed in some clump of bushes or buried in the ground.

They went far into the jungle, but by noon they had not seen any trace of it. Then panic seized Dr. Wiseman. It was obvious that it would soon be 3 p.m., but he would not know when the exact hour struck, so as to take his heart tablets. If he took them before or more than ten minutes after the hour, he would instantly suffer an attack and die.

"Let us return to the house at once", he said to Kotokro.

"Why, Doctor, aren't you interested any more in finding the iron trunk?"

"I am. But it is obvious that we cannot find it before 3 p.m. when I must take my heart tablets or die. Since the table clock is inside the trunk and we cannot therefore know when the precise hour strikes, it means I am doomed to die soon. I do not wish to die on the ground. That is why I want us to return to the house. If I must die I must do so inside the house in the tree, out of the reach of any wild beast, so that my corpse may not end in the belly of some carnivorous creature."

"But if you die in the house in the trees, then where shall I sleep, since I cannot lie beside your dead body?"

"You can build another house in the trees for yourself. I have showed you how to do that."

"No, Doctor, there won't be sufficient time for me to build a house in the trees before nightfall, so that I would be obliged to sleep up there with you for this night at least. Besides", he added jokingly "how do you know that if I happen to be on the verge of starvation you will not end in my own stomach rather than in the stomach of some wild beast?"

"I know you won't do that, for I am now convinced that you are not a cannibal. But your objection concerning lying down beside my corpse is worth considering. I would suggest that you sleep on the ground, as we did on the first night, until you are able to build for yourself another house in the trees."

"No, Doctor; that won't do", objected Kotokro. "If your problem is simply a matter of finding the correct time I can easily help you to solve it."

"How?"

"I can find the time for you."

"Can you? Then let me have it at once, and no more monkeys business."

"I mean I can ascertain for you the exact hour. One doesn't need a watch to be able to tell the time."

Dr. Wiseman's hope rekindled. He had heard that the Negro could tell the exact time by just looking at the sun. Perhaps there was some truth in it, or Kotokro wouldn't be saying it.

"What is the time then?" he asked.

"I cannot tell you now. I need to see the sun; so let us return to the house as you suggested. From there I shall go to the hunters' camp, where there is a clearing from where the sun can be seen."

They quickly made their way back to the house. Arrived there Kotokro asked Dr. Wiseman to wait for him while he proceeded to the abandoned hunters' camp.

There he found the sun shining brightly from a cloudless sky. It had already inclined a considerable angle to the West. With the cutlass which he had brought he cleared a circular space with a diameter measuring a foot longer than the length of his shadow. Then standing at the western rim of the circle with his back towards the sun, he slowly stepped forward until his shadow touched the eastern rim. From where he now stood, he advanced towards where his shadow had touched, counting his steps. He counted ten; from which he concluded, by calculation, that the time was nearly 3 p.m. He quickly dashed back to the house.

"It's 3 p.m., Doctor. Quick, run to the stream and take your tablets." he cried to Dr. Wiseman.

The Doctor whose heart had begun to beat fast quickly rose to his feet and rushed towards the stream. He was in such a hurry that he fell several times before he arrived there. It was then almost five minutes past three. He quickly swallowed the tablet and drank water. A few minutes later his heart beat resumed its normal rhythm, and he felt that he had indeed been saved. And so it turned out to be; for nothing happened to him by nightfall, by which he knew that he had taken the tablets at the right moment.

Meantime they had to find something to eat. Only a single cluster of bananas, consisting of twelve fingers, still remained. Dr. Wiseman wanted them to eat these for lunch, but Kotokro said that if they did they would have nothing with which to induce the monkeys, when they found them with the trunk, to surrender it to them.

"What shall we eat then?" asked the Doctor.

"The roots I brought"

"What! Can we eat raw roots?"

"We shall roast them"

"With what fire?"

"It's quite easy to make fire", replied Kotokro.

"How?"

"You will see presently."

With that he brought down from the house some of the dry banana fibre that covered the floor. Then he looked round and collected several dry twigs. He wound some of the dry fibre round a dry twig, leaving part of the twig bare. Then he took another dry twig and began to rub it vigorously over the bare part of the first twig. Soon the friction began to cause smoke. Suddenly the dry fibre caught fire. He put more fibre upon the fire, and soon there was a full blaze.

Kotokro made a big bonfire with which he roasted some of the wild yam for lunch. He kept the fire burning by adding pieces of dry wood. In the evening he again roasted more of the wild yam and they had it for dinner. Having concealed the remaining bananas in the ground they climbed up into the house, when the night came, and lay down to sleep.

CHAPTER SIX
THE DESTRUCTIVE STORM

When they woke up the next morning there were signs of another bright day. The jungle was well illuminated with the light of the sun coming from a clear sky. No breath of wind disturbed the leaves on the trees. All was so quiet and peaceful that the stream could be heard bubbling over the pebbles.

Kotokro was the first to wake up, and he aroused Dr. Wiseman who was still fast asleep. The previous day's hard search for the missing trunk had exhausted his energy.

"Get up, Doctor", he said, tapping him gently on the shoulder. "We have a busy day before us. We must try and discover the trunk by all means today."

Dr. Wiseman sprang up at once with a clenched fist, as though he were about to aim a blow at Kotokro. He had been dreaming that he was in his office in London looking over the first edition of a book which he had written on the "Intelligence Quotient of the Negro." The book had just come from the printers. He found it full of very vexatious misprints. Again and again the printers had substituted the name "Dr. Wiseman" for "Kotokro." He would not have minded if the passages in which these misprints occurred were saying anything complimentary about him. But that was not the case. "The tests proved conclusively that Dr. Wiseman had an inherited disposition to indolence, dishonesty, larceny and mendacity" ran one passage. "It revealed that Dr. Wiseman was congenitally unintelligent, puerile and pusillanimous," ran another. "It showed beyond every reasonable doubt that Dr. Wiseman's lesser deficiencies were greed, arrogance and selfishness" said a third.

These printing mistakes made Dr. Wiseman so angry that he immediately proceeded to the Manager's office and confronted him.

"What the hell do you mean by making such stupid and insulting mistakes in my book?" he demanded.

"We made no mistakes," replied the Manager calmly, "It was you who made the mistakes and we corrected them for you."

"Nonsense! You had no right to correct any mistakes in my manuscript."

"Well, we have done it. And what do you intend to do about that?" challenged the Manager.

Dr. Wiseman was so incensed that, without any more waste of words, he immediately aimed a blow at the Manager's left ear. Unfortunately for him it missed its target, flying over the Manager's head instead. In response the Manager sent a blow which landed fairly and squarely upon the Doctor's right shoulder.

This was actually the touch of Kotokro's hand as he aroused the Doctor from sleep. He immediately sprang to his feet with the clenched fist which he had intended for the Manager in retaliation.

"Thank God I was only dreaming," he said with a sigh of relief, relaxing his fist.

"Why, were you fighting in your dream?" asked Kotokro.

"Yes, some ass of a manager had annoyed me beyond endurance," he replied.

"What exactly did he do?"

"Never mind. It was only a dream," he evaded.

"Well, I suggest that before we begin our day's work, we first go to the stream and take a bath, since we have not performed that necessary ablution for many days now."

"You can go down and take a bath if you want to" replied Dr. Wiseman. "I don't need it. My grandfather performed that ritual only once in a year, and my father once in six months: and they were both the healthier for it. I normally take a bath once in three months, and we have not yet been here for that period of time."

"But here, in this jungle, if you take a bath only once in three months you will soon be dirty and full of unbearable stench," Kotokro pointed out.

"Not at all" disagreed Dr. Wiseman. "Only the black skin is liable to such conditions when it lacks a bath. That is why you Negroes need to have a bath ever so often."

"A human skin is a human skin, Doctor," disagreed Kotokro. "Why then should only the Negro's skin require constant wash to keep it from being dirty?"

"The explanation is simple," replied Dr. Wiseman. "You see, dirt is black in colour. Now, there is what we call "The law of Homogeneous Attraction," which means that substances of the same kind attract one another. So because the skin of the Negro is black it easily attracts dirt, which is also black. That is why only Negro's need to have a bath every day. When they don't, they smell."

"So all dirt is black?" asked Kotokro.

"Of course. Who ever heard of white dirt?"

"I see. It means then that if your dress were bespattered with black soil you would say that it is dirty?"

"Yes, of course."

"But if it were bespattered with white earth, such as clay, then you would not say that it is dirty?"

"White clay? It would be dirty, of course."

"So there is white as well as black dirt?"

"Yes. But right now my skin is not dirty and therefore needs no wash."

Without further argument Kotokro descended and hurried to the stream. Arrived there he plucked a leaf from a tree which his people called "Saporo." The leaf produced a kind of lather when it was rubbed and was used in place of sponge and soap whenever these were lacking. He scrubbed his body with the leaf and had a bath as best he could.

He returned to the house to find that Dr. Wiseman had also descended and was roasting some of the roots in the fire which he had kept burning all night.

After they had eaten Kotokro went and dug up the rest of the bananas which he had hidden in the ground. They then set out to look for the missing trunk.

They scoured the forest over a wide area. Kotokro kept looking up all the time, but Dr. Wiseman resumed his concentration upon the ground. He still found it difficult to believe that the trunk could have been carried away by monkeys. Although so much trouble had already been taken by both of them in looking for it, he still entertained some doubt about Kotokro's innocence. The boy could be merely putting up a show of innocence knowing all the while where he had hidden the trunk, he thought. So he kept scrutinising the ground at every step.

It was a good thing he did so. Kotokro, who was leading had gone past a tangled undergrowth without taking any notice of it. Soon Dr. Wiseman came by. It looked such an ideal place for hiding things. He stopped and peered into it. There was no trunk, but something else caught his attention. He looked again, straining his eyes. He saw what appeared like several big round stones neatly arranged on a bed of dry leaves. They were all white, each as big as a mango. He called to Kotokro.

"Hey, come and see something in that clump of bushes", he said, pointing.

Kotokro came back at once and looked.

"They are the eggs of a giant partridge!" he exclaimed excitedly. "Let us take some at once. They are very good to eat"

"Take some? We must take all away," replied Dr. Wiseman, who was even fonder of eggs than of bananas.

"No, no. If we take all away the partridge will never come to lay here again. Immediately it lays ten eggs it goes to brood. But as long as it does not see ten eggs it will go on laying. So let us take away two eggs now and come for two every other day, so that we shall always have eggs to eat."

"All right. You go and bring two then" agreed Dr. Wiseman, "but count how many there are."

Kotokro obeyed and started crawling on his knees towards the eggs. Dr. Wiseman stood watching him;

"Use your brains, my boy", he said to Kotokro, observing how he advanced with difficulty. "You have a cutlass. Why don't you cut your way through the bush with it? You would progress much more quickly."

"No, Doctor", declined Kotokro. "If I did that and the bird came to find this place disturbed it would know that someone had been here. It would then take away all its eggs."

"All right. Hurry then, we must resume our search quickly."

It was not long before Kotokro had reached where the eggs lay. Having counted them he removed two. They were such fresh and lovely eggs.

"Did you count how many there were?" asked Dr. Wiseman when Kotokro returned with the two.

"Yes; there were five." he replied.

From where he stood Dr. Wiseman had been able to count the eggs even before Kotokro came to them and had counted seven. He was therefore surprised that the boy could say there were only five. He said nothing, however, but it confirmed his suspicion of the boy's honesty and left him more convinced than ever before that he had stolen and hidden the iron trunk. "He means to come and take the extra two eggs for himself without my knowledge" he said to himself.

"Let us resume our search for the missing trunk then" was all he said to Kotokro.

They continued the search for a long time without success. Just as they were thinking of returning for lunch Kotokro suddenly heard the chattering of monkeys from the distance. He stopped and strained his ears to listen. As he did so a sound, as of the irregular beating of a drum, came over the air from the same direction. He asked Dr. Wiseman, who had also halted, whether he heard anything.

"Nothing," he replied. "All is so still and quiet that there can be no sound or movement for miles around."

Kotokro was certain, however, that he had heard the chattering of monkeys and the sound of a drum. He concluded that the Doctor's hearing was not so good. He resumed his advance in the direction of the sound, with Dr. Wiseman following. The two sounds grew louder and louder. At last Dr. Wiseman said:

"Oh yes, I hear some sounds now. It must be some natives drumming and singing. I am sure they are dancing as well. It is either a funeral or a festive occasion. With natives, particularly the Negroes, both occasions indifferently call for drumming, singing and dancing. Let us hurry to reach there. Thank God we are arriving at a human habitation at last. We shall soon find our way back home."

"No, no, Doctor" said Kotokro. "These are not sounds made by any human beings."

"Who else could be making such sounds – ghosts?"

"I don't know. We shall soon find out."

The sounds grew louder and louder. Suddenly they ceased. Wondering why, Kotokro halted again and gazed upwards. There, in the topmost branches of the very tree under which he stood, sat a family of chimpanzees, holding the iron trunk. There were seven of them, namely a father, a mother, and five children. The mother and three of the children were holding the trunk between them while the father, a huge fellow with a bottom as hard as an ancient rock and a mouth like a saucer, had his right hand uplifted for a strike on the trunk. They were the authors of the sounds which Kotokro had heard, being assiduously engaged in trying to open the trunk. They had been at it for two days now, when they suddenly espied the owners of their booty approaching. They had accordingly suspended operation in order to escape notice. They discovered to their surprise, however, that Kotokro had sharper ears and keener eyes than they had anticipated.

"Hey, Doctor I told you it was the monkeys," exclaimed Kotokro immediately he set eyes upon them. "look, there they are, holding the trunk on top of the tree."

"Where are they?" asked Dr. Wiseman, coming up.

"Up there," he replied, pointing.

Dr. Wiseman raised his head and looked. Yes, there was the trunk, held tightly by four monkeys. A fifth was sitting by with a raised arm, while two young ones watched the drama with eyes full of curiosity and expectation.

"You detestable pilferers!" shouted Dr. Wiseman, "surrender the trunk at once or prepare for war!" And with that he cast about for a stick with which to make good his threat.

"Don't, Doctor," said Kotokro, restraining him. "Remember that only bananas can induce these creatures to comply with any demand. Being out of reach they have no regard for threats. So let us try bananas first."

"But there are so many of them now that resort to bananas will be of no avail. If you throw any to them only one or two of them will try to catch it, while the rest hold on to their illegal acquisition."

"That is true" conceded Kotokro. "Then we must think of another way to get the trunk from them."

"I have a plan," said Dr. Wiseman. "Let both of us start throwing the bananas to them simultaneously. Our throw should be so fast that all of them will try to catch them at the same time. In this way they will be obliged to let go the trunk."

"That is an excellent idea, Doctor" commended Kotokro. "except that, in that case, the trunk will crash to the ground, since we cannot catch it before it falls; and the things in it, particularly the table watch, will hardly escape damage."

"How else can we get the trunk then? You surely don't mean to tell me that we can somehow persuade them to descend gently with it and deliver it into our hands?"

"I think we can" replied Kotokro.

"What!" exclaimed Dr. Wiseman incredulously.

"I think we can persuade them to do exactly as you say."

"All right. Persuade them then. What are you waiting for?"

"What we must do is this: We must place all these bananas under the tree and pretend to go away, leaving them behind. After we have taken a few steps, you will pretend to deliver a blow at my head. I shall fall to the ground and feign death. Then leave me with my cutlass within easy reach and go away until you are out of their sight. You will see what will happen then."

Dr. Wiseman did not have much confidence in the strategem, but he decided to let the boy have his way. If it did not work they would have to resort to other means. Once they had been able to trace the trunk thus far, there was no way the monkeys would be able to disappear with it again. If he had to chase them from tree to tree he would not hesitate to do so. They would be tired of the unrelenting pursuit and decide to end it by surrendering their booty.

"All right, do as you say" he agreed.

At once Kotokro separated the bananas, finger by finger, and placed them here and there in singles. That done, he started going away as already arranged.

Dr Wiseman quickly rushed from behind and struck him lightly on the head; where upon he fell to the ground and let go his cutlass. It fell only about four inches away from his grasp. Then Dr. Wiseman pretended to examine him. Apparently finding him dead, the Doctor departed without looking back.

The monkeys had been attentively watching these proceedings, imagining that all was genuine. No sooner was the Doctor out of sight, therefore, than they descended to the ground with unwonted rapidity, bringing the iron trunk with them. They gently deposited it at the foot of the tree and immediately proceeded to collect the bananas, each hurriedly devouring its find.

"Hey, you incorrigible thieves" shouted Kotokro, snatching the cutlass and springing to his feet. "Woe betide you today."

The monkeys, being completely taken by surprise, abandoned all thoughts of the trunk, and even of the bananas, their only concern now being for their personal safety. Then they rushed towards the tree and were all clambering up in the twinkle of an eye, leaving the trunk behind. Thereupon Kotokro lifted it up in triumph. Placing it upon his head he called to Dr. Wiseman.

"Doctor, I have got the trunk from those rascals," he said.

Dr. Wiseman hurriedly turned back to meet him and was surprised to see that the boy had indeed succeeded in retrieving the trunk undamaged. They returned to their house where they opened it and discovered that everything in it was intact.

And now it was time for lunch. Dr. Wiseman asked Kotokro to roast some of the roots and one of the two partridge's eggs. The eggs were so big that one would be quite sufficient to serve the two of them for a meal.

"I can roast the roots, Doctor," replied Kotokro "but the egg will not bear roasting. It would burst in the fire and go to waste."

"Let's tie it up in a leaf then," suggested Dr. Wiseman.

"We would have the same result."

"What are we to do then?" "I am unaccustomed to eating eggs raw. Perhaps you are."

"I cannot eat it raw either."

"Well, what must we do then?"

"Yes, Doctor, what must we do?" echoed Kotokro, looking up at him expectantly.

Dr. Wiseman scratched his head for a solution. Then he said;

"I have thought of a way. Bring the corned beef tin. We shall boil it in it."

Kotokro did as he had instructed. But when he placed the egg on top of the tin it immediately tilted it and rolled into the fire. He had to retrieve it quickly, or it would have burst in the flames. Then the Doctor said that he should try the same device once more. He did so, with the same result.

"You must find some stones to keep the tin steady," Dr. Wiseman next advised.

"No, no, Doctor. It's no use." said Kotokro. "I have thought of a better way."

"What way?"

"Let us dig a hole in the ground and put the egg into it. Then we shall cover it lightly with soil and make fire upon the spot. In this way the egg will cook without bursting."

Dr. Wiseman was not sure that this device would work satisfactorily, but he decided to let the boy have his way.

"All right. Go ahead and do as you suggest," he said.

Kotokro immediately dug a hole and placed the two eggs in it, having wrapped them in leaves. He explained that it was better to have both cooked at once to avoid the trouble of having to cook them one by one. They would eat one and leave the other for the next day. Then he covered them up and made a big fire on the spot. While the fire was burning he placed some of the roots on it at the same time to roast. They were also enough to last them for two days.

After the roots were well roasted Kotokro removed the fire from the spot and dug up the eggs. When he shelled one of them he found it to be beautifully cooked. They divided it up and ate it with half of the roots, leaving the other half for the next day. It was a good thing they thus made provision for the next day as subsequent events were to show.

After they had rested Dr. Wiseman said that they should try and make the house more secure from intruders. They could not continue to sleep with their things in it in the way it was. The monkeys might come once more and steal them while they slept.

"What we are going to do is this," he explained. We must cover the top with a network of stout ropes. With the same kind of ropes we must also make a door for closing the entrance when we go to bed. In this way we shall make it impossible for any creature to enter while we sleep."

Kotokro had nothing to say against this suggestion, so they proceeded to put it into execution. They went and cut several stout climbers for use as ropes. Then they climbed up into the house with them and began the work, Dr. Wiseman doing the greater part of it.

It was hard work, but long before sunset they had completed it. Dr. Wiseman surveyed it with satisfaction and said:

"We shall now sleep in peace and be safe from the reach of those arboreal brigands."

"Yes, Doctor," agreed Kotokro "But we shall not be safe from the rain. It is going to rain cats and dogs tonight and we shall be soaked to the skin unless we can roof that house."

"What do you mean it is going to rain cats and dogs?" disagreed Dr. Wiseman. "Have we experienced a finer day than this ever since we have been here?"

"That is why it is going rain so hard." replied Kotokro. "Whenever the sun shines so brightly in the morning, with no breath of wind, and it remains fair the whole day, a heavy rain invariably follows in the night. At least that is what happens in Kantoma."

"Well, here is not Kantoma" replied Dr. Wiseman. "it does not follow that what happens in your village must necessarily happen everywhere else in the world. If you had the least knowledge of Geography you wouldn't draw such a conclusion."

"All the same, please let us roof the house," pleaded Kotokro. "We shall at least be protected from the night dew."

"It is too late now to do that. In any case I am too tired to do any further work on this house today." replied Dr. Wiseman, unmoved.

"All right, Doctor," said Kotokro. "Then I shall go and harvest the other bunch of bananas, since we still have some two hours to go before nightfall. I shall bury them in the ground as before, so that we shall have more bananas to eat in two days time."

"You may do that," agreed Dr. Wiseman.

Kotokro took his cutlass and proceeded to the abandoned hunters' camp. There he cut down the second banana tree that had mature fruits. He lopped off the bunch of bananas and cut six of the leaves. They were very broad, each measuring about six feet long by three feet wide. Then he conveyed the bunch of bananas to the house and buried it in the ground. After that he went back for the leaves.

"Just pack them somewhere. We cannot roof the house today," said Dr. Wiseman when he arrived with them.

Kotokro piled them up on top of one another and weighed them down with firewood, to prevent them from being blown away should there be a violent storm. Then they ate more of the roasted roots for dinner and rested until it was time to go to bed.

Before they retired for the night Kotokro made fire with two big logs and protected it from any possible rain by constructing a little shed over it with some of the banana leaves. Then they climbed up to go to bed.

Before they slept they closed the entrance with the door made of wicker-work and secured it firmly with stout ropes, so that no intruder could easily gain access into the house. Soon they were fast asleep.

They must have slept for about three hours, when Dr. Wiseman suddenly woke up. He had been dreaming that he was sitting in a plane on his way to a conference in Australia when a violent storm suddenly arose. It seized the plane and began to toss it up and down most violently. The plane was about to crash when he suddenly woke up out of fright.

He looked around him. The night was pitch dark. Kotokro was fast asleep, as he could tell from his heavy breathing. The house was rocking gently. There was a gentle wind blowing. All of a sudden the jungle was illuminated for an instant by a flash of lightning, followed soon after by distant rumblings in the sky.

The flash of lightning became more and more frequent, and the roar of thunder grew louder and louder. A storm was fast approaching. He felt for the torch-light and switched it on Kotokro. The boy was still fast asleep. He wondered if he should wake him up and tell him it was going to rain. But again it occurred to him that the rain might die away before it reached where they were, so he decided to wait.

All of a sudden the entire jungle seemed to be thrown into frenzy. The trees swayed this way and that, rocking their house in no gentle manner. Kotokro was still fast asleep. In fact the rocking seemed to be lulling him into deeper slumber.

The winds continued to gain in intensity. Suddenly complete pandemonium broke loose in the jungle. The trees ran riot, lashing one another with their branches. Then there was a blinding flash, followed by ear-splitting thunder and the loud patter of rain. It seemed as if all the sluices of heaven had been thrown open, resulting in a heavy deluge.

The house was tossed like a canoe caught in a sea of billows. It shot from side to side, up and down. The cutlasses were hurled against the iron trunk. One of them bounced on the floor and the handle struck Kotokro on the jaw, whereupon he sprang up at once.

"It's raining, Doctor!" he cried "Let's descend at once."

The words were hardly out of his mouth when there was another flash of lightning, more blinding than all the previous ones. It struck one of the trees supporting the house and sent it crashing to the ground. At once the rope which secured the house to the tree was severed and the house tilted one side downwards, throwing its occupants and everything in it to that side.

Dr. Wiseman and Kotokro struggled to stand up. It was difficult. It was as if they were caught in a net. Fortunately the two trees between which lay the entrance still stood, and so the ladder was also still intact. With difficulty Kotokro crawled to the entrance and ripped the door open with a cutlass.

Quickly descending to the ground he fetched one of the stout ropes which had been left over from the previous day's work. He climbed back with it. Then tying one end of it to one of the two trees at the entrance, he let down the other end to Dr. Wiseman, just as he had done when rescuing him from the ravine. The Doctor caught hold of it and climbed to the entrance from where they both quickly descended to the ground.

All this time the rain had been beating them mercilessly. But as soon as they reached the ground Kotokro fetched two of the banana leaves and they used these as umbrellas; for, as has already been said, each was large enough for this purpose. In fact, even one could have provided adequate shelter for both of them.

It continued to rain heavily with uninterrupted lightning and thunder, as they stood there shivering in their wet clothes. Had they not been under the cover of those banana leaves they would certainly have endured a hard ordeal.

It rained steadily for a very long time. Towards dawn the winds began to abate and the rain to decrease in intensity.

The flash of lightning and the roar of thunder slowly receded into the distance. Gradually the darkness grew lighter and lighter as the rain began to peter out. At last the song of birds sounded an "all clear", like the sound of siren after an air raid. The sun slowly re-appeared in the east, scattering the remnants of darkness and bringing warmth again to the cold and wet jungle.

Dr. Wiseman and Kotokro put away the banana leaves under which they had been sheltering and examined the havoc wrought by the storm. The tree which had been struck by the lightning had broken only a few inches below the rope that tied the house to it. Without their knowing, that point had been rendered weak by wood-peckers who had made their home there. Had the Doctor constructed the house even a foot lower down, it would not have been affected by the destruction of the tree.

"Damn those accursed birds!" shouted Dr. Wiseman in exasperation when he realised the cause of their predicament.

"Don't damn them, Doctor," pleaded Kotokro. "After all they had made their abode in this tree before we decided to join them. We should have remembered that there are other creatures besides ourselves whose dwellings are more properly in the trees."

"Nonsense! " remarked Dr. Wiseman;

The trunk and the second cutlass were trapped in the house and had to be retrieved. At Kotokro's suggestion both of them climbed up again to the entrance. Then letting himself down to the corner of the house where the iron trunk and the cutlass lay, Kotokro tied to the trunk that end of the rope by which the Doctor had ascended from the house to the entrance. Dr. Wiseman then pulled it up and let it down to the ground, using the same rope. He went down and untied the trunk. Then he climbed up again and let down the end of that rope to Kotokro, who was still waiting in the dangling house. Taking hold of it the boy climbed up to the entrance at once, holding the cutlass. Then they both descended once more to the ground.

The fire which Kotokro had made the previous evening was still burning despite the heavy downpour, having been well protected by the shed which he had constructed over it. That crude shelter had withstood the force of the storm, for he had secured it firmly by ropes to some of the trees standing by. They took off their clothes and hang them near the fire to dry.

When they opened the iron trunk they found that no water had entered it and that nothing in it was damaged. There were the table clock, the bananas, the cooked partridge's egg, the roasted roots and Dr. Wiseman's a brief-case. They ate the bananas for breakfast, reserving the roasted roots and the egg for lunch and dinner.

After this Dr. Wiseman went to take a good look at the house to see if it could in any way be repaired. He found that the only way this could be done was to bring the whole structure to about two feet lower down. This would enable the stump of the broken tree to be used as a support for the fourth corner. This however, would not be an easy task to accomplish without first dismantling the whole house, so he gave up the idea. As he started to think of what else could be done, Kotokro who had been observing him, suddenly asked:

Doctor, I don't suppose there were monkeys and violent storms on that island where Mr. Robinson built his house in the trees?"

"Probably not. But why do you ask?"

"Well, here, as you can see, there are monkeys (and very mischievous ones at that) as well as destructive storms. So I don't think it would be a good idea to try and live again in a house in the trees. We have not fared at all well in doing so."

"I was thinking so too, my boy," Dr. Wiseman readily agreed for the first time. "But where else can we be safe from the monkeys and violent storms?"

"In a house on the ground, or in a cave." replied Kotokro "But a house is out of the question, since we cannot build one in a hurry; so I suggest we look for a cave."

"I think that is a good idea, if we can find one."

"Let us try then. I am sure we are bound to discover one; for there is no jungle that has no hole in the ground as well as in the trunks of trees."

108

CHAPTER SEVEN
DR. WISEMAN'S GREAT DISCOVERY

Leaving the iron trunk and its contents under a tree Dr. Wiseman and Kotokro took up their cutlasses and set out to look for a cave. There was no fear that the monkeys would steal the trunk again while they were away, for they apparently did so only at night.

They searched for a long time, following the upward slope of the land towards the west. They came across holes in the ground and underneath overhanging boulders, but none was large enough to serve as a shelter even from rain, not to talk of wild beasts.

At last they arrived at a spot where the land rose up precipitously into a steep hill. It was heavily wooded, with many of the giant tree sending their roots down from the top of the steep declivity to the ground below. If they were likely to find a cave anywhere it was here, so they began to explore the place diligently.

It was Kotokro who first discovered what they were looking for. He had crawled under a tangled growth, close to the steepest side of the hill, when he suddenly saw a hole stretching from the ground level to about five feet up the rise.

"Come, Doctor," he cried to Dr. Wiseman who was following some distance away. "I have discovered a hole here. It looks like the entrance to a cave."

The Doctor doubled his pace and soon stood beside him.

"Where is it?" he asked.

"There," replied Kotokro, pointing.

Dr. Wiseman looked and saw it too. It was partly concealed behind a tangled growth of weeds. Kotokro at once began to clear away the weeds, and soon revealed the broad entrance to a deep cave.

"Let us enter at once and explore the interior," said Dr. Wiseman.

With that he switched on the torch-light which he had brought for such a purpose and began to move forward with little caution.

"Stop, Doctor," said Kotokro, pulling him back. "It is not safe to enter a cave just like that. You never know what may be lurking in it."

"What are we to do then? Must we leave it unexplored?"

"We shall explore it after we have assured ourselves that it is safe."

"How can we assure ourselves that it is safe without first entering it?"

"We don't have to enter to find that out. We shall send a smoke into it. If nothing dangerous issues out after some time we can then enter, for it would then be an indication that no harmful creature dwells within."

"But where shall we have fire? There is no dry wood in this jungle after last night's heavy rain."

"We can't make fire here. I shall have to run back to our house and bring a smouldering brand."

"It is a long way off," Dr. Wiseman pointed out. And you may even lose your way."

"No, I shall not lose my way. It will be easier than finding my way in London. Here in the jungle no two trees are alike. So just wait for me here. I shall be back soon."

With that Kotokro set off. He had carefully noted their trail by the appearance of the trees that they passed by on their way and so was able to retrace their track without the slightest difficulty. It was not long before he arrived at their base. He found the fire still burning and at once took a brand. Holding it like an athlete at the beginning of the Olympics he ran back to the hill. There he found Dr. Wiseman anxiously waiting for him.

"Well done, my boy," he could not help saying, not having expected that Kotokro would be back so soon, considering how long it had taken them to arrive at the place from their base.

"How did you manage to find your way there and back so soon?"

"I told you it was easier for me to find my way here in the jungle than in London," he replied.

"Well, what exactly do you propose to do now?"

"I am going to make a fire at the entrance, as I have already said. If nothing comes out of it then it is safe, and we can enter."

So saying Kotokro gathered wet leaves and twigs and heaped them all up on the firebrand at the entrance, a little way inside the cave. When they began to burn he put on the heap more of wet leaves and twigs.

Thick black smoke soon began to rise and make its way into the cave, propelled by a gentle breeze.

"Quick, Doctor," cried Kotokro. "Let us climb a tree at once. You never know what may be coming out."

Dr. Wiseman did not hesitate to do as he had said. Seizing the nearest tree he began to clamber up and was soon sitted high up in a branch. Kotokro also climbed into a tree only about six feet away from the Doctor's. They looked anxiously on as the smoke gathered volume and began to invade the innermost recesses of the cave.

Suddenly they heard a sound of agony, as of some wild creatures in pain. It was coming from inside the cave. It quickly increased in volume until it reverberated most alarmingly throughout the jungle.

"What is it, Kotokro?" asked Dr. Wiseman anxiously.

"Don't be frightened, Doctor", he replied. "It is the combined roars of only a few lions."

The words were scarcely out of his mouth when two huge tawny lions darted out of the cave, followed by three young cubs. They looked to neither right nor left but bounded straight ahead and were soon lost in the jungle.

Dr. Wiseman was about to address Kotokro again when the words were driven out of his head by the appearance of a most frightful sight. A huge snake, which Dr. Wiseman at once identified as a python, from the one he had seen in the London Zoo, issued from the cave, writhing with agony. It must have been at least eighty feet long, for it took quite some time before it was completely out of the cave. It had spots of black and brown, with a most hideous head and eyes reddened with the smoke. Dr. Wiseman held tight to the tree, unable to decide what to do should the monstrous creature take it into its wicked head to follow him up where he sat. Fortunately for him the giant serpent was too blinded by the smoke to think of climbing a tree, so it simply glided off on the ground like a living cable.

The dreadful creature was scarcely out of sight when there was a weird cry like the simultaneous wailing of a thousand ghosts and a large army of vampire bats sallied out, flapping their wings and baring their teeth most savagely. They were soon swarming over a wide area, in search of the perpetrators of the arson.

Dr. Wiseman flung his arm about to ward off one that was flying in close proximity to his ear, whereupon the dentate bird bit the ear most cruelly. Screaming with pain the Doctor raised his arm once more to strike at his unprovoked assailant.

"Keep still, Doctor," Kotokro shouted to him. "They are all blind and cannot see you. They can only detect movements and attack their sources accordingly. So don't move."

The Doctor did as he was told. Several of the horrible monsters flew round and round him, sometimes approaching so close to his face that it seemed they would pluck out his eyes. But although he was by now bleeding quite profusely from the wound in his ear, and the pain was almost insufferable, he remained motionless. The blood kept dripping on to his shirt until it was thoroughly soaked.

The desperate drama continued for a long time. Meanwhile the fire which had burst into flames had begun to burn itself out. Gradually only a heap of ashes could be seen, with little or no embers in it.

After what seemed an endless ordeal those winged quadrupeds began to return into the cave, still keeping up their frightful clamour. Gradually their cries ceased as they settled once more in their ancient abode, where they and their ancestors had lived undisturbed from time immemorial. After the last of them had disappeared into the cave Dr. Wiseman and Kotokro descended from the trees.

"Well, Doctor," said Kotokro. "It is evident that we cannot live in this cave, for co-existence with those little flying crocodiles will not be possible. So let us continue our search for a safer haven."

"But they apparently lived in peace with the lions and the python?" Dr. Wiseman pointed out.

"They are all dumb creatures. Their common enemy is man," replied Kotokro.

Dr. Wiseman was greatly astonished at Kotokro's knowledge of the ways of animals. Young as he was, he sometimes displayed the knowledge of an experienced adult in matters relating to jungle life. He began to wonder why the boy's Intelligence Quotient was so low.

"Well, let us look for another place then," was all he said.

They searched for a long time without finding any more caves. Instead, they came again and again upon a large hollow in the trunk of a tree. Some of them were big enough to provide shelter for the two of them and their luggage if it was raining, but none was sufficiently spacious enough to accommodate them if they had to lie down to sleep.

At last they saw a huge tree with a trunk several meters in girth. It was the African species of BANYAN, a tree mostly found in India. It had scores of roots shooting down from the trunk from a height of about twenty feet. The roots were flat and overlapping at the top, forming a perfect roof. At the bottom, however, they broke up into a lattice-work all round the stem, at a distance of about twenty-four feet. They provided ample room, all round, for shelter. It was quite an ideal place for protection from the rain and dangerous animals.

But there was no entrance to the room it provided. So using his cutlass Kotokro opened an entrance about six feet high and three feet wide. He cut it very neatly, so that what came off could be used as a door to close it again. In order that it might not slide into the room when it was used to close up the entrance, he crossed the top and bottom with sticks about four feet long, and tied them up firmly, so that when the entrance was closed they acted as wedges to prevent the door from falling in.

When the work was completed Kotokro went to fetch the iron trunk, fire and the banana leaves. Having brought them he also went and brought soft plantain fibre for their beds. Then they cleaned the room, which was entirely devoid of weeds, and made two beds by fixing forked sticks in the ground and crossing them with other sticks. When they had finished Dr. Wiseman surveyed their work with satisfaction and said:

"Now we have constructed a perfect home. We shall be safe from the monkeys and other unwelcome visitors, as well as from the rain, while we shall not lack fresh air, as we would have done in a cave, for we shall have plentiful supply through the lattice-work at the bottom."

"Yes, Doctor," replied Kotokro. "But I think we shall not be entirely safe from the rain if there is a fierce storm like the one last night, for then water will come in through the lattice-work and wet the floor. We need therefore to find a way of making the house more waterproof. I suggest we cover up the lattice-work with banana leaves."

"But if we did that we would be keeping out fresh air too," the Doctor pointed out.

"Well, we can't have it both ways. Either we exclude the rain and the fresh air, or admit both together," replied Kotokro. "And I think it would be better to exclude both, because I am sure we shall survive with the air that will already be in the house when we go in to sleep, seeing what a large room it is."

"All right. Go and bring more banana leaves then," agreed Dr. Wiseman. "What we have here are not enough for the work."

Kotokro went and brought as many banana leaves as he could carry. He went about three times, until Dr. Wiseman said that what he had brought would be quite sufficient for the work. Then on the Doctor's instruction he went to fetch two more of the partridge's eggs and to bring more roots. The Doctor said that if he did not do that they would have nothing to eat for breakfast next morning, not to speak of lunch and dinner.

Meanwhile Dr. Wiseman proceeded to cover up the lattice-work with the banana leaves. He did so by making the leaves overlap one another both vertically and horizontally, beginning from the top. It was like roofing a gabled roof from the top. Like most specialists in the more intellectual disciplines, Dr. Wiseman had never had much respect for manual labour, certainly not for carpentry, which he had always regarded as one of the fields of the intellectually inferior.

He had almost completed the work when Kotokro returned, bringing plenty of wild yams and two of the partridge's eggs. At first he did not notice what the Doctor had done, being too tired to pay much attention. But when he had sat down and rested for a while he suddenly noticed that there was something wrong with the work. He looked again and saw exactly what was wrong. Without saying anything he laughed and laughed.

"What is so funny?" asked Dr. Wiseman resentfully, unable to comprehend the source of the boy's amusement.

Kotokro continued to laugh and laugh. This made the Doctor the more angry. If there was one thing he detested most in the Negro it was his addiction to laughter. From the oldest Head of State to the youngest urchin in the street the Negro was incapable of serious thought and dignified gravity. He was always ready to laugh even when his risible faculty had received no particular provocation. Some people said that it was a demonstration of his resilience to adversities, but he considered it to be a revelation of his lack of intelligence. Whatever it was, he did not like it, and it always aroused in him the deepest feeling of resentment whenever it was exhibited.

"Stop that chatter at once!" he shouted, as Kotokro continued to laugh.

Kotokro suppressed his mirth, for he perceived that the Doctor's face had become very red. Dr. Wiseman's face always turned red when he was very angry.

"Does it rain from the earth to the sky, Doctor?" he asked, trying hard to preserve his countenance.

"Why do you ask such a nonsensical question?" asked Dr. Wiseman, getting more angry.

"Because the way you have covered up the lattice-work would seem to suggest that that is what happens."

"How?"

"You have done it upside down, in a way that will admit the rain and exclude the air," he explained.

"Nonsense! I have done nothing of the sort!"

"You have, Sir. Just look at it again."

Dr. Wiseman straightened himself up, put his hands akimbo and examined his handiwork closely. He perceived at once that what the boy said was true.

"I see what you mean, my boy. You are quite right," he admitted. "But you should have told me at once without prefacing it with laughter."

"It was funny, Sir. I cannot help laughing at funny situations."

"Why not?"

"I don't know. Funny things make me want to laugh, just as sad things make me want to cry."

"It means you have no control over your emotions?"

"Control over my emotions? What does that mean?"

"It means when you feel like laughing you just laugh, and when you feel like weeping you just go right ahead."

"Exactly, Sir. That's what I do."

"Well, I am not surprised. It is characteristic of your race. The Negro likes fun too much, and is easily upset by adversity. It all springs from the lack of intelligence.

"Is that so?" Kotokro asked doubtfully "What about the way you have covered up the lattice work?"

"And what about it?"

"Must we not try to correct it?"

"Not now. I am tired and hungry. Besides it is too late now. We can do that tomorrow, so bring the food and let us have something to eat."

Kotokro produced the roots and the egg, both of which had been cooked the previous day. It was a good thing they already had them to fall upon, both of them being very tired after their hard work. At the approach of darkness they ate the rest of the food for dinner and went to bed.

They had a peaceful night, undisturbed by monkeys or rain. And when they woke up the next morning another beautiful day was on the offing. The jungle was fully illuminated with the sun's rays and the birds were singing happily in the trees. They cooked the partridge's egg and roasted some of the roots as on the previous day.

After they had had breakfast they set to work to rectify the mistake which Dr. Wiseman had made in covering up the lattice-work. They began by first removing carefully the banana leaves, so that they were not torn and could be used again. Then they arranged them from top to bottom making each successive leaf go under the previous one by about two inches.

Suddenly Kotokro, who had been supplying the Doctor with the leaves as fast as the latter could put each in place, said:

"Stop, Doctor. I don't think that this will do either."

"What do you mean?" asked Dr. Wiseman impatiently.

"Water will still come in," he explained.

"In what way?"

"When it rains water will still pass between the roots and the banana leaves into the room."

Dr. Wiseman stood back and examined the work carefully to see if the boy was right. He found once more that what he had said was true.

"Well, what can we do then?" he asked. "I can't see any other way of covering up this lattice-work so as to keep water out altogether."

"I think I can see a way," said Kotokro. "It will be a bit laborious, but that is the only way, as far as I can see."

"What is it?"

"We shall have to cover it up to the top, and we must do it inside the room from the bottom upwards."

"What will hold the banana leaves together? You don't mean to tell me that you could produce nails to nail them, assuming that they would even take nailing?"

"No. What we must do is this: We must cut sticks and construct a framework from the ground to a point slightly above where the flat overlapping roots cease from forming a roof. It is this framework that we shall have to cover with the banana leaves, so that when the water descends upon them from above, it will run off to the floor. To prevent the floor from flooding we shall also have to construct a shallow gutter round the base to take away the water that comes in."

"I don't quite understand what you mean, but let us proceed," said Dr. Wiseman. "I shall discover, as we go along, if there is sense in the plan you suggest."

"Let us go and cut the sticks then," said Kotokro.

They did not have to go far before they found and cut all the sticks they needed for the work in the way Kotokro had described. They planted twenty of the sticks all round the room, about a foot away from the base of the lattice-work, making them slant towards one another, so that they formed a cone. Then they crossed them with other sticks, using ropes to tie them up. Having thus constructed a framework, in the shape of a wigwam, they set to work to cover it all round with the banana leaves, beginning from the bottom. When they had finished, the structure that was formed could, in itself, have provided shelter from rain if it stood anywhere outside and had the apex also covered.

The work was truly laborious and had taken several hours. But it was worth all the trouble, for there was no doubt that it was as good as any house built with concrete, in respect of its ability to withstand rain and the force of wind. They made it even more waterproof by digging a gutter all round the base, as Kotokro had suggested, to carry away any water that might come through the lattice-work.

By the time they had completed the work it was past noon. They had lunch and being very tired, lay down to rest. In the evening they had the rest of the food for dinner and as soon as darkness came, they went to sleep for the night.

After breakfast the next morning Dr. Wiseman announced, to the surprise of Kotokro, that he was going to the stream to take a bath and wash his shirt which had been badly stained with blood when his ear was bitten by the vampire bat.

"Why, Doctor, we have not yet been here for three months," Kotokro pointed out.

"We haven't. And so what?"

"So I am surprised that you think it is time for you to take a bath."

"Nonsense! Do I have to wait three months before taking a bath even when I am so obviously dirty?"

"I don't see you dirty. You are still white."

"And you don't also see my shirt dirty?"

"I see it dirty, because it is stained with your blood."

"And you don't see that there is need for me to wash it too?"

"There is. Dirt from blood needs to be washed away at once."

"All right. Then you understand why there is need for me to take a wash now. The blood went on my body too."

"I now understand, Doctor," Kotokro said. "Then you may go, and do as you say, while I go to bring more roots and fetch two of the partridge's eggs. We shall need them for lunch and dinner."

Having come to this understanding they parted, the Doctor taking the way towards the stream and Kotokro going in the opposite direction.

It was just past noon when Kotokro returned, bringing some wild yams and two of the partridge's eggs. Dr. Wiseman had not yet returned from the stream. He made fire and roasted some yams and cooked the two eggs, following the method they had used on the two previous occasions. It took about one and half hours getting the lunch ready. But long after Kotokro had eaten his portion Dr. Wiseman had still not returned.

Kotokro began to get anxious. The distance to the stream was not at all far, and since the Doctor had only his shirt and trousers to launder, he should have returned within two hours at the most. Was it because he was waiting for them to dry? But there was no need for that. He had taken his coat also with him, with a view to wrapping it around his waist after the laundry, and should have returned to the base by now to dry the washed clothes. Or had he washed the coat too and was waiting for all three to dry? No, it was unlikely that the Doctor would do such a thing, since he must have been aware that those clothes could not dry in less than four or five hours. He would not wait, long after it was past lunch time, for them to dry first.

Concluding that something must be wrong Kotokro set out with an anxious heart to find the Doctor. He went to the stream, but there was no sign that he had been there. Then he retraced his steps towards the house. About midway between the stream and the house he suddenly saw what appeared to be the Doctor's foot-prints on the ground. It was obvious that he had not gone to the stream at all but had strayed off to somewhere else. Had he done that intentionally or had he simply missed his way?, he wondered.

He followed the Doctor's trail, keeping his gaze firmly fixed on the ground. Suddenly he heard a rustling sound. Raising his head he saw Dr. Wiseman running towards him. The Doctor looked so excited.

"Oh Kotokro!" he shouted as soon as he set eyes upon the boy. "Guess what I have found."

"What is it?," Kotokro asked anxiously.

"Oh, you can never guess it. You can never guess it!" continued the Doctor in the most excited tone. He was almost on the point of setting his feet in motion for a dance.

"Tell me, Doctor. What is it?" asked Kotokro again.

"I have made the greatest anthropological find in this century. My name will go down in history as the man who discovered the relics of the world's most ancient civilization."

"What is it?"

"It is a whole city, with the most magnificent buildings anyone has ever seen. It must have been built thousands of years before the Christian era, in the remotest antiquity. The buildings, which are almost all alike, show an architectural skill unrivalled anywhere in the world. I missed my way to the stream, and this is the discovery I have providentially made in the process."

"What are the buildings like?" asked Kotokro.

"They are all multi-storied buildings, cone-shaped and rising several feet above the ground. They are built of the most durable material, in the form of hard-baked clay. Each building has several spires and chimneys and looks exactly like a castle."

"Are people still living in them?"

"Of course not. They must have been abandoned thousands of years ago. But they are so well preserved that you would think they were built not more than a decade ago."

"But what makes you think that this is not a modern city?"

"Two things. First of all, no one lives in them, as I have already said. Secondly all the buildings are placed haphazardly without streets or inter-connecting foot-paths, and the whole city is hidden under what appears to be a virgin forest. That forest must have come into existence not later than ten thousand years ago. "

"Doctor, your discovery seems to be very interesting," observed Kotokro. "Please let us go and see it at once. I am dying to have a look at it."

"Let's go. You will be simply amazed when you see it."

As they went along Dr. Wiseman kept repeating what a great discovery he had made. Not only would scientists from all over the world be flocking to study it, but tourists from all the five continents would come in their thousands to see the greatest wonder of the world.

"I shall claim proprietary right over the find and will soon become a multi-millionaire," he added.

"And what does that mean?" asked Kotokro.

"It means I shall have millions and millions of money."

"And what would you do with millions and millions of money?"

"A lot of things. I shall build or buy mansions in different parts of the world - in Paris, in Rome, London, New York, Berlin, Melbourne, Rio de Janeiro, Ottawa, Tokyo and in all the sea-side resorts in the world. I shall also buy a luxury yacht, a private aeroplane, a helicopter, a fleet of cars, including Rolls Royce, Mercedes-Benz 600, and many other cars from all over the world. I shall construct Zoos and swimming pools in all the mansions I build or buy."

"And when you have done all these, what will you be doing next?" asked Kotokro.

"I shall travel from place to place, and wherever I go I shall hold big parties, in the course of which the most delicious foods and drinks will be served, for I shall keep scores of cooks and servants in all my mansions."

"What will become of your research on Intelligence Quotients then?"

"I wont have time for that. I shall leave it to Dr. Springfield and the others to carry on."

"And for how long will you be enjoying yourself?"

"For as long as possible."

"I suggest you give some of the money to Dr. Stockdale, so that he will bring you back to life any time you die. In that way you will be able to enjoy your wealth for a long time."

"There will be no need for that. With all the good food I shall be eating and the luxurious life I shall be living I am bound to live for many years."

They had been advancing as they talked. But suddenly Kotokro halted and burst out laughing.

"Oh Doctor," he said. "You remind me of the story that old Mangodo told of Mr. Spider and his children."

"What did he say?"

"He said that one day Mr. Splider, who was a very poor and lazy man, with nothing to sleep on, sat in his hut surrounded by his eight little children, the oldest of whom was only ten years old. Mr. Spider said to his children:

"I shall make a big maize farm and reap a bumper harvest. I shall sell the maize and get a large amount of money. With the money I shall buy the most expensive blanket in the world to sleep on.

"Daddy, I shall sleep with you at the head of the blanket," said his sixth son.

"No, you shan't," replied his eldest son. "I shall sleep at the head of the blanket, because I am the eldest."

"And I shall sleep at the right side of the blanket," said his fifth son.

"No, you shan't" replied his second son "I shall sleep on the right side of the blanket, because I am older than you.

"And I shall sleep at the left side of the blanket" said his seventh son.

"No, you shan't," replied his third son. "I shall sleep at the left side of the blanket, because I was born before you."

"And I shall sleep at the bottom of the blanket" said his eighth son."

"No, you shan't" replied his fourth son. "I shall sleep at the bottom of the blanket because I am senior to you."

"Hearing the children thus quarrelling over the blanket Mr. Spider said angrily: "Hey, go away, all of you, and leave my blanket alone. You are tearing it."

Dr. Wiseman laughed heartily. It was the first time Kotokro had seen him do that. Was the story all that funny? he wondered. Or was it the prospect of becoming rich that had suddenly released the Doctor's risibility?

"Mr. Spider was a great day-dreamer," the Doctor remarked after a pause. "He must have been always building castles in the air. But I am not. I shall really get all the money I want and live comfortably all the rest of my life."

"And what will you give me? After all, we came here together?" asked Kotokro.

"Oh , don't you worry. Your needs are few and can easily be satisfied. I shall give you all the pen-knives you want for yourself and all the cutlasses and corned beef and cloths that you want for your parents."

"Will you, indeed?" asked Kotokro delightedly.

"Trust me, I will."

Kotokro was almost frisking with joy as they went along. It would have been difficult for an observer to determine whether he or Dr. Wiseman was the happier of the two as they leapt across rough grounds and dodged under fallen trees on their way to their joyful destination.

They had proceeded for some distance in silence when Kotokro suddenly slackened his pace; but Dr. Wiseman, who was leading, continued to advance at the same pace, so that the distance between them had begun to widen without the latter knowing it. Suddenly Kotokro said:

"Doctor, it seems we have been day-dreaming too, like Mr. Spider."

It was an unexpected pronouncement, and the Doctor turned round to look at him. He saw the boy looking very despondent.

"Why do you say so, my boy?" he asked.

"We have been making plans that may never come true."

"Why do you say so?"

"You see, there is no guarantee that we shall ever get out of this place alive, so that we may never profit from your find."

"Ho, ho!" sniggered Dr. Wiseman. "Is that all? When did you ever hear that anyone got permanently lost in the jungle?"

"Sometime people do. Old Konkro once went into the forest at Kantoma and never came back. It is said that he got lost in the forest."

"But our case is different. We didn't just set out to go into the forest. We air-crashed while travelling, just as Robinson Crusoe and the Swiss Family Robinson were shipwrecked while on a voyage. They were all able to return home eventually."

"You have told me about Mr. Robinson, but who was Robinson Crusoe?" asked Kotokro.

"He was an Englishman who was shipwrecked on an uninhabited island. He stayed there for several years, but was eventually able to return home, bringing with him a native whom he called 'Friday'."

"What is a native?"

"A native meant an original inhabitant of the land," explained Dr. Wiseman. "But it is now used to mean a primitive person."

"And what is a primitive person?"

"A primitive person is an uncivilized person."

Kotokro laughed.

"Ah, Doctor," he said. "I still don't understand what you are trying to tell me. I find each explanation even more difficult to understand. What is an uncivilized person?"

"An uncivilized person is a person who does not know how to build and live in a beautiful house, how to make and ride in a car, how to weave and wear beautiful clothes and how to prepare and eat nice foods."

"Oh, I see" replied Kotokro. "Like you and me, eh?"

"Well, like you, but not me."

"Why, Doctor" asked Kotokro. "Can you build and live in a beautiful house, make and ride in a car, weave and wear beautiful clothes or prepare and eat nice food?"

"No, but my people can do all those things, so they are civilized. And because they are civilized I am also civilized."

"I see. And because my own people cannot do all these things they are not civilized?"

"Quite so."

"And because they are not civilized I am also not civilized?"

"Correct."

"And Robinson Crouse's man, Friday: Was he also uncivilized and was that why he was called a native?"

"So."

"And was he like me?"

"Yes."

"But I have a name, and you call me by it in a shortened form. So why did Robinson Crouse call this man, Friday? Did the man say he had no name?"

"He probably had; but it was perhaps to long for Crusoe to be able to pronounce it, so he simply called him Friday. It was the day on which he rescued him from his fellow savages."

"Savages?"

"Yes, savages."

"What does it mean?"

"It is another word for a primitive person, especially one who kills his own kind without good reason. He is bad and blood-thirsty."

"I see. Did he answer gladly to that name of Friday?"

"He did. We are not told that he ever objected."

"Well, let us hope we shall be able to get out of this place then like Robinson Crusoe and the Swiss Family Robinson." Kotokro said in a doubtful voice.

"We certainly will; and you will be my man, Friday. I mean I shall return with you to Britain and make you very happy. You can stay with me and visit your parents as often as you like, taking for them presents; for money will be no object."

"I will not like to be your man, Friday." refused Kotokro "I shall just return to my village and live with my father and mother. You will have to go and bring me the things you have promised."

"That would be no problem. I would send them through the British High Commissioner in Blaft, if I can't come myself. So cheer up, my boy. We are going to live very happily for the rest of our lives. We deserve it, seeing all the troubles we have gone through."

They had continued to advance as they talked, and it was not long before they arrived at their destination; or so the Doctor said.

"There you are" said Dr. Wiseman, pointing triumphantly. "Did you ever dream of a city so splendid?"

Kotokro's heart sank. It was as if he had suddenly awakened from a pleasant dream to find himself grovelling in misery. He said nothing.

"Why, aren't you happy to see this wonderful sight?" asked Dr. Wiseman, observing his mood.

"No, Doctor", replied Kotokro gloomily. "This is no ancient city at all. All these structures you see are ant-hills."

"What!" Dr. Wiseman shouted so loudly that his voice rang through the forest. "Do you mean to tell me that buildings of such artistic construction and highly sophisticated design are nothing but ant-hills?"

"They are just ant-hills, Doctor," insisted Kotokro.

"How do you know."

"We have some in the forest at Kantoma too."

"Impossible. I can't believe it."

"Look at them carefully and tell me" said Kotokro. "Do they have entrances into them?"

The question raised a point which the Doctor had overlooked. It jolted him a bit, but he refused to accept that this was an important consideration.

"Does that really matter? I am sure there is a good explanation for it."

"No explanation," repeated Kotokro emphatically. "They are anti-hills pure and simple."

"Prove it," challenged Dr. Wiseman, still clinging hard to his belief.

"All right. I am going to show you" said Kotokro. And he immediately cut a stick and sharpened it. He advanced towards the nearest structure and stuck it into it. When he pulled it out again it left a hole through which thousands of white ants began to pour out.

"Do you see that?" he said. "All these others are just ant-hills. As I have said, we have them also in Kantoma, except that ours are not quite so huge."

The truth came as a shock to Dr. Wiseman. All the castles he had been building high up in the air came crashing down over his ears. His heart which had been as light as air, providing plenty of room for mirth, suddenly became as heavy as lead. It was all he could do to remain standing. His knees tottered and his eyes reeled. His face became as white as snow in the Arctic, all the blood having suddenly fled from it. His heart-beat lost its rhythm. He felt a kind of weakness in all his limbs, in a way that he had never felt before.

For some time he stood speechless. Then he sat down and propped his head on his knees, feeling utterly dejected.

"Cheer up, Doctor", said Kotokro, who had by now begun to recover from his own deep disappointment. "After all, we don't really need all those things we were talking about. What we do need we already have. My father has always said that it is unwise to throw away what one has for what one cannot have. At least we have our health and strength, which are very precious. We must not throw them away by brooding over our disappointment."

Kotokro's words seemed to have some effect. Dr. Wiseman slowly rose to his feet again with a forced smile and said:

"Let us go back to the house. I am very tired."

They slowly made their way back to the house. It took them a long time to get there, as they now found the obstacles on the way, such as fallen trees, overhanging branches and tree stumps, very obstructive, no longer having the spirit and energy with which they had come. But eventually they arrived back at their base.

Dr. Wiseman ate his lunch with little appetite, even though he was very hungry. He was surprised to see how adversely his palate had been affected by his disappointment. Even the partridge's egg which he had always eaten with great relish now tasted like rubber in his mouth. After he had swallowed a few morsels with difficulty he told Kotokro that he was going to bed.

"Wont you go to the stream to have a bath first?" asked Kotokro.

"No, I have no desire to do that now," replied Dr. Wiseman.

"Well, let me go and wash your clothes for you then." Kotokro offered, "for we still have some hours to go before sunset. They may not dry today, but they will certainly do so by tomorrow morning, if no rain falls in the night."

"Thank you" said Dr. Wiseman.

Taking off his shirt and trousers he gave them to Kotokro. He said that he would keep the coat for covering himself up.

"There is no need" said Kotokro. "You can tear a piece from one of the cloths in the trunk for that purpose."

Dr. Wiseman declined, saying that he did not want to damage what he had given the boy as a present for his parents. But upon Kotokro's insistence he at last consented and tore a piece, with which he covered himself up. Then Kotokro went to the stream with the Doctor's coat, trousers and shirt and laundered them as best he could without soap. They came out at least cleaner than they had been before.

He brought them back to the house and constructed a clothes-line with sticks and a rope and hang them out to dry.

Dr. Wiseman slept the whole afternoon and did not wake up until it was dark. He always slept more than he was wont to do whenever he was overcome with grief, being quite the opposite of some people whom asleep always eludes whenever they have anything weighing down on their mind. In normal circumstances, however, he did not find it so easy to sleep.

Meanwhile, Kotokro who did not want to disturb him, ate his portion of the dinner, consisting of the roasted roots and half of the partridge's egg. On waking up again the Doctor said that he had still no appetite for food, so he lay down once more and slept. Kotokro did the same.

CHAPTER EIGHT
DR. WISEMAN'S OBSESSION

Kotokro slept very soundly throughout the night. When he woke up the next morning there was the beginning of another bright and sunny day. The jungle was well lit with the sun's rays penetrating here and there through the leafy canopy of the giant trees. The air was still and motionless, not disturbing a single leaf on the trees.

He looked round for Dr. Wiseman. The Doctor was not in his bed. He opened the door and went out. His clothes which he had left drying on the line were not there. What had happened to him? He entered the room again and examined the Doctor's bed. He found the piece of cloth with which the Doctor had covered himself up neatly folded and placed at the head of the bed.

It was obvious that Dr. Wiseman had got up and gone somewhere while Kotokro was asleep. But where could he have gone? He had probably gone down to the stream to have a bath, he thought. The previous day's high elation and subsequent deep disappointment over his find had robbed him of any desire to take a bath that day. But having recovered his normal composure he had probably gone to perform that ablution now.

He decided to go to the stream and find out. He could not take anything for granted, especially as the Doctor had never behaved in this manner ever since they found themselves in that jungle, apart from the night when his stomach ran.

He ran down to the stream, but there was no sign of Dr. Wiseman. He had probably gone to bring some of the partridge's eggs. He must follow him there. There was no sign of the Doctor when he arrived there. He counted the eggs and found that the bird had come to lay one more. None had been taken away. Removing two he retraced his steps towards the house.

Suddenly the thought occurred to him that the Doctor might have gone back to see the ant-hills. It was true he had shown a high degree of disappointment when it was proved to him that what he imagined to be the work of highly skilled architects were merely the handiwork of those little unintelligent creatures; but he apparently still thought that the proof was inconclusive. He must have returned there, therefore, for double assurance.

Kotokro soon became absolutely certain that the Doctor had, indeed, gone back to see the ant-hills; for, looking on the ground, he discovered several foot-prints. He counted them and found that there were eight pointing in the direction of the ant-hills and six pointing away from it. This meant that, of the eight, six had been made by him and the Doctor when they both went to see the place the day before; and the other two were left by the Doctor only this morning.

He was confirmed in this conclusion on examining the foot-prints more closely. Two of them had definitely been made only this morning, for they were fresher. There was no doubt that the Doctor had gone this way.

Kotokro was quite right. After Dr. Wiseman woke up the previous evening he had not been able to sleep well again. This was because his mind had immediately gone back to the ant-hills, and he had begun to think that he had made a mistake in accepting Kotokro's opinion about the place so easily. It occurred to him that he should have conducted a closer examination of, at least, three of the buildings before coming away with him, for the fact that all the structures he had seen contained no entrances and that white ants had poured out from the first one which Kotokro had pierced with a stake, could possibly be explained on other grounds. With such thoughts agitating his mind he kept waking up again and again throughout the better part of the night.

At last, just before dawn, he fell into a deep slumber, in the course of which he had a dream. In this dream he remembered that he had once read from an ancient historian (Herodotus, it seemed) that there had existed, between the years 12,000 - 8,000 B.C., a kingdom somewhere in the centre of Africa, called Walinki or "The Land of Precious stones." The people of Walinki had attained to a very high degree of civilisation and were particularly gifted in architecture as well as in art and craft. Their capital, Lokodi, contained the most splendid buildings that were ever seen anywhere in the world. They were all built in the shape of cones, several storeys high, with chimneys and spires artistically constructed. The whole city was surrounded by high walls.

During the reign of its last king, Emperor Akibonga VI, a barbarous tribe to the North over-ran the country and laid siege to Lokodi. For several years the inhabitants bravely withstood the siege. But at last, overcome by famine and superior forces, they decided to surrender.

Before they did so, however, they conveyed into ten of their public buildings, situated in various parts of the city, all their treasures, both private and public. These consisted of several tons of gold, diamond and silver, as well as of innumerable collections of gold and silver artefacts, including plates, cups, knives and forks, and a host of other things wrought from precious stones. The Emperor's treasures were separately stored in the eleventh building. These also consisted of gold and silver sceptres, several pieces of diadems studded with all kinds of precious stones, and an innumerable collection of jewellery.

After that they brought out all their other possessions and piled them up in the centre of the city. Then they sealed up the entrances to all the buildings, both private and public. They set fire to the pile and flung upon it the corpses of all the inhabitants who had died from famine but had not yet been buried.

While the pile was in flames they sent a message to the enemy, saying that they were prepared to come out of the city in surrender. One old man, however, advised against this course of action, saying that the enemy would not spare them. When they paid no heed to him he refused to go out with them, declaring that he would rather die inside the city than outside it.

Truly enough, as soon as the gate of the city was thrown open and the people came out, the enemy fell upon them and slaughtered them all to the last baby. Then they entered the city and found the old man sitting beside the blazing pyre. They asked him what was the meaning of the fire and he told them that a dreadful plague had descended upon the city in fulfilment of a prophecy which had also foretold of their coming. It had already claimed the lives of half of the population, and that was why the other half had decided to surrender, preferring to die at once by the sword than slowly through the hideous affliction, the seeds of which would remain in the city for eight thousand years.

On hearing this the barbarians immediately slew the old man and fled from the city as fast as they could go.

On remembering this story in his dream Dr. Wiseman, still dreaming, immediately took a pick-axe and spade and set off towards the city of ant-hills. Arrived there he set to work. Inside the first building into which he made an entrance he discovered a huge amount of diamond, gold and silver. In the second he found an innumerable collection of jewellery of the finest craftsmanship. He was so excited that he clapped his hands and jumped for joy; whereupon he jumped clean out of bed, and found that he had only been dreaming.

He concluded, however, that this dream must have a basis in physical existence, for it had seemed so vivid and real. Destiny had obviously brought him there for the purpose of discovering the hidden treasures, especially when he found by calculation that the eight thousand years which had been foretold as the duration of the seeds of the plague in that city had only elapsed by twenty years.

By now dawn was approaching. Dr. Wiseman rose up and, seizing his cutlass, stole out of the room on tiptoe, not wishing to disturb Kotokro who was still fast asleep. He immediately set out for the city of ant-hills.

Arrived there he cut a stick and sharpened it. Using it as a pick-axe he began to make an entrance into the first ant-hill that he came across. He worked very hard, for the walls were as strong as baked bricks. At the first stroke a host of white ants began to pour out; but this did not deter Dr. Wiseman. He persevered and eventually succeeded in opening a wide entrance into the structure. He gazed into it and found that it contained nothing but the hives of white ants, such as harbour their queens.

Disappointed but by no means frustrated he went on to a second structure. Here again he succeeded in opening an entrance after very hard work, but he only found in it hives similar to the first. He was industriously engaged on a third structure when Kotokro, who had followed his trail, suddenly appeared on the scene.

"What are you doing Doctor?" asked Kotokro.

"I am searching for treasures hidden in these buildings" he replied.

"Who told you that treasures are hidden in these ant-hills?"

"These are no ant-hills," replied Dr. Wiseman. "They are ancient buildings in the legendary city of Lokodi, described long ago by a Greek historian."

Kotokro laughed until the tears ran down his cheeks.

"What are you laughing at so foolishly?" Dr. Wiseman asked angrily.

"You are very funny, Doctor," replied Kotokro, hardly able to contain himself. "These structures are not buildings constructed by any human hands. As I told you yesterday, they are just ant-hills. They may look like buildings, but they were constructed by white ants. I am sure several are even now in the process of being built."

"Where? show me."

"All right; come along then. Let us traverse the city, and I am sure we shall find some of the buildings still in the process or being constructed. You will learn all about them from the builders."

This was a challenge Dr. Wiseman could not refuse. It seemed quite ridiculous to suggest that some of these ancient buildings were still in the process of construction with the builders even now on the job.

"Let us go straightway," he agreed, and immediately picked up his sharpened stick and the cutlass.

They went through the city for a long time without seeing any new structures, until Kotokro began to think that he was probably mistaken in his conclusion, and Dr. Wiseman was on the point of calling a halt to their fruitless search. Suddenly Kotokro espied a small ant-hill that was just emerging from the ground. The next instant he saw another one which had risen about two feet above ground; then a third which had gone up a little higher still. Dr. Wiseman saw them too, and his heart at once sank; for it was now quite clear to him that the boy had been right.

"There are some of your ancient buildings rising up even now, Doctor" Kotokro said. "The architects are even now on the job. Let us enquire from them who built the ones we saw before."

Dr. Wiseman did not reply. He stuck into the smallest of the structures the sharpened stick which he carried. At once an army of white ants began to pour out.

"Let us go away from here at once," he said to Kotokro in utter dejection and immediately turned round and began to retreat.

Kotokro followed, bubbling with laughter. He was sorry to see the Doctor so badly disappointed, but to him the situation appeared more comic than tragic.

CHAPTER NINE
ESCAPE FROM TWO DANGERS

On their return to the house Dr. Wiseman said that he would now go to the stream to have a bath, as he had originally intended to do when he missed his way and found himself in the city of ant-hills. He had forgotten to do so the previous day before going to bed, due to his excitement over his supposed great discovery.

To make sure that he would not miss his way again Kotokro offered to accompany him; so taking the cutlass, which he always carried with him whenever he ventured out of the house, he followed the Doctor.

They had covered about half the way when Kotokro, who had always been in the habit of occasionally looking up into the trees whenever he was walking through the forest, suddenly espied something that looked like a huge climber entwined round the trunk of a tree underneath which their path lay. He looked again. At first he could not see where it began from the ground or ended in the tree. But as he continued to gaze at it, he suddenly discovered that it was moving. The next instant he saw the ugly head of a serpent that looked like a boar-constrictor. He realised at once that it was a python. It was the python that had issued out of the cave in which were the lions and the vampire bats. He recognised it by the colour of the skin and the white circle on its head.

It had raised its head and was watching Dr. Wiseman intently as the latter unwarily advanced towards it. No sooner did Kotokro perceive the danger ahead than he said to Dr. Wiseman in a whisper:

"Doctor, please stop where you are. Don't move and don't turn round to look at me. There is a python on the tree ahead of you."

Dr. Wiseman immediately stopped and raised up his head for the first time to look into the trees. He discovered, to his horror, that he was only a few yards away from where the formidable creature was lying in wait for him. The dreadful monster was looking straight into his eyes. He hardly knew what to do.

"Now, listen carefully, Doctor," said Kotokro in the manner of a teacher giving instructions to a hard-learning pupil. "Retreat slowly backwards, keeping your gaze fixed upon the snake all the time. It will then follow you only slowly, so that the distance between the two of you will widen. Then when you are sufficiently out of reach you may turn round again and flee as fast as your legs can carry you."

Dr. Wiseman had followed Kotokro's instruction closely. He began moving backwards slowly, keeping his gaze fixed continuously upon the serpent. The latter followed slowly from tree to tree as Kotokro had predicted, and the distance between them had begun to widen. Kotokro himself, who had set the example of backward retreat, was even further away from the snake by now. Suddenly as he took a step backwards Dr. Wiseman stumbled against the stump of a tree and fell on his back. Rising up at once to his feet he forgot all about Kotokro's advice and took to his heels.

The python began to chase with incredible speed, shooting from tree to tree. Before Dr. Wiseman could advance about twenty yards it was upon him. The deadly creature immediately wound itself around the Doctor and bore him irresistibly to the ground. Then it began to tighten its grip and to squeeze the breath out of its victim. Doctor Wiseman felt as if his ribs were crushing. He gave himself up for dead.

However, fate had not yet decreed that the unfortunate Doctor should thus end his life. Kotokro, who had been watching the dreadful drama with deep horror at once summoned courage and rushed forward with his cutlass. Without any thought of danger to himself he started to slash the serpent again and again most savagely. Then with one desperate stroke he almost severed off the head of the terrible monster. It immediately relaxed its grip on the Doctor and slipped off his body, dead.

With difficulty Dr. Wiseman rose up to his feet, badly shaken. He hardly knew what to say to Kotokro.

"Thank you, my boy, thank you. You are very brave," he said in a quivering voice, forgetting what he had said of the boy's behaviour when Kotokro wrested the lady's hand-bag from the thug and restored it to its owner. He had then said to Mrs. Casely: "You see, I have always told you that this boy has no intelligence. What business had he to follow the thief when he knew he might easily get lost? Besides, he could easily have been stabbed." Neither did Kotokro forget what Mrs. Casely said to him on the same occasion; "Some people would even call it fool-hardiness. You exposed yourself to danger. The thief could easily have stabbed you." He wondered what Mrs. Casely would have said if she were here.

They proceeded to the stream where Dr. Wiseman had a wash as best as he could without soap. On their way back to the house, Kotokro stopped where the python's carcase lay and proceeded to cut it up into big chunks. Dr. Wiseman watched with horror and revulsion.

"What are you doing that for?" he asked.

"It is very nice meat," replied Kotokro. "I shall smoke and take it with me to Kantoma when we are going away from here. All the people in Kantoma will have a big feast when I arrive with it, for we shall make a big party and invite everybody."

"You will make a big party with python's meat?" asked Dr. Wiseman incredulously.

"Yes, it is a special delicacy, just like frogs and water scorpions which some people like so much."

"Which people like frogs and water scorpions?"

"The French and the British."

"You have got it all wrong, my boy," said Dr. Wiseman. "Those are not ordinary frogs and water scorpions. They are aquatic frogs and lobsters. They are quite edible."

"Not by me," replied Kotokro, making a wry face.

"Well, my boy, I guess a man will always eat whatever he is brought up to eat and enjoy it too."

"Yes, Doctor," agreed Kotokro. "And also he will always live the life he is brought up to live and find nothing wrong with it."

"Queer, isn't it?"

"Yes," Kotokro agreed again.

Kotokro took a long time in cutting up the python, for it was really a creature of immense proportions. Then he cut ropes and wove a rough basket into which he collected as much of the meat as he could carry.

They returned to the house, and after they had had breakfast consisting of the usual partridge's egg and roasted roots, Kotokro went back for the rest of the python's meat. He went six times before he was able to bring all. Then he constructed a barbecue with sticks and spreading the chunks of flesh on it, made a fire underneath to smoke them dry.

Meantime he also collected dry firewood and stored them inside the house. When Dr. Wiseman asked him what he was doing that for, he explained that it was in anticipation of an impending rain.

"How do you know it is going to rain?" asked Dr. Wiseman.

"Because we have now the kind of weather we had three days ago when it rained so hard," he replied.

"Does that kind of weather always herald rain?" he asked.

"Yes."

"All right, we shall see if it does."

By the evening the chunks of python's meat were well smoked and were dripping most appetizingly with fat. They looked and smelt so nice, but the very thought of anyone putting some in his mouth to eat made Dr. Wiseman's skin bristle with goose pimples. When Kotokro therefore took some to eat with his supper Dr. Wiseman could not endure the very sight of it and turned his eyes away. Kotokro, however, ate it with great relish. Dr. Wiseman had to make do with more of the partridge's egg and roasted roots.

After they had eaten Kotokro wove three large baskets with ropes into which he collected the smoked chunks of meat and conveyed them into the room for the night. He said that he could not leave them outside, lest some carnivorous creatures should come and help themselves to them while they slept. And it was well he did that, for that was exactly what would have happened.

It must have been about five hours after they had lain down to sleep when Dr. Wiseman was suddenly awakened by a loud and angry howl close behind the walls of the house. As the inside was all lined with banana leaves he could not see what animal had uttered that frightful sound. Before he could guess what it was he heard the sound again. There was no doubt about it. It was the roar of a lion. Almost simultaneously three or four other lions also began to roar in concert. Their combined voices produced a most fearful din.

Dr. Wiseman switched on the torch-light and found that Kotokro was still fast asleep. The sound had not disturbed him in any way. Going up to him he shook him gently and whispered.

"Hey, Kotokro, listen," he said.

The boy opened his eyes and listened.

"They are lions, Doctor," he said. "They want to come in."

He had hardly said so when they heard the door to the house shaking violently. Dr. Wiseman switched on the torch-light towards it. The light fell on the banana leaves with which the door was also lined, so that he could not see what was happening behind it. He moved forward and tore a hole through the banana leaves. Then he switched on the torch-light again and looked outside through the hole. The light fell upon the flashing eyes of three lions who were frantically pulling at the door in an effort to secure entry. Kotokro saw them too.

The door had been strongly secured with stout ropes, but if the ferocious beasts persevered in their attempt it was obvious that they would soon succeed in pulling it apart. Dr. Wiseman seized his cutlass and prepared to sell his life dear, in case the beasts succeeded in coming into the room; for he had no doubt but that if they entered they would prefer the raw flesh of the two living beings to the smoked meat of the python.

"Do not bother, Doctor," Kotokro said calmly to him. "They will be satisfied with some of the smoked python's meat. If they have it they will leave us alone."

"But how can you let them have it without letting them in first?" asked Dr. Wiseman. "And if they enter it will not be left to us to decide what they will rather have."

"I agree, but they will not enter. I am going to throw some of the meat to them through that hole."

So saying Kotokro opened one of the three baskets and took out the chunks of meat. He piled them close to the hole and began to throw them out through it one by one. As they came out the lions pounced upon them and began to devour them greedily. Before they could finish one basketful, however, they were quite satisfied and could eat no more. So they walked quietly away.

Not long after they had departed, signs of an impending storm appeared. It began with the blowing of a cool and gentle breeze which came in through the hole torn in the door. Gradually the breeze turned into a violent wind which began to sweep through the forest, buffeting the trees most ferociously. The cry of frightened monkeys and other creatures of the jungle added to the din, producing an indescribable feeling of imminent danger.

Suddenly there was a blinding flash, followed almost immediately by a deafening explosion and fearful roar of thunder. Rain began to patter as when the intermittent beating of a drum ushers in the beginning of a frenzied dance. Soon the patters turned into a regular downpour, which began to gather strength until the whole jungle seemed to be under the savage impact of a mighty deluge.

Lightning and thunder flashed and exploded as though a fierce battle were being waged in the sky.

On and on the fearful din continued unabated. The water rushing through the lattice-work of the tree's grotesque roots struck the banana leaves that lined the walls of the room and flowed down and out, so that the room would have remained completely dry but for the little hole in the door. As they had no device for closing it now, some water passed through it to the floor of the room. Kotokro quickly dug a gutter at this part of the room to divert the water outside. In this way the floor continued dry.

The downpour continued with lightning and thunder and heavy wind until well towards dawn, so that Dr. Wiseman and Kotokro were deprived of a good night's rest. But the next day began with a glorious sky. The morning was bright and cool, with a gentle breeze rustling the leaves and fanning the entire jungle. Kotokro forecast from these indications that there would be no rain that day and the next. And so it turned out.

CHAPTER TEN
FIRST ATTEMPT TO ESCAPE

Dr. Wiseman could not overcome his disappointment over the city of ant-hills so easily. Throughout that night, in spite of the distraction of the lions followed by the heavy rainfall, his mind kept going back again and again to the ant-hills. He concluded that even if they were really anti-hills they were of such strange and marvellous construction that they could become objects of tourist attraction. If he could find his way back to London he would publicize his discovery and lay claim to it. After all, British explorers like Cecil Rhodes and others had discovered lands in Africa to which they had laid claim. He would eventually form a company to administer it, making himself the Director of that company. He would yet become rich. He started making plans for the future.

He became so obsessed with his plans that he now found his enforced stay in the jungle quite intolerable. He wanted to get back home as soon as possible. So immediately after breakfast that morning he said to Kotokro:

"We must try to get out of this place by all means today."

"Do you mean we must quit this house?" asked Kotokro incredulously.

"No, I mean we must quit this jungle altogether and return home."

Kotokro laughed.

"Ah, Doctor," he said. "You talk as if we chose to stay in this jungle of our own free will. If we could have gone away, why do we still remain here? You know we have tried every means to get out but have failed. Why do you think that we can get out today of all days?"

"I have thought of a plan," replied Dr. Wiseman. "Where there is a river there will always be human dwellings. If we sail along that stream we are eventually bound to arrive at a human habitation. I am sure we shall then be able to find our way back home."

"But how can we sail along that stream when we have no canoe?"

"We can easily construct something that will be as good as a canoe, in fact even better than a canoe."

"What is it?"

"We shall construct a raft by lashing together several pieces of log. You know that as water flows downstream it gathers volume until it forms a big river. The beginning of our voyage may be beset with difficulties on account of the smallness of the stream, but we shall soon begin to sail on a big river and will have no difficulty at all in making progress."

"All right, Doctor," said Kotokro. "Let us try your plan then."

They fell four tree, each about eight inches in diameter, and cut them up into ten pieces, each twelve feet long. They conveyed them all to the side of the stream where they lashed them together into a raft measuring twelve feet long by seven feet wide.

"When we push this into the water it will float," explained Dr. Wiseman who had directed its construction. "So let us get ready to embark."

"What about the crocodiles, Doctor?" asked Kotokro. "If we stand on this and sail down the river the crocodiles can easily attack us if we happen to meet them on the way."

"Quite right, my boy," agreed Dr. Wiseman. "But we shall have to take our chance. We shall protect ourselves with clubs and cutlasses. If we are attacked we shall sell our lives dear."

Kotokro did not at all relish the prospect of having to sell his life to any creature, whether dear or cheap, but it seemed there was no better alternative, so he accompanied Dr. Wiseman through the forest looking for suitable trees for use as clubs.

They did not have to look far before they secured four stout sticks with heavy knobs which they quickly shaped into clubs. Dr. Wiseman took the two heavy ones for himself and gave the two light ones to Kotokro.

It was well past mid-day when they finished the work and Dr. Wiseman would have wished to set sail immediately but Kotokro suddenly came up with an idea which seemed very sensible, although it led to further delay. He suggested that they should construct a wall round the raft as a defence against any attack by the crocodiles.

It was not difficult to imagine how this might be done and they at once set to work. They cut several sticks and chopped them up into pieces about four feet long. With these they constructed a protective railing all round the raft. They then tied other sticks across them horizontally and so succeeded in building a strong fence. When they had finished, the whole thing looked like a huge oblong basket of wicker-work. They lined the bottom again with other sticks, so that when the structure was lowered into the stream no water came in through the floor as it floated.

By this time night was approaching, so they decided to postpone their departure until the next morning.

Before they went to bed that night Kotokro placed some of the python's meat outside the house, so that if the lions came again they might eat them and go away without disturbing their sleep. And it was a good thing he did so; for they were so tired when they went to bed that they forgot to secure the door with stout ropes, an omission which would have cost them dear if Kotokro had not thought of this measure. As it was, when the lions came they did not bother to try to enter, for they found their food already waiting for them outside. They simply ate and went away, for the pieces were more than sufficient as a meal for all four of them.

Dr. Wiseman was the first to wake up next morning. He immediately went down to bring the partridge's eggs, for he could not reconcile himself to the idea of having to leave them behind when the time would come for them to depart. He counted seven eggs, although Kotokro had said that there were five when he went to bring two the previous evening after the partridge had laid one more egg for the day. He took all seven and chuckled to himself as he carried them back to the house. There were two reasons for his feeling of satisfaction. The first was the surprise and embarrassment which he visualized Kotokro would show when he confronted him with the indisputable evidence, in the form of those eggs, that he had been lying to him; and the second was the discomfiture which he imagined the partridge would feel when it came to find all its eggs gone. Not that Dr. Wiseman was normally a man of ill-will, but the disappointment and frustration which he had suffered in connection with the ant-hills had greatly affected his moral perception.

Kotokro was still asleep when he returned to the house. He woke him up and told him that he had gone for all the rest of the eggs, since they were departing for good that day.

"Oh, Doctor!" Kotokro exclaimed. "Why did you do that? The partridge will not come there to lay again when it comes to find all its eggs gone."

"Well, what would that matter, since we are going away for good?"

"But suppose we are unable to get away…?"

"We shall get away" interrupted Dr. Wiseman. "We are bound to come to some human dwelling if we sail along this river. From there we shall reach home."

"All right, Doctor" said Kotokro. "Let us take away the eggs then. I hope your optimism will be justified."

"Guess how many eggs I found there?" asked Dr. Wiseman, ignoring Kotokro's implied expression of doubt.

"Five," he replied promptly.

"Wrong! There were seven. Here they are."

Kotokro counted them.

"One, two, six, seven, four, three, five." he said, turning to Dr. Wiseman triumphantly. "I told you there were five eggs."

"Who taught you to count this way?" Dr. Wiseman asked with surprise.

"Old Rakito," replied Kotokro. "He is the only one in Kantoma who knows how to count in the white man's language."

"And how did he teach you to count?"

"He said one, two, six, seven, four, three, five, nine, eight, ten, eleven, twelve, sixteen, seventeen, fourteen, thirteen fifteen, nineteen , eighteen, twenty… and so on."

Dr. Wiseman laughed.

"Oh, Kotokro, you will be the death of me! I don't know what other poison old Rakito has put into your head!" he said.

"Poison? He did not put any poison into my head," replied Kotokro. "The only other thing he did was to teach me the alphabet."

"And how did he teach you to say them?"

"He said they are a, v, c, p; g, f, e, h; y, j, q, l; n, m, o, b; k, r, s, d; u, t, w, x, i, z."

Dr. Wiseman laughed again.

"Can you spell me KOTOKRO then," he asked.

"Yes. It is KOTOKRO."

"Correct. But you have mixed up the letters hopelessly."

"Have I? Well, what does it matter, as long as I can spell correctly?"

Dr. Wiseman thought for a moment.

"Well, I guess it doesn't really matter in what order you say them as long as you know what sound each letter stands for," he conceded.

"And it doesn't matter in what order I say the numbers, as long as I can add and subtract correctly?"

"No, there it matters greatly," disagreed Dr. Wiseman. "For example, you said there were five eggs, when actually there were seven, a mistake which you made on account of your wrong way of counting."

"But when I said five, I had in mind what you call seven, so that you and I were agreed in our minds about the number of eggs that there were. It was only in naming the number that we differed."

"Never mind," said Dr. Wiseman. "This is not the time to argue about this or anything else. We must get ready to go away. We need, first of all, to cut poles for punting the raft in shallow waters, and oars for rowing it when we get into deeper parts. So let us set to work at once."

They went near the stream and cut two bamboo poles. They were long and straight and very light but strong. They also cut two sticks and shaped them into oars.

When all was ready Kotokro carried all their possessions into the raft. These consisted of the rest of the bananas, the one and half basketfuls of python's meat and the iron trunk into which they had packed Dr. Wiseman's brief-case, the cloths and the seven partridge's eggs. The table clock had long ceased to function and been thrown away by the Doctor. Kotokro still had his pen-knife in his pocket and they kept the cutlasses for emergencies.

They climbed into the raft and, using the bamboo poles, they shoved it into the middle of the stream. They were soon on their way.

From the beginning their voyage was beset with difficulties. Now and again their progress was hindered by creepers and tree branches overhanging the surface of the water. They had to cut these away with the cutlass before they could advance. In some places huge boulders and large roots jutting from near-by trees impeded their progress and they had to overcome these with difficulty. But gradually the stream became bigger and deeper until they found themselves on a large river, free from any impediments.

Soon they had no more use for the poles, except in preventing the raft from going too close to the shore and running aground. They now had to make use of the oars, as the water was too deep for the poles to reach the bottom.

The river continued to grow bigger and bigger until they found themselves sailing on what appeared like a large lake, stretching about two miles from shore to shore. They kept as close as possible to the land, looking intently not only for human dwellings but also for foot-paths and other accesses that might lead to a human dwelling. But it was all in vain. The river flowed through a complete wilderness, untouched by man. Only birds of divers plumes and sizes disported on the surface or flew along the shores. Now and again the river was joined by streams that served as tributaries.

They had sailed for a long time without any incident when all at once the wide expanse of water began to narrow, as the banks began to rise up higher and higher. The strands gradually disappeared until the land on either side rose up to form a step precipice. They seemed to have entered a ravine.

The ravine continued for a very long distance, getting narrower and narrower and obliterating from view the rays of the sun. Then they began to fear lest they might eventually find themselves sailing upon an underground water as with ever-increasing speed the raft glided over the surface of a river of immense volume.

After a long time the river began to widen once more and the banks to lose their steepness. The sun came overhead again spraying the surface of the water with brilliant rays. Strands began to re-emerge as the river grew bigger and bigger.

Suddenly the roar of water-fall came faintly from the distance. They were seized with panic as they contemplated the terrifying possibility of being dashed to pieces on their arrival at that perilous spot. They tried to slow down with the oars the speed of the raft as it was borne along by a swift current, but it proved to be a strenuous task. Then an idea occurred to Kotokro.

"Doctor, let us keep very close to the shore where the water is shallow, so that we can use the poles to slow down our advance," he said.

Dr. Wiseman agreed to the suggestion and they began to paddle ashore.

But they had hardly advanced a few yards when, upon looking back over his shoulder, Kotokro suddenly perceived a shoal of crocodiles making towards them with incredible speed. It was the first time they had fallen in with those savage amphibians and Dr. Wiseman expressed surprise that they could have appeared from behind in that part of the river which they had already traversed.

"They must have come from one of the tributaries that we passed on the way" explained Kotokro.

The dreadful reptiles gained rapidly upon them. Soon they were only a few yards away. They opened and shut their long snouts, displaying their serrated teeth in the most menacing manner. Panic seized Dr. Wiseman, who now found himself once more in that terrible danger from which he had miraculously escaped when he fell into the river from the plane. If only the boy had been up there on the upper ground to bring him succour as he had done on that occasion, he might yet be saved, he thought. But now the danger was inescapable, for the two of them were literally and metaphorically in the same boat.

"Have no fear, Doctor," said Kotokro, observing him. "We may yet escape from danger."

"How can we?" asked Dr. Wiseman incredulously. "Behind us are those savage creatures, and before us is a dangerous waterfall. We are between Scylla and Charibdis!"

"What are Scylla and Charibdis?" asked Kotokro.

"It is a long story. I cannot explain it now," replied Dr. Wiseman. "But it is an expression which means that we are between the Devil and the deep blue sea."

"Oh, I understand," said Kotokro. "It means we are between the crocodiles and the dangerous waterfall."

"Correct and apt, my boy," commended Dr. Wiseman. "It shows you have some understanding, even though you lack intelligence."

"What is intelligence?" asked Kotokro.

"It is that mental faculty in which you and your race are lacking. When you have it you can make machines to speed with you over the land, under and over the water and through the air. You can also do other wonderful things."

"Like killing people and bringing them back to life?"

"Exactly."

"But not like escaping from the jaws of crocodiles?"

"No, that one depends upon sheer luck."

"But we don't have to depend upon sheer luck to deliver us from the jaws of these pursuing crocodiles, do we?"

"What else can bring us deliverance from these formidable monsters?"

"Our own energy and resourcefulness."

"How? Do you mean we can defend ourselves with these clubs and cutlass? The best we can do with them is to sell our lives dear."

"We can do better than that."

"In what way?"

Kotokro had no time to explain, for by now the crocodiles were within a striking distance, and the foremost of them had already seized the railing around the raft and was trying hard to tear it apart. Before it could do much damage to it, however, Kotokro opened the basket that was half full of python's meat and threw two large chunks out. The ravenous creatures at once put up a savage fight as they contended for the unexpected hand-out, the one tugging at the railing being among the first to go for a bite. They fought for their food for a long time, lashing one another with their serrated tails. And even after they had consumed the meat the fight continued for some time between those who had managed to have a helping and those who had struggled in vain. This gained time for their intended victims, who rowed strenuously in flight.

Soon, however, the savage brutes somehow managed to compose their quarrels. Then once more they turned their attention to their quarry. They pursued with haste, and it was not long before they were once more within a striking distance. But before they could approach any further Kotokro again threw to them another two pieces of the python's meat. Once more the amphibious reptiles fell upon the hand-out with rapacity, and upon one another with combatant tails. They fought and lashed one another without giving any quarter. At last they somehow settled their quarrels as before and resumed their pursuit of the fugitives.

When they came dangerously near Kotokro again threw to them another two pieces of the apple of discord. Once more they repeated the performance and thus enabled their prospective victims to gain further time.

This went on for a long time until the first basket was exhausted of its contents and Kotokro had to open the other for a continuation of the drama. Again and again he threw the meat to them until only two remained in this basket also.

They had been concentrating their attention so much upon the pursuing creatures that they had not noticed that the river was rapidly rising in volume. But, suddenly, as Kotokro took his eyes off the crocodiles and gazed towards the shore, he discovered, to his horror, that the strand close to which they were sailing had disappeared, being covered by water. This meant that should they decide to pull ashore they would have no firm ground on which to land. Then, for the first time he gazed across the river to the opposite bank to see if there was land. There was not, but he discovered two huge rocks rising above the surface of the water close to the shore. All at once he recognised them as the rocks he had seen when he came to rescue Dr. Wiseman from the ravine.

"See, Doctor, this is where you fell into the river from the plane," he said to Dr. Wiseman.

The Doctor looked and saw the two rocks standing side by side, but as he had not noticed them on the previous occasion he was unable to recognise them.

"Where did you stand to throw down the rope to me?" he asked instead.

Without replying Kotokro gazed intently ahead, scrutinizing the cliff which now rose steeply from the river. Their raft now seemed very close to the waterfall, for the roar became almost deafening. Suddenly Kotokro perceived what appeared like a rope hanging down from the top of the ravine and touching the surface of the water.

"See, Doctor," he said. "There is something over there which I seem to recognise. Let us paddle towards that cliff."

By now the crocodiles had finished devouring the python's meat which Kotokro had thrown to them and had resumed their pursuit, after composing the quarrel which invariably followed. Kotokro threw to them the last two pieces, and once more they immediately started fighting over them as before. Then Dr. Wiseman and Kotokro rowed with all their might towards the cliff. Soon they were near enough to the object which Kotokro had seen from afar to recognise its true nature. It was no other than the second rope which Kotokro had thrown to Dr. Wiseman when he saw the crocodiles coming to pull down the first. This meant that the little stream upon which they had started their voyage had brought them back to the very point from which they had first set out into the jungle. The river had risen much higher than on that occasion, due to heavy rains upstream, hence the rope now touched the surface of the water.

They quickly made for the rope and had soon caught hold of it. They secured the raft to it and thus prevented it from being borne along by the swift current. Then Kotokro pulled out the pen-knife from his pocket and offered it to Dr. Wiseman, saying:

"Here, Doctor, take this and ascend quickly to the upper ground. Then cut and bring a second rope and throw one end of it to me while you hold the other end. I shall tie the iron trunk to it so that you will then pull it up while I ascend by this rope."

Dr. Wiseman needed no second bidding, for he realised that the crocodiles would soon be upon them again. He was relieved to have had this means of escape and he grabbed the opportunity with alacrity. Having quickly caught hold of the rope he began to ascend with great agility. Soon he had reached the upper ground and had disappeared from view.

Kotokro waited and waited without the Doctor re-appearing. Meanwhile the last two pieces of python's meat which he had thrown to the crocodiles had been devoured by those oviparous carnivores, who now turned their attention to him and his curious craft. With swift paddling feet they sailed towards their prey.

Nearer and nearer they came. Kotokro could have seized the rope to which the raft was tied and climbed out to safety, but he could not contemplate with equanimity the prospect of abandoning the iron trunk which contained what he and the Doctor valued most in their necessitous situation. So he continued to watch them coming and to cast anxious glances at the top of the cliff to see if the Doctor had returned. Suddenly he heard the Doctor calling from above.

"Hey, Kotokro," came his voice. "Here is the rope. Catch hold of it at once." And he immediately lowered one end of it down to the boy while he held the other end. Kotokro seized the rope as soon as it touched the bottom of the raft and tied it to the iron trunk. Then he called to Dr. Wiseman to pull it up. Immediately the Doctor began to do so he seized the rope that was already tied to the tree above and the raft below and began to climb with great speed.

It was only just in time. He had scarcely reached half-way when the wild creatures seized the raft with their teeth and began to drag it downstream. They tugged hard at it, but it was so stoutly built that it would not give way. At last the fence round it began to break up, providing an entrance into the raft. Whereupon two of the crocodiles dashed into it and tried to seize the rope by which Kotokro was climbing, but it was too high above the surface of the water for them to reach it, having been tied to the top of the railing which rose about four feet from the top of the raft, as has already been explained. Then they swam back and began, with the others, to tug at the raft again with all their might.

At last the rope began to crack. All at once it snapped only an inch below Kotokro's grasp. The boy found himself dangling at the side of the cliff with no rope to rest his feet on. He was now safe from the crocodiles but hardly out of danger yet. He had to hold fast to the rope and plant his feet firmly against the wall of the cliff as he pulled himself upwards.

While all this was happening Dr. Wiseman had been hauling up with the greatest difficulty the load which Kotokro had tied to the end of the rope. Soon the Doctor became so exhausted that, after a time, he just stood there clinging to the rope, unable to pull up the burden any longer. Gradually he became dazed, and it seemed as if he would either have to let go the rope and the iron trunk or be pulled down into the river by them.

Just at this moment, however, Kotokro succeeded in climbing out of the ravine. He quickly ran to the Doctor and seizing the rope from him, tied it to the trunk of the tree. Having thus secured it he took his time to pull it up.

As soon as Kotokro took the rope from him Dr. Wiseman sat down to rest, for all his strength had deserted him. The reason for the Doctor's swift exhaustion was not hard to find. At home he had been accustomed to taking rich and heavy meals at short intervals. His breakfast consisted of a large bowl of either corn flakes or Quaker oats or wheat bran or shredded wheat, soaked in a pint of fresh milk and sweetened with four table spoonfuls of Cuban sugar. This was followed by two thick slices of bacon, three eggs, a tin of baked beans and three fat French sausages, all in the company of four thick slices of toasted bread well plastered with creamy Danish butter. He topped all these with further four slices of toasted bread and butter and jam, and washed the whole down with three cups of Sri-Lankan tea. Three hours later, at 11 a.m., he filled his stomach again with four slices of thickly-buttered bread, half-a-pound of Danish cheese, a dozen slabs of Canadian biscuit and half-a-tin of Kenyan peanuts. He diluted all these with three cups of tea and milk to ensure easy assimilation. At one o' clock in the afternoon he filled his stomach for the third time with a three-course meal, prefaced with three glasses of Scottish whisky and soda, to stimulate his flagging appetite. The first course was chicken broth followed, by way of a second course, with a plate of boiled Irish potatoes, a pound of English beef-steak, an assortment of welsh vegetables; and by a third course of steamed pudding and milk and custard. The first two courses were interspersed with copious draughts of Moroccan wine, and the last course was capped with Brazilian coffee.

Another three hours later he reflated his stomach for the fourth time with buttered English bread, cakes, biscuits, cheese and Nigerian cashew-nuts, all of which be sent down with four cups of Chinese tea. At seven in the evening he replenished his deflating paunch for the fifth time with a three-course meal of mushroom soup, Australian lamb, Irish potatoes, Korean rice, Brussels sprouts and Italian asparagus; all of which he ushered in with large drafts of whisky and soda and topped with three cups of Ugandan coffee. Before he lay down to rest three hours later on his soft and cosy bed he capped the day's gorge with two cups of ovaltine and hot milk, to induce undisturbed sleep.

Dr. Wiseman had thus maintained a pampered stomach and a petted body all his life until he found himself in the jungle in the company of this hardened urchin whose daily intake had, by way of balanced diet, consisted of roasted plantain in the morning, rice and stew in the afternoon, and stew and rice in the evening, followed almost immediately by a stretch on a hard mat spread on the bare floor of his father's hut.

It is not difficult to visualize then what effect their dependence now on bananas, roasted roots and half-a-partridge's egg a day had on their bodies and energies. Dr. Wiseman's bulging stomach had folded up with inanition and his soft flesh had begun to shrivel up on his bones, while Kotokro, who now fed and rested no worse than he had been accustomed to do at home, still retained his bodily appearance and physical strength.

CHAPTER ELEVEN
BACK TO BASE

After Kotokro had pulled up the iron trunk he also sat down to rest, for he was slightly out of breath. But it was not long before he was up on his feet again. Then he said to Dr. Wiseman who was still far from recovering from his exhaustion:

"Where do we go from here, Doctor?"

"I do not know," he replied. "For I can see no way out of here."

"Neither do I," agreed Kotokro, "short of going back to our base."

"Do you mean we must complete the circle in a futile search for an exit out of this jungle?"

"We have already done that, for this was our starting point."

"Then we shall never get out of here?"

"So it seems, unless someone shall find us instead of our finding someone. So I suggest we go back to our base and stay there until fortune sends rescue."

"All right," agreed Dr. Wiseman. "But let us rest a bit first. I cannot stand on my feet as yet, much less march on them.."

"All right, Doctor," agreed Kotokro. "Then I must also sit down again and rest."

And with that he sat down and propping his head against the trunk of the tree in the shade of which they had both taken shelter from the sun, was soon fast asleep.

As Dr. Wiseman watched him his heart was filled with envy. The boy could sleep anywhere and under any circumstances, while sleep often disserted him even in his regular hours of rest, especially when his mind was burdened with care. Right now he was even more tired than the boy, and yet his limbs could not dissolve in slumber, due to the latest danger from which they had both escaped and anxiety for the future. If this was the difference between the possession of high intelligence and the lack of it then he would rather do without it. This was not a serious wish of course, but a momentary thought induced by frustration.

It was a long time before he felt strong enough to walk. Then he woke up Kotokro and told him they must be going, for the day was far spent. The boy immediately sprang to his feet and placing the iron trunk on his head, led the way.

Their progress was much easier now than when they first set out from this spot; for the track which they had left behind was still visible and all they had to do was to follow it. Dr. Wiseman, however, now found the going rather difficult. His shoes had begun to wear out at the soles, beginning from the toes, on account of which he could only tread with his heels. Whenever he attempted a normal walk his toes were stung most painfully by thorns and other objects sticking out from the ground. They could not, therefore, advance as fast as they would otherwise have done.

When they arrived at the spot where the "Krampana" climbers grew Kotokro cut two again, rolled them up and put them into the trunk. He explained to Dr. Wiseman that they might come in handy sooner or later.

The Doctor was in a very despondent mood as they went along. Not only had his hope of escape from the jungle been dashed but here he was, unable to use fully his feet which had been more accustomed to press on brakes and clutches and accelerators than tread on the firm ground. Besides, as their track lay through the scene of the plane's crash he would soon find himself again at that gruesome spot, where corpses and severed human hands and heads would by now be rotting on the ground. The very thought of it made him feel sick.

On and on they went. At last they reached a spot which Kotokro recognised at once as the place where he had first found his iron trunk and some of its contents.

"We are not very far from the scene of the plane's crash, Doctor," he said to Dr. Wiseman, who could only identify streets and buildings whenever he travelled.

"How do you know?" asked the Doctor, not at all convinced that this was so.

"Do you see this clump of trees?" he said, pointing. "It marks the place where I found my iron trunk."

Dr. Wiseman looked. But although the boy had pointed it out to him before, when they were first coming from the ravine, he found it no different from any other clump of trees.

Next they came to the tree from the branch of which he had found the Doctor's brief-case suspended. He pointed this also out to the Doctor, but again he failed to recognise it. Not long afterwards they arrived at the spot where they had found the severed lady's arm with a watch upon the wrist, and he again pointed the spot out to Doctor Wiseman. The Doctor looked all round, but could find no human hand.

"Now I know you have been lying all along," said he. "For if this is the spot then where is the lady's arm?"

"It is no longer here," replied Kotokro. "Some animal must have eaten it."

"With the wrist-watch and all?

"Possibly, or it must have eaten the arm and left the wrist-watch."

"What!" exclaimed Dr. Wiseman. "What kind of animal could have done that? With what could it have first unstrapped the wrist-watch from the hand?"

"With the teeth."

"Ridiculous! Not even you could have done that, much as you are able to open a tin of corned beef with that natural instrument of yours."

The words were hardly out of the Doctor's mouth when, looking hard upon the ground, Kotokro saw the wrist-watch lying only a few feet away from where he stood. He immediately picked it up.

"See, Doctor, I was right," he said holding it up. "This is the wrist-watch."

The Doctor examined it closely. There was no doubt about it. It was the very wrist-watch which he had seen on the lady's severed arm. The strap was cut on one side, but the two strips of leather belt that held it were still joined together by the connecting buckle.

"Now I see you are right, my boy," acknowledged Dr. Wiseman. "You are really very observant."

"We are not likely to find any more severed limbs or corpses" remarked Kotokro as they resumed their journey.

"Why?" asked Dr. Wiseman, not without some feeling of relief.

"Because they must all have been devoured by wild beasts."

The Doctor said nothing, only entertaining the hope that the boy would be proved right again. And so it turned out. They traversed the area without seeing any of the horrible sights of carnage which they had seen on their first journey here.

They next came to the spot where the plane had burst into flames when it struck the ground. There was still the iron skeleton of that flying monster, the only surviving relic of the fatal accident. Even the ashes which it had left behind when it was consumed with all its contents in a mighty conflagration, had been washed away by the heavy rains that had fallen subsequently.

Before they left the vicinity Kotokro suggested that they should construct some signs on their trail to guide any search party that might come looking for them. Dr. Wiseman agreed that this was a good idea; that, in fact, he was about to make that suggestion himself when Kotokro spoke.

"What we must do is this," continued the Doctor. "We must plant arrows pointing to the direction we have taken, so that they will have no difficulty in following and finding us."

Having said so he began at once to cut sticks, which he shaped into arrows. Then he cut other sticks and planting them on the ground, slit their tops and inserted the arrows, making them point in the direction they were going. He had planted only three such sign-posts at intervals of some twenty yards when they came to a large tree close to whose trunk their path lay. Kotokro at once pulled out his pen-knife from his pocket and began to make carvings on the bark.

"What are you up to?" asked Dr. Wiseman.

"Doctor, it is better to leave more durable signs," he replied. "There is no guarantee that the arrows we have planted will not be blown down in a storm and be eaten by white ants before any search party arrives on our trail. What I am doing then is carving the image of you and me on the bark of this tree, together with an arrow showing where we have gone."

"That is an excellent idea. Let me see," said Dr. Wiseman, approaching the tree and watching the boy at work.

Kotokro carved neatly a tall white man with a prominent stomach, smartly clad in a lounge suit. He had a square chin, a medium-sized mouth with bristling moustaches on his upper lip, which was overhung with a large hooked nose that took its source from the middle-ground of two fierce-looking eyes. A high forehead terminating at the border of a luxuriant growth of straight hair towered above his nose like a cliff. He held in his hand a brief-case.

When Kotokro had completed his work, Dr. Wiseman looked at it and shaking his head, said:

"This is not me at all."

"You are right, Doctor," agreed Kotokro. "It is not you now, but it is you as you were before."

Without a word Dr. Wiseman opened his brief-case and took out his Passport. He opened it and looked at his photograph in it. Then he looked again at the boy's carving.

"You are really an artist, my boy," he commented. "If only you had intelligence you would be a genius."

Kotokro said nothing, but went on to carve the image of himself walking in front of the Doctor. It depicted a lanky boy of about eight, barefooted, with bony limbs and a protuberant stomach. He had a big mouth and a nose that rose only moderately from his face. His receding forehead ended where his pate was crowned with thick woolly hair. He was half-naked, with only a little piece of cloth covering his loins.

Dr. Wiseman looked at it. It was exactly as he had seen the boy when he first met him at Kantoma.

"But you no longer look like this," he said with a smile. "You look much more handsome now."

"I know," replied Kotokro. "I looked even handsomer when we were leaving London."

"Why then did you not make yourself to look as you were at that time? After all, that is what you have done in my case."

"The explanation is simple, Doctor," replied Kotokro.

"I want anyone who sees these carvings to know at once that they represent a white man and a black boy. If I made myself look as I was when we were leaving London, clad in a suit and with shoes on, anyone would not know whether I was black or white, since these carvings do not show any colour. It is only by my lanky body, protruding stomach, bare feet and half-nakedness that anyone could easily conclude that this is a black boy."

"I understand now. Please proceed" said Dr. Wiseman.

Kotokro went on to carve an arrow pointing to the direction in which they were going. When he had finished he turned to Dr. Wiseman and asked:

"How is it, Doctor?"

"Superb'" he commented. "But let me add something else."

With that he took the pen-knife from Kotokro and wrote immediately above the two images: "Two Air-crash Survivors." Then he also wrote underneath: "Dr. Wiseman and Kotokro."

"That will ensure that if any literate person chances to arrive here he will have no difficulty in knowing who we are," he said when he had finished.

After this they resumed their journey. At every few intervals they stopped at a tree and repeated the operation on its bark. They continued to do this until they arrived at the abandoned hunters' camp. There Kotokro examined the palm trees and found that two of them had ripe fruits on them. He was highly excited.

"Now we can have palm oil," he said to Dr. Wiseman.

"How?" he asked.

"I shall harvest these nuts and extract oil from them," he explained.

"Can you, indeed? And what use shall we have for it if you do?"

"You will see when the time comes."

"Then you are not going to harvest them now?"

"No, not now. I shall come for them later."

They continued their journey until they eventually arrived back at their base. By now Dr. Wiseman was very tired and hungry. While he rested Kotokro went and brought some yam tubers, which he roasted. They had them for lunch, together with one of the seven partridge's eggs which Kotokro had kept in the iron trunk. When the evening came they again had roasted yam and egg for dinner and retired for the night as soon as darkness fell.

They must have slept for about six hours when they were suddenly awakened by the roar of a lion. It was obvious that the lions had come again for their daily supply of python's meat. But now Dr. Wiseman and Kotokro had none to give them, having fed all to the ravenous crocodiles.

They sensed the great danger in which they stood. If nothing was done to satisfy those carnivorous beasts they would end by eating them. Dr. Wiseman began to think fast. Suddenly an idea occurred to him..

"There are five of the partridge's eggs left," he whispered to Kotokro. "Let us throw these to them, so that they may eat and leave us in peace."

"No, Doctor," replied the boy. "Lions do not eat eggs. They prefer flesh. So if they don't have meat to eat they will eat us."

"Then we must prevent them from entering, for if they succeed in coming in I am sure you wont be a mouthful for them. They will fall upon me as well."

"True," agreed Kotokro, unless, of course, they first begin with you."

"God forbid." said Dr. Wiseman with a shudder.

"But don't worry, Doctor," continued Kotokro. "They will not eat you or me, for we shall prevent them from coming in."

"How?"

"Just switch on the torch-light for me," was all he would say.

Dr. Wiseman groped for the torch-light and switched it on. It illuminated the room but did not penetrate through to the outside on account of the banana leaves that curtained the walls. Guided by its light Kotokro pulled out one of the stakes that formed the pillars for the inside structure. With his cutlass he sharpened one end of it. Then standing close to the hole which Dr. Wiseman had made in the banana leaves curtain on the first night that the lions came, he asked the Doctor to point the torch-light through it.

Dr. Wiseman did so, and the light immediately fell upon the bright eyes of a lion that stood ready to pounce upon any meat that might be thrown out. As no meat came out, the lion came closer to the hole, blinking at the light that issued from it instead. Kotokro, who stood with the sharpened stake raised for a strike, immediately plunged the weapon straight into the beast's right eye. It happened to be the male lion. Howling with pain it turned round at once and bounded off, followed by the lioness and its two cubs, all of whom had come to partake of the regular dinner.

"They will never come to trouble us again, unless I am much mistaken," said Kotokro. "They will give us a wide berth."

His prophecy came true. From now on the beasts never came to the base again to trouble them. The next time that the wounded brute came to that house again it was for a very different purpose, as will be seen later. Meanwhile they lay down to sleep again in peace and did not wake up until the next morning.

CHAPTER TWELVE
SETTLING DOWN

"Doctor, it is evident that we shall continue to stay here for a long time yet; so let us provide ourselves with all the things we need to make life more tolerable," said Kotokro immediately after their usual breakfast of partridge's egg and roasted roots the next morning.

Dr. Wiseman did not answer. Any suggestion that they were destined to remain in that jungle for many more days always filled him with alarm. He no longer took comfort or derived hope from the comparison of their situation with that of Robinson Crusoe or the Swiss Family Robinson, and the fact that those were able to return home eventually. The hope which he had derived from that comparison had arisen from the happy prospect of becoming a multi-millionaire as a result of his supposedly unique discovery. And now that that prospect had proved to be illusory the hope it engendered had also been dashed.

"The first thing we shall need are utensils, including water and cooking-pots, drinking cups and dishes," continued Kotokro.

"And from where do you think we are going to be able to purchase all these?" asked Dr. Wiseman sullenly.

"We shall make them ourselves."

"Do you know how to make them?"

"Yes, I learnt from my mother."

"Go ahead then," said the Doctor, not at all sure that the boy would be able to produce anything useful.

Kotokro set to work at once. Going down to the stream he searched along the bank until he found a spot where there was plenty of white clay. It was devoid of any stones or pebbles and was better than any that his mother ever used in making earthen ware. Using his cutlass he dug up several large chunks and carried them to the house. Then he looked for and found a fallen tree quite close to their abode. Having slightly hollowed the upper part of it for use as a mortar he cut a stick and shaped it into a pestle. Then he brought and pounded the clay in it until it was all very soft and malleable.

He conveyed the prepared clay back to the house and prepared the ground for his ceramic works. Sitting down he moulded four large water pots, six dishes, four mugs, four cooking pots (one of them very large) and two other pots for fetching water. He also fashioned a coal-pot by making a dish with little holes at the bottom for ventilation and a cylindrical pot with a flat bottom and a hole at the side, also for ventilation. When he placed the dish on top of the pot they formed, together, a kind of coal-pot. Having moulded all these earthen-ware he put them out to dry.

Dr. Wiseman had sat watching Kotokro with interest as he toiled at his handicraft, wondering whether the boy would really make a success of it. It was true that the ware he had fashioned were rather crude, but there was no doubt, he thought, that they showed a certain degree of ingenuity, particularly in a boy of his age. They would undoubtedly be useful if he could render them hard and impermeable.

Besides this display of ingenuity the boy's industry also surprised the learned Doctor. He recalled the many stories he had heard of the Negro's laziness. It occurred to him that if the Negro was really lazy then it was not constitutional, but was due to the absence of incentives. No man desired work for its own sake but only in response to a felt need. Kotokro was proving this beyond all doubts.

In the evening they had their usual dinner and went to bed early. They did not wake up until late in the morning when the sun was already close to the zenith. The previous day's hard work had made Kotokro very tired; and, as for Dr. Wiseman, he had no particular desire to be up early and doing, for there was, in fact, nothing for him to do. Besides, he was now thoroughly fed up with their monotonous meals and preferred sleep to what they would have for breakfast that morning.

It was Kotokro who first got up from sleep. Then he aroused the Doctor who was still fast asleep, dreaming of home. There was hardly a night when the learned Doctor slept without dreaming, owing to the many thoughts that always ran through his mind. This time he was dreaming about breakfast. His wife had prepared a delicious plate of bacon, eggs, baked beans and sausages. The tea to wash them down was already brewing in the pot. The sight of them whetted the Doctor's appetite enormously as he sat at table and was preparing to begin with a plate of shredded wheat and fresh milk. He had just taken a spoonful and was about to put it into his mouth when Kotokro tapped him on the shoulder and woke him up.

"Oh, you have deprived me of my nice breakfast," he complained on waking up.

"How?" asked Kotokro.

"I was just about to eat a delicious breakfast when you woke me up." he explained.

"Do you mean you were dreaming of breakfast?"

"Yes, and of a much better breakfast than the one to which we are here condemned."

"It is a good thing you did not eat that breakfast, Doctor," said Kotokro. "It is not good to eat food in a dream. At least that is what my father says."

"Why not?"

"He says that if you eat in a dream it means you have been fed by witches. Anything unpleasant can happen to you."

"Superstitious nonsense!" exclaimed Dr. Wiseman. "Why are you Negroes so superstitious?"

"Don't you believe it is true?"

"It is not true that when you dream of eating it means the witches have fed you."

"What does it mean then?"

"Nothing, it is only a dream, which means that it is as real as the story you told about Mr Spider and his blanket."

"I know that Mr. Spider didn't really exist, any more than his blanket. It is only a story which old Mangodo fashioned in his head. It is not the same as your dream. You really did dream, didn't you?"

"I did, but it has no meaning, because the food in the dream didn't really exist."

"And you too didn't exist in the dream?"

"No."

"And you don't exist now also?"

"I exist now."

"How do you know that you exist now but did not exist in the dream?"

"Because I now see everything clearly and they make sense."

"Didn't you see everything clearly in your dream, and did they not make sense?"

"They made sense in the dream, but they don't make sense now."

"Is it not possible then that what makes sense to you now may not make sense when you reflect on them in a dream?"

"Stop this unnecessary argument!" shouted Dr. Wiseman in exasperation. "Anyone with a modicum of intelligence knows that a dream is only a dream and nothing else. In any case this is not the time or place to argue about dreams. I am hungry and therefore more interested in what to eat for breakfast. Let us therefore find something to eat, and it must be better than roasted wild yam and partridge's egg."

"All right, Doctor," said Kotokro. "I came upon water coco-yams yesterday when I was searching for clay upstream. I also saw some crab-holes. I am going to bring some for breakfast." So saying Kotokro took his cutlass and set out.

He proceeded to the stream where he dug up six tubers of water coco-yam. They were large and pink, each weighing about eight pounds and enough for two meals for the two of them. Then he went on to search for crabs. From the very first hole he came across he pulled out a huge crab with a toe as big as a pair of pliers. He was able to collect four in all. Having washed both the crabs and the water coco-yam thoroughly in the stream he brought them to the house.

Dr. Wiseman had been anxiously awaiting his return and was glad to see him come back with what promised to provide a more palatable meal. Although he had never before tasted water coco-yam and crabs he found most welcome the promised change of diet.

Kotokro made fire and at once proceeded to roast the water coco-yam and two of the crabs. They all smelt so good that Dr. Wiseman's appetite was keenly whetted long before they were ready. Kotokro removed them from the fire as soon as they were done and set the Doctor's portion before him.

Dr. Wiseman tasted the water coco-yam. It was very soft and nice. But when it came to the crab he was uncertain how to proceed. Kotokro set him the example, however, by tearing his share piece by piece and chewing them with shell and all. But no sooner did Dr. Wiseman try to do the same than one of his front teeth broke. The shell of the crustacean had been too strong for the Doctor's teeth which had not been accustomed to cracking anything so hard.

Indeed at home Dr. Wiseman's teeth never touched anything that would task their strength. First of all, he used tooth-paste and tooth-brush for cleaning his teeth in the morning and evening, unlike Kotokro who always vigorously employed chewing-sticks for that purpose. The Doctor never chewed bones either, preferring to feed them to his dog, Robin-hood, who always chewed them with avidity and was thankful to his Maker that the learned Doctor did not know what he was missing. Nor had the Doctor's teeth improved by the food they had had to live on since they found themselves in that jungle, and the fact that he had not been able to brush them for the past two months or so, his tooth-paste having finished in less than a fortnight after he fell from the plane.

As for Kotokro, since he had always maintained a healthy set of teeth with chewing-sticks until he came to London, he had no difficulty at all in this matter, there being an abundant supply of his requirement in that place of undisturbed nature. In vain had he tried to persuade the Doctor to abandon his old habit and learn to use chewing-sticks. The latter had resorted to washing his mouth with water only, so that by now his teeth, which had been none too strong before, had become quite brittle. It is a great wonder then that at the first encounter with a crab's shell only one of them gave way.

Dr. Wiseman was not able to enjoy his meal after this minor but very painful injury and left Kotokro to finish it all up. Then the boy turned to him and said:

"Doctor, we have a few more things to do in order to make our lives here more pleasant. We cannot have the comfort of your house in London, but we can make this place as habitable as my father's house in Kantoma."

"What do you want us to do?" asked Dr. Wiseman, the pang of hunger and the pain of a broken tooth still racking his feelings.

"I suggest we curtain the inside of the house with bamboos instead of banana leaves. They are nicer and more durable. We also need chairs and benches to sit on. We can again make these with bamboo canes."

"Why should we take all that trouble when the duration of our stay here is so uncertain?" replied Dr. Wiseman "We may be rescued from here any day, you know."

"Please, Doctor," pleaded Kotokro, "do not adopt the mental attitude of old Yaloma."

"What do you mean?"

"It is said that old Yaloma's father died at the age of forty and left him his farm and house. Yaloma, who was then twenty and unmarried, gladly took over the farm and the house but did nothing to maintain and improve them. After a time the farm was choked with weeds and the house began to collapse. Still Yaloma paid no attention to them. When people asked why he was so neglectful of his inheritance he replied that he did not see the use of troubling himself over them. After all, he would soon die as his father had died. Even if he lived beyond the forty years that had been his father's span he could not live up to sixty.

And so the days and weeks and months and years passed by, and Yaloma continued to live unconcerned, until he had no farm to live on and his house fell into ruins. He is now over one hundred and twenty years old and sees no death in sight. He is so poor that he only lives on hand-outs from kind-hearted neighbours and on foods which little children steal for him from their parents in exchange for the stories he tells them. Surely you don't want us to end up like old Yaloma?"

"Well, my boy, this is not a very cheerful story, but I guess there is some wisdom in it." replied Dr. Wiseman. "I agree it would be foolish for us to adopt the attitude of old Yaloma. So let us do as you say."

Kotokro was very glad to hear this and immediately took up his cutlass. "There are plenty of bamboo canes near the stream," he said. "Let us go and cut some."

Reluctantly Dr. Wiseman followed him to the stream. They cut several canes and conveyed them to the house. Then they splitted some and removing the banana leaves from the framework inside the house, they replaced them with the bamboos. Again, using some of the bamboos, they lined the floor and carpeted it with soft banana fibre. They did it all so neatly that it was a delightful sight when they had finished.

They took the whole day working on the house. In the evening they again had roasted coco-yam and crab for dinner. As before, only Kotokro was able to eat the crabs. Dr. Wiseman had to make do with the roasted coco-yam only.

When the night came they went to bed. They slept much more soundly than they had done for a long time. It was not only the exhaustion from the day's work but the comfort of the place that now deepened their relaxation.

After breakfast the next morning they continued work on the house. Upon Kotokro's suggestion they constructed a stockade to enclose the entrance, measuring about twenty-four feet long by sixteen feet wide by six feet high. It had a gate to it and provided a spacious compound where they could sit for some hours at night in safety before going to bed. Then they built two long benches in the yard, with backs and arm-rests, and also made two arm-chairs and a table in the room - all with bamboo canes.

When they had completed the work Dr. Wiseman, who had never owned a house before but had always lived in a rented premises, surveyed it with satisfaction. It was like the day he first bought a car, it being the first time he was owing something of value in this life. It made him feel very proud.

"Well, it is not much of a house, but it is a house all the same," he commented with delight.

"Yes, Doctor," agreed Kotokro. "It is much finer than my father's house at Kantoma. If it were not because I miss my parents and friends I wouldn't mind staying here all the rest of my life."

"Quite right, my boy," responded Dr. Wiseman, "I feel so too. Were it not for my wife and child I would be happy to stay here for a very long time. After all a man's home is wherever his house is, be it on the Arabian Desert or in the African jungle."

They lived much more comfortably for several days after this. Their main problem now was food; or, to be more precise, food was Dr. Wiseman's main problem. He had come to dislike roasted wild yam, and although he rather preferred water coco-yam it did not quite agree with his stomach. And as for roasted crabs his teeth dreaded them. Kotokro, however, had no such problem. He had always enjoyed water coco-yam even in Kantoma, and as for crabs they were his special delicacy, boiled or roasted. By now, however, he too had begun to lose his appetite for both, due to their monotony.

About three weeks after Kotokro had made the earthen-ware they were dry enough for firing. He collected them together and stacked them with plenty of dry firewood. He set fire to them and a big bonfire ensued. He kept on plying more and more firewood until all the earthen-ware began to glow with heat. As the fire burned he collected quite a large amount of the charcoal that was formed and stored it in a corner of the room for rainy days. Then he waited until the rest of the firewood had turned into ashes. Thereupon he removed the ware and took them to the stream where he washed them clean. He conveyed them all back to the house. Dr. Wiseman was very happy to see them.

"You are very clever, my boy," he commented as he examined them one by one. "Where did you learn to do this?"

"I always watched my mother when she was making them" he replied.

"Well, let us test and see if they can serve their purpose. I suggest you fetch water from the stream with that water-pot."

Kotokro did not wait for a second bidding. He immediately took one medium-sized pot and ran down to the stream. In no time he was back with a pot of water. He poured it into the big water-pot which he had placed at a corner of the room. He went for more water until the big pot was full. Dr. Wiseman took a cup and poured himself some of the water and drank. He was now convinced that Kotokro's earthen-ware were as hard and useful as any china he could have bought from the most expensive shop in London.

"And now," said Kotokro, when he saw that the Doctor was fully satisfied with his products, "we can improve on our diet."

"What do you mean?" Dr. Wiseman asked.

"Instead of living on roasted foods all the time we can now eat something boiled." he exclaimed.

"I can't see much difference," replied Dr. Wiseman. "In what way will boiled crabs be different from roasted crabs?"

"They will make excellent soup; so that you will have something to eat with your water coco-yam while I crack their shells. Besides, your stomach will find boiled food more digestible than roasted ones, I am sure."

"All right. Let us try boiled food for dinner then."

When Kotokro went to the stream to bring more crabs he discovered, for the first time, that there were also far more fish in it than he had imagined. He saw a large shoal of huge mud-fish and many other kinds of fish disporting in the cool sparkling water. They seemed to have migrated there from somewhere. However, try as hard as he could he was unable to catch any, so he had to content himself with the crabs, which were easier to catch because they lived in holes on the bank. When he returned to the house he told Dr. Wiseman what he had seen.

"Good. Then we can have some fish to eat instead of these flinty creatures."

"I shall have to make fish-traps to catch them" Kotokro informed him.

"Fish traps? No, all we need is a string and a hook."

"And from where can we get them?" asked Kotokro

"You will see" he replied with the air of one who had a surprise up his sleeves. "Just let me have your pen-knife."

Kotokro pulled out his pen-knife from his pocket and handed it to him. The Doctor immediately disappeared into the bush. He was soon back with a stick and a thin but strong rope which he had cut from a climber. He sat down and carefully shaped the stick into an arrow. He attached the string to it.

"This is a hook and a line," he said to Kotokro. "We shall cover the barbed point with food and throw it into the stream. One of those big fish will at once pick it up and swallow. When I pull it up you will see what will happen."

"Oh, Doctor, this hook is too big" replied Kotokro "The fish will easily see it and will be afraid to pick the food from it."

"There you are mistaken, my boy" said Dr. Wiseman "A small fish may see and evade it, but not such big ones as you say you saw in the stream."

"Not even a fish as big as a crocodile will swallow that arrow even if you conceal it in a chunk of meat."

"We have a saying in English that the sweetness of the pudding is in the eating." said Dr. Wiseman simply.

"What does it mean?" asked Kotokro

"It means if you want to know whether something is true or not, put it to the test." he replied. "So let us stop arguing and rather go down to the stream and see if this hook and line will not catch fish."

So saying Dr. Wiseman took a piece of roasted coco-yam and, covering the barb of the arrow with it, led the way to the stream, followed by Kotokro. When they arrived there he discovered, to his delight, that there were, in fact, many more and bigger fish than Kotokro had described. They were swimming and diving and chasing one another in sportive revelry. The Doctor at once threw the bait into the water. Almost all the fish made a rush for it simultaneously, and soon not a vestige of the water coco-yam remained. They had snatched it all up from the arrow which served as a hook.

Dr. Wiseman tried again with more of the water coco-yam, but with the same result. The fish ate it all up without any of them being so greedy as to swallow the improvised hook in addition. At last there was nothing left to be used as a bait and the Doctor had to give up any further attempt to catch the fish in this way.

"I told you, you could not catch any fish with this device, Doctor," said Kotokro. "These fish are more intelligent than you give them credit for."

"Intelligent!" exclaimed Dr. Wiseman "Whoever heard of a fish being intelligent. It means you don't understand the meaning of that word. If you did you would know that intelligence is reserved for only the highest creatures. These fish act and re-act from instinct only."

"And who are the highest creatures?" asked Kotokro.

"Human beings, of course, and the most developed among them."

"And who are the most developed among them?"

"The Caucasian race."

"And who are the Caucasian race?"

"That is the anthropological name for the white race. They are the most developed. The others are only now beginning to develop. They are the developing nations."

"What are they developing into?"

"Full-fledged, intelligent and civilized human beings."

"And if they develop into full-fledged, intelligent and civilised human beings, then what?"

"Then they will be able to live in freedom from poverty, filth and squalor."

"And if they are able to live in freedom from poverty, filth and squalor, then what?" asked Kotokro again.

"Then they will be happy."

"Oh, I see" said Kotokro, his face lighting up. "Then they will be able to eat, sleep and laugh and have no cares, just like the people in Kantoma?"

"No, not that," replied Dr. Wiseman.

"But what?"

"Look here, you wont understand these things, because of your lack of intelligence. So stop asking questions and let us rather consider how else we can catch fish from this stream."

"All right, Doctor," agreed Kotokro. "We shall try another device for catching them then. I guess yours is too intelligent for them."

"What other device?"

"Something less intelligent, as you will see."

"What is it? Show me."

"I cannot show you now," replied Kotokro. "For it is too late. I shall do so tomorrow, so let us return home."

They went back to the house, and Kotokro now boiled some of the water coco-yam and made crab-soup for their dinner. Dr. Wiseman enjoyed the coco-yam and the soup but not the crabs, as it was to be expected. Boiling had, if anything, only further hardened the shells of those flesh-less creatures. But the flavour which their marrows infused into the soup made it quite palatable. As for Kotokro he greatly enjoyed the meal, even though the soup lacked salt and pepper. His stay in London, where most of what he ate was devoid of these condiments, followed by his enforced stay in the jungle, where they were non-existent, had taught his appetite to do without them.

When night came Kotokro made a bonfire in the yard and they sat on the benches telling stories until it was time to go to bed. Dr. Wiseman told of the exploits of "Br'er Rabbit" and of "Reynard The Fox", and Kotokro told of the clever tricks of "Cunning Rabbit" and "Mr. Spider." They laughed at each other's stories, and when they got up to go to bed Kotokro suddenly asked:

"Doctor, were Br'er Rabbit and Reynard The Fox supposed to be white or black?"

"They could be black or white. The stories don't say."

"But were they supposed to be intelligent?"

"Yes, they were supposed to be very clever and intelligent."

"Then they couldn't have been black. They were white. That is rather funny, isn't it?"

"Why?" asked Dr. Wiseman.

"Because they behaved exactly the same way as Cunning Rabbit and Mr. Spider, who are black."

Dr. Wiseman made no reply.

CHAPTER THIRTEEN
DIVERSIFYING MEALS

The next morning Dr. Wiseman and Kotokro ate roasted coco-yam and egg for breakfast. Then Kotokro took his cutlass and, telling the Doctor that he would soon be back, set out for the abandoned hunters' camp. Arrived there he harvested the two ripe bunches of palm-nuts and cut some palm branches. He brought these to the house.

"What are you going to do with them?" asked Dr. Wiseman.

"I am going to extract palm-oil from these palm-nuts; and from these palm branches I shall weave baskets and fish-traps in the way my father does," he explained.

Dr. Wiseman said nothing, but looked on with interest as the boy proceeded to put his words into action. He first cut up the two bunches of palm-nuts and picked out the nuts, which he boiled in one of the cooking pots. Next he pounded the boiled nuts in the hollow which he had carved out of the fallen tree. Then having separated the kernels from the resulting pulp, he mixed the latter with water and placed it on the fire to boil. As it boiled, the fragrant oil began to gather at the surface, which he carefully skimmed off with a corned beef tin. He was able to extract nearly two gallons of oil from the nuts, which he stored in one big pot.

Next he sat down and, producing his pen-knife, began to work on the palm branches. He made from them three baskets of varying sizes and three fish-traps. Then he said to Dr. Wiseman who had sat all the while marvelling at the boy's skill and ingenuity;

"Doctor, from now on our lives will be even more pleasant. With these traps we shall be able to catch fish from the stream, which we can either boil for soup or fry in palm-oil for stew. With the palm-oil we can also make soap for bath and to wash our clothes."

Again the Doctor said nothing, but looked on to see how the boy would translate his words into deeds. Kotokro got up and at once proceeded to the stream with the three fish-traps, taking with him several slices of water coco-yam. Arrived there he put some of the coco-yam into each of the traps and placed all three in different parts of the stream. Then he returned to the house, where he sliced and fried some of the water coco-yam in palm-oil for lunch.

Dr. Wiseman found the fried coco-yam so delicious that he asked Kotokro to produce more. The boy did so and the Doctor ate it all with great relish.

In the evening they again had fried coco-yam for dinner and sat telling stories, as on the previous day, until late in the night, when they went to bed.

Early next morning, while Dr. Wiseman still slept, Kotokro got up and, taking a basket, went down to the stream to inspect the traps. He found all three crowded with fish which were trying in vain to escape. He released them into his basket and reset the traps.

Dr. Wiseman was still asleep when he returned to the house with his catch. Without waking him up he made fire and proceeded to fry some of the fish and coco-yam for breakfast. He had almost finished frying sufficient quantity when the Doctor woke up from sleep. He breathed in with pleasure the delicious fragrance that was wafted through the air from the pot, wondering whence could be its source. He soon found out.

Emerging from the room he saw Kotokro removing from the sizzling oil the last batch of fish which he had been frying.

"So you really did catch fish?" he asked with delight.

"Yes, Doctor. And plenty of it too, just look inside the basket."

The Doctor looked into the basket and discovered, to his surprise, that it contained enough fish to last them for several days.

"This can last for weeks, with careful management," he commented.

"We don't have to manage, Doctor," replied Kotokro "I have re-set the traps and, unless the fish in that stream take it into their empty heads to leave the place I am sure we can have as much more of them tomorrow. In fact, if I re-set the traps every day for three days we wont be able to eat for a year the quantity of fish that will be caught."

"Good, my boy. You have done very well" commended Dr. Wiseman. But first let us see how your breakfast tastes."

Kotokro served the fried fish and coco-yam in two separate dishes, one of which he placed before Dr. Wiseman while he kept the other for himself. They soon had a most appetizing breakfast. Indeed Dr. Wiseman, who had by now forgotten what a real English breakfast tasted like, thought he had never before tasted anything so good.

"And now, Doctor," said Kotokro when they had finished eating "you just relax while I do something very important and necessary."

"What are you going to do?" he asked.

"I am going to make soap. We need soap badly, both for bath and for washing our clothes. You and I could do with some personal hygiene."

It was true. Although Kotokro had gone to take a bath in the stream every day, from the day that they first discovered it, itches had begun to appear on his body. His clothes too, which were now torn in many places, were anything but clean.

As for Dr. Wiseman who had insisted on having a bath only once a month even in that hot and humid climate his body was full of sores which had developed from scratched itches. His long hair and unkempt beard had also become the habitat of trouble-some lice; and his clothes, which were also in tatters, were grimy and ill-smelling. All this had been the result of the lack of soap. The Doctor knew this well and was, therefore, relieved to hear Kotokro say that he could manufacture this indispensable detergent. He was by now convinced that the boy could do many simple but necessary things which he had learned from his father and mother.

Kotokro took the largest of the three baskets and went into the jungle. It was not long before he was back with a basket-full of the dry bark of a tree which he said, was the kind used for making soap. Heaping it up on the ground he set fire to it and burnt it to ashes. He collected the ashes and dissolved them in a pot of water. Then he sieved the water through one of the baskets, thus removing all hard substances from it and leaving behind a fine sediment. He put this on fire and boiled until all the water had evaporated. Then he added palm-oil to the sediment that was left behind and boiled again until a hard substance was formed in the pot. He removed and formed these into little round balls, each the size of an orange.

"I have made soap now, Doctor," he said to Dr. Wiseman when he had finished.

The Doctor took one and examined it. He could not believe that this was soap, for it had a pungent smell and looked black. He had no faith in any object that looked black.

"Are you sure that this is soap?" he asked doubtfully.

"It is soap, and very good soap too" replied Kotokro "for it is also medicinal."

"In what way?" he asked.

"It can cure the itches and sores on your body."

The Doctor shook his head. "I can't believe that this is soap," he said. "And I wont try it. Why, it may worsen my condition."

"You once said that the sweetness of the pudding is in the eating, Doctor" Kotokro reminded.

"Yes, I said so."

"Well, I suggest we put this thing to the test to ascertain whether or not it is soap."

"You may do that. I don't propose to offer myself as a guinea-pig for your doubtful experiment."

Kotokro immediately brought water in a pot and rubbing some of the soap on his hands, begun to wash them. It produced very white and copious lather, to the surprise of Dr. Wiseman. Still, however, the Doctor was anything but convinced.

"Are you sure it is harmless?" he asked.

"Absolutely. Not only is it harmless but it is also medicinal, as I have said. It can cure itches."

"All right. Then use it on your body and let us see the effect by tomorrow."

Kotokro agreed to this suggestion and immediately went to the stream. There be washed his body clean with the soap and laundered his clothes. He returned to the house and, in the presence of Dr. Wiseman, rubbed some of the soap all over his body.

They again had fried coco-yam and fish for lunch and dinner and sat telling stories in the evening until it was time to go to bed. Kotokro slept more soundly than ever before, but Dr. Wiseman lay sleepless for the better part of the night, scratching the many itches on his body. At last he too was overcome by sleep.

Kotokro was the first to wake up the next morning. He immediately went into the bush where he searched for and discovered a kind of creeper used for sponge. He cut four short pieces, each about a foot long. He placed these on the fallen tree one by one and beat them with a stick until they came out in very fine fibres. He took them to the stream and washed them with soap. He had made excellent sponges.

On his return to the house again he found Dr. Wiseman still asleep. He went and sharpened his pen-knife on a stone until the edge became as keen as a razor-blade. Returning to the house for the third time he found the Doctor now awake.

"Doctor, you must make yourself clean today," he said. "I have got everything ready for your bodily hygiene."

"What and what?" he asked.

"Here is a razor for getting rid of your beard; and there are soap and sponge for removing the grease from your body. I shall also launder your clothes to dissolve the grime and expel the odour."

"Let us first see what effect that primitive product of yours has had on your body," said the Doctor.

"Oh, yes. I forgot," replied Kotokro, stripping himself to the waist.

Dr. Wiseman examined him closely. Yes, there was no doubt about it. Most of his itches had disappeared; and those that had been scratched into sores had almost healed up already.

"Is it your soap that did this?" asked Dr. Wiseman incredulously.

"Sure, it is," replied Kotokro.

"Then I shall try it," yielded the Doctor at last.

Kotokro offered him the sponge and some of the soap and, together, they went down to the stream where the Doctor shaved his bushy beard and had a good bath and gave his clothes to Kotokro to launder. Then he rubbed his body all over with some of the soap and, tying a cloth around his loins, he and Kotokro returned to the house.

They had plenty of fish and water coco-yam for breakfast. After that while Dr. Wiseman rested, Kotokro took his cutlass and one of the pots and, telling the Doctor that he would be back soon proceeded to the abandoned hunters' camp. Arrived there he climbed one of the palm-trees and made a notch a few inches below the top-most branch and inserted a reed pipe. He placed the pot below the pipe and secured it with a rope to catch any juice that might flow through the pipe. Then he climbed down and returned home.

They had boiled yam and fried fish for lunch, and the same again for dinner, and went to bed late in the night.

When Dr. Wiseman woke up the next morning he was surprised to see that the itches had disappeared from his body and that most of the sores had either healed or were in the process of healing. Kotokro's black soap had done the trick.

After breakfast Kotokro went to see the palm-tree and discovered that it had filled the pot to over-flowing with frothy palm-wine. He tasted it and found it very pleasant. It was like apple cider of the highest quality. Having collected it into another pot which he had brought for the purpose, he brought it to the house.

"What is this?" asked Dr. Wiseman when he saw it.

"It is palm-wine. I tapped it from one of the palm-trees at the abandoned hunters' camp." Kotokro replied.

Dr. Wiseman had heard much of that famous drink of the West African Negro. It had featured in the accounts of nearly every white traveller returning from that part of the world. Some had extolled its excellent quality, others had decried its inordinate consumption by the natives which, they said, rendered them lazy and improvident. He was glad he now had the opportunity to discover the truth for himself.

"Is it good to drink?" he asked.

"It is simply wonderful," Kotokro assured him. "Just taste it and see."

He poured a cupful and handed it to the Doctor. The latter tasted it. It was so nice and refreshing. He asked for more, and Kotokro again poured him a cupful. He gulped it down and called for a third helping.

"No, no, Doctor," refused Kotokro "You have had enough. "If you take more it will make your brains revolve in your head."

By now Dr. Wiseman was feeling so fine from the effect of the alcohol that if only Kotokro had obliged him he would not have minded whatever his brains did in his head. The boy however stoutly refused to give him more. Whereupon he rose up from his seat and, seizing the pot, tried to pour for himself. But, as it often happens in a state of inebriety, his hands refused to second his inclination. The pot fell to the ground and broke into pieces, spilling the delicious intoxicant.

Kotokro laughed.

"I told you, Doctor, that you had had enough. See what is already happening to you," he said.

"Nothing is happening to me. My Intelligence Quotient still remains high" replied Dr. Wiseman in a drawling voice, his tongue having also been rendered torpid by the alcohol.

Kotokro wondered whether under the influence of alcohol any man's Intelligence Quotient could remain unaffected. He asked the Doctor.

"Only the Negro's intelligence can be affected by alcohol," he replied "because he has very little of it, to begin with."

"Do you mean when white people get drunk their intelligence still remains the same?" he asked again with incredulity.

"Yes, it remains the same. In most cases it is even sharpened still further."

Kotokro did not contradict. He knew that when he was under the influence of alcohol his own brains ceased to function properly. Perhaps the white man's brains were made of different material, he said to himself.

By lunch time Dr. Wiseman was still feeling on top of the world, with an appetite so liberal and undiscriminating that when Kotokro set the usual meal of boiled coco-yam and fried fish before him he fell upon it with the abandon of a blind man beating a drum. He filled his stomach to repletion and rose up feeling very lethargic. Then he laid down to rest and did not get up again until late in the evening. Even then the hang-over still persisted, so that he went to bed again without any more food for the day.

Dr. Wiseman woke up the next morning, however, feeling very vigorous and ready, with a keen appetite, for breakfast.

He was greatly surprised. At home, whenever he had a hang-over from an over-doze of alcohol the condition persisted for several hours, with the loss of both appetite and energy at the end of it.

"This palm-wine is really a wonderful beverage," he said to himself. "No wonder the blacks are so addicted to it."

They continued to live on roots and fish until Dr. Wiseman grew tired of both. He missed the absence of what he termed "civilised diet", which for him meant the alternation of edibles from the four corners of the globe, including Irish potatoes, Chinese rice, Danish milk, English bread, Argentinean salmon and meat- particularly meat of all kinds, be it bird, pork, beef, lamb or venison. So one morning, a week after his first taste of palm-wine, he said to Kotokro.

"I think we must try and get some meat to eat as well. We cannot live monotonously on roots and fish. It is not good for one's intelligence and system."

"Yes, Doctor," Kotokro agreed, although he could not see how the monotony of their diet could affect the Doctor's intelligence when alcohol could not prevail against it. "It will be easy to get meat too, for there are plenty of game in this jungle, as can be seen from their numerous foot-prints."

"Then we must start hunting for them," suggested the Doctor.

"But we have no guns," replied Kotokro.

"We can use bows and arrows."

"Do you know how to make them?" asked Kotokro.

"Of course. It is very easy. Just bring me a cutlass."

Kotokro fetched him the cutlass; where-upon telling him that he would be back soon, Dr. Wiseman disappeared into the forest. It was not long before he returned with four slender sticks and two strong ropes. Then he sat down and, while Kotokro looked on, he proceeded to make bows and arrows out of these. He used Kotokro's pen-knife and took less than three hours in making two beautiful bows, a big one for himself and a smaller one for Kotokro, together with eight sharp arrows.

Meantime Kotokro had gone for more palm-wine. After they had drunk they had lunch, and Dr. Wiseman suggested that they should rest for sometime and then go to hunt with the bows and arrows. The Doctor drank quite moderately this time, as he wanted to remain sober enough for the hunt.

After they had rested for about an hour they set out. There was no doubt at all that there was plenty of game in that jungle. The foot-prints of all kinds and sizes of wild animals, from buffalos to bush rats, were clearly visible on the ground.

The only problem for Dr. Wiseman was, however, that on account of the wearing out of his shoes at the toes he could only tread with his heels, a mode of progression that was at once slow and painful. However, for the purpose of hunting, which involved stalking one's prey, it was perhaps the most suited to the occasion.

It happened, however, that there was no prey to stalk. They wandered through the forest for the whole day without sighting even a mouse, although there were foot-prints of animals everywhere as has already been pointed out.

Then Kotokro said:

"Doctor," let us abandon the hunt and go back home, for I think we have only been wasting our time."

"Why do you say so?" asked Dr. Wiseman.

"Because although we have seen many foot-print of animals we have hunted for several hours now without setting eyes upon even a rat. You also see that except for monkeys, the lions, the python and the vampire bats, the last three of whom we only stirred up from their abode, we have never espied any animal in this jungle ever since we have been here. What does this mean then? It means that although there are many animals here, they only come out at night. This is borne out by the fact that on the day you climbed down from our house in the trees to go to toilet you saw what appeared to be some animal, which scampered off when you threw a twig at it. We are not therefore likely to see any animal during the day. We can only do so at night."

"But we cannot go to hunt at night," Dr. Wiseman pointed out. "not only because we cannot then see the animals to shoot but also because it would be dangerous for us to do so, for we then run the risk of meeting with a lion or some other wild beast against whom bows and arrows can provide no protection."

"Quite true, Doctor" agreed Kotokro. "So we must not try to go out to hunt at night. We must find some other way of getting the animals."

"What other way?"

"We must set traps."

"That is a good idea. But do you know how to do it?"

"Of course. But I must have some food for a bait; so let us first go back to the house."

They returned to the house and, while Dr. Wiseman slaked his thirst with some of the palm-wine that Kotokro had gone to bring in another pot, the boy took some wild yam and his cutlass and set out again for the bush. He looked for and saw the tracks of four different animals, namely a bush-pig, an antelope, a deer and a grass-cutter. He set a trap on each track by bending down a stake and attaching a noose to the end of it, so that when the animal put its head through the noose the bent stake would at once spring up and hoist it up by the neck. To induce the animal to take the risk of so doing, he placed slices of coco-yam on either side of each noose. Darkness was approaching when he finished the operation and returned home.

He found Dr. Wiseman lying on one of the two benches in the yard, fast asleep. Close beside him stood the pot of palm-wine, empty. While Kotokro was away he had kept gratifying his appetite as it called for more and more of the sweet intoxicant, until not a drop was left. Then as the alcohol went to his head and loosened his limbs he stretched himself on the bench and was soon dissolved in sleep.

Kotokro prepared their dinner and woke him up. The Doctor sat to it with rekindled appetite. After they had finished eating he asked Kotokro about the traps. The latter explained to him what he had done.

"Are you sure they will catch animals during the night?" he asked.

"Quite sure. If they don't there will have to be some explanation for it."

"Such as?"

"Such as that the animals posses more intelligence than me."

Dr. Wiseman had wanted to say that, that would be hardly surprising; but he managed to check himself just when the words were at the tip of his tongue. The idea that Kotokro had no intelligence was so deeply rooted in his mind that even though by now it had been considerably shaken by the boy's repeated display of genius and resourcefulness it had by no means been completed eradicated, a cherished belief being always difficult to part with.

They went to bed earlier than usual, for Kotokro was feeling rather tired after the day's hard work in making and setting traps.

Early next morning, while Dr. Wiseman still slept, he got up and went to inspect the traps. The ones for the bush-pig and the grass-cutter had caught their intended victims. Both were hanging by the neck, quite dead. He loosened them and went on to inspect the other two traps. The one for the antelope was still intact, indicating that the animal had not passed on the trail that night, but the one for the deer had missed its prey. Having re-set the traps on fresh trails he returned to the house with his two catches.

Dr. Wiseman was delighted to see Kotokro back with the bush pig and the grass-cutter. They had their usual breakfast of fried fish and boiled roots, after which the boy proceeded to cut up the two animals. He fried some of the meat and put the rest on fire to dry by smoke.

That day they had a sumptuous dinner, which was made the more palatable by being preceded with copious draughts of palm-wine for appetite.

CHAPTER FOURTEEN
THE GORILLA AND THE LION

Almost one year had gone by since Dr. Wiseman and Kotokro's abortive attempt to escape from the jungle by sailing down the river. They had continued to live on fish, meat and roots, with occasional bananas for desert. By way of diversification Kotokro sometimes prepared palm-soup with the usual meat and fish and with crabs, whose shells continued to defy the strength of Dr. Wiseman's teeth although they provided very welcome flavour for his palate.

Whether from the simplicity of their diet or the enforced cessation from mental labour and too much physical exertion, Dr. Wiseman had begun to feel like a young man again. His stomach had considerably decreased in size and he felt a kind of vigour he had not known for a long time. His heart-tablets had finished for the past seven months, but he had had no further trouble with his heart. The day after he had taken the last tablet he had given himself only one more day of survival, since he would have none to take again unless they were rescued before the next two days had elapsed. But when the two days came and went and nothing happened to him he took courage. And when after a week he was still alive and well he became certain that he had got rid of the malady altogether. And so he had; for, without knowing it, his heart condition had been occasioned by the "civilised" foods on which he had battened while in his native land.

The only problem that faced the Doctor now in their enforced condition of life concerned his clothes and shoes. Both were now completely worn out. His shirt, coat and trousers hang on him in tatters; and as for his shoes he might as well not be wearing them, for the soles were completely gone and he put them on only for the purpose of reminding himself that he was still a civilised man, for he could not walk in them without enduring great pain.

"Why don't you dispense with them altogether and learn to go barefoot as I am doing?" asked Kotokro one day. "It is much more comfortable that way, you know."

"No, I can't go barefooted," replied Dr. Wiseman. "Only animals and natives do that."

And so he continued to wear his shoes, which now consisted of the upper leather only. It was rather an unusual way of providing protection for one's feet, but Dr. Wiseman insisted that it was better than nothing. In the end the soles of his feet got firmly acquainted with the earth and he was able to tread on the ground with no less ease than Kotokro. He had come to do as the boy had suggested without consciously learning to do so.

As for Kotokro that one year or so in the jungle had added considerably to his mental and physical development. He had increased his height by several inches and could now undertake labours that had previously defied his strength, such as carrying large bundles of firewood and fetching water in a big pot. He was also more mentally alert and could reason and act in a more mature manner.

Although like Dr. Wiseman his clothes were tattered and hung in shreds on his body, it made little difference to him, since before going to London he had not worn anything better.

Their lives had not been unpleasant, for they had much to eat and drink and plenty of time for rest.

After several months in this state of Epicurean existence, however, they began to feel bored, particularly Dr. Wiseman. He yearned for the excitement of "civilised" life and the change of seasons and sceneries. From now on he began to look anxiously forward to the arrival of a search party. He would sit in front of the house every day with his eyes and ears wide open, expecting to see or hear something.

This over-anxiety to be rescued was the cause of an incident that nearly cost the two of them their very lives. It happened in this ways:

As the Doctor sat in front of the house one afternoon, straining his ears and eyes to catch the approach of a search party a strange sound reverberated through the jungle. It came from the direction of their marked trail.

"Hawool! Hawool!" was the sound he heard.

It sounded to him like a human voice and the anxious Doctor immediately concluded that it was a search party calling to them.

"Halloo! Halloo." he answered back.

Kotokro, who had been taking a nap on one of the benches in the yard, at once sat up.

"What is it, Doctor?" he asked.

"Someone is calling. Listen," he replied.

Kotokro listened.

"Hawool! Hawool!" the sound was repeated.

"Halloo! Halloo!" the Doctor responded at once.

"Hawool! Hawool!" came the sound again in an increasing volume. Whoever was making it was fast approaching.

"Halloo! Halloo!" Dr. Wiseman responded once more before Kotokro could say anything.

"Do not reply again, Doctor" Kotokro cautioned. "That sound doesn't appear to me to be that of a human being."

"What else could it be?" asked Dr. Wiseman.

It could be the voice of some beast."

"What!" exclaimed Dr. Wiseman "Your suggestion is simply ridiculous, my boy. What beast could call out like that?"

"But this is certainly not the voice of a human being" the boy persisted.

"Well, we always say that the sweetness of the pudding is in the eating," replied Dr. Wiseman. "Whether it is a human being, a beast or a ghost we shall soon find out; for whoever is making that sound is fast approaching and will soon be here, unless I am much mistaken."

"Suppose whoever is making the sound arrives here and is found not to be a human being, what will you do?"

"Well, it certainly cannot be a ghost, much as you and your people believe in such things. And if it is an animal it certainly cannot be a lion or a tiger, the only beasts I fear."

Just as the Doctor finished speaking, the voice came again, sounding much nearer than before.

"Hawool! Hawool!"

"Halloo! Halloo!" responded Dr. Wiseman.

"Hawool! Hawool!" came the voice for the fifth time, followed by the rustling of leaves. The caller was almost in sight.

"Halloo! Halloo! We are here. Glad to see you!" replied Dr Wiseman with the joy of a released hostage.

"Quick, Doctor! It is not a human being or a ghost," shouted Kotokro "It is a gorilla!"

The words were scarcely out of his mouth when a huge beast in the form of a male gorilla emerged from the bush.

"Hawool! Hawool! Hawool." it called angrily, displaying a threatening row of powerful teeth.

The response which he was about to make immediately died in the Doctor's throat. He was so terrified by the appearance of the hirsute anthropoid that he stood dazed for some time. Then recovering himself he dashed into the yard and seized his bow and arrows. As the man-like creature continued to advance, taking measured steps, the Doctor at once let fly an arrow in the direction of its hairy chest. But it did not reach its target, for the dextrous creature caught it in mid-air and, breaking it in two, threw it away.

Dr. Wiseman discharged another arrow at it with the same result. Then seeing that his weapon was of no avail against the powerful monster, he seized his cutlass and rushed to the attack in utter desperation. But, as he raised up the weapon to strike, the beast seized and crushed it in its iron grip.

"Oh, Doctor, come into the room at once:" shouted Kotokro, who had already fled into the room for refuge as soon as he saw the frightful beast emerge from the bush.

Sensing the danger in which he stood Dr. Wiseman did not stop to argue. He immediately dashed into the room before the gorilla could lay its hands on him. Kotokro at once closed the door and fastened it with two stakes laid across it at the top and bottom.

The gorilla continued to advance slowly. It was in no hurry, for it knew that its victims were caught cooped up and had no chance of escape. It soon reached the door and, with one powerful blow, sent it crashing into the room, leaving the entrance wide open.

Just at this moment, however, a most miraculous thing happened. As the beast was about to enter the room in which its intended victims were now crouching in fear, they heard the roar of a lion. The gorilla heard it too and turned round to look for the intruder. As it did so a huge lion with a shaggy main also emerged from the bush in the direction from which the gorilla had come. It had apparently been following the gorilla as it made its way towards the house in response to Dr. Wiseman's calls.

A fierce fight immediately ensued. The lion flew at the gorilla. It first bit it on the head, tearing off the skin. The gorilla fell to the ground. Then the lion buried its fangs in its throat. While it was clinging tenaciously to it, the gorilla also held the neck of the fierce beast in both hands and began to squeeze its throat in its terrible grip. As each tried to free itself the other tightened its hold the harder. At last the gorilla's hold began to take effect. The lion became dazed, its eyes began to swim and its jaws gradually relaxed. The gorilla shook itself free and, with one powerful blow, splitted the lion's skull. The carnivorous quadruped breathed no more.

The gorilla rose to its feet with a staggering gait. It took a few steps towards the door again and bent down to enter. Suddenly it slumped to the ground and lay hurdled up. It was dead. The bleeding from the head and neck had had its effect.

Both Dr. Wiseman and Kotokro had been watching the deadly fight in great terror, knowing that their lives would still be in danger whichever side emerged victorious. They had not at all expected that it would end in the death of both contestants and thus leave them safe.

They came out from their hide-out and dragged the two dead beasts away from the yard. It was hard work, for both were very heavy creatures. But after tugging repeatedly they succeeded in dragging them some distance away from their abode.

On close examination Kotokro discovered that the lion was blind in one eye. He recognised it at once as the lion whose eye he had pierced with a sharpened stake when it tried to attack them in the night. Dr. Wiseman recognised it too when Kotokro pointed it out to him.

"Is it not strange, Doctor," asked Kotokro "that the gorilla to whom we have done no wrong should have come to harm us, and the lion to whom we had done no good should have come to save us?"

"Well, that is the inscrutable way of nature," replied Dr. Wiseman. "She often acts in a way that defies human reason."

"She?" asked Kotokro with a puzzled brow.

"Yes, she. That is to say, Nature."

"Nature? Who is Nature?"

"By Nature we mean the whole universe and everything in it."

"And the whole universe and everything in it cause things to happen in this way?"

"No, it is God who causes things to happen in this way."

"Then why didn't you say that that is the inscrutable way of God?"

"Because you wouldn't know anything about God. Only white people know and worship him. Heathens only know about woods and stones, to which they bow in homage."

"But whites also bow in homage to woods and stones." Kotokro disagreed.

"Where did you ever see whites bow to woods and stones?"

"In the church to which Mrs. Casely took me and the other boys."

"My boy, it is blasphemous to say such a thing," replied Dr. Wiseman, horrified. "They were not bowing to woods and stones. It was to the crucifix behind the altar that they were bowing."

"And what is the crucifix made of?"

"Never mind what it is made of. It is simply the image of Christ on the cross."

"What was he doing on the cross?"

"He was not doing anything. His enemies hung him there."

"For doing what?"

"For claiming to be the son of God."

"Did they believe his claim?"

"They did not."

"Is that why they hung him there?"

"Yes."

"What kind of men were they, white or black?"

"They were white men, of course."

"What do you call men who kill their own kind without good reason? If I remember correctly you said they were called savages?"

"Yes, we call them savages."

"They were savages then. Why, old Sodoro in our village claims to be the uncle of God, and no one has harmed him for that. We only laugh, for we find his claim highly entertaining. If we believed him we would have worshipped him instead. So if those white men believed his claim then they should have worshipped Him; and if they did not believed it, then they should have only laughed.

"It is not only because he had claimed to be God's son," continued Dr. Wiseman. "They also said that he had claimed to be able to destroy and re-build in three days their place of worship which they had taken several years to build. And, above all, because he had also said that he was their king."

"Why didn't they challenge him to destroy the building and re-build it in three days? Were they afraid he would be able to do so? Then they should have worshipped Him. And as for his claim that he was their king, could they not have simply asked him who installed him as their king? You see, old Sodoro also said similar things. He said that he could make our river dry up at his command; and also that he was our chief. We challenged him to make the river dry up, and he couldn't do it. And as for his claim that he was our chief we simply asked him who installed him as such? He could not answer. The result of all this was that he only provided good entertainment for us. No one laid a finger on him. We rather came to like him."

"All that you have said is absolute trash!" commented Dr. Wiseman in exasperation. "It clearly shows that you have not an iota of intelligence."

"What is iota?" asked Kotokro.

"The smallest amount."

"All right, Doctor" said Kotokro "let us only consider then what to do about these two creatures. We cannot bury them, for we have no implements to dig a grave deep enough to accommodate both, and we cannot leave them here to rot, for the stench would be unbearable."

"We must consume them in a bonfire" replied Dr. Wiseman.

"That would be very difficult" Kotokro pointed out. "For we would require more firewood than you and I can bring together, and it would take several hours, if not days, to reduce them to ashes."

"Well, what else can we do, short of cutting them up to eat? Perhaps you could do that, but I cannot. I have never in my life tasted a gorilla's or a lion's flesh and I do not intend to begin doing so now, especially as I have more civilised meat to feed upon."

"I have an idea," replied Kotokro. "We can cut them up for eating, but not for eating by me or you; for I alone could not eat such a large amount of meat even if I wanted to."

"Who is to eat them then?"

"The same as disposed of the corpses of the victims of the plane crash, namely the carnivorous denizens of this forest."

"You mean the wild beasts?"

"Exactly."

"Why don't you simply leave them there to be eaten by them at night then?"

"That is not a bad idea, but we must first remove the skins. They will come in handy."

It occurred to Dr. Wiseman that the boy was right. Why, he himself should have thought of that. If such rare animal skins arrived in London they would fetch no small sum of money.

"All right, carry on then?" said the Doctor, foreseeing that he was more likely to profit from them than the boy.

Kotokro brought out his pen-knife and cutlass and set to work. He began with the lion. He first cut off the head, which had been badly shattered by the gorilla's blow. Then he made a slit in front from the neck to the tail and carefully removed the flesh and bones from the skin. When he had finished he proceeded to deal with the gorilla in the same way. He cut off the head, with its damaged skin, and made a slit in front from the neck to the bottom and removed the flesh and bones. He did all this to the appreciation of Dr. Wiseman, who now began to reckon how much he was likely to receive from the two skins. He estimated that they would, on arrival in London, bring him not less than a thousand pounds sterling, a no inconsiderable sum of money.

After Kotokro had finished flaying the two beasts he took a cutlass and began to cut up their carcasses into big chunks of meat. That done he conveyed it all to the abandoned hunters' camp which was about a quarter of a mile away. There he scattered them on the ground.

He came back and began to work on the two skins. He first made small slits at close intervals on either side of the lines of incision to enable him lace up the skins after they were dry. Next he put each in a big pot and poured water on it to soak. Then he went into the bush and brought the bark of a tree which he said was used for tanning leather. He cut it into bits and added them to the water in either pot.

Dr. Wiseman had been watching with curiosity as Kotokro performed these operations, and congratulated him on his performance when he had finished.

"But are you sure they will be soft, with the hair still remaining on them when they are dry?," he asked.

"Sure," replied Kotokro. "They will be like mink coats."

And so they turned out to be, after they had soaked for three days and Kotokro, having scraped the bits of flesh that still clung to them in the inside, had pegged them out to dry.

Meantime they repaired the broken door of their room and got rid of the gore which both animals had left in the yard. They first scraped and buried it in the ground and then scattered fresh soil on the spot to cover up all traces of it. Kotokro said that if they did not do so they would again be invaded by soldier ants during the night.

That evening they went to bed earlier than usual, but they were awakened in the middle of the night by loud and hideous howls emanating from the direction of the abandoned hunters' camp. It was obvious that scores of wild beasts-tigers, lions and leopards- were fighting over the meat which Kotokro had conveyed to the spot.

When Kotokro passed there the next morning on his way to inspect the traps, there was no trace of a single chunk of meat. The wild beasts had devoured every bit of it, leaving soldier ants to clean up the mess left behind.

For the first time Kotokro returned to the house without any game. He had found all the traps intact, no animal having ventured to come out that night, due to the noise made by the wild beasts. However, they had no problem with their meal, for they already had an abundance of meat and fish to fall back upon.

CHAPTER FIFTEEN
SECOND ATTEMPT To ESCAPE

For several days Dr. Wiseman was unable to get over his perilous encounter with the gorilla. Any time he remembered the incident he shuddered to think of what would have happened to him if the lion had not providentially intervened in the very nick of time. "It would have splitted my skull in the way it did to the lion," he said to himself "thus spilling my brain and all the intelligence in it." So immediately after breakfast a fortnight after the incident he said to Kotokro:

"My boy, it is more than one and half years now since we returned here following our unprofitable voyage down the river, during which period of time the only being that has come to look for us is the gorilla. Think of where you and I would have been today if that hideous creature had laid its monstrous hands on us. We must therefore try again to get away from here before a similar fate succeeds in overtaking us."

"Which direction shall we take?" asked Kotokro.

"I suggest we go upstream this time. We cannot, of course, sail, since the stream gets narrower and narrower from this point; but we can skirt it until we eventually arrive at its source. I am sure we are bound to come upon some human habitation before then."

"All right, Doctor," agreed Kotokro. "There is no harm in trying, although I still think our only hope of escape from this place lies in someone coming to find us."

"If we continue waiting here someone is bound to come and find us all right; and we shall then escape not only from this place but also from this world altogether."

"Well, let us depart then at our own free will," replied Kotokro.

With that he began to collect into the iron trunk all the articles that they could not leave behind. These were one of the two cutlasses, his three ropes, the two skins, which were now as dry and soft as mink coats, Dr. Wiseman's brief-case and its contents, two drinking cups and their two bed sheets which were by now worn out. He also packed some fried fish and meat and some cooked tubers into one of the pots and covered the pot with a dish.

What they were leaving behind were all the other earthen ware, the palm oil, the rest of the meat and fish, the bows and arrows, the empty corned beef tins and the torch-light which was by now useless, the batteries in it having long become dead.

"Doctor, I cannot carry the iron trunk and the pot, so you will have to assist me with one of them," said Kotokro to Dr. Wiseman when everything was ready for their departure.

"How can I assist you?" asked Dr. Wiseman. "I cannot hold either the pot or the iron trunk in my hand. Both are too heavy. And I cannot carry either of them on my head. Even as a child I never carried things on my head. Only blacks and other primitive people do that. That is why they have little or no intelligence."

"How?" asked Kotokro, unable to see the connection between intelligence and the carrying of things on the head.

"Because as the load presses upon their pate it stifles the growth of intelligence." he explained.

"Oh, I see," said Kotokro. "Then I shall carry the pot on my head, as it already has no intelligence. With my right hand I shall hold one end of the trunk by the handle while you also hold the other end by the handle. This means that I shall have both hands engaged, while you will have one hand free. Which again means that you will have to take the lead and use your free hand in clearing the way with the cutlass whenever we encounter any impediment."

"That will make for slow progress, but let us do as you say; for it will be better than staying put on this accursed spot."

Kotokro put the pot on his head as he had suggested. Then he took hold of one end of the trunk while Dr. Wiseman held the other. As they went along Dr. Wiseman, who was leading, cleared their way every now and then with the second cutlass which he was holding. Again and again he complained that his hand was straining with the load and that he needed rest. Whereupon they would put down the iron trunk, while Kotokro also deposited the pot on the ground. After resting for a while they would get up again and resume their advance.

This manner of going retarded their progress considerably, so that by noon they had covered a distance of some two miles or so only, having by then been journeying for about four hours.

They had been keeping as close as possible to the course of the stream, which became narrower and narrower as they went along. At last they began to ascend a high ground. Suddenly they came upon a narrow gorge. At the head of the gorge was a huge boulder from underneath which a spring of water was bubbling. They had arrived at the source of the stream without coming across any human dwelling. Kotokro was greatly disappointed.

"We have made a useless journey, Doctor," he said. "We have arrived at the source of the river without coming across any human settlement. I suggest we go back to our base. At least there we have shelter."

"Cheer up, my boy," encouraged Dr. Wiseman. "Our journey has not been as useless as you think. At least we have discovered the source of that river upon which you and I sailed, or at least I have discovered it. This is a great achievement in exploration. It will make me famous, for I shall name the river after me. It will be called River Wiseman."

"But why do you say you have discovered it?" asked Kotokro. "Did we not discover it together?"

"We did. But you, as a black, don't need fame. Only white men do."

"And what would you do with fame?" asked Kotokro.

"Nothing. Except that I shall be respected wherever I go, and my name will be for ever remembered even when I am dead."

"Oh, is that all?"

"That is all."

Kotokro laughed.

"Ah, I wouldn't like to bestow my name upon a river. It is too precious." he said. "Besides it does not even belong to me. It is my grandfather's. And I wouldn't care to be remembered when I am dead. No one remembered me when I was not born and it made no difference to me."

"Of course, you wouldn't know about these things. But, believe me, it means a great deal, even though it brings no material benefit."

"Are all rivers and their sources discovered by somebody?" asked Kotokro.

"Yes, all rivers."

"Was River Thames discovered by Dr. Thames?"

"No, no. Rivers and mountains in civilised countries are not discovered. They have existed from time immemorial."

"Then how did it get the name Thames?"

"I don't know. It has always been called so."

"What about my suggestion that we should go back?" asked Kotokro, changing the subject.

"We cannot go back to that dangerous abode. Let us rather go forward, for we are bound to arrive somewhere."

They had sat down to rest as they talked, but at the suggestion that they should continue their way forward Kotokro got up and, placing the pot on his head once more, asked Dr. Wiseman if he was ready.

"Of course," he replied. And with that he rose up and lifted the trunk by one end while Kotokro held the other end as before.

They were able to proceed more quickly this time, as the vegetation from here was not as rank as the parts close to the stream which they had already traversed. Still they would have been able to make faster progress if they had not been holding the iron trunk.

They continued to go up the high ground until they reached the summit and began to descend. Then Dr. Wiseman said that he was tired and hungry, and so they should rest and have some food. Kotokro was not averse to the suggestion, as he himself was beginning to feel the pangs of hunger. He also reckoned that after they would have eaten some of the food, the pot would be lighter and therefore easier to carry. So they sat down and ate. After resting for a while they resumed their journey.

Kotokro found his burden considerably lightened, just as he had expected; for they had helped themselves to a large portion of the food. They were now able to proceed more briskly than before, as they had also had their energies renewed.

Upon descending to the bottom of the hill they suddenly came upon a spot in the valley which appeared to be a river completely covered with weeds. It was not very wide, being only about twenty feet across. Dr. Wiseman was about to wade into it when Kotokro said:

"Stop, Doctor. You may be taking a dangerous step, for we do not know how deep it is."

"What must we do then? Must we turn back?" asked the Doctor.

"Well, if we have to turn back we would be surer of our safety than venturing into this unknown."

"I know what we will do," said Dr. Wiseman after considering for a moment what Kotokro had said. "I am going to cut a stick with which to measure the depth as we go along. If it proves to be too deep then we shall have to find some other way of crossing it."

So saying he let down his end of the trunk and cut a stick, about six feet long, from a nearby plant. Then lifting up his end of the trunk once more he told Kotokro to hold the other end as before. He would measure the depth of the river as they waded through, he explained.

"No, no, Doctor," Kotokro disagreed. "Let us not proceed in this manner. I suggest you first find out the depth by yourself alone. If it proves to be safe we shall then cross together."

"All right, I shall do that if you are afraid to go in with me" agreed Dr. Wiseman.

"But you must not rely on the stick only," Kotokro advised. "You may unexpectedly strike a spot deeper than the length of this stick."

"What do you want me to do then?"

"It would be advisable to tie one end of a rope to your waist while I tie the other end to this tree, so that in case you suddenly fall into a depth you may be able to pull yourself up again and not drown."

It was with great difficulty that Kotokro could persuade Dr. Wiseman to agree to his suggestion, for he refused to have a rope tied around his waist, saying that he was not a monkey and had no inclination to look like one.

"You will not look like a monkey," Kotokro assured him. "And even if you did, what would it matter, as long as you did not behave like one?"

"Are you happy then that you look so much like a monkey?" asked Dr. Wiseman bluntly.

"Ah, Doctor," exclaimed Kotokro. "No monkey would consider that as a compliment. Any monkey hearing you say that he and I look alike would feel deeply insulted, because.........?"

"Because what?" interrupted Dr. Wiseman.

"Because every monkey thinks that any human being, whether black or white, being a glabrous animal or isn't that the word? without the elegant adornment of a tail, and with a trunk split in two midway upwards for legs, on which it stands erect like a palm-tree even when in motion, as well as a head that is not only roofed with woollen thatch but is also studded with funny protrusions and riddled with holes is the ugliest creature on earth."

"Rubbish !" shouted Dr. Wiseman. "No white man can be ugly."

"That is a matter of opinion on which any monkey would beg to differ. After all, beauty, as they say in my language and I believe in yours too, is in the eye of the beholder. In other words even your white beauty queen may be the very incarnation of ugliness in the eyes of any monkey. And even in my own human eyes, whenever I contemplate the breathing pipe of any human being, which goes by the name of NOSE sticking aggressively out his face, I find it very funny.

"All right, all right, my little empty-headed rage," replied Dr. Wiseman, "there is no need to say more. I am prepared to do as you say if only to please you."

"Good," said Kotokro. And with that he opened the iron trunk and took out his three ropes.

One of them was long enough to stretch across the river and beyond. He tied one end of it to Dr. Wiseman's waist as he had suggested, and the other end to the trunk of the tree that stood quite close to the brink.

"Well, you can go in now, Doctor," he Said when all was ready.

Dr. Wiseman stepped forward into the supposed river. Alas! it proved not to be a river but a bog. But it did not appear to be deep, for the stick sank down about two feet only when it touched the bottom. He stepped forward again and sounded the depth. It was the same. He grew more confident and began to advance with little caution. He had almost reached the middle of it, with the stick still showing a depth of two feet, when suddenly, as he planted the stick in front of him again, the ground under the bog immediately gave way and he plunged headlong into the treacherous quagmire.

"Help! Help, Kotokro!" he shouted as he began to sink.

The boy held the rope at once and tried to pull him back, but he could not. The Doctor was too heavy for him.

"I can't" he said. "Pull yourself back by the rope."

Dr. Wiseman tried to do as he had suggested, but that part of the rope having been covered with slime from the mire proved to be too slippery for his grasp. And now he was submerged up to his shoulder. Then his shoulder rapidly disappeared, leaving only his neck above the surface. Gradually his neck also began to disappear. And now he was in it up to his chin and mouth, with the top of his head scarcely showing among the covering weeds. Then as he opened his mouth to shout for help again the viscous fluid entered it, choking his voice.

Meantime Kotokro had quickly unloosened the other end of the rope and wound it round the trunk of the tree. Then using this as a fulcrum, he began to pull the Doctor with all his might, just as the latter's head was also in the process of disappearing from sight. Slowly the Doctor began to re-emerge, still clinging to the rope. Kotokro pulled and pulled until the Doctor's feet stood once more on firm ground underneath the shallower part of the bog at a depth of two feet.

Dr. Wiseman escaped from those jaws of death, covered with mud from head to heels. He spat out the mud from his mouth and wiped his face with his hand. But his dress, like every part of his body, was plastered with that sticky substance, so that he had to undress, leaving nothing on.

Whereupon Kotokro also stripped himself naked and gave him his ragged clothes to wipe himself. Next the boy opened the iron trunk and took out his tattered bed-sheet and, tearing it, gave a piece to Dr. Wiseman to wrap around his waist, while he himself remained naked.

"We must turn back, Doctor," advised Kotokro, seeing the hopelessness of their situation, "for it is obvious that we cannot cross this bog."

"I cannot go back to that wretched place until we have tried all other means of crossing this morass," he refused.

"What other means?"

"Let us cross from a spot a little further down there" he replied, pointing to a point that looked slightly narrower.

"If we have to cross then we must think of another way of doing so" replied Kotokro, "for we cannot adopt the method which we have already tried with such near tragedy."

"What other method?" asked Dr. Wiseman.

"I have an idea. It is this: We must tie a rope from the branch of this tree to the branch of that tree across the bog. We can then cross by this rope."

"How is that to be done?"

"Just watch and see."

So saying he tied the three ropes around his waist and began to ascend the tree. He climbed up to its top most branch, which was about thirty feet above the ground, and stretched over the bog for a distance of about five feet. He firmly tied one end of one of the ropes to the overhanging branch. Then he untied the other two ropes from his waist and secured them to the trunk of the tree. That done he held the rope which he had securely tied to the branch and swung himself on it with great force towards the other bank. He landed only about two feet away from the brink of the bog on the other side. Still holding the other end of the rope he climbed the other tree which also stood close to the bog and tied it to a branch about twenty feet above the ground.

Having thus firmly secured the rope from tree to tree he worked his way back on it to the tree on the other side where Dr. Wiseman was still waiting for him. There he removed a second rope from the trunk of the tree and knotted it around the stretched rope, making a loop, so that it could easily slide down over it.

Then he threw the other end of it down to Dr. Wiseman and asked him to hold it and rail himself across the bog to the other side. When the Doctor had climbed about half-way up the rope Kotokro, who was holding the other end, suddenly let go. The Doctor at once began to slide down very rapidly on the rope and soon found himself on the other side.

Kotokro tied up their wet dresses into a bundle and threw it across the bog to Dr. Wiseman. Alas! the Doctor failed to catch it. It bounded on the ground and jumped into the middle of the bog. It was soon swallowed out of sight.

Without interrupting his operation Kotokro also slid down on the rope to that side and brought back the second rope by which the Doctor had crossed over. He tied the third rope to it just about six inches below the stretched rope and secured it to the trunk of the tree, so that the second rope would not slide down when he let go. Then he descended to the ground and climbed the tree again with the iron trunk up to a height of about ten feet above the ground. There he tied the sliding rope to it and, loosening the third rope from the trunk of the tree, allowed the iron trunk to slide down gently towards the other side.

Dr. Wiseman untied it and set it down. Then Kotokro pulled the rope back to his side and tied the pot of food to it by the neck. He gently slid it down to the other side in the same manner as he had done the trunk. Lastly he himself slid down the rope to the other side.

And now both of them had crossed with the iron trunk and pot of food, as well as two of the three ropes. The third rope was still stretched across the bog from tree to tree.

"How are you going to get back that rope?" asked Dr. Wiseman when the boy stood beside him.

"It wouldn't be difficult," he replied. "But I must not try to take it away, for it is useful here as a bridge across the bog."

"How? When we are going away for good?"

"We may not be going away for good," replied Kotokro. "Anything could happen to make us turn back."

"Nothing can happen to make me turn back," declared Dr. Wiseman firmly. "I have burnt my boat."

"What does that mean?"

"It means there is no turning back for me."

"All right, Doctor; then let us hurry to go forward, for the day is already far spent and we have not made much progress."

So saying he put the pot on his head once more and held one end of the iron trunk. Dr. Wiseman also held the other end and they resumed their journey as before.

It was not long before they were ascending a hill again. They climbed and climbed until they reached the summit. It was much higher than the one from which they had descended to the edge of the bog. Then they began to descend precipitously. They went down and down until they suddenly burst upon a wide expanse of what appeared to be another bog. It was about four hundred yards across. Its surface was covered with weeds like the one they had just crossed.

"This may be a river and not a bog," suggested Dr. Wiseman. "So let us first make sure what it is."

"Even if it proves to be a river how can we cross it?" asked Kotokro.

"It may not be deep, so that we may be able to wade through."

"All right. Let us try and find out then."

Dr. Wiseman cut a stick and plunged it into it, to sound the depth. It was so deep, even at the brink, that had he leaned forward as he did so, he would have fallen headlong into it. As it was, he was leaning backwards as he probed it with the stick. It was revealed at once that it was also a dangerous quagmire.

Dr. Wiseman stood despondent. He surveyed the bog right and left. It stretched endlessly in a semi-circle in both directions, so that it seemed to join the first bog at both ends.

"We are completely surrounded by the two bogs, Doctor," said Kotokro "so that we either have to go back or else make our abode here."

"Make our abode here!" exclaimed the Doctor. "How can we make our abode in a place where we have nothing for shelter and do not even have water to drink? No, let us return to our base. There at least we have both."

"Let us first have something to eat then" replied Kotokro, "for I am tired and hungry."

Dr. Wiseman also said that he was tired and hungry; so they sat down and ate as much of the food as they could. Then Kotokro said that as they were going back to their base, where they had left plenty of food behind, there was no need for him to carry the remaining food back. There was no need also to return with the pot, as they had left two behind.

Dr. Wiseman agreed with this, adding that it would even make for more rapid progress, since Kotokro could now carry the iron trunk on his head and leave him free of any encumbrance.

The sun was setting behind the trees when they set out to return to their base. Kotokro carried the iron trunk on his head and held one of the cutlasses in his hand, while Dr. Wiseman led the way with the other cutlass. Now that both of them were relieved from holding the iron trunk they were able to advance more rapidly, especially after they had climbed back over that precipitous hill.

Darkness had already begun to fall when they arrived back at the first bog. As the rope was still stretched across it they did not spend much time in re-crossing. Kotokro simply climbed the tree and untied this end of the rope which was about twenty feet above the ground. He took it further ten feet up the tree and tied it there, so that it now ran parallel to the surface of the bog. Then he went over it to the other side. There he untied the other end and brought it ten feet lower down the tree, where he again secured it to the tree, thus making it slope once more from the other side.

Having thus reversed the slant of the rope he came back to the other side where Dr. Wiseman was still waiting for him. There he secured a second rope in a loop to the outstretched rope and railed the Doctor across, as he had done when they were first crossing it. Next followed the iron trunk.

While Kotokro was thus engaged he noticed that a sudden gust of wind had begun to blow through the forest. It quickly gathered force and momentum. Soon the whole place was seized with pandemonium just as he was crossing over by the rope. The trees swayed and bowed under the irresistible force of a fierce storm. Blinding flashes of lightning slashed the sky, followed by deafening explosions of thunder. The two trees between which the rope was stretched across the bog swayed in frenzy, now tensing now slackening their hold.

At last just as Kotokro had crossed over and was about to descend, the rope snapped from the other tree, as if severed with a knife, and fell to his side. He quickly untied it from the tree and dropped it to the ground.

Then he hurriedly descended and, picking it up, folded and put it into the iron trunk.

"Let us go at once, Doctor," he said "for the rain will soon be here. "

He had scarcely said so when loud patters struck the tree-tops. Soon a heavy deluge began to pour from the loaded sky, drenching the forest and everything underneath. Both Dr. Wiseman and Kotokro were soon soaked to the skin. For the Doctor, however, this was a blessing in disguise, for the water quickly washed away the slime which had stuck to his body when he fell into the bog. Although Kotokro had wiped it away with his clothes some had still remained.

And now the sun had completely deserted the sky, leaving it to pitch darkness, so that they could no longer have found their way but for the successive flashes of lightning which continuously illuminated the forest. The trail which they had blazed on the outward journey also helped in keeping them to the right track.

On and on they went. At last they came to the source of the river which the Doctor had proposed to name after himself. They descended the hill from which it flowed and continued along the trail which skirted the stream.

They had not gone far when they began to wade through water. The river had overflowed its banks and was fast invading their track.

"We must hurry, Doctor," said Kotokro. "The flood keeps on rising, and we may soon find ourselves in deep water unless we reach our base quickly."

Dr. Wiseman tried to hurry, but now he was unable to see the way any longer. The water, which had come up to his knees and submerged Kotokro up to his chest, had almost obliterated their track.

"I can no longer see my way forward," he said after taking a few more steps, "for all the marks I made are no longer visible."

"Let me lead the way then," said Kotokro "for I can still identify our track."

So saying he went past the Doctor and began to lead the way. Although their track was now hidden under water he was able to tell where their way lay, by observing the trees which they had passed on their outward journey. He had always said that no two trees in the forest looked exactly alike.

On and on they went, and the water kept on rising continuously.

And now Kotokro was up to his neck, and Dr. Wiseman to his shoulders, in water.

"Help, 0 Doctor, help! I am drowning," cried Kotokro, being now submerged up to his chin.

"What can I do?" replied Dr. Wiseman. "I myself have as much difficulty in wading through this flood."

"Just relieve me of the iron trunk and I shall swim if need be," he replied.

"Let the flood take it away," said Dr. Wiseman, "for there is no way I can help you. I cannot hold it, and my head is not used to carrying things."

Kotokro could no longer continue to hold the cutlass. He let go, and it was immediately carried away by the swift current.

Just at this moment, however, he saw a tree which marked the point from which their track turned away from the river towards the land. He quickly made for it and turned, followed by Dr. Wiseman. Soon they had begun to climb the hill on which their house stood. As they went along they found themselves gradually re-emerging from the water. It came down to Kotokro's neck, then to his chest, then to his waist and then to his feet. Finally they found themselves on firm ground.

After advancing for a further two hundred yards or so they arrived safely at their base. Owing to the storm no wild beast had come out that night, so that they had stood in no other danger. By now the rain had stopped falling where they were, but was continuing in the distance. Flashes of lightning still came from across the sky and brightened the forest, so that they were able to make their way into the compound. They found the place very muddy and slippery from the rain, but when they entered their room it was as dry and cosy as ever. Not a drop of water had leaked through the roof.

Kotokro groped his way to the corner of the room where he had stored the charcoal, the coal-pot and dry twigs and fibre. He filled the coal-pot with charcoal and brought it outside into the yard, where he placed it on one of the benches. Then he brought some fibre and dry twigs and lighted it. When the charcoal had caught fire and begun to glow, he took the coal-pot back into the room, where it gave an illumination bright enough to make them see their way about.

Dr. Wiseman who had been sitting in the room all the while, shivering with cold, at once drew near and began to warm himself. While he did so Kotokro put some meat and yam on the charcoal to roast. By the time they had finished eating it was past mid-night, for they had arrived back quite late. They lay down to sleep and did not wake up until the next morning, when the sun was already high up in the sky.

CHAPTER SIXTEEN
AMONG THE WAPITIS

Another six months had gone by since Dr. Wiseman and Kotokro failed in their second attempt to get away. They had continued to live as before, feeding upon wild tubers and meat and fish trapped by Kotokro. No harmful creature had come to molest them, nor had any monkey come to play tricks upon them. Their lives had been quite peaceful and uneventful. From day to day they had expected to see a search party emerge from the direction in which they had blazed a trail with arrows and carvings on tree barks, looking for them. But no living creature had come from that direction, nor indeed from anywhere else.

But now economic necessity had begun to overtake them. The roots and tubers on which they were living had become scarce in their immediate vicinity and they had to search very far before they could find any. The fish had also migrated from their usual abode and only one or two stragglers could be caught now and then. As for the animals they all seemed to have learnt to recognise Kotokro's traps and to give them a wide berth, and only a few ignorant or thick-headed ones allowed themselves to be caught once in a while.

At last life became extremely boring and food very scarce. They managed to cheer and regale themselves with palm-wine, but when this also became no longer available, owing to the exhaustion of the sap from repeated tapings of all the trees, their life in the jungle became altogether intolerable. Then Dr. Wiseman said to Kotokro:

"My boy, we can no longer continue to live in this jungle. If we do we shall die here, one of us at least providing food for the carnivorous beasts. So let us make one desperate effort to get away before we become too weak to move. "

"I agree, Doctor," replied Kotokro. "It would be better to die at once attempting to escape than end our days here slowly in this wretched state of existence."

Having thus made up their minds to go away they set out early next morning immediately after breakfast. Kotokro carried on his head the iron trunk which now contained only Dr. Wiseman's brief-case, the two skins and the three ropes. The two bed-sheets had both been torn and only a little piece still covered the Doctor's loins. As for Kotokro he had remained in his birthday suit ever since he gave his clothes to Dr. Wiseman to wipe himself and subsequently lost it in the bog.

Kotokro suggested that since in their first and second attempts to get away they had sailed downstream and skirted the river upstream, both to no avail, they should now cross the river and head away from it altogether. They were bound either to arrive somewhere or die in their attempt. Dr. Wiseman agreed, adding, however, that God forbid that he should end in the wild jungle where his corpse would not even receive a civilised burial.

"What does it matter where or how a man is buried, Doctor?" asked Kotokro.

"It matters a great deal where and how a man is buried" disagreed Dr. Wiseman. "How would you like to be buried with your head upside down in a rubbish dump?"

"Is that why a certain great white King's bones were taken for burial in his native city centuries after he had been buried in a different place?"

"Who told you?"

"Mrs. Casely."

"Well, that shows you that white men care about where and how they are buried, if you Negroes don't."

They had been advancing towards the stream as they talked. Soon they had come to it and were wading across, with Kotokro leading and Dr. Wiseman following. It was not deep, coming up only slightly above the waist of Dr. Wiseman and the chest of Kotokro. The current, however, was very swift, for it had rained upstream only the night before and the flood had not yet receded. The unexpected result was that Dr. Wiseman emerged from the water quite naked. The little piece of cloth which he had tied around his loins had been carried away by the rushing water without his knowledge, for he had not tied it firmly enough.

"Stop, Kotokro," he called to the boy who, having stepped once more on dry land, had begun to pursue his way vigorously without looking back to see if the Doctor was still following. "I am completely naked like you."

"What happened, Doctor?" asked Kotokro, turning round to look at him.

"The piece of cloth which I tied around my loins has been washed away by the current," he explained.

"Did you not see it go?"

"I did not. And I am sure it cannot now be retrieved."

"Well, what does it matter? It only means that we are both naked now. It makes for better company."

"We must find something to cover ourselves. We must not be seen like this."

"Why, what crime do we commit by going naked?"

"It is criminal. At least in my country one commits a crime by going naked. It is punishable by imprisonment."

"Does it mean no one goes naked in your country?"

"No, civilised people do not go naked. It is only in Africa that you find naked people."

"But Mrs. Casely said that white men and women in Aping Forest do ape chimpanzees and baboons and orang-utans by going naked, and no one punishes them?"

"It is Epping Forest, not Aping Forest," he corrected. "And they are not punished because it is a place set aside for people to go naked if they want to."

"So there are people in your country who want to go naked?"

"Yes; they are cranks and faddists who don't know what they are about."

"I see. And the Africans who go naked are also cranks and faddists who don't know what they are about?"

"No, they are simply the unspoiled children of nature. They are like Adam and Eve in the Garden of Eden."

"Who are Adam and Eve?" asked Kotokro.

"They are the first man and woman whom God created as husband and wife. They dwelt naked in the Garden of Eden and were not ashamed until the Devil, in the form of a serpent, persuaded them to eat of the forbidden fruit. Then they became aware of their nakedness and were ashamed."

"Before whom were they ashamed?" asked Kotokro.

"They were ashamed before God and before each other."

"Why were they ashamed before God? Did they not know that it was he who created them naked? And why should they be ashamed before each other, when they were husband and wife? At least my father and mother are not shamed before each other. They bath together and sleep together."

"Look here, you ask too many questions. It is a sign of your lack of intelligence. If you had intelligence you would understand things at once and would not be asking so many silly questions."

"True, Doctor, there are many things that your people do and say that I do not understand. I really wish I had intelligence."

"Well, cheer up, my boy. It is not your fault. The Creator did not endow you and your people with any.

"May I ask one question then?"

"Yes. What is it?"

"You say that it is only cranks and faddists and the unspoiled children of nature that go naked. But you and I are going naked now. To which of the two categories do we belong?"

"We don't belong to either. We are naked by necessity."

"What does that mean?"

"It means we *are* naked because we cannot help it. If we had something to wear we wouldn't go naked."

"But we have something to wear."

"Where is it?"

"Here in this iron trunk" he replied. So saying he put down the trunk and proceeded to open it. Dr. Wiseman looked on, wondering what he was going to bring out. Kotokro took out the gorilla's and the lion's skins.

"Here they are" he said, handing the gorilla's skin to Dr. Wiseman. At the same time he himself began to don the lion's skin.

Dr. Wiseman hesitated. The idea of wearing a gorilla's skin for a dress did not appeal to him, but he was even less happy at the prospect of being seen naked by other people. Without a word he accepted it and began to put it on. After both of them had put on the skins and laced them up they looked exactly like a gorilla and a lion. It was only when you looked carefully and saw human heads peeping through the skins that you would conclude that these were no ordinary gorilla and lion.

Thus attired but, of course, standing erect on their two feet, they resumed their journey through the unbroken jungle.

They must have covered a distance of about four miles when they suddenly struck into a foot-path running at right angles to their line of advance. This was the first time that they had come across a foot-path since they had been in that jungle, and they were highly excited. It meant there was now the prospect of coming into contact with other human beings at last.

Kotokro suggested that they should turn to the left, but Dr. Wiseman said that when you were not sure which way to go you should always turn to the right, and you would be right. Kotokro had nothing to say against this, so they turned to the right and continued their journey in a high degree of expectation. A foot-path must always lead to a human dwelling. Once they fell in with other men they would eventually find their way back home.

The path grew narrower and narrower as they advanced, and did not appear to be frequently used, as would be the case with one connecting two villages, but it was a foot-path all right, and it kept their hopes high.

At last they came upon a tree that had fallen across the path. The tree was so huge that it must have been about nine feet in diameter. It was impossible for anyone to climb over it without the aid of a ladder, of which there was, of course, none. Fortunately the trunk did not quite touch the ground at the part where it crossed the path. There was enough room for crawling under, but you had to go on your belly to be able to do so.

"Let us go back and take the opposite direction, Doctor," said Kotokro "for it seems to me that this end of the path does not lead to a human dwelling."

"Where else can it lead to?" asked Dr. Wiseman. "A path must always lead to a human dwelling."

"Not necessarily. It depends upon which direction you take. It may lead to a farm, you know."

"I don't know about that. But even if it leads to a farm it must surely come from a human dwelling?"

"I don't dispute that. It seems to me that this path we are following is leading to a farm from a human dwelling."

"Well, let us follow it then. If we arrive at a farm we shall turn back."

Kotokro thought it would be a waste of time and energy to arrive at a farm and then turn back; but Dr. Wiseman was so certain it would lead to a village that he was not prepared to listen to anything to the contrary, so there was nothing he could do but agree to their continuing forward. But there was the tree trunk to be crossed.

"Let us crawl under," suggested Kotokro.

"No, I can't" replied Dr. Wiseman. "You can crawl under if you like, but I must find some other way of getting to the other side."

"What other way?" asked Kotokro.

Dr. Wiseman looked round and saw a very faint track that seemed to go round the fallen tree.

"There seems to be a detour here," he said. "I must follow it."

"All right, Doctor," said Kotokro. "You may do so if you wish. But I shall cross by crawling under the trunk. It is a short cut."

"Short cuts are dangerous," reminded Dr. Wiseman. "So be careful."

"I shall" replied Kotokro.

Kotokro put down the iron trunk he was carrying and pushed it forward under the fallen tree. Then he lay down on his stomach and began to crawl under, pushing the trunk before him as he advanced.

It was not long before he was on the other side. Then he straightened himself up and sat down on top of the box, waiting for the Doctor. Doctor Wiseman for his part, had by now almost reached the base of the fallen tree and was about to rejoin the path. From where he sat, however, Kotokro could not see him, nor could he also see Kotokro. Suddenly, as Kotokro raised up his head to look for him, he saw the Doctor appear high up in the air, with his feet pointing to the sky. At the same time he heard him calling loudly:

"Help! Kotokro, help!"

Kotokro saw at once the Doctor's predicament. He had been caught in a booby-trap which had hoisted him high up by the two feet. Kotokro quickly crawled back under the fallen tree and ran towards the Doctor. He was dangling by his feet from a rope tied to the top of a medium-sized tree which had been bent down to touch the ground and had sprung up with him immediately he stepped into a noose that held it. Kotokro saw at once what he must do to rescue the Doctor from his trying position. He ran back to the path once more and, crawling again under the fallen tree, he brought back the iron trunk. Opening it he took out one of the three ropes and ran with it towards the Doctor.

And now Dr. Wiseman began to demonstrate quite unwittingly that in a position of inverted suspension one's high I.Q. is apt to turn into Q.I., that is to say into Questionable Intelligence; for he proceeded to give instructions to Kotokro, any of which, if the boy had carried out, would have resulted in the learned Doctor's intellectual, if not physical, demise.

"Climb the tree at once and cut me down, for my head is spinning," he called to Kotokro.

"No, Doctor," refused the boy. "If I cut you down you will land on your head and break your neck."

"Then hew down the tree at once, so that I may fall to the ground."

"No, Doctor. If I do that the result will be the same. Your head will be the first to greet the earth and that will do your intelligence no good."

"Then do whatever you think fit to get me down. If you delay another minute everything inside me will rush down into my head."

Kotokro did not delay. There was a very tall tree whose branch overhung the tree on which the doctor was suspended. He quickly climbed this with the rope and tied one end of it to the branch. Then he let the other end down to the doctor and said:

"Doctor, hold this rope and right yourself up."

Dr. Wiseman caught hold of the rope at once and pulled himself up until he found his head facing the sky once more, with his legs still tied to the booby-trap. Then Kotokro quickly descended from the tree.

"Where is the cutlass, Doctor," he enquired.

"It dropped from my hand when I was hoisted up," he replied. "It must be lying somewhere down there. Look for it."

Kotokro searched and searched but could not find it.

At last, just as he was thinking of climbing the tree to untie with his hands the rope which held the Doctor, he espied the cutlass some distance away from the booby-trap. It had been hurled from the Doctor's grasp when the trap sprang up with him. It was fortunate that it landed in an open spot, or Kotokro would never have found it, for almost everywhere here was thick bush.

Kotokro retrieved it at once and proceeded to cut down the tree to which the Doctor was now tied by the feet. It was not a large tree, being only about four inches in diameter, so that it was not long before he brought it down. As it fell, Doctor Wiseman slid down the rope with it and stood on the ground again with his feet. Then Kotokro severed the rope with his pen-knife and set the Doctor free.

"Do you see now, Doctor," said Kotokro "that sometimes it is long cuts that are dangerous? If you had taken the short cut by crawling under the fallen tree with me, you would not have found yourself in that awkward and excruciating position."

"True, my boy," conceded Dr. Wiseman. "One should not take every saying at its face value. If you do you will often land upon your head."

"Which direction shall we take now?" asked Kotokro.

"Let us turn back," replied the Doctor, "for I cannot crawl under the fallen tree and I have no intention of getting myself hoisted up again by taking this detour."

Kotokro at once put the iron trunk on his head once more and they turned back in the direction from which they had come. Dr. Wiseman could only limp along, for he had suffered a sprain in one leg when he was so violently and unceremoniously seized by the trap. Indeed had it not been for the gorilla's skin which protected him he would have been seriously injured in both feet. As it was, he suffered only a sprain in the other foot.

They had gone only a short distance along the path when they heard voices coming from the opposite direction. Kotokro was the first to hear them and he halted and asked Dr. Wiseman to stop and listen. The Doctor listened and confirmed that they were, indeed, human voices.

"We must hail them at once, so that they may know we are here" the Doctor added.

"No, Doctor," Kotokro disagreed. "we must not hail them until we see what kind of people they are."

"Nonsense! If we wait to see them before we decide what to do, don't you think they would have seen us too, so that our lives would be in danger if they turn out to be savages?"

"They will not see us at the same time that we see them."

"How?"

Kotokro had no time to explain, for by now the voices sounded so close that the people, whoever they were, appeared to be almost in sight.

"Quick, Doctor," he said. "Let us hide in that clump of bushes."

With that he made for a clump of bushes that stood quite close to the foot-path. The Doctor followed him still limping. They crawled silently to get into it, so as not to make any sound or disturbance that might betray their presence.

They had hardly settled down and turned to keep watch over the foot-path when two men appeared. They were as naked as the day they were born, and each carried a bow and arrows. They went past where Dr. Wiseman and Kotokro lay concealed without casting a glance in their direction, for they did not seem to have noticed anything unusual. Soon they had reached where the booby-trap had seized Dr. Wiseman. Then exclamations of surprise and anger rent the air. They had apparently come to inspect the trap which they had set for a big game and were amazed and mortified to discover that it had been destroyed by what was obviously a human hand.

They began to talk excitedly in a gibberish tongue, which neither Dr. Wiseman nor Kotokro could understand. They seemed to be swearing and issuing threats against the culprits. After a while they turned round to go back in the direction from which they had come.

All this time Dr. Wiseman and Kotokro had been lying flat on their stomachs as they observed what was going on. But just as the men were about to reach again where they lay concealed, Dr. Wiseman suddenly raised himself up to observe them more closely. Alas! there was a nest of hornets hanging just above him into which he bumped his head. Highly resenting this unprovoked aggression the ireful insects at once fell upon both the Doctor and the unoffending Kotokro in a fierce onslaught. They stung both of them most ferociously.

Screaming with pain the two at once rushed out of their hiding place, forgetful of their fearful appearance and the need to avoid detection. At the sight of them the two naked men immediately turned round and fled with all their might, screaming with terror. Both Kotokro and the Doctor ran after them, calling to them to halt, but the louder they called the faster the two frightened men ran. In a trice they had darted under the fallen tree and were sprinting for dear life. Soon they were out of sight.

It happened that the two naked men were hunters who had come to the bush in the company of ten others who were presently encamped abut half-a-mile away. They had left the camp to inspect a trap which they had set for a buffalo. It was the trap in which Dr. Wiseman had been caught and Kotokro had destroyed by cutting him down.

The two fugitives did not halt until they looked back and saw no one pursuing and no longer heard what they took to be the roar of a lion and a gorilla.

The path by which they were fleeing ended at the brink of a river and led nowhere. So as soon as they felt safe from pursuit they wheeled round and quietly returned through the bush to their camp. They arrived back looking all bruised and like men scared out of their wits.

Flocking around them their companions asked what was the matter. They related the incident, saying that they had gone to inspect their trap only to discover that it had been destroyed by someone. They were returning to the camp when a most extraordinary thing happened. A gorilla and a lion suddenly dashed out of a thicket and, roaring most frightfully, began to chase them. Had they not made the maximum use of their legs their souls and bodies would by now have parted company, the former going to their ancestors and the latter into the belly of the lion.

"But how can a gorilla and a lion travel in company?" their companions asked, not believing their story.

The two swore that they were not lying.

"If you do not believe us then take up your spears and bows and arrows and follow us to the spot. If we don't find them there we shall organise a hunt for them," they said.

The others agreed and immediately seized their weapons and followed them. And so it happened that as Dr. Wiseman and Kotokro were on their way back along the foot-path they suddenly began to hear loud voices coming from the opposite direction.

"It is the cry of hunters, Doctor," said Kotokro. "We are in mortal danger, for they are obviously coming after us."

"What have we done to make anyone come after us?"

"We have scared those two naked men out of their wits by our appearance. I am sure it is they who have gone to tell their companions about our presence and persuaded them to come after us."

Dr. Wiseman saw at once the gravity of the situation.

"Quick, let us run into hiding," he said to Kotokro.

"No, Doctor, these are hunters. If we go into hiding, they will scour the bush until they find us."

"What are we to do then?"

"We must go forward and meet them."

"What! Do you mean I must expose my life to these savages just like that? Do you think I am ignorant of what happens to white men who fall in with savages in Africa? Maybe you may be spared, but certainly not me. Once they lay their hands on me, I shall certainly end in their cooking pot."

Kotokro laughed.

"Oh Doctor," he said. "who told you that all people in Africa who do not wear clothes are savages and will eat you if you happen to come among them?"

"I have seen it in movies and heard it from the authentic accounts of white travellers from Africa."

"I am sure these naked men will not harm us if they discover that we are human beings like themselves. The two men who saw us think we are a gorilla and a lion, and that is why they fled from us and have apparently gone to tell their companions and persuaded them to come after us."

"Well, you bet, at the sight of us they will discharge their arrows into us first and ask questions afterwards; and neither you nor I will be able to answer any of these questions, for the simple reason that our lips will be sealed for ever."

"I am sure they will not do that. They will ask questions first and when we give them answers they will not harm us."

Dr. Wiseman would have insisted on going into hiding, but he was not given the choice; for just at this moment shouts seemed to come from every direction. It was evident that they were beating the bush all around them. In such a situation hiding would be of no avail and might even be more dangerous than going to meet them as Kotokro had suggested.

"Quick, Doctor. Let us undress at once." Kotokro advised.

"Do you mean we must go naked like those savages?" asked Dr. Wiseman incredulously.

"Yes, for if they see us in the guise of animals like this they will slay us before asking any questions."

Very reluctantly Dr. Wiseman unlaced the gorilla's skin and slipped it off. Kotokro did the same with the lion's skin, and at once put both back into the iron trunk and closed it. He had hardly finished doing so when they saw six naked men coming from one direction and another six from another. They were soon surrounded by twelve men who started talking simultaneously, so that it would have been impossible to know what they were saying even if they had spoken in English or in Kotokro's native tongue. As it was, they spoke in a very strange language. It was full of gutturals and sibilants and conveyed no meaning whatsoever to either the Doctor or Kotokro.

Kotokro made signs that they did not understand what they were saying, whereupon they stopped talking and resorted to the use of signs too. They asked what manner of men were the Doctor and Kotokro and where they had come from.

Kotokro replied that they were human beings like themselves and had fallen from the sky in a plane crash, which their interlocutors took to mean that they had come from the sky. A tall young man of about thirty, who happened to be the owner of the booby-trap which had seized Dr. Wiseman, asked if they were the ones who had destroyed the trap. Kotokro replied that they were, and went on to explain the circumstances. The young man became very angry. He asked whether Dr. Wiseman was so lazy that he could not have crawled under the fallen tree and had to go round it by a buffalo's track, with the consequent destruction of his booby-trap which he had set with so much difficulty. Both Dr. Wiseman and Kotokro apologised for what they had done, but it was the intervention of an elderly man of about fifty which prevented the young man from doing them harm. His name was Elder Oloko, as the Doctor and Kotokro learned afterwards.

"Leave them alone," he said to the young man, whose name was Yamogi "for they did not set out deliberately to cause you a loss. And you should rather be sorry for the pain this white man has suffered."

In deference to his admonition Yamogi stayed his hand, but it was evident that he continued to bear resentment, particularly against the Doctor.

The men next asked Dr. Wiseman and Kotokro whether they had seen a gorilla and a lion there. Kotokro replied that they had not. They turned to Yamogi and his friend, Dankida by name, and asked whether these were not the men whom they had seen and had mistaken for a gorilla and a lion. The two swore that these were not. They had seen an actual gorilla and a lion emerging from the bush like two good friends who had immediately rushed to attack them, roaring most frightfully. Had they not fled as fast as they could, they would not have been standing there now to testify to what they had seen. The gorilla was black and the lion had a tawny skin, they added.

Kotokro laughed.

"This is the first time I have heard of a gorilla and a lion travelling together like two friends," he said. "In fact they are two great enemies, who will always fight when they meet, for each claims to be the King of the Forest."

The people laughed too and nodded their heads in agreement. But the two men insisted that what they were saying was true. Whereupon the others burst out into even more hilarious laughter, saying that these two were cowardly men who, through unaccountable fear, had mistaken two human beings for a gorilla and a lion and taken to their heels in consequence.

"If you say you saw a gorilla and a lion then go after them," they added. "But we will not waste our time on a wild goose chase, for we have other things to do in the camp."

With that they turned to go away, taking Dr. Wiseman and Kotokro with them. Yamogi and Dankida also turned and followed them, saying that they alone would not be a match for a gorilla and a lion and would not, therefore, go in pursuit of them.

Dr. Wiseman felt very embarrassed as he and Kotokro followed the men. Hitherto only Kotokro had seen him naked and he was only a boy. He had never appeared naked among so many grown-ups. It was true that the men themselves were naked, but they were used to it and didn't seem to mind. He wondered whether he would also grow used to going naked in the course of time.

After advancing along the foot-path for about a mile they emerged into a large clearing in the middle of the forest. It proved to be the men's hunting camp. There were a dozen single-roomed huts, all disposed in a circle round a shady tree, under which a number of rough wooden benches had been placed.

About ten women, all stark naked, were performing various household chores. Some were cooking, some were sweeping and others were weaving fish-traps.

At the sight of Dr. Wiseman and Kotokro they all stopped working and gazed at them with keen interest. Dr. Wiseman felt so embarrassed that he covered his private parts with his palm and hang down his head like one caught in the commission of a serious crime. Thereupon one of the ladies, a very beautiful young woman in her late twenties, at once rushed forward and, before anyone knew what she was about, removed the Doctor' s hand from under his belly. All the other women at once burst into laughter, which was immediately taken up by the men. They laughed and laughed until the tears ran down the cheeks of some of them. This added so much to the Doctor's embarrassment that he wished with all his heart that the ground would open there and then and swallow him out of sight.

Suddenly he observed that no one paid any attention to Kotokro who was also naked. He wondered why. Was it because he was only a boy? All at once he remembered what Kotokro had said when he was arguing with him about the jig-saw puzzle during the intelligence test: "Where people go naked they don't take any interest in one another's nakedness." Were they taking interest in his nakedness because he had drawn attention to himself by trying to cover up his private parts? he wondered.

He concluded that, that must be the case. If so he must do something to correct the situation.

By now the laughter had died down. The Doctor raised his head and smiled. Then he stepped forward and, before anyone could guess what he was up to, embraced the young woman who had removed his hand from under his belly. He had meant to appear friendly, but alas: he had committed an unforgivable social crime.

The people of Wapito, a tribe in the interior of the Republic of Muccaso to the west, were among the most hospitable of men. If a stranger happened to come among them they would do everything in their power to make him feel at home. If he was a man, his host would even share with him his wife, out of a genuine desire to please without looking for anything in return. It was taboo, however, to touch another man's wife without his permission, even if you went no further than mere embrace. It was among this simple-hearted but morally strict tribe that Dr. Wiseman and Kotokro had found themselves without knowing.

What made the Doctor's crime even worse was that the young woman whom he had embraced was the wife of the very man whose trap had hoisted him up when he stepped into it. This man, Yamogi, still harboured resentment against the Doctor for the destruction of his trap and was anything but mollified by this further act of transgression on the part of Dr. Wiseman. Springing up with indignation he seized two spears, one of which he hurled at the Doctor's feet.

Doctor Wiseman did not know what this meant. He supposed that the man had aimed it at him in a friendly game. Whereupon he picked it up and, in a spirit of friendliness, offered it back to him with a smile. Yamogi angrily snatched it from him and hurled it again at his feet.

"Hey, what does he want?" asked the Doctor, unable to comprehend the man's attitude.

"I think he wants a fight", replied Kotokro.

"A fight? But I have no quarrel with him?"

"No. But I believe he has with you."

"For what?"

"I don't know. But I shall find out."

With that Kotokro turned to the man nearest him and asked, by the use of signs, what that man wanted with the Doctor.

"He is challenging him to a fight with spears," he replied.

"For what?"

"For embracing his wife without his permission."

Kotokro turned round and told Dr. Wiseman.

"You mean he wants to fight a duel with me?" asked the Doctor.

"Yes, a duel. I believe you fight duels in your own country, don't you? Mrs. Casely said that you do."

"Mrs. Casely told you a lot of rubbish. We don't fight duels these days. Only occasionally do you hear of some crazy individual wanting to fight a duel."

"Well, I don't think this man is crazy. It seems to me he is sane and means business."

"Look here, tell him I am sorry. I meant no offence. I merely wanted to be friendly." said Dr. Wiseman.

Kotokro interpreted it to the offended young man.

"He has a strange way of showing friendship," he snapped. "He will not get away with it."

Kotokro told Dr. Wiseman what the man had said; whereupon the Doctor plucked the spear from the ground and threw it away. Then approaching the angry young man he presented his chest to him and said to Kotokro:

"Tell him to kill me. I shall not fight him."

In normal circumstances this brave act of defiance would have been enough to disarm the Doctor's adversary, for the people of Wapito were as chivalrous as they were hospitable and would never strike an unarmed opponent. But the young man was labouring under such a strong sense of injury, fuelled by the laughter which Kotokro's remark had evoked at his expense, that he forgot about all social norms. He raised his spear and, leaning backwards, poised to hurl it at the Doctor's chest. Before he could do so, however, their leader, Elder Oloko, quickly sprang forward and, snatching it from him, broke it into two.

"Shame on you!" he said. "Are you so cowardly and so unmindful of custom that you would strike an unarmed man and a stranger? Remember that this man, who has come from the sky, could not have known anything about our custom, so that he acted in ignorance. And we do not exact penalty from a man who acts in ignorance."

"What did he say?" Dr. Wiseman asked Kotokro.

"I did not quite understand what he said. But it seems to me he told the man that he should not harm you because you acted in ignorance.

"Of course I acted in ignorance. He should have known that," said Dr. Wiseman.

"But, Doctor, is it not said in your own country that ignorance of the law is no excuse?"

"Who told you that?"

"Mrs. Casely."

"Well, we say ignorance of the law, not of custom."

"What is the difference?"

"The difference is that law is written custom, which every member of the community is expected to observe. Custom is unwritten law. Civilised men live by law, but savages like these live by custom."

"I see. It is a lucky thing then that their custom is not written. Otherwise there would have been no excuse for you."

"But I apologised, and he should have been satisfied with that if he were a civilised person."

Meanwhile the angry young man had gone to sit under the tree at the centre of the camp, sulking. Soon afterwards one of the women brought food in a dish and placed it on one of the benches and told Dr. Wiseman and Kotokro that the leader, Elder Oloko, had sent it for them. By now the sun had begun to set and they had not eaten anything since breakfast in the morning, so that they were very hungry. Dr. Wiseman looked at the food. It was some mashed roots with soup and plenty of meat. It looked and smelt good, but he was repelled by the idea of having to eat from the same dish with Kotokro. He did not know what to do.

"Doctor, you may eat as much of it as you like and leave the rest for me," said Kotokro, observing him.

"Are you sure you like it that way?" asked Dr. Wiseman.

"Sure."

Washing his hands Dr. Wiseman fell to. He was so hungry that he demolished more than a fair share of the food before he remembered that he must leave some for Kotokro. But he had no need for regret; for as Kotokro was sitting down to eat what was left, the woman brought more food, so that the boy had more than enough to assuage his hunger.

Kotokro had hardly finished eating when three large dishes filled with the same kind of food were brought by other women and placed on the ground beneath the tree. Thereupon all the men gathered round and started to eat, four to a dish. As Dr. Wiseman watched them he began to wonder how they managed to avoid communicating their diseases to one another.

After everyone had eaten, the men made a bonfire and sat round it to chat. Then their leader asked Dr. Wiseman and Kotokro to tell them more precisely how they happened to fall from the sky. With some difficulty Kotokro managed to recount, by means of signs, how the Doctor had come and taken him from his home to the white man's country; how he had stayed there for one year; how he was bringing him back through the air when the machine in which they were travelling crashed to the ground; how he and the Doctor were the only survivors out of more than a hundred passengers, how they had stayed in the jungle for more than two years, after repeated failures to find their way to some human habitation, and how in their third serious attempt they had at last succeeded in coming among them.

"So you come from Gamberia and this man from the whiteman's country?" they asked when he had finished.

"Yes,"

"Why then do you speak the same language?"

"The language we speak is the white man's language. I learnt it when I was in his country."

"You were able to learn it in one year?"

"Yes.

"Then it must be a very easy language."

Kotokro replied that it was not at all easy. They had so many words for expressing the same idea that, unless you had a very large vocabulary, you might not be able to understand half the things they said.

After this Kotokro was also able to extract from them some information about themselves, all through the use of signs. They told him they belonged to the Wapito tribe in the Republic of Muccaso which bordered on the east of the Republic of Gamberia. Their village, called Fomaki, was a day's journey away from the camp. They had come from there to hunt and trap animals, and they usually remained in camp for a week before returning home with their catches. They had come only the day before and might have to remain there for another six days before returning, unless they were able to bag enough game sooner. They came to the camp once every month, and after six months they took their catches, in the form of smoked meat, to the Republic of Blohim, which bordered on the west of Muccaso, to sell for gold. They remained there for about four months. When they eventually returned to their village they rested for another two months, after which they set out for the Republic of Gamberia to buy salt and other articles with their gold.

Kotokro asked how far away was their village from the border with Gamberia. They replied that it was a month's journey away. They had to go by foot-paths and sleep in villages on the way. If one did not know the way one could very easily get lost. They bought the salt and other merchandise from the trading centre of Hoba on the River Mambadimpo, inside Gamberia and four day's journey away from the Gamberia-Muccaso border.

Both Dr. Wiseman and Kotokro were delighted to hear this, for they knew that once they arrived at Hoba they would be as good as back home. It was clear, however, that they had many more months to wait before that could happen; for they had to spend six more days in the jungle, twelve months at the village of Fomaki and one month on the way to Hoba, making a total of thirteen months and six days.

They asked if upon their return to Fomaki they would not get a guide to take them to Hoba at once, as they would find it tedious to wait for them until they were going to Hoba. They replied that it was not a journey that could be performed by three or even four men, for it was full of many hazards. Not less than a dozen men travelled on every occasion. Dr. Wiseman and Kotokro concluded, therefore, that they had no option but to wait.

They had supper just before sunset. Then Elder Oloko showed them into a room in one of the huts, where they slept on deer skins with stuffed antelope skins as pillows for their heads.

CHAPTER SEVENTEEN
DR. WISEMAN GETS LOST IN THE JUNGLE

During the following five days Kotokro always followed the men to the hunt and the inspection of their traps, while Dr. Wiseman stayed behind in the camp with the women. They always left early in the morning, taking their food with them, and returned late in the afternoon.

Dr. Wiseman tried to occupy his time with learning the Wapito language while the men were away. He had as his tutor the wife of elder Oloko, Madam Fantani. He, however, made little progress, for he found the language very difficult, so that in five days he had only learnt to say "Wotu dika?," meaning "How do you do?"

Kotokro, on the other hand, learnt the language very quickly. He had no formal instruction but picked it up simply by listening to the men's conversation as they went through the bush. In three days he had managed to learn all the greetings and many simple words of command.

And now the time came for the men to return home. The sixth day after Dr. Wiseman and Kotokro came into the camp Elder Oloko informed them that they would depart very early on the morning of the day after the morrow. Dr. Wiseman and Kotokro were very happy to hear this, although they knew that even after they reached the village of Fomaki they would still have to spend more than a year there before setting out for Gamberia. However they found welcome the prospect of living in a more permanent abode and among many more people than with only a few men and women in a camp in the bush. Besides, it might even be possible to find some means of leaving the place earlier than they had been told.

As Dr. Wiseman lay in bed that night he tried hard to fall asleep, so that the night would pass quickly by, bringing back another day. But instead of falling asleep thoughts began to chase themselves interminably in his mind. He thought of all he and Kotokro had had to endure since they suffered the air-crash in the jungle, his mind dwelling more particularly on their miraculous escape from dangers and his disappointment over the city of ant-hills. Suddenly, just before daybreak, he fell asleep.

He woke up late the next morning and found that Kotokro and the men had already left for the hunt. Then he remembered their impending departure from the camp the next day and thought of all he would have to tell of their long stay in the jungle when he eventually arrived back in London - how he nearly ended in the belly of a python, how he was saved by a lion from the deadly blow of a gorilla, and all the many perils and bizarre adventures he and Kotokro had gone through. It occurred to him, there and then, that he had made a mistake in not bringing with him some of the artefacts he and Kotokro had made. These would have gone a long way in gaining credibility for his story. But at the time they were leaving he had only thought of his safety, not of the story he would tell once back home. Anyhow it was not too late, he decided. A whole day still remained before their departure. He could go back to their house in the jungle and bring some of those objects before noon.

Having thus made up his mind Dr. Wiseman immediately set out without informing anyone, so that when Elder Oloko's wife brought him his breakfast he was nowhere to be seen. The lady concluded that he had gone into the bush to attend nature's call, so she set his food down in the hut and went away.

Meanwhile Dr. Wiseman was vigorously pursuing his way back to their jungle home, still thinking of how valuable those artefacts would be, once he managed to get them to London. He might even be able to sell them for large sums of money if he wished. Any collector of primitive art would happily grab them for almost any amount he would ask for.

He was so preoccupied with thoughts of his impending return to safety and to fortune that he went past the place where they had emerged into the foot-path without noticing it. On and on he went, until he was only a short distance away from where he fell into the booby-trap. Then he saw a faint track which he immediately mistook for that by which they had come. Branching into it he continued his way as briskly as he could, determined to be back even before the men returned to the camp.

He proceeded for a long distance without reaching the river which they had crossed when they set out from their abode. Then he began to get worried, for by calculation he should have arrived at his destination long ago.

The trail grew fainter and fainter until it was no longer visible. Then for the first time it dawned upon him that he was lost. Panic seized him. And now he began to wish he had come with Kotokro; for the boy could find his way through the jungle as well as any animal in the bush. But it was now too late. He should have thought of it the previous evening and informed him, so that he would not have gone away with the men in the morning. Well, he must try and find his way as best he could. Kotokro had said that no two trees in the jungle were exactly alike. But to him they all appeared the same and he had never learnt to notice any difference. If only he had, he would not have been in this predicament.

He tried to retrace his steps. He could not, for he had blazed no trail as he went along, not having brought the cutlass with him. He became more and more confused, not knowing what direction to take. At last he decided to just keep on going. He was bound to arrive somewhere. Who knew, he might even unexpectedly arrive back in the camp.

By now he had been gone for about four hours and was traversing a part of the jungle that looked distinctly different. The trees were smaller and grew more sparsely, but with thick undergrowths. The undergrowths were so thick that they concealed the ground completely and he had to tread without knowing what he might be stepping on.

How he wished he had brought the cutlass, so that he could at least have cut his way through them.

He had not advanced for more than half-an-hour in this terrain when he suddenly burst upon a bog. It was about four hundred yards across and seemed to curve convexly in a semi-circle. Looking across he discovered that it was the other side of the very bog from which he and Kotokro had retreated when they made their second unsuccessful attempt to escape from the jungle. If only he could cross it and get to the other side he was sure he would be able to find the way to his destination. But there was no way he could cross that formidable morass. And even if he could do so, how would he be able to cross the smaller one which he and Kotokro had crossed by ropes?

He thought and thought. He could find no way out. Then it occurred to him that his best course of action would be to skirt the bog. Since he had unexpectedly found himself on the other side of it, it meant that it did not stretch endlessly; otherwise they would have come across it again in their third attempt to get away. Having arrived at this decision he immediately turned to his right and proceeded along, keeping as close as possible to the border of the treacherous slough.

The ground continued to be hidden by thick undergrowths, making it very difficult for him to hurry. And now the day was far spent and the night was closing in. He became more and more alarmed. He must return to the camp before nightfall or give up any hope of survival. With so many wild beasts prowling the jungle at night, it would be a miracle if he lived to see another day. He quickened his pace, not caring very much what he might be stepping on, for now it was so dark that he could hardly see the ground.

Suddenly, as he took a step forward, the ground gave way under his feet. Before he could recover his balance he found himself going down, down as if into the bowels of the earth. He had fallen into a pit. He landed at the bottom, with a thud, on a heap of leaves that had accumulated there over a long period of time. It was a pit dug by hunters for trapping big game. Fortunately for him it was not too deep, being only about eleven feet below the ground.

He tried to climb back. He could not, for the sides were sheer and very slippery with moss. What was he to do now? Out of panic he started to yell for help. But his voice only reverberated from side to side in the pit without coming out, so that even if someone had happened to be nearby he could hardly have been heard. How he wished Kotokro had been around. The boy could easily have rescued him with one of his ropes. He now realised for the first time how much he had owed his survival in the jungle to that unintelligent boy. From the time he fell into the ravine from the plane, to the time they arrived in the hunters' camp the boy had always been his saviour from mortal dangers.

Meantime there was alarm in the hunters' camp. When the men returned from the bush late in the afternoon Kotokro was surprised to see the Doctor's breakfast sitting in the hut untouched.

The Doctor himself was not around. He asked where he had gone, but no one seemed to know. Madam Fantani explained that when she brought the breakfast that morning the Doctor was not in the hut, but she had imagined that he had only gone to the bush to attend nature's call and would soon be back. When he was not back by mid-day she and all the other women had concluded that he had joined the men and would return with them in the late afternoon. She was surprised to see them return without him.

Kotokro became greatly alarmed. Where could the Doctor have gone the whole day? He decided to inform Elder Oloko and implore him to organise a search for him without delay, for the day was already far spent and darkness would soon set in.

Elder Oloko was equally concerned when Kotokro told him what had happened. He immediately summoned the men and arranged that they should divide themselves into two parties of six, one party to take the path leading to the north and the other the path leading to the south, in search of the missing Doctor.

Kotokro decided to join the party going to the south, for that was the direction from which he and the Doctor had come into the camp. It occurred to him that Dr. Wiseman might have gone back to their house in the jungle to retrieve something he had left behind, although he could not imagine what it could be. He quickly led the men to the place. They arrived there just when the sun was going down, only to find that the Doctor was not there. Kotokro became even more alarmed. Unless Dr. Wiseman returned to the camp before nightfall there was little hope of his survival in that beast-infested jungle.

When they returned to the camp darkness had already set in. They found that the others had also come back without the Doctor.

That evening Kotokro was unable to eat his food, due to anxiety, and was hardly able to sleep throughout the night. He kept on waking and pricking up his ears at the least sound emanating from outside, in the expectation that the Doctor had returned.

On waking up again well after mid-night he detected a faint sound seeming to come from far away. He strained his ears to listen. Yes, there was no doubt about it. It was the growl of wolves. A pang of fear shot through his heart. The Doctor must have fallen among those carnivorous beasts who were growling as they struggled over his carcase.

The growl continued for a long time. Then all of a sudden he heard the roar of a lion. Thereupon the growling ceased and was followed, soon afterwards, by a piercing cry, as of some animal in pain. It had hardly died down when a strong wind arose, followed by lightning and thunder and the loud patter of rain. Soon a heavy downpour descended from the sky. It rained very hard but intermittently until daybreak. Kotokro had been unable to close his eyes in sleep for the rest of the night.

As for Dr. Wiseman, as soon as he realised the hopelessness of his situation he stopped calling for help; for he began to fear lest his shouts would only invite some dangerous animal to where he was, with terrible consequence to his life. But alas! his shouts had already had that effect. A pack of wolves prowling some distance away from where he was, heard him and made for that direction.

It was not long before they smelt precisely his whereabouts, even after he ceased calling.

Being quite exhausted with his long walk through the jungle he had stretched himself on the cushion of leaves at the bottom of the pit to rest when he suddenly heard the growl of a wolf coming from the ground above. He looked up and saw, to his horror, the dim figure of some huge beast standing at the brink and looking down into the pit. He rose to his feet at once; whereupon there was an even fiercer growl, which was immediately joined by the fearful cry of a pack of wolves.

The Doctor gave himself up for lost. At any moment those savage creatures would jump down into the pit and make an end of him. He shut his eyes and awaited his doom.

He waited and waited, but nothing happened. Instead the growling grew in volume as more and more of those dreadful beasts seemed to join the pack. Then he began to wonder what they were waiting for. Why had none of them jumped down into the pit? Was it because they all feared lest he might put up a fight?

Suddenly there was silence. Then he faintly heard a sound which he recognised at once as that of a lion. A few moments later he heard the cry of pain from some animal in the distance. This lasted only a few seconds, when there was silence again.

Dr. Wiseman had no idea of what had happened. But whatever it was, it brought him some hope that all might not yet be lost, and that at least he might still live a few hours longer.

What had actually happened was that as soon as the wolves heard the roar of a lion they were all seized with panic, as one of their most dreaded enemies is a lion. They fled helter and skelter. But alas! the lion had already espied them and gave chase. It had no difficulty at all in grabbing one of them. Thereupon the unfortunate creature set up a cry of anguish as the pitiless brute assuaged its hunger in the same way as its victim would have filled its stomach with the flesh of Dr. Wiseman. It was this last sound which, unpleasant as it was to the Doctor's ears, had brought a pleasant end to his immediate predicament.

But Dr. Wiseman was scarcely out of danger yet, as he himself fully realised. Yet when the danger came it was hardly of the kind or from the quarter he had anticipated.

It had been warm and damp in the pit when he fell into it. But not long after the sound ceased he felt a gentle breeze playing around his naked body. Then the inside of the pit began to cool. It was a great relief, for he had been sweating profusely. But when the significance suddenly dawned upon him panic seized him once more. It became clear to him that this meant a sudden change in the weather, heralding the coming of rain. Not only would he be soaked to the skin, but if it rained hard for a long period of time, as African rains are wont to do, he might drown from the water that would surely fill the pit.

He had hardly arrived at this conclusion when he heard a violent wind raging through the wood above. He could hear the trees lashing one another with their branches as they swayed this way and that. Now and again there was the sound of a snapping branch and the heavy groan of a tree as it gave way to the irresistible force of the wind and came crashing down.

Suddenly a bright light flashed in the pit, followed almost immediately by a loud explosion and protracted rumblings in the sky. A storm was fast approaching. The flash of lightning, the explosion and the rumbling increased in intensity until he suddenly heard the loud patter of rain throughout the jungle. Drops struck his forehead, then his pate, then his shoulders, then all over his body. And now it seemed as if a sluice in the sky had been opened. The rain came down in torrents, pouring upon him in a heavy deluge.

Water began to rush into the pit. At first it came only in trickles over the sides, then the trickles turned into a stream and then into a flood. And now the water began to fill the pit. It came up to Dr. Wiseman's feet, then to his knees, then to his waist, then to his stomach and finally to his neck. Only his head rose above the water now. He got ready to swim.

Suddenly the rain stopped. Gradually the water in the pit began to seep into the soil, decreasing in volume. It dropped down to his shoulders, then to his waist, then to his knees. Dr. Wiseman's hope of survival began to revive.

All of a sudden the lull was broken again and the heavy downpour resumed. The pit began to fill up once more. The water came up to his waist again, then to his shoulders and then to his neck. Still the downpour continued. Finally the water was deep enough to cover him up completely. At this point he began to swim, thus managing to float at the surface.

And now the water had carried him almost up to the brink. He stretched out his hand but it failed to grasp the upper edge of the pit, for he was still about three feet away from the ground above. He began to hope that the rain would continue, so as to fill the pit completely and so bring him out of danger.

Alas! His hope was soon dashed again. For just at this moment the rain began to die down and once more the water in the pit started to seep through the soil as before, until, when he stretched his legs, they touched the bottom of the pit once more. He was back to where he had started.

The water had hardly disappeared again from the pit when the rain recommenced for the third time. It began to fill the pit as before, until it came up to his neck again. Suddenly the rain ceased altogether. The water in the pit came down and down again until he stood at the bottom of the pit for the fourth time.

By now it was almost dawn, as he could tell by the light that dimly penetrated into the pit. It was not long before bright daylight fully illuminated his open grave. Very tired and shivering with cold he sat down on the wet leaves to rest.

Meantime Kotokro had risen out of bed and gone to implore Elder Oloko to ask his men to delay their departure for the day, so that they might organise a search for the Doctor as on the previous evening. The latter replied that he did not think the men would agree to this, as they had already made preparations for setting out that morning. However, he would put his request to them and hear what they would say.

Having summoned the men together Elder Oloko informed them of Kotokro's request. The first to reply was Yamogi. He said that it was asking too much to ask that the men should delay their departure for another day merely on account of a stranger who had walked away from the camp for reasons best known to himself. They had already organised a thorough search for him the previous day without success. With so many wild beasts prowling the jungle, and with the heavy rain that had fallen during the night, it was impossible that the man would still be alive. It would therefore be a waste of time to go searching for him once more.

He was supported by his companion, Dankida, who added that even before the rain began he had heard the wolves growling in the forest, as if they had caught and were devouring a prey. He was sure it was the Doctor they were feasting upon. They should therefore forget about organising another search for him. If they did they would not be able to find even a bone belonging to the Doctor. Those ravenous creatures were particularly fond of bones and would leave none of the Doctor's as a remnant after devouring his flesh.

Kotokro disagreed with both of them. He remained hopeful that the Doctor was still alive.

"I heard the growl of the wolves too," he confirmed "but this lasted for some time and was followed by the roar of a lion. Now, it is common knowledge, at least in my country, that wolves do not growl when they have caught a prey. Like dogs, who are their kin, they growl when they have their prey at bay. After seizing it they no longer growl or howl as they struggle for its flesh. My conclusion, therefore, is that they must have seen the Doctor sitting on top of a tree, quite out of their reach. They set up the growl to scare him down, but they must have fled immediately they heard the roar of a lion."

"Now that you mention it, I remember hearing the roar of a lion too, followed soon after by a piercing cry," said Dankida. "That conclusively proves that even if the Doctor managed to avoid being devoured by the wolves he eventually ended in the belly of a lion."

"Not necessarily," disagreed Kotokro again. "The cry of anguish that followed the roar of the lion was not that of a man. It was the cry of a beast, and must have come from one of the wolves as it was being devoured by the lion. No, if the Doctor had sought refuge on top of a tree, as I am sure he must have done, no wild beast could have got at him, and he must still be alive."

"You forget that leopards and other wild beasts can climb trees, even if wolves and lions can't" intervened Yamogi. "So even if he was safe from the wolves and the lions, he could not have escaped the jaws of those other man-eaters, of whom there is quite a large population in this jungle."

"Yes," agreed Dankida. "And even if he managed to escape being devoured by any wild beast by climbing a tree, remember that there was a fierce storm during the night, as Yamogi has pointed out. Only a witch could live through that storm to see another day. Altogether I think we are only wasting our time by discussing this matter. The man is dead and gone, and nothing we say or do can bring him back."

"You say that only a witch could live through that storm to see another day," rejoined Kotokro. "But both the Doctor and I lived through even worse storms in the jungle for over a period of more than one and half years."

"Then you two must be witches," pronounced Yamogi.

"No, we are not," replied Kotokro "Only the gorilla and the lion which you saw walking hand in hand, like two good friends, could be witches."

This rejoinder provoked immediate and prolonged laughter from the rest of the men who had hitherto remained silent listeners to the exchanges between Kotokro, on the one hand, and Yamogi and Dankida on the other. It was obviously a jibe directed at the two men, and it had the desired effect of shutting them up.

"And now," resumed Kotokro when the laughter had died down "since it seems no one is prepared to sacrifice his time to help me find the Doctor I shall do so alone. You can all go away and leave me here to manage as best I can. Good bye." And with that he turned to go away.

"Stop, boy" one young man of about twenty-five said, stepping forward. He was the younger brother of Yamogi's wife. His name was Securri. "I see sense in everything this boy has said," he continued, turning to Elder Oloko. "I shall therefore go with him to look for the white man. We cannot leave him here alone, because he may not be able to find his way to our village even if he succeeds in finding his companion. Let the others, therefore, go away. I shall remain with him."

"I am glad you have volunteered to remain with the boy," Elder Oloko said, speaking for the first time. "Whether his hope of finding his companion is justified or not we cannot refuse him help, as a stranger; for the gods have divers ways of putting to the test the virtues which men profess, and they often do this through strangers. Remain with him, therefore, and help him to look for his companion. We all pray that you may find him alive and bring him safe and sound to our village where warm welcome awaits every stranger."

The others agreed to this arrangement. As for Yamogi and his friend, Dankida, they were far from satisfied. If they had had their way Kotokro would have been left there to perish with the Doctor. Yamogi resented the Doctor for the two wrongs he had done him, by being the cause of the destruction of his trap and by embracing his wife without his permission; and both he and Dankida hated Kotokro for the jokes which he was always cracking at their expense. However, there was nothing they could do against the will of the others, so they held their peace.

Immediately after breakfast the hunters and their wives set out on their return to their village, leaving Kotokro and Securri behind. They also left for them enough food to last them and the Doctor, in case they found him, for three days.

Kotokro and Securri set out almost at the same time to look for Dr. Wiseman. The former took with him two ropes and the cutlass, while the latter carried a spear and a bow and arrows.

It occurred to Kotokro that Dr. Wiseman might have gone back to the city of ant-hills. The Doctor had not yet given up his grandiose plans concerning the place and had referred again and again to the enormous wealth that he would make from turning it into a tourist attraction. He had probably gone there to take a last look and had lost his way. They must, therefore, turn their search in that direction. He explained it to Securri, who agreed that they must, indeed, look for the Doctor there.

They advanced along the path leading to the fallen tree, close to which Dr. Wiseman had been caught in Yamogi's booby-trap. It was not long before they arrived at the place where Kotokro and the Doctor had first emerged from the bush into the foot-path. In spite of the night's heavy rain which had obliterated their track, Kotokro was able to find his way towards their destination by just observing and recognising the trees which he and the Doctor had come across on their way from their abode in the jungle.

They soon came to the river and did not have much difficulty in crossing it, even though it was now in floods from the previous night's heavy rain. Securri, who was a very tall young man, being over six feet, simply carried Kotokro on his shoulders and waded with him through it. At its deepest point the water came up only to his chest, so that Kotokro did not get wet in any way. It was a fortunate thing that this young man came with him, otherwise he would have had to turn back or take the highly dangerous risk of swimming across that turbulent water.

Landing on the other side of the river they quickly made their way towards the city of ant-hills. They arrived there just before noon, only to find that the Doctor had not been there, for they examined the whole place minutely without finding any trace of him. They retraced their steps and crossed the river again to the other side.

And now Kotokro could not decide which way to turn in search of the missing Doctor. He looked all round and could see no track anywhere, save that by which they themselves had come. After some deliberation with himself he turned downstream and asked Securri to follow.

They went on and on until they found themselves in a terrain quite different from any they had traversed so far. The trees were smaller and more sparse, with undergrowths which were so thick that they concealed the ground completely. With his cutlass, however, Kotokro who was leading, began to cut their way through the undergrowths.

Suddenly something attracted his attention. He saw a spot in the undergrowths that seemed deeply crushed as if some heavy object had fallen there. Almost at the same time he also saw a short tree stump which looked as if someone had stumbled against it.

"Look," he said, turning to Securri who had been following closely behind. "Some creature must have stumbled against this stump and fallen down there. I don't think it was a gorilla. It must be a man, because no gorilla could have stumbled and fallen down. It could only have lain down here if it wanted to rest. But if so, it would have first made a bed with twigs. There is no such bed here, so this cannot be the work of a gorilla. A man must have fallen or lain here to rest."

Just as he finished speaking he saw several broken twigs marking a trail forward.

"Ah, yes," he continued. "It is definitely a man. I see several broken twigs. A gorilla does not blaze a trail like that when it goes through the bush."

"You are quite right," agreed Securri. "A gorilla normally moves along fixed tracks and does not mark a new trail through an unknown terrain. Let us hail your friend then. If he is anywhere nearby he will respond."

Kotokro agreed, and together they set up a shout for the Doctor. For some time there was no response. But as they continued to advance along the trail marked by the broken twigs Kotokro suddenly heard a faint sound. He stopped to listen. It was not repeated. He turned round to Securri and asked if had heard the sound. He confirmed that he had.

"Let us call again," suggested Kotokro.

They did so. A faint sound was heard in response, which continued even after they stopped calling. Kotokro was now certain that it was the Doctor who was answering. However, he decided to be cautious, in case it proved to be a gorilla; for he remembered how that terrible beast came to their house in the jungle when Dr. Wiseman responded to its calls. However, as the voice became more and more audible as they approached its source, it became quite clear that it did not come from a gorilla. It definitely came from a man.

And now they were close to the source of that sound. They were not sure, however, whether it was coming from the ground or the top of a tree.

"Where are you, Doctor?" shouted Kotokro.

"I am here" replied Dr. Wiseman feebly.

"Where"

"In this pit."

Kotokro kept his eyes fixed upon the ground. Guided by the Doctor's continued responses he and Securri soon found themselves at the brink of the pit in which the unfortunate man stood shivering with cold and hunger. Using the two ropes which Kotokro had brought they soon hauled him up to safety.

Dr. Wiseman's joy knew no bounds. He rushed forward and hugged Kotokro and patted his crinkled hair.

"Thank you, thank you, my boy," he said repeatedly. "I never expected to get out of this pit alive, for I reckoned that you had already gone away with those natives and that I was doomed to perish in this open grave."

Kotokro narrated to him all that had happened since he was found missing: how they had organised a search for him the previous day without success; how when the time came for the men to go away he had tried to get them all to search for him again but had been opposed by Yamogi and Dankida, and how Securri had been the only one who had offered to assist him in a renewed search.

Dr. Wiseman shook hands with Securri when Kotokro had finished and told him that he had done well.

"When I get back to England I shall send you a beautiful coat and trousers together with a pair of shoes, a shirt, a tie and a bowler hat to match, so that you will be dressed, like a civilised man," he promised him.

"I don't want to be dressed, like a civilised man!" snapped Securri.

"Strange," commented Dr. Wiseman. "You mean you are happy to go about like this, with your bell tolling in front of you?"

Securri replied that he was, for he had nothing to hide or be ashamed of. Only those who had unsightly blemishes on their bodies concealed them with clothes.

"Ah well, that settles it then" replied Dr. Wiseman with a shrug of the shoulders. "Anyhow I thank you all the same for your help."

"Thank you too, for thanking me." replied Securri; "for that was all I needed from you."

Kotokro asked the Doctor what had made him leave the camp to come and fall into a pit. He told him.

"Why didn't you ask me instead to go for them?" asked Kotokro.

"I thought of it only after you had gone with the men," he replied. "And I could not wait for you to return, for then it would have been too late."

"Do you still want those articles then?"

"I do. They will be worth thousands of Pounds in London."

"All right; I shall fetch them for you then. Meantime you can return to the camp with Securri while I go for them."

"No, let us all go together," replied Dr. Wiseman. "I must not be left alone in the company of this savage. He may be a cannibal, you know. And you may return to find me gone."

"But I was left alone in his company, and not only did nothing happen to me but he also proved very kind and helpful."

"You are different. You are his kind, being black like himself."

"Then between the two of us you will provide an excellent meal," Kotokro replied, laughing.

"I know I am safe when you are around" replied Dr Wiseman "for your acquaintance with our civilized way of life has made you reasonable and humane?"

"Are these people then, who know nothing about your civilised way of life, not reasonable and humane?" asked Kotokro.

"Who ever heard of savages being reasonable and humane? If they were they wouldn't be savages."

"What are you two talking about?" asked Securri who had stood listening to their conversation without the faintest idea as to what they were discussing.

"We are discussing whether all three of us should go to our house in the jungle for those handicraft which the Doctor wants to take away with him, or whether he and I should do so while you go back to the camp to await our return," replied Kotokro.

"Nonsense" said Securri. "The Doctor must be very tired and hungry after his ordeal in this pit. So you two must return to the camp in order that he may have some food and rest. I shall go to your house in the jungle and fetch the articles he wants."

Kotokro interpreted to Dr. Wiseman what he had said.

"Does he know the place?" asked the Doctor.

"He does," replied Kotokro, "for I went there with him in the company of four others when we were searching for you yesterday."

"Good. Then let him go and bring them. What I want are all the earthenware you made, the fish traps and the bow and arrows. He must put them all into the big basket which you wove."

"They are too many, Doctor," Kotokro pointed out. "We cannot carry all those things away."

"What do you mean we cannot carry all those things away?" asked Dr. Wiseman. "We are not going to carry them. It is this savage who is going to do so for us, and he is strong enough to carry twice as much."

"But suppose after bringing them to the camp he refuses to carry them any further, how can we take them all with us, when you cannot carry any?"

"Never mind about that. He will not refuse to carry them further after bringing them to the camp. If he does we shall then take with us the few that you can carry and leave the rest behind. But we must not leave some in the house in the expectation that we cannot convey them all from the camp to this man's village."

"But we still have to consider that even if I carry some to this man's village I may not be able to convey them to Gamberia, for as these men have told us, it is a month's journey away from their village."

"My boy," said Dr. Wiseman impatiently. "Do not cross your bridge before you reach it. At any point that we have to leave some or all behind, we shall do so."

"All right, Doctor," Kotokro yielded at last. "Let him bring all, as you say. I shall tell him so."

With that he turned to Securri and told him what the Doctor had said.

"Are they many?" asked Securri.

"They are. But the Doctor thinks you are strong enough to bring them all."

"All right, I shall try, provided they will not break my neck."

"What does he say?" asked Dr. Wiseman.

"He says he will try to bring them all."

"I knew he would."

Kotokro and Dr. Wiseman set out for the camp while Securri went to bring the handicraft as promised. When they reached the camp they ate some of the food that had been left for them and rested.

Securri did not return to the camp until towards sunset. He came looking very tired. His neck was almost breaking under the heavy load of pots, plates, water-pots and drinking cups which he carried. Besides what he had on his head Dr. Wiseman's bow and arrows also hung from his shoulders.

He deposited them on the ground under the shady tree and sat down holding his neck in his hands and sweating profusely. It was Kotokro who first spoke.

"Well done," he said. "I never thought you would be able to bring all these articles. Why didn't you bring only as much as you could conveniently carry?"

"A promise is a promise", he replied. "I promised to bring them all provided I would not break my neck. Well, I did not know whether or not I would break my neck until I was actually carrying them. And, as you see, I did not break my neck, although I was not very far from doing so."

"Thank you very much then. You have been very helpful" said Kotokro.

"What are you two talking about?" asked Dr. Wiseman who had not said a word hitherto.

Kotokro told him.

"I knew that, that brawny neck of his wouldn't break under any amount of load," he commented. "And I am sure it wont break when he carries them for us on our journey to the village."

Kotokro said nothing. And he was glad when Securri did not ask him to tell him what the Doctor had said. He would have either had to lie or tell him exactly what he had said. Either alternative would have made him feel very uncomfortable indeed.

After Securri had eaten he said that it was now too late for them to think of setting out for the village. If they did, they would have to travel in the night and that could be very risky, for many wild beast prowled on the path at night. The men knew that they would not be able to leave for the village that day, whether they found the Doctor or not, and that was why they had left enough food to last them for three days. They should, therefore, spend the night there and set out the next morning.

There was nothing Dr. Wiseman and Kotokro could do but abide by Securri's advice. So they went to bed early that evening in eager expectation of the morrow.

When they opened their eyes again it was daybreak. Kotokro woke up Securri who was still fast asleep. The previous day's labour had truly affected his energy, for he was normally an early riser.

After they had performed their morning ablutions and taken breakfast they got ready to set out for the village of Fomaki. Dr. Wiseman suggested that Kotokro should carry the trunk while Securri carried the basket of artefacts. He himself would hold the bow and arrows and the cutlass. Kotokro interpreted it to Securri.

"I will not carry for him one hair from his beard," snapped Securri.

"He says he cannot carry them," Kotokro interpreted it to Dr. Wiseman.

"Do you see that?" commented Dr. Wiseman. "These people are unreasonable. After conveying these articles all the way to this camp he refuses to carry them any further. Why did he bring them when he knew that he would not carry them further?"

"What did he say?" asked Securri, who had been watching the Doctor's lips as he spoke.

"He said that you should not have brought them if you knew that you would not carry them to the village," Kotokro interpreted.

"Did I bargain with him to convey them from here to the village? I only promised to bring them to this place and I have fulfilled that promise."

"Well, never mind," said Dr. Wiseman with resignation when it was interpreted to him. "I shall carry the bow and arrows and the cutlass. And you, Kotokro, may bring with you in the trunk as much of the handicraft as you can carry."

Kotokro could add only three plates and two cups to what he already had in the iron trunk, for even when empty, the trunk was heavy enough. They had to leave behind all the rest of the articles, much to Dr. Wiseman's anger with Securri for thus making him lose so much fortune. Then the three of them set out for Fomaki, with Securri leading the way and Dr. Wiseman bringing up the rear.

The journey to Fomaki proved to be long and arduous. The foot-path by which they were travelling was narrow and even appeared in places like mere hunter's trail, several of which branched from it, so that without Securri to lead them Dr. Wiseman and Kotokro could not easily have found their way. Many trees had also fallen across the path, and they had to crawl under, cross over, or go round some of them by detours.

Now and again they came upon a stream through which they had to wade. One or two were so swollen with floods that they could not have crossed without the assistance of Securri, who occasionally carried both Kotokro and his trunk on his shoulder when the water was too deep for him, and supported Dr. Wiseman by holding his hand when he was in danger of being swept away.

Towards noon they came upon a sight that shattered once and for all, Dr. Wiseman's dream of making a fortune out of the city of ant-hills. This was no less than miles and miles of open tract covered with thousands of ant-hills that were much bigger and more artistically wrought than any he had yet set eyes upon. When he first caught sight of them he thought that they had arrived at their destination.

"This is capital!" he exclaimed with admiration.

"No, it can't be their capital," contradicted Kotokro who had misunderstood what he meant. "It is merely another city of ant-hills, more splendid than the one you saw."

Securri confirmed that it was as Kotokro had said, and that there were many more like this scattered all over Wapito-land, and even far beyond into the neighbouring territories.

"Truly ex Africa a liquid semper novi," murmured Dr. Wiseman under his breath.

"What does that mean?" asked Kotokro whose sharp ears had caught the Doctor's words but could extract no meaning from them.

"It means there are many surprises in Africa."

"And this is one of them?"

"And this is one of them"

"Are there no surprises in your own country?" asked Kotokro.

"Certainly not. Who ever heard of surprises in a civilised country?"

"What do you mean by surprises then?" asked Kotokro.

"By surprises we mean things that are strange and unexpected."

"Strange to whom?"

"Strange to the beholder who has never seen the like before."

"And is there nothing in your country which a beholder from elsewhere has never seen before?"

"Certainly not."

"But I saw a Zoo, an underground railway and the Stonehenge, which I had never seen before."

"You did. But there was nothing strange about those."

By now they were just about to re-enter the forest from the open terrain. Kotokro was going to say something again when Securri suddenly stopped and pricked up his ears.

"Listen," he said, turning to Kotokro.

Kotokro listened but could hear nothing at first. Then gradually a droning sound, as of an aeroplane flying at a great height, began to gain upon his ears. A few seconds later, as the sound increased in volume, Dr. Wiseman heard it too.

"It is an aeroplane," he exclaimed. "They must be searching for us. Let us do something to attract their attention."

"No, Doctor," said Kotokro. "This is not the sound of an aeroplane. It is something more sinister, unless I am much mistaken."

Securri confirmed that it was something from which they rather ought to run away if they knew where best to find a hiding place.

"What is it?" asked Kotokro who knew what it was not, but not exactly what it was.

"It is a huge army of bees that have left their hive after their honey has been pillaged. They are now very angry and will attack with utmost ferocity any human being they see. They are known to put a whole army to rout, inflicting thousands of casualties."

"What must we do then?" asked Kotokro.

"We must hide under a tree until they fly past. If they see us we are as good as dead."

So saying he darted under the canopy of the nearest tree, dragging Kotokro with him. Dr. Wiseman followed instinctively, wondering if the two blacks were not playing some practical joke on him.

It was only just in time, for soon the sky overhead darkened in a way that could not have resulted from any number of aeroplanes flying overhead. Dr. Wiseman still did not know what it was, as Kotokro had not had time to explain to him what Securri had said, but he was now convinced that it could not be an aeroplane or any number of that flying machine.

Gradually, the droning sound decreased in volume as the sky began to clear once more, bringing back the sun's light.

"What was it?" asked Dr. Wiseman of Kotokro when the phenomenon had passed off.

Kotokro told him.

"I wonder where they are heading for" he said.

"They don't have any particular destination" Kotokro explained. "We shall be lucky if we don't encounter them again on the way."

"How?" asked Dr. Wiseman.

"When they fly like this they are looking for human beings to punish and they usually hang together in a big cluster from the branch of a tree overhanging the most frequented path leading from a village. When an unwary traveller passes underneath them they suddenly fall upon him and sting him to death. We shall be lucky if we don't meet them ambushing over this path before we arrive at our destination."

"That would be terrible," said Dr. Wiseman with a shudder, "especially when we are so completely naked and have no clothes to protect ourselves."

"Clothes would even avail us nothing," explained Kotokro. "A few days before you came to our village, one of the chief's wives was returning from her farm with a baby on her back when she happened to pass under one of those dangerous clusters of angry bees. They immediately fell upon her and the baby, and she had to save herself by abandoning the baby and fleeing to the village to cry for help. The baby was clad from head to foot in thick cotton clothes. When the men went to the rescue, they found it completely buried under the swarm of bees. It was already dead. They had to beat a hasty retreat lest they themselves might be the object of next attack. When they returned to the spot the next day, the swarm of bees had disappeared, leaving behind only the child's skeleton."

"Dear me" exclaimed Dr. Wiseman. "Africa abounds not only in surprises but also in terrible dangers. What shall we do if we happen to meet anything like that on the way?"

"You said that we must not cross our bridge until we come to it, Doctor." Kotokro reminded.

"I did. But this is a very serious danger against which we must take timely precaution."

"What have you two been talking about?" asked Securri who had hitherto paid no attention to their conversation.

"We have been discussing the bees that have just passed overhead," Kotokro replied. "What can we do if we happen to find them hanging over our path?"

"You seem to know much about the habit of bees," replied Securri. "We shall simply avoid them."

Just as he spoke, Kotokro heard the crow of a cock. "Are we about to arrive at Fomaki?" he asked, "Yes, we are almost there," Securri confirmed.

His heart filled with joy. They were about to accomplish the first, part of their journey to freedom. Dr. Wiseman was also happy to hear that they were about to arrive at their destination. Their joy, however, was soon succeeded by fear and anxiety, for they had taken only a few more steps forward when Securri suddenly stopped short and pointed:

"Look" he said.

Kotokro and Dr. Wiseman looked in the direction to which he was pointing. They saw two dark objects in the form of cylinders, one about four feet long and a foot in diameter, the other about half that size, both suspended from the branch of a tree that overhung the foot-path.

"What are they?" asked Kotokro.

"They are swarms of bees that have clustered together." replied Securri. "They must be the bees that passed us on the way."

Kotokro was greatly astonished. He had often seen clusters of bees hanging from the branch of a tree, but in magnitude these went far beyond anything he had ever seen or heard of.

"They are very dangerous", continued Securri. "If we try to pass under them they will fall upon us and sting us to death."

"What must we do then?" asked Kotokro.

"We must turn back and try to reach the village by a detour."

Kotokro interpreted to Dr. Wiseman what he had said.

"How far are we from the village?" asked the Doctor.

Securri replied that it was just round the corner, and that were it not for the bees they would be there before he could count twenty.

"And how long will it take us to get there by the detour?" he next asked.

"About a quarter of the time it has taken us to get here." he replied.

"What" exclaimed Dr. Wiseman. "It means we would arrive there just before nightfall?"

Securri replied that that was the case.

"No, we must not go by any detour then," objected the Doctor, "I am already too tired. We must think of some means of passing under them without being stung."

"What means can you think of, Doctor?" asked Kotokro.

Dr. Wiseman thought for a while.

"I have an idea," he said. "We must make use of the lion and gorilla skins."

"How?" asked Kotokro.

"You and I will cover ourselves with the skins and so pass under them in safety, for then even if they fall upon us they cannot sting us through those thick and hairy vestments. After we have crossed to a safe distance I shall then divest myself of the gorilla skin and you will take it to Securri, who will wear it and so come with you in safety."

"It is not a good idea, Doctor," Kotokro replied at once.

"Why not?" asked Dr. Wiseman.

"For two reasons: First, because we do not want Securri or anyone else to know that we have these skins. Secondly, because these skins cannot protect us, since they do not cover the head, the most vital part of the body. No, we have no alternative but to follow Securri's advice."

"What are you discussing?" asked Securri who had been waiting for their reaction to his suggestion.

"The Doctor says he is very tired, nevertheless if there is no other way of avoiding being stung by these bees he has no objection to your suggestion that we should turn back and go by a detour."

"All right, let us go then, for there is no other way," said Securri, and at once turned back and began to lead the way. Kotokro followed, with Dr. Wiseman bringing up the rear as before.

After advancing for some distance they came to a faint track that branched off the foot-path. Securri turned into it. Kotokro and Dr. Wiseman followed. They went on and on without seeing or hearing any sign that they were about to arrive in the village. By now Dr. Wiseman was so tired that he could hardly take another step forward. Suddenly they heard the crow of a cock.

"Try and endure a little more," Securri said encouragingly to Dr. Wiseman, observing how he walked with difficulty. "We are about to arrive at our destination."

The information had a revitalising effect upon the Doctor's depleted energy, for he immediately began to move with quicker steps and great agility. Soon they heard the voices of children at play, the barking of dogs and the bleating of goats. A few moments later the village of Fomaki came into view.

Soon they arrived at an extensive clearing right in the middle of that thick jungle, covered with scores of houses built without any regular formation. Each house consisted of three or more round huts placed in a circle and joined by high walls to form a compound. They were exactly like the houses at Kantoma, Kotokro's village, except that they looked finer and stood on much cleaner grounds. Each hut was neatly thatched with palm leaves and had the walls plastered with white clay, both inside and outside.

Men, women and children thronged to see them as they made their way to the Chief's house, where Securri said they must first report. The men who had returned from the camp the previous day had already told the people in the village that Securri had been left behind with a little black boy to search for his missing white companion and that he was expected to return the next day with or without the two.

Actually they had had no hope that Dr. Wiseman would be found. At least that had been the expectation of Yamogi and his friend Dankida, and they had made everyone believe that the Doctor had already perished in the jungle. Everyone else was therefore happy to see Securri return with the Doctor and Kotokro, except Yamogi and his friend, who were sorely disappointed and unhappy at the turn of events. However, they had to pretend that they shared in the general joy and relief.

A large crowd, including Yamogi and Dankida, followed them to the chief's compound, where they found Chief Dogobisa and his Elders, including Elder Oloko, at a council meeting. Elder Oloko was very happy to see them and rose up at once to embrace Securri.

"Well done, my lad," he said. "You have brought credit to our tribe by your brave and humane act. Yamogi and his friend Dankida said that you acted foolishly by offering to remain behind with this boy and his companion who, for all they knew, might have contrived to lure one of us into destruction. They added that they would be greatly surprised if you ever came back alive."

"Well, I am alive all right and have brought the two strangers," replied Securri, casting triumphant glances in the direction of Yamogi and Dankida. "What do they have to say now?"

All eyes turned to look at the two men. They said nothing. It was evident that they felt greatly embarrassed, for they hang their heads in shame and, as soon as attention was directed away from them, they sneaked away from the crowd.

Securri narrated all that happened after the men left him and Kotokro behind to search for the white man: and when he had finished Chief Dogobisa added his commendation to that of Elder Oloko. Then Securri told them of the clusters of bees that had come to hang only a short distance away from the village. Thereupon Chief Dogobisa caused a gong-gong to be beaten, informing all the people that no one should go along that path until the dangerous insects had departed of their own free will.

"It is those two witches, the white stranger and his little black friend, that have brought them," commented Yamogi and Dankida when they heard the announcement, "for never before has any such thing happened in this village."

That evening Chief Dogobisa offered his half-completed guest-house, consisting of two round huts, as accommodation for Dr. Wiseman and Kotokro. They were to occupy one of the huts and Securri was to sleep in the other to keep them company. Not that he feared lest some harm might come to them if they were left to themselves, but the norms of hospitality required that they should have one of the villagers to be by them to administer to their needs, and Chief Dogobisa could find no one better fitted to perform that office than Securri.

CHAPTER EIGHTEEN
EVENTFUL SOJOURN AT FOMAKI

Although the news that clusters of bees had come to hang over the path leading from the village brought fear into the heart of everyone in Fomaki, and most of the people thought that the presence of that phenomenon signified some impending disaster, no one associated it with Dr. Wiseman and Kotokro, except Yamogi and his friend Dankida.

"It is said that the bees are in two clusters, one big and the other small," said Yamogi. "That clearly shows that they are connected with the white stranger and his little black companion, for their statures are also in that proportion. Indeed those bees are the very embodiments of their witchcraft. Never mind that one is white and the other is black, while all the bees are black in colour. Colour is of no consequence in witch-dom. The important thing is that they speak the same language."

"Quite right," agreed Dankida, "for how else could they have survived for years in that jungle, as they claim, and the white stranger also lived through that night of extreme danger when he got lost, if they were no witches? They certainly are, and are responsible for this phenomenon."

"We must do something about it then," suggested Yamogi, "We cannot allow those bees to hang there until they leave of their own free will as Chief Dogobisa has said; for we do not know how long they intend to stay; and meanwhile no one in this village dares to pass along that path to go to his farm."

"I agree we must do something about it" said Dankida. "But what can we do?"

"I have an idea," said Yamogi, "we can burn or drive them away with fire."

"How?"

"We must set fire to the bush immediately below where they are hanging. The flames and smoke will either kill or drive them away."

Dankida agreed that that was a very good idea, and they decided to put it into execution early next morning, just before dawn. And so they did.

As soon as they heard the last crow of the cock before dawn they got up and proceeded along the path where the bees were, taking a lighted torch with them. The village was still buried in sleep, so that they were sure no one would see them.

Arrived at the spot they quickly set alight the bush immediately beneath the bees. The place was heavily covered with dry leaves, which at once caught fire. Soon the whole area was in flames. It was some time, however, before the insects began to feel the heat. By then their two assailants were fleeing back to the village with utmost speed.

The bees gave chase, nevertheless, and soon several of them had overtaken the miscreants. They fell upon them as they still ran and stung them without mercy. Then the two set up a yell which had the effect of arousing the whole village. People ran out of their houses to see what was happening, only to be met by a hail of bees that began to attack them with great fury. They ran back helter and skelter. And as they did so they too screamed with agony, so that the whole village was thrown into turmoil.

Securri was asleep when he was suddenly awakened by the loud hullabaloo. He got up and rushed out of the house to see what was happening. He saw people screaming and running in all directions. As he stood looking on and wondering what could be the matter, he saw a man running at full speed towards him and flinging his hands wildly about his head. The next instant he saw a large swarm of bees in pursuit. Some had overtaken him and were inflicting painful stings upon all the exposed parts of his body.

Securri took to his heels and ran as fast as he could towards the house. But before he could cover half the distance some of the terrible insects had overtaken him and had begun to sting him on his neck and ears. Many more would have descended upon him with dire consequences had not something quite unexpected intervened. As the bees were chasing him, a flock of sheep that had just broken loose from their pen came rushing towards him. Immediately upon meeting them the bees transferred their attention to these, thus enabling Securri to flee in safety.

While all this was going on Dr. Wiseman and Kotokro were still fast asleep. They were so tired after the previous day's journey that mere screams could not have awakened them. But as Securri's room had no door of any description to the entrance, he made, instead, for the room in which the two were sleeping. That room at least had a mat covering the entrance. Arrived there he threw aside the mat and went in, allowing it to fall back. Kotokro and Dr. Wiseman were still fast asleep, but the former woke up at once.

"What is it?" he asked, rubbing his eyes.

"It's the bees! Oh, those abominable insects," he gasped, "They are all over the place."

Ever as he spoke Kotokro and Dr. Wiseman, who had by now also awakened from sleep, heard loud screams and wailings from every quarter of the village. They were mingled with the bleating of sheep and goats and the cackle of fowls and barking of dogs. The noise continued for a long time, but gradually it began to die down.

Suddenly cries of panic burst forth again from the village, as a loud crackling sound came over the air. This was soon followed by choking smoke which penetrated into the room.

"It seems there is fire!" said Kotokro. "Let us go out at once and see what is happening."

They rushed out and saw, to their horror, that the whole village was engulfed in a pall of smoke. It was coming from a big conflagration that was raging from the bush along the path where the bees had settled. As they looked on, large sparks began to shoot into the sky and land on the roofs of the nearest huts. These caught fire at once and began to blaze furiously.

218

The whole village would undoubtedly have been burnt to ashes if the people had not exerted themselves to the utmost to limit the spread of the flames. Men, women and children ran to the stream, which was fortunately close by, and brought water again and again, which was dashed upon the devouring blaze. They also poured some upon the roofs of the houses that had not yet been touched, and in this way protected them from being consumed by the leaping inferno.

It took a long time before the fire was put out. By then several houses had been burnt to ashes. Among them were three out of the four rooms in the hut of Yamogi and two rooms of his friend Dankida, thus confirming the truth of the saying that "he who sets an evil trap risks being caught by it." As their huts were at the outskirts of the village, close to where the bush was burning, they were among the first to which the flames spread. But for the water which the villagers poured upon them all their rooms would have been burnt to ashes. They had not, of course, anticipated that the fire would thus make for the village when they embarked upon their evil venture.

There was great lamentation in Fomaki that day, not only on account of the burnt houses, but more especially because of the harm done by the bees. Two children, the daughters of Chief Dogobisa, were stung to death outright, while six men and five women suffered so seriously that they were laid up for several weeks. As for Yamogi and his friend, in addition to the loss of their huts the bees also inflicted on them no small punishment. They were so stung on the head that these swelled up like balloons, with their mouths, noses and ears dotted on them like little knobs.

In spite of their sorry condition, however, Yamogi and Dankida were as mischievous and talkative as ever. Going to the chief's house they began to sympathize with him on the loss of his two daughters and to put the blame on Dr. Wiseman and Kotokro.

"It is these two strangers that have brought this misfortune upon us all," they charged. "They led the bees here, being witches, and caused the fire to burn and destroy our houses. We must punish and expel them from the village at once."

Chief Dogobisa found it difficult to believe their accusation, for it did not make much sense to him. However, he sent for his Elders and put it to them. They in turn found it difficult to believe it. Nevertheless they decided to summon Dr. Wiseman and Kotokro and hear what they had to say.

And so it happened that as they and Securri were sitting down to breakfast, a messenger came to say that chief Dogobisa and his Elders wanted to see them immediately. Covering up their food they rose up and followed him, accompanied by Securri.

They arrived at Chief Dogobisa's palace to find him seated with his Elders, surrounded by a large crowd of people, among them being Yamogi and his friend Dankida. The messenger had told one or two people about the case as he went along to call Dr. Wiseman and Kotokro, and the news had spread like wild fire, thus bringing the crowd of on-lookers to the palace.

When Dr. Wiseman and Kotokro stood before Chief Dogobisa and his Elders their two accusers were asked to repeat what they had said. Thereupon Yamogi stepped forward and said:

"Chief Dogobisa, Elders and people of Fomaki, you are all aware of the great calamity that has befallen our village today. Not only have we been subjected to the vicious and unprovoked attack of bees, resulting in the death of two of the daughters of our beloved chief and in serious injuries to many of us, but we have also been invaded by fire which has destroyed many of our houses. Such a combination of disasters has never been known in this village ever since our ancestors came to dwell here. How then do we account for their occurrence now?

"We have a saying that disasters do not come from the clouds. Every misfortune that befalls a man is the work of some evil genius. Some person or persons, are therefore, responsible for our sufferings today. And I say categorically and without the mincing of words that they can be no other than the two strangers that came into our midst yesterday, namely the white man and his little black companion. They are witches and are the ones who brought the bees and the fire that have, together, brought deep sorrow into our hearts this day."

"Why do I accuse them of being witches? The reasons are simple and easy to see by any man with sense. First of all, by their own account these men stayed in the jungle for a period of more than one and half years and yet came to no harm. Any man that can do that must surely be a witch, considering the many wild beasts that infest the jungle and render it unsafe to stay there for even a night. Secondly, these men were seen at the same place where Dankida and myself were chased by a gorilla and a lion, yet they were unharmed by those two terrible creatures. Either they were able to escape their notice through witchcraft or they themselves were the ones who changed themselves into those two dangerous beasts. Thirdly, one of them, the white stranger, was able to survive in the jungle through a night of unprecedented storm and fierce howls of wolves and angry roars of lions. Only a witch can do that. It is evident then that these two strangers are, in fact, witches, and that they are the ones who brought the bees to our village and caused the fire that has inflicted so much damage upon our houses. They must therefore be punished for their crimes and expelled from this village before they proceed to do their worst."

Everyone had been listening to him attentively, and when he had finished there was continued silence, as if people were weighing his words. Then Chief Dogobisa broke the silence and asked Dr. Wiseman and Kotokro if they had anything to say.

All eyes turned at once upon Dr. Wiseman, to whom Kotokro had been interpreting all that Yamogi had been saying.

"Tell them that we are not witches - at least I am not - and that what he had said is absolute nonsense," began the Doctor. "In my own country no one believes in witchcraft. It is true that there was a time when our people also believed in its existence and they used to burn those who were suspected of its practice. But that was quite a long time ago, when our people were primitive and highly superstitions, as you are today. It was the days of ignorance. All that he has said, therefore, is trash. There are no such things as witches. It is particularly stupid of him to suggest that we could have brought the bees here and caused the fire at the same time. We ourselves had to run away from those insects and come to this village by a detour when we saw them hanging over the path. Why would we have run away from something that we ourselves brought, assuming that we could have brought them? As for the fire, since it is said to have been started this morning, when we were asleep, in what way could we have been the cause of it? Altogether I consider his accusation very preposterous and hardly deserving of any lengthy reply."

Kotokro waited until Dr. Wiseman had finished saying all that he wanted to say, instead of translating his speech sentence by sentence as he normally did on most occasions. Then he turned to the Doctor and said:

"Doctor, I don't think they will be pleased to hear what you have said, so let us think of something better."

"Who cares whether they will be pleased to hear it or not? It is the truth, and they should jolly well take or leave it."

"What did he say?," asked Chief Dogobisa, when it seemed to him that Kotokro was hesitating to interpret what the Doctor had said.

"He said he did not quite understand what I had interpreted and was asking me to repeat it."

"Is that all he said in so many words?" asked Chief Dogobisa again incredulously.

"Yes" replied Kotokro.

"Strange. The language must be really difficult; why, all that could have been said in four words in Wapiti." said Chief Dogobisa.

"Chief Dogobisa, Elders and people of Fomaki," said Securri, suddenly stepping forward and interrupting, "there is no need for us to wait to hear any defence from these strangers. We all know that what my brother-in-law, Yamogi, has said is nonsensical in the extreme. I do not blame him. The stings which the bees have inflicted on his head must have affected his reasoning power sadly. He charges these strangers with being witches and with being the cause of our double misfortune today, but he has not put forward any reasons that can convince any man with a normal head and normal brains. None of the reasons he gives for concluding that they are witches can stand up to scrutiny. First of all, he says they are witches because they were able to dwell in safety in the jungle for more than one and half years. We ourselves as hunters are able to remain in the jungle for at least a week every month and could have stayed longer if we wished. Are we, therefore, witches? I have seen the house which these two strangers built in the jungle and in which they lived. And I can assure you that it can much better withstand the attack of any beast or man than our own huts, and that any of you could stay in it for years in safety."

"But these two strangers did not stay in the jungle voluntarily. They did so because they were unable to do otherwise. They got lost in the jungle and could not find their way to any human abode. Could they have got lost if they were witches?"

"Secondly, Yamogi says that since these strangers were not harmed by the gorilla and the lion which he and Dankida claim to have seen, it proves that they are witches, because either they themselves were the two creatures or they were able to escape their notice by means of their witchcraft. The answer to that is that all of us who went to look for the two creatures arrived at the conclusion that it was these two strangers whom, in their cowardly fear, they had mistaken for a lion and a gorilla.

"Thirdly, he says that the white stranger at least must be a witch, because he was able to live through a fierce storm and a night of prowling beasts. I myself saw what enabled him to live through that night. He fell into a pit, as I said here yesterday, and that is why the beasts were unable to get at him. Had he been a witch he would not have spent the night in a pit and waited for us to come to his rescue. He would not have fallen into it in the first place, and if he did he could easily have come out again without anyone's assistance.

"Lastly Yamogi accuses them of having brought the bees that stung two daughters of Chief Dogobisa to death and of having been the cause of the fire that has destroyed some of our huts. This is the most illogical part of his accusation. If they are the ones who brought the bees, why would they have tried to burn them with fire? For it is evident that it was in the attempt to burn them with fire that someone set ablaze the bush underneath them, resulting in the spreading of the flames to our village.

"No, these strangers are no witches, but unfortunate men who got lost in the forest and were delivered by Providence into our protection and hospitality. I spent one night alone with them in the jungle and came to no harm. Were they evil men they would not have suffered me to return home alive, bringing them with me.

Let Yamogi therefore seek another explanation for the disasters that have overtaken this village this day."

Everyone had been listening to him attentively as he spoke, and there were loud cheers when he had finished. Then Elder Oloko also spoke and said:

"There is no doubt that Yamogi and his friend Dankida brought this charge against the strangers out of malice. Yamogi has borne them a grudge ever since they admitted having destroyed his trap, even though he knows full well that they did not do so wantonly. They had to do it to save this white stranger's life. It was that grudge that led him to forget the norms of hospitality and to attempt to slay the same white stranger when he embraced his wife in ignorance of our custom. And now, having been baulked in his attempt to take unjust revenge, he brings this frivolous charge and altogether senseless accusation against them. Let him go away and see how he can reduce his swollen head to a normal size with the help of Tobi, the medicine-man, and thus restore his power of reasoning."

There was laughter as Elder Oloko concluded his speech. Then Chief Dogobisa called for silence and asked:

"Does anyone here hold a contrary view from what Securri and Elder Oloko have said?"

"No, no, we agree with them," came a chorus of voices from all sides.

Then Chief Dogobisa turned to Yamogi and Dankida and said:

"Do you see that no one here agrees with what you have said? I myself saw no sense in any of the reasons you gave for your accusation and was only waiting to hear what others would say. Even if these two strangers were witches, which I do not believe they are, they could not have brought the bees here and set fire to them at the same time. The bees came of their own accord and someone else from this village must have tried to burn them by setting fire to the bush immediately underneath them, with the result that the fire spread to our huts. You would do well then to try and find out who caused the fire instead of wasting our time with baseless accusations against innocent people."

Chief Dogobisa had hardly finished speaking when someone with a small voice suddenly said:

"I saw the people who set fire to the bush."

All eyes turned to look at him. He was a little boy of about six, big-headed and spindle-legged, with a stomach like a little inflated balloon.

"Hey you, what did you say?" asked Chief Dogobisa.

"I saw the people who did it," the boy repeated.

"Whom did you see?" asked Chief Dogobisa again, looking hard at him.

"I saw two men, like papa Yamogi and Papa Dankida. They were going along the path on which the bees were said to be, and one of them was holding a lighted torch."

"Why do you say like Papa Yamogi and Papa Dankida?" asked Elder Oloko. "Did you not see them clearly?"

"No, it was a bit dark, so I could not see them clearly. But they were of the height and stature of Papa Yamogi and Papa Dankida."

"What were you doing outside the house at that early hour of the morning when you saw them?" Chief Dogobisa asked again.

"I had got up to go to the bush to ease myself. I had a pain in the stomach."

"And did you see them return to the village?"

"I did not. I was afraid of the darkness, so I hurried up and returned to the house quickly."

The crowd had begun to murmur as the boy spoke and was being questioned. But now there was a hush, as all eyes turned once more upon Yamogi and his friend.

"Who should give credence to the cooked-up story of a little silly boy like that?" said Yamogi. "It's a lie."

"I am not lying. It's true" persisted the boy.

"Never mind" Chief Dogobisa interrupted. "Whether it is true or not we shall soon find out."

"It is true" repeated the boy. "I am not lying. They are the ones who did it."

"Well, we need not waste any more time here" said Chief Dogobisa, rising up.

The Elders rose up too, and the crowd began to disperse.

"Let's go and finish our breakfast," said Securri to Dr. Wiseman and Kotokro "I am sure the child knows what he is talking about. We are all aware of the wicked ways of those two men."

On their way back to the house, Dr. Wiseman asked Kotokro what Securri had said in their defence. He told him briefly, adding, "He is a clever young man. Without him we would have stood in great danger."

"What could they have done to us?" asked Dr. Wiseman.

"Anything. They could have burnt us or stoned us to death."

"What" exclaimed Dr. Wiseman in disbelief. "Are there still people here in Africa so primitive as to believe in witchcraft to the extent of putting to death those whom they suspect to be witches?"

"Yes, Doctor," replied Kotokro "Many people in Africa still believe in witchcraft. I learn that even in your own country there are still people who believe in witchcraft."

"Who told you?"

"Mrs. Casely."

"Those are psychopaths."

"What are psychopaths?"

"They are people who are sick in mind. They do not know what they talk about."

"What exactly does that mean? Does it mean they don't know witchcraft, which is what they talk about?"

"No, no. It means that their minds are not functioning normally, so that they believe and talk about things that do not exist."

"But how can anyone believe and talk about things that do not exist? A thing must exist somewhere, either in one's mind or in the outside world, before one can believe and talk about it?"

"Nonsense! If a thing exists in one's mind then does it exist?"

"Yes. My thoughts exist in my mind, so they exist. In the same way, if witchcraft exists in people's minds then it exists."

"You reason like these savages, my boy." said Dr. Wiseman "Anyone with a bit of intelligence will see at once that there is no logic at all in what you say."

They had been advancing as they talked, and by now they had arrived back in the hut. Kotokro was too hungry for further argument, so he uncovered his food and sat down to eat. Dr. Wiseman and Securri did the same.

After breakfast Dr. Wiseman and Kotokro sat discussing the morning's events.

"Does it mean, Doctor, that you did not understand any of the things that were said there?" asked Kotokro.

"What do you mean?"

"I mean did you not catch any of the things Yamogi and Securri said in the Wapiti language?"

"How could I? I know only a few words in Wapiti and can recognise them only when they are spoken slowly. In that voluble and torrential way in which they spoke, how could my ears have caught any of the words?"

"Then let us try and learn the language. I myself have not yet perfected my knowledge of it, but I know enough to be able to teach you."

"What use shall I have for a barbarous tongue like that after I leave here?" asked Dr. Wiseman. "After all we are going to be here for just about a year at the most, so why should I take all the trouble of learning such a difficult language, for which I shall have no use after I leave here?"

"But I learned the English language when I was in your country, even though I knew I would have no use for it after I returned to Kantoma, since no one in my village speaks English."

"You needed it for the intelligence test. And, in any case, you will always find it useful, for it is spoken in all the four corners of the world."

"I did not need it for any intelligence test," Kotokro disagreed. "If you really wanted to test my intelligence then you should have tested me in my own language and about things connected with where I was born and brought up. As for the English language being spoken in all the corners of the world, as you say, that may be so. I have no means of knowing. What I do know is that it is not spoken in my corner, Kantoma, where I was born and where I intend to live all the rest of my life."

"All right, all right, my boy," said Dr. Wiseman, "I shall try to learn it just to please you and to while away the time: for I guess it will be boring, eating and sleeping all the time for a period of one year or more, without any mental or physical exertion. So let us learn it. When do we start?"

"Right now," replied Kotokro.

For more than five months Dr. Wiseman battled heroically to acquire the Wapiti language, while Kotokro sought to perfect his own by engaging in long conversations with Securri. The Doctor insisted that the easiest way for him to remember the words was to write them down with the equivalent English translations, and he had enough paper and pen in his brief-case for doing this. But after one gruelling session with Kotokro one evening, he at last threw in his hand and said:

"I cannot learn any more. The language is much too difficult."

"Why, Doctor," said Kotokro "it is much easier than English."

"That's not true," Dr. Wiseman disagreed. "Look at this word, "molinkeda" for example; which you have just taught me. You say that when you pronounce it molinkeda (that is, with the accent on the first syllable) it means either a rivulet or a goat or drizzle. But when you say molinkeda (that is, with the accent on the second syllable), then it means <u>dark night</u> or <u>ant-hill</u> or <u>spear</u> or <u>foot-print</u> or <u>roof</u> or the sentence "<u>I am sick</u>". Again if you say <u>molinkeda</u> (that is, with the accent on the third syllable) then it means either <u>milk</u> or <u>market</u> or <u>gorilla</u> or <u>seller</u> or <u>cave</u> or the sentence '<u>she is sleeping</u>! Yet again if you say molinkeda" (that, is, with the accent on the last syllable) then it means either <u>a flute</u> or a <u>stool</u> or <u>a baby-girl</u> or <u>a dunce</u> or <u>groundnut soup</u>. Thus this words "<u>milinkeda</u>" alone stands for twenty different things, all of which are unrelated in any way. How can anyone learn a language like this, which is purely tonal and depends, for its meaning, upon how you pronounce the word? It is highly confusing."

"But I was able to learn it easily," Kotokro pointed out.

"You did, because your own language is also tonal and has the same syntactical structure."

"What does that mean?" asked Kotokro.

"It means it is based on the use of the voice and follows the same rules of construction as this barbarous Wapiti tongue!"

"But I was also able to learn the English language in a short time, although it is not like my language in any way," Kotokro pointed out.

"So did my parrot," replied Dr. Wiseman "The ability to learn a language is a gift of the lower breed. It has nothing to do with intelligence or mental capacity."

"And was your parrot able to reason in English?" asked Kotokro.

"It had no need to. Its needs were simple, and it was able to communicate them in it."

"All right, Doctor," said Kotokro. "But your own needs are not simple and you are unable to communicate them in Wapiti. So let us leave it at that?"

"As long as you are around I don't have to bother."

Dr. Wiseman was quite right. As long as Kotokro was around he did not have to bother. But had providence not intervened a few days later, Kotokro would not have been around when his life was in mortal danger. It happened in this way:

Elder Oloko and his men, including Securri, had continued to spend the first week in every month away from the village, hunting and inspecting their traps. As Kotokro was busy teaching Dr. Wiseman the Wapiti language, he had never been able to go with them. But when the Doctor refused to learn the language any more, on the grounds that it was too difficult Kotokro made Securri know that he would accompany them on their next trip to the jungle. He took this decision because he thought it would be too boring to just eat and sleep with nothing else to do; for, thanks to the hospitality of Elder Oloko , both he and Dr. Wiseman were amply supplied with food every day and did not have to exert themselves in any way in order to earn a living.

Now Yamogi and his friend Dankida had never forgiven Dr. Wiseman and Kotokro from the day they met them in the jungle. As we have seen, Yamogi had reasons to resent Dr. Wiseman in particular. He had not only been the cause of his trap being destroyed, but he had also embraced his wife without his permission, refused him the satisfaction of a duel and, what was even more unpardonable, proved by all his actions that he was a witch. Had he not survived alone in the jungle at night and brought bees to the village, in the attempt to destroy which he and Dankida had caused fire that had spread to burn their huts instead? In his eyes Dr. Wiseman was a witch who ought to be destroyed before he brought further misfortune upon him and the whole of Fomaki. Kotokro was a witch too, but he was less harmful than his white companion. The need to do away with him was not so urgent. He could be taken care of later.

As for Dankida he had no particular reason to hate either Dr. Wiseman or Kotokro. Neither of them had wronged him personally, except when they used their witchcraft to let the fire burn his house too. However, Yamogi was his closest friend, and anything that touched him was a concern to him too.

Such being their feelings towards Dr. Wiseman and Kotokro it is little wonder that they decided to look for an opportunity to get rid of the two. That opportunity came when they heard that Kotokro would accompany their party to the hunt on the next occasion.

"It means the white stranger will be left in the house alone for a week at least," said Yamogi when he first heard the news.

"Excellent," Dankida replied with joy. "We shall have the opportunity to get rid of him."

"How?" asked Yamogi.

"We shall not go with the men to the hunt," he explained. "We shall say that we are sick. After they have gone and left us behind we shall have a golden opportunity to slay him undetected."

"But if we stay behind and he gets killed wont suspicion fall upon us?"

"No, we shall do so the very morning his black companion leaves him, so that it will appear as if he slew him before departing with the men."

"But it will look very suspicious if both of us say that we are sick at the same time, and the white stranger is subsequently found slain, wont it?"

"You will pretend to be sick three days before the men are due to leave, and I just the day before. In this way our excuses will appear genuine."

Having decided upon this strategem the two men put it into execution when the time came. Three days before the men were due to depart, Yamogi complained that he was sick. He had a severe attack of malaria. He began to shake like one possessed and to cause his teeth to chatter in his head most uncontrollably. Then he went and sat in the sun, saying that he was feeling terribly cold. After a while he began to sweat profusely. Then he went into his hut and slept. When his wife brought his meal he refused to eat, saying that he had no appetite. His friend, Dankida, however contrived to bring him food unknown to his wife, so that the poor woman thought that her husband was really in a bad way.

Just the day before the men were due to set out Dankida also said that he was sick. He had caught the sickness that afflicted his friend. He too began to shake his body convulsively and to make his teeth chatter in his head. He went and sat in the hot sun until he was drenched with sweat. Then he went indoors and slept. When his wife brought his meal he ate only a little bit of it and said that that was as much as he could take in.

And now the day came for the men to depart. Kotokro had not been feeling well when he went to bed the previous night. He was feeling cold and had a splitting head-ache. He knew at once that he was going to have an attack of malaria fever.

"It seems there is an outbreak of malaria fever," he said to himself "First Yamogi, then Dankida and now myself." He decided that he would not be able to go with the men after all.

The men always set out from the village about two hours before dawn, so as to be able to reach the camp by the late afternoon and have enough rest before the next day's hard labour. Kotokro had arranged with Securri to wake him up the next morning for the journey. But when Securri knocked at his door and said that it was time to go, Kotokro informed him, to his disappointment, that he was sick and could not go with them after all. He hoped he would be well enough to go with them on the next occasion.

And so Securri had to go without him. When he joined the others they asked him where was his friend, Kotokro.

"He too has caught the malaria fever and says he cannot come with us," he replied.

Some of the men had had some doubt about Yamogi and Dankida's claim to be sick, but when they heard that Kotokro too was sick they changed their minds.

"Well, this proves that they are really sick," they said.

And so it happened that the men set out for the camp without Yamogi and his friend Dankida and Kotokro. Yamogi and Dankida, however, did not know that Kotokro had not gone with the men after all.

Dankida had been on the lookout for their departure. As soon as he heard that they had gone away he went to Yamogi's hut and woke him up.

"They have all gone away," he said. "Let's go and finish that white witch quickly before people begin to wake up."

Yamogi got up and seized his spear. Dankida was also carrying a spear. They proceeded stealthily to the hut in which Dr. Wiseman and Kotokro were sleeping. The moon was shining brightly from a cloudless sky. Soon they stood behind the hut.

Just at this moment, however, it occurred to them that there might be some difficulty in slaying the Doctor undetected. First of all, to get into the hut they would have to enter the compound first. This was not so easy, as it was enclosed with a high wall. Then after they would have entered the compound and the hut in which the Doctor slept, they would have to slay him in such a way that it would look as if Kotokro did it while the Doctor was asleep. They could not use a spear, as everyone knew that Kotokro had no such weapon. They would have to slay him with either a cutlass or an arrow. Kotokro and the Doctor were known to have brought these. But they themselves had now only brought spears. Yamogi suggested, therefore, that Dankida should go back and bring either a cutlass or an arrow.

While they were discussing this in whispers Kotokro, who had been having terrible nightmares, due to the high fever which he had contracted, suddenly woke up from one of those frightful mental presentations. Hearing voices immediately behind the hut he pricked up his ears to listen. Then he heard Yamogi say:

"When you come back you can stand on my shoulders and climb over the wall into the compound. You will then open the gate and let me in. After that our work will be easy. I shall stealthily enter the hut and make my way as quietly as possible towards him, taking care not to wake him up. I shall then use the weapon you bring to slay him. You should bring a cutlass, for it will be an easier weapon to work with. Hurry, go now and be back quickly. I am waiting."

Silence followed, and Kotokro concluded that Dankida had gone to bring the weapon, and that Yamogi was still waiting for him behind the hut. He decided to wake up Dr. Wiseman and let him know what was happening. He had to do so very quietly and make sure that the Doctor did not make any noise on waking up. So putting his hand to the Doctor's lips he shook him gently. He woke up and, before he could say anything Kotokro whispered into his ear:

"Quiet, Doctor," he said. "There are some people outside, seeking to come in and murder us."

Then he went on to explain, still in whispers, what he had heard. He added that one of them had gone back to bring a weapon for their murderous purpose and was expected to be back soon.

"Let us prepare to defend ourselves then," suggested Dr. Wiseman. "We have the bow and arrows as well as the cutlass."

"No, Doctor," replied Kotokro. "We must not use any weapons. If we do and we slay them our lives might be in danger, for even though we would have done so in self defence, some people might not understand and would not forgive us."

"Must we allow these wicked savages to take our lives then without resistance?" asked Dr. Wiseman in surprise. "I am not prepared to be slain like a lamb led to the slaughter, if you are."

"We shall not allow them to slay us," Kotokro replied calmly.

"And how are you going to prevent that?"

Without replying Kotokro bent down and began to open the iron trunk which he always placed at the head of his bed. Guided by the moonlight which penetrated through the mat into the room he took out the gorilla's and the lion's skins. He threw the former to Dr. Wiseman and said:

"Here, don this at once."

At the same time he slipped the lion's skin over himself and laced it up. By the time he had finished dressing the Doctor had also put on the gorilla's skin.

"Now we are ready for them," whispered Kotokro. "What we are going to do is this: We shall wait until they have entered the compound and opened the gate. We shall then rush out suddenly and cry like the animals we are supposed to be. We must, however, not do that too loudly, for we must not be heard by the villagers."

"Do you think that this plan will work?" asked Dr. Wiseman doubtfully.

"You bet it will" Kotokro assured him.

They had hardly finished their preparations when Kotokro heard voices again behind the hut. Dankida had returned. He heard him saying: "I couldn't find a cutlass; but I have brought an arrow."

"Good," replied Yamogi. "It will do just as well. Let's go."

Breathlessly Dr. Wiseman and Kotokro waited as the two men proceeded to put their plan into execution. First, Yamogi placed both hands against the wall while Dankida climbed over his shoulders to the top. Then he jumped down into the compound and proceeded to open the gate. It took some time before he could unfasten all the ropes that bound the door to the stakes planted on both sides of the gateway as door posts. Then Yamogi came in and both men began to tiptoe cautiously towards the hut in which Dr. Wiseman and Kotokro were waiting for them, with Yamogi leading the way.

Just as they were about to reach the entrance Dr. Wiseman and Kotokro suddenly rushed out of the hut.

"Hawool! Hawool! Hooi! Hooi" they cried simultaneously.

Yamogi and Dankida were so terrified at the sudden and unexpected appearance that they turned round and, yelling with fright, bumped into each other as they tried to escape. Dankida fell to the ground and lay unconscious. Yamogi however, managed to flee, screaming with terror.

Soon the whole village was astir. People ran to meet him wondering what could be the matter. He could hardly explain.

"He has changed! He has changed!" he cried again and again.

"Who has changed?" they asked.

"The white man. He has changed."

"What has he changed?"

"The white man has changed himself into a gorilla and a lion?"

"The whiteman has changed into a gorilla and a lion?" they asked incredulously.

"Yes, he has. He is a witch - a big, big witch."

"How can one man change himself into two beasts at the same time, even if he is a witch?" they asked.

"Go and see. He is in the hut. You will see him changed into a gorilla and a lion. Seeing is believing."

Without more ado the people ran to the hut in which Dr. Wiseman and Kotokro were. Everyone was eager to see this wonderful phenomenon of one man changed into two mutually hostile beasts.

Meantime, as soon as Dr. Wiseman and Kotokro had put the two men to flight, they quickly divested themselves of the animal skins and stood once more in their birthday suits. Then seeing Dankida lying stretched on the ground they proceeded to examine him. They found that he was not dead, for he was still breathing. They brought water and began to pour it over him in order to revive him.

They were thus engaged when the crowd arrived, led by Yamogi. He was shaking so violently that he could hardly remain on his feet. He had to be supported by four men. As soon as he set eyes upon Dr. Wiseman and Kotokro he began to scream again.

"There he is! He has changed himself again into two human beings."

"Who has changed himself again into two human beings?" they asked.

"The white man. He has. Yes, he has changed himself again into two human beings! The dreadful, dreadful witch!"

The people were greatly puzzled. They could not at all understand what he was taking about. They looked at one another and shook their heads.

"He has not been well," his wife explained. "He has had a severe attack of malaria fever, and that must have unsettled his brains."

"Who says I have not been well, silly woman." asked Yamogi angrily.

"Why, who doesn't know that you have been sick for three days now and that that is why you did not go to the hunt with the men today?" many asked.

"I have not been sick. I am perfectly well. And I tell you he is a witch," he persisted.

"This is really serious?" said his sister. "Please help me to take him to Papa Tobi, the medicine man."

"I am not going to any medicine man. I am not sick. I am well and say that the white man is a witch."

"He is raving. We must take him to papa Tobi at once," said many of the spectators.

The four men who were supporting him at once bundled him up and started to take him away. He struggled and tried to free himself, but all in vain. Many more people came to hold his hands and his feet. They took him to Papa Tobi, the medicine man, protesting in vain that he was not sick.

By now the day had completely dawned and everyone was up. They found Papa Tobi in his hut getting ready to go to the bush to look for medicinal herbs. This was something he did first thing every morning. The leaves which he gathered for his medicinal concoctions must have the morning dew on them.

"What's the matter with him?" he asked as soon as Yamogi was deposited on the ground before him.

"He is raving mad," they replied. "He needs your cure."

"Bring him into the hut," said Papa Tobi.

They bundled him inside, still protesting vehemently. Then Papa Tobi examined him and asked if he had had malaria fever.

"Yes, he has been sick for the past three days," his wife confirmed.

"It's a lie. I have not been sick," he protested.

"Never mind" said Papa Tobi. "If you have not been sick you are sick now. You need a cure."

"I don't need any cure."

"Oh yes, you do," Papa Tobi said emphatically.

With that he produced some liquid concoction in a calabash and offered him to drink.

"I wont drink it," he refused. "I swear I am not sick."

"Hold him," Papa Tobi ordered. "If we don't force him he will not drink. It is the usual behaviour of people afflicted with this kind of sickness."

The people tightened their grip on him. Papa Tobi then opened his mouth by force and poured the medicine into it. It was twice more bitter than quinine and contained ninety per cent alcohol.

He spat it out. Then Papa Tobi held his nose tightly and gave him a second doze. He was unable to spit it out now and had to swallow it.

"Good," said Papa Tobi, straightening himself up. "He will be all right now. Let him go."

It was not long before the alcohol had gone to Yamogi's head. He began to laugh hilariously. Then he beat his chest and said:

"To hell with all of you. I don't fear any of you - gorilla or lion or witch. Damn you all."

"Don't mind his raving," said Papa Tobi. "He will eventually calm down. But before then he will reach a stage of destructive violence. So take him to his house and put him in stocks. He will go to sleep after some time. And when he wakes up he will be calm and sober again."

He gave them some of the over-bitter concoction and instructed that if he continued to behave abnormally after waking up they must force him to drink more of it. They must continue to do so until he was completely cured.

Still raving and saying that he did not fear anything under the sun or above it, he was led away to his house and put in stocks, as Papa Tobi had directed. He of course put up a stiff resistance, but he was overpowered by the combined strength of his captors and the effect of the alcohol. He gradually began to calm down and, after a while, fell into a peaceful slumber.

Meanwhile his friend, Dankida, was in a worse condition. When the crowd found Dr. Wiseman and Kotokro pouring water on him they asked what was the matter. Kotokro explained that he was just coming out of the hut to go to toilet when he saw the two men in the compound. He did not know what they had come there for. Immediately upon seeing him they had taken to their heels. But as they did so, Yamogi, who was following Dankida, tripped the latter and he fell to the ground unconscious. That was why they were trying to revive him.

"They must have come for some sinister purpose," said Gotiplo, the village crier, "for why should they have come into somebody's compound at this hour of the morning and then taken to flight at the sight of this boy?"

He had hardly said so when, upon looking around he espied an arrow on the ground. It was the arrow which Dankida had brought and which Yamogi had thrown away as he fled. He picked it up.

"They must have come with this arrow to harm the white man," he said.

Everyone agreed that that must be so. Then they conveyed Dankida, still unconscious, to his house. Having tried in vain to revive him they summoned Papa Tobi, the medicine man. When he came he examined Dankida carefully, listening to his heart-beat and gazing into his eyes. Then he straightened himself up and shook his head.

"He will not recover," he said. "He is as good as dead." He was right. Dankida never opened his eyes again. In less than two hours after Papa Tobi had left him he breathed his last.

There was much lamentation in Fomaki that day. He was buried in the evening.

Both Dr. Wiseman and Kotokro were sorry for the tragedy that had befallen Yamogi and his friend, even though it had been of the latters' own making. It brought home to them the harm that blind superstition could bring to those who laboured under it. What surprised Dr. Wiseman however, was that two men in that state of primitive existence, men whom he regarded as savages, could be so ill-disposed as to plot the destruction of a fellow man in the way those two had done. He had always thought that only civilised people were capable of premeditated crimes. "Where is your noble savage that the philosopher wrote about?" he said to himself, more than to Kotokro.

"What do you mean?" Kotokro asked, overhearing him.

"I mean I don't see any difference between the civilised and the uncivilised person in respect of crime. Wickedness is not the prerogative of civilised life."

"Of course not; nor cleverness. Don't you see how cleverly they plotted?"

The next morning they went to see how Yamogi was getting on. He had recovered from the previous day's excitement and was calmly sitting down to breakfast, though still in stocks. But at the sight of them he immediately started yelling again.

"There they are - the gorilla and the lion," he shouted. "They are coming to get me. Bring spears and kill them."

His wife concluded that he had still not recovered, so she tried to persuade him to drink more of the medicine which Papa Tobi had prescribed for him. He refused. Where-upon she summoned four hefty young men. They held him and compelled him to swallow it. Within a few minutes the alcohol in the drug had gone to his head again and he was talking and raving as before. After sometime he calmed down again and went to sleep.

As soon as he woke up again he enquired where were the two beasts into which the white man had changed himself. Once more his wife concluded that

233

he was still unwell, so she called in the four young men again and he was compelled to drink the bitter potion.

This went on for four days, until realising that the enforced imbibition of that abominable liquid was the inevitable sequel to any repetition of his accusation, Yamogi decided to adopt a new strategy. So upon waking up the fourth time he called his wife and said:

"What a terrible ordeal I have been through: I have had a long bout of nightmares, due to the high fever that has afflicted me for days now. But why am I in stocks?"

His wife replied that he had been behaving violently as if he had lost his mind, and that Papa Tobi the medicine man had accordingly instructed that he should be put in stocks.

"Come and loosen me then. I am on the way to recovery," he said.

They removed him from the stocks and, after he had eaten, he enquired after his friend Dankida. He was informed that he was dead. He had died four days before, after being found lying unconscious in the compound where Dr. Wiseman and Kotokro lived.

Yamogi was visibly affected upon hearing the news, but he bore it bravely.

"What did he go to do there?" he asked.

"You should know," replied his wife. "Didn't you go there with him?"

"Did I indeed?" he asked, feigning ignorance.

"Of course you did. And you came screaming that you had seen the white man changed into a gorilla and a lion."

"How absurd! The fever must have run very high in my blood."

From now on, out of fear of unpleasant consequences Yamogi never again referred to Dr. Wiseman as a witch and never claimed to have seen him changed into a gorilla and a lion. So everyone concluded that he had been cured by Papa Tobi's treatment. And so indeed he had, sarcastically speaking.

Three days after Yamogi was seen to regain his sanity the men returned from the hunt. Securri brought with him all the handicraft which he had refused to carry when he and his two strangers were leaving the camp. Dr. Wiseman was very happy to have them, but wondered what had made Securri change his mind.

"Were you afraid that if you did not bring them I would harm you by my witchcraft?" he asked.

"Me? I do not fear your person, not to talk of your witchcraft, if indeed you have any. I brought them because I did not want you to think that I wanted them for myself; for if you had gone away, leaving them behind, you would have thought that I wanted you to do so, in order that I might have them for myself after your departure."

"Well, you are still going to have them if you do not help us to take them away when we are leaving here," said Dr. Wiseman.

"You will have to find someone else to carry them for you when you are leaving here. I am not the only one in the village.

Securri and the other men were shocked to learn of the tragedy that had befallen Yamogi and his friend; but they said that as for Yamogi he deserved it. His rabid hatred of the two strangers had boomeranged on him by the injury it inflicted upon his own mind. "Nothing is more destructive of mental health than rancour," they said. "It is that which has unsettled his brain and made him see a gorilla and a lion where there was only one human being."

As for Yamogi, upon learning for the first time that Kotokro had not gone with the hunters after all, but had remained behind with Dr. Wiseman, he became even more certain that he had indeed seen two creatures, namely a gorilla and a lion. However, he dared not repeat his claim for fear of dire consequences. So he stuck to his explanation that his queer behaviour had been occasioned by his sickness.

CHAPTER NINETEEN
DR. WISEMAN ACQUIRES YELLOW METALS

A fortnight after the men returned from the hunt they got ready to take their meat to the Republic of Blohim to sell. Dr. Wiseman and Kotokro were surprised when Securri brought out a pair of shorts and hung it up to dry.

"Have you had this all the time?" Dr. Wiseman asked him through Kotokro.

"Yes," he replied.

"Why didn't you wear it then?"

"Because I had no need to," he replied.

"But why have you brought it out now?"

"I am taking it to Blohim," he replied. "I shall not be allowed to cross the border into Blohim unless I wear it."

"Who will not allow you?"

"The Blohim border-guards. They do not allow anyone to enter their country unless they hide their private parts."

"Very sensible people," declared Dr. Wiseman.

"Sensible? I think they are rather dishonest, preferring to appear different from what they really are."

"Do all the others have something to cover themselves up when they travel outside Wapito-land?" asked Dr. Wiseman again.

"Yes, they have."

"Where can we get something to cover ourselves up when we are going away from here?"

"They sell all sorts of garments at the border with Gamberia. You can buy some when you arrive there," he informed him.

Dr. Wiseman was heartened to know that he would remain naked only in Wapito-land, where everyone was naked, but would be able to get some clothes to conceal his parts before he arrived in the Republic of Gamberia.

As for Kotokro it made little difference to him. He did not mind much if he had to arrive back home naked as he was. Although the people in Kantoma would be surprised to see him thus, no one would care much about it, particularly when they would have learned the circumstances.

The next morning the men set out. Each carried a heavy load of smoked meat in a skin bag slung over his shoulder. Yamogi, who had by now recovered to all intents and purposes, accompanied them. He had sufficient meat to sell too, despite the fact that he did not go with them to the hunt on the last occasion.

The men were away for about four months, with Dr. Wiseman and Kotokro waiting anxiously for their return. When they came back they brought plenty of gold. Securri had eight large nuggets, each weighing about ten kilos, and twenty others, each of the size of a chicken's egg. Some of the men had slightly less than this, but others, including Yamogi, had even more. He had ten large nuggets of the same size as Securri's, and thirty smaller ones.

Dr. Wiseman gasped and his eyes popped out at the sight of so much gold. He had never seen the like in all his waking life, nor even dreamt of such in his sleep. He estimated that even the smallest in Securri's collection would fetch not less than one hundred thousand Pounds Sterling in London. If the young man could arrive with his gold in Britain he would be one of the richest millionaires in all Europe.

"What are you going to do with all this gold?" he asked.

"I am taking it to Gamberia to buy salt, mirror, matches and other articles brought there from the white man's country." he replied.

Dr. Wiseman was very sorry that he had none of those articles to sell. If he could lay hands on even the two smallest ones he would never lack money all the rest of his life. But now he had no means of getting any, since he had absolutely nothing to sell. Suddenly it occurred to him that Securri might be interested in his brief-case, the only thing he had apart from the papers and the bank notes. Securri would obviously have no use for the papers and bank notes, both of which were, of course precious to him. Well, he could dispense with the brief-case if Securri would like to buy it; for he could easily purchase one to replace it on arrival at Blaft. He put the proposition to Kotokro and asked for his opinion.

"I doubt if he will want to buy it," he replied. "Anyhow ask him."

"Bring it then," said Dr. Wiseman.

Kotokro went into the room, opened the iron trunk and brought out the brief-case. Dr. Wiseman removed the papers and bank notes from it and showed it to Securri.

"I want to sell this," he said. "How much will you offer for it?"

Securri took and examined it.

"I don't want it," he said, handing it back to him. "I have my leather bag. It is bigger and stronger than this."

Seeing the disappointment in Dr. Wiseman's face he added: "If you would rather sell to me your iron trunk I would buy it. I am sure Yamogi would also like to buy your cutlass and your pen-knife. He said he was going to buy some from Gamberia."

"No, I cannot sell any of them" replied Dr. Wiseman ruefully. "They are not mine." And he glanced expectantly at Kotokro.

"We cannot sell the iron trunk, Doctor" Kotokro said, "because it contains our gorilla and our lion skins and we do not want them to see these. But you can sell the cutlass and the pen-knife, for I see you strongly desire to have gold."

"But they are yours" Dr. Wiseman pointed out, not un-expecting a hopeful reply.

"They are and they are not," replied Kotokro. "You bought them for me. You can have them, for my need for them is much less than your desire for the gold."

Dr. Wiseman was glad of the offer and thanked Kotokro.

"I shall buy you many more to replace them as soon as I arrive back in London," he promised.

Securri took them to Yamogi and said that the white man wanted to sell them. At first Yamogi would have nothing to do with them, saying that he did not want to possess a witch's articles. But he consented to buy them when Securri pointed out that if truly Dr. Wiseman and Kotokro were witches then the best way of depriving them of their powers was to take from them their instruments of destruction, which a cutlass and a pen-knife obviously were.

"Will he accept four big nuggets of gold?" he asked.

"Add four smaller ones" Securri urged. "I think they are worth much more than that."

Yamogi handed him four large nuggets each weighing ten kilos, and four small ones. Securri said that he was taking them to the white man to see if he would accept them.

When he came back and showed Dr. Wiseman what Yamogi had offered the latter could hardly believe it. He had not expected that the man would offer for them even one smaller nugget.

"Tell him to add another small one," said Kotokro to Securri, pretending that they were not enough. Dr. Wiseman said nothing.

Securri went back and told Yamogi that the white man had said that he could have them for one more small nugget. The latter was very happy to hear this and brought out one more, which Securri took to Dr. Wiseman.

"He was very happy to have had them for four large nugget and five smaller ones," he told Dr. Wiseman.

After Securri had left them Dr. Wiseman began to wonder if he had made a good bargain. Perhaps these things that looked like gold were, in reality, not gold at all, but some worthless metal. He could not see how anyone in his right mind could exchange such a large amount of gold for just an ordinary cutlass and a pen-knife. He called Kotokro and asked him to take a good look at them.

"Are they real gold?" he asked

"I do not know, Doctor," he replied. "I have never seen gold in my life and have no idea what it looks like or what it is used for. You may remember that when I first saw the asphalt in London I thought it was gold."

"Real gold is a very precious metal, yellow in colour, which can be used for all sorts of things," Dr. Wiseman explained.

"Can you eat or drink it?" asked Kotokro.

"What a silly question to ask!" shouted Dr. Wiseman. "If it is like these ones you see, how can anyone eat or drink it?"

"I see. But maybe you can wear it for dress, or sit on it as a chair, or sleep on it for a bed, or lie under it as a roof?"

"Nonsense! Only a mad man would think of doing any of those things with gold!"

"Of what use is gold then, if you cannot do any of those things with it?"

"It is very useful. You can use it for replacing a lost tooth, as well as for making jewellery and all sorts of ornaments."

"Why would anyone want to replace a lost tooth with gold?" asked Kotokro. "Would not ivory or something else be a better replacement? In any case, I would not like to be seen with gold for a tooth, if gold is as yellow as this. Why, it would make me look like a real witch!"

"Well, in my country people like to be seen with gold in their mouths. It makes them appear wealthy and elegant."

"And the jewellery. What do they use them for?"

"They wear them on their bodies and clothes, to make them appear wealthy and important."

"And what do they do with the ornaments?"

"They decorate their houses with them."

"For what purpose?"

"To make them appear wealthy."

"So gold is used for appearances only?"

"Yes, mostly."

Kotokro was greatly surprised to hear this but said nothing.

That evening Securri informed them that the men would set out for Gamberia in about two months time. Dr. Wiseman was highly excited. He began to imagine his arrival back in London with that large amount of gold. They would fetch him millions upon millions of Pounds Sterling.

Again and again momentary doubts and deep gloom took the place of elation in his heart. The metals looked like gold all right. But how could they really be gold when they were so cheap? He would wake up in the middle of the night trembling and sweating profusely. He had dreamt that he had arrived with them in London only to be told that all of them together were not worth a penny.

When Securri informed them of the impending journey to Gamberia he had also told them of the difficulties on the way. It was a long journey that usually took about a month to accomplish, he had said. There were many obstacles on the way, two of which were particularly difficult to overcome. The first was the passage through a terrain infested with scorpions. You had to go on stilts in order to avoid being stung to death by them. If while you were crossing on the stilts you happened to stumble and fall you would have no chance of getting up again alive, for they would instantly fall upon you and plunge their poisonous tails into your body. The second obstacle was a long tunnel at the end of which you stepped into Gamberian territory. It was very narrow and dark and winding, so that you ran the risk of bumping into the sides and injuring yourself unless you groped your way forward carefully as you went along. What was more, there was a gate at the end of the tunnel through which you were not allowed to pass unless you were able to give a pass-word. This consisted of a set of words which you had to repeat correctly.

Dr. Wiseman was greatly troubled when he heard this, for he did not know how to walk on stilts. How then would he be able to cross the terrain of scorpions and eventually arrive back in London with his precious gold?

"Do not worry, Doctor," said Kotokro, observing him. "It is not difficult to walk on stilts. I shall teach you how to do it."

"Will you indeed?" asked Dr. Wiseman hopefully.

"Yes. We can start right now."

"But what about the pass-word? Does Securri know?"

Kotokro asked Securri what was the pass-word.

"I do not know," he replied. "It changes every day, and it is transmitted from the gate at the Gamberian border to the beginning of the tunnel for those wanting to enter to learn it before they start doing so."

"Does it mean then that we shall not know what it is until we arrive at the beginning of the tunnel?" asked Kotokro.

"Exactly."

Kotokro told Dr. Wiseman and added encouragingly: "I am sure it will not be difficult for you to learn."

Kotokro borrowed stilts from Securri and began teaching Dr. Wiseman how to walk on them. It was not at all easy for the learned Doctor. He kept on falling any time he tried to stand up on them. It took him more than a week before he could stand up erect on them. Then he tried to walk. Upon taking the first step he came crashing down. He bruised his knees and sprained his right arm, and it took a fortnight before he was sufficiently recovered to resume the lesson. By the end of the seventh week he could only manage to totter along for some distance before falling, rather in the manner of a youngster learning to ride a bicycle. At last he said to Kotokro:

"I don't think I can learn it. It is much too difficult. It is not a skill that an intellectual like me can acquire. It is easier for people without high intelligence, such as blacks and acrobats."

"Then it sometimes pays to be without high intelligence," replied Kotokro, "for it is obvious that you can never return safely to London with your gold."

"Why?"

"Because you cannot learn to walk on stilts on account of your high intelligence. That means that you can never traverse the terrain infested with scorpions and will have to stay behind."

Dr. Wiseman saw at once that what Kotokro had said was true. Unless he learned to walk on stilts he would be doomed to remain in Wapito-land forever. He shuddered at the prospect.

"Well, I will try hard. Maybe I shall succeed," he said.

"I am sure you will," replied Kotokro encouragingly. "It took me only three days to learn it."

Dr. Wiseman resumed the lessons, determined more than ever before to succeed. He fell to the ground again and again, but he never gave up. At the end of the eighth week he could walk a fairly long distance without falling down. He was delighted.

And now the day for their departure came. Dr. Wiseman removed the papers and bank notes from his brief-case and gave them to Kotokro to put them in his iron trunk. Then he filled the brief-case with the gold which he had obtained from Yamogi. He wanted to carry this himself to make sure it remained safe.

The problem now was with the earthen ware which Securri had brought to the village on the men's last visit to the hunt. Securri would not carry them for Dr. Wiseman, neither would anyone else, for they all had their own loads to carry. The Doctor was greatly upset, for he was faced with the painful prospect of having to leave them behind. He calculated that if he was able to arrive in London with them they would fetch not less than some Forty Thousand Pounds Sterling at an auction at Christies. What a loss it would be if he had to go without them.

He implored Securri, through Kotokro, to carry for him just two dishes, two cups and two water pots, promising that he would give him Five Pounds Sterling in bank notes on arrival at the Gamberian boarder.

"I wont carry for you even one cup for all your bank notes" snapped Securri. "I told you I would not carry them one step beyond this village and I mean to keep my word." Then observing the look of deep disappointment on the Doctor's face he added: "I'll tell you what I can do. If you like I shall buy them, together with the ones Kotokro brought with him in the iron trunk. Not that I particularly want them for anything, but just to help you."

"What would you pay for them?" asked Dr. Wiseman eagerly.

"Ten small nuggets of gold for the whole lot of them." replied Securri.

Dr. Wiseman's heart leapt for joy. He could hardly believe it. He had seen the nuggets of gold which Securri had brought and knew that any of the small ones would fetch a large sum of money on the London market.

"Make it twelve," he haggled, taking his cue from Kotokro.

"No, ten, take or leave it."

Dr. Wiseman did not attempt to bargain further, lest Securri might change his mind and withdraw his offer. He seemed to him to be so unpredictable, like most blacks.

"All right, I accept your offer," he said quickly.

Securri at once handed him ten of his small nuggets of gold and took away all the earthen-ware. Dr. Wiseman added them to his collection in the brief-case. By now the brief-case was so heavy that he could hardly lift it up, much less travel with it. He was determined, however, to go away with it even if it cost him his life.

It was about six o'clock next morning when Dr. Wiseman and Kotokro said good-bye to Elder Oloko and Chief Dogobisa and set out with the men. There were ten of them, including Securri. Yamogi did not go, because he had already purchased from Dr. Wiseman the two most important things he was going to buy. Besides, even if he had not had them he would have hesitated to travel in the company of the two strangers whom he still regarded as witches. As far as he was concerned their departure was good riddance, and he did not regret being the only one among the men to be left behind.

CHAPTER TWENTY
THE JOURNEY TO GAMBERIA

From the start Dr. Wiseman found the going difficult. He kept depositing his brief-case on the ground at every few steps to regain his breath and rest his arm that was straining under that heavy load. This retarded their progress greatly, for they had to travel in company and could not leave the Doctor and Kotokro behind. At last Securri offered to help.

"No, I shall manage," the Doctor declined, fearing Securri might disappear with it once he laid his hands upon it. Kotokro he could trust to some extent, because his brief acquaintance with the white man's ways had taught him a certain amount of honesty, but not this raw child of nature to whom right and wrong were like identical twins.

Soon Dr. Wiseman was so tired that he sat down to rest. Then the men became impatient and threatened to leave him behind. He rose up to his feet again and took up the brief-case. But he had hardly taken two more steps forward when he stumbled and fell prostrate on the ground. The brief-case at once flew from his hand and landed some distance away. Securri ran towards it with the intention of retrieving it for the Doctor.

"Stop him!," yelled Dr. Wiseman. "He will run away with my gold!"

No one paid any attention to him, for the Doctor's queer behaviour had made them all jump to the conclusion that he was not quite himself, being over-excited at the prospect of returning home. Before he could rise to his feet again Securri stood beside him with the brief-case.

"Here is your precious possession" he said contemptuously handing it to him. "I have no use for it or its contents."

Dr. Wiseman perceived now that his suspicion had not been justified. If Securri could bring the brief-case to him when he was down on his belly, it was most unlikely that he would try to make off with it when he stood firmly on his two feet and was in a more advantageous position for pursuit.

"Please carry it for me," he pleaded with Securri, "for now I see the weight is beyond my strength."

At first Securri would not oblige him. But when Kotokro added his voice and the others also said that if he did not the Doctor would retard their progress, he at last consented to do so. After this they were able to proceed more rapidly.

They travelled the whole day and, towards nightfall, came to a little village of about twenty houses deep in the heart of the thick jungle. They decided to spend the night here and continue their journey the next day. As they made their way to the chief's house to ask for accommodation a large crowd of men, women and children, all naked, followed them, being attracted by the sight of a white man among them.

"He is an albino," some said.

"No, he is not," others disagreed. "Don't you see his straight hair?"

"He is wearing a wig of horse hair," the others explained.

They spoke in a tongue slightly different from the Wapito language, but Kotokro was able to catch most of what they said and to interpret it to Dr. Wiseman, who found it all amusing.

Suddenly, as they kept on arguing about Dr. Wiseman's hair, a little urchin of about four stepped forward and, before anyone could suspect what he was up to, pulled the Doctor's hair so hard that he winced. Thereupon his mother, who was standing by, seized and spanked him until he yelled with pain.

"Stop beating him!" shouted Dr. Wiseman.

"He is a very naughty boy," said his mother, "he is always up to some mischief."

"Well, you were all arguing about the nature of my hair," said Dr. Wiseman, "he wanted to put it to the test."

"Is that a mark of intelligence?" asked Kotokro.

"That could have been a mark of intelligence in a white child" replied Dr. Wiseman. "But I think the boy is really mischievous as his mother says."

They spent the night at the chief's compound and resumed their journey early next morning. For over two weeks they travelled through a dense jungle, spending the nights in villages and little hamlets along the way. They crossed rivers and climbed over or crawled under fallen trees, some of which were of unimaginable size. On occasions the trees were so gigantic and lay so firmly on the ground that they could neither cross over nor crawl under them. Then they had to make a detour round them. Some of the trees had just fallen during a heavy storm, so that there were no beaten tracks round them and they had to go round them through tangled undergrowths.

On the twentieth day after leaving Fomaki they found themselves in a more open terrain, where the trees grew more sparsely and were of lesser girth and height. There were now fewer impediments in their way, but they were more exposed to the fierce rays of the sun and found their day's journey more exhausting.

They continued to spend the nights from village to village. At last they arrived in a small town of about eight hundred inhabitants. It was called Nampatu. It was at the bank of a wide but shallow river called River Banjo.

"We are now about to arrive at the land of the scorpions" Securri informed them. "Only this river separates it from that place."

"Since we did not bring any stilts how are we going to cross?" asked Kotokro.

"We didn't have to bring stilts," replied Securri. "In the first place it would have been difficult to carry them all the way to Tonko and back. Secondly we can purchase some from here. They are very cheap."

"Then what do we do with them after we have crossed the scorpions' territory?"

"We can sell them at the other side."

Securri had hardly finished speaking when several of the inhabitants, both young and old, came running towards them. Everyone of them carried stilts for sale. Securri handed Dr. Wiseman his brief-case. One old man of about sixty approached the Doctor and shoved him several pairs of stilts, some short others long.

"Which one do you want?" he asked.

"I want a pair of the short ones," he replied. "I can't walk on long stilts."

The man gave him a short pair.

"How much is it?" asked Dr. Wiseman.

"How much will you pay?" the man asked in turn.

"One Pound," he replied.

"What is one Pound?"

Dr. Wiseman asked Kotokro to open the iron trunk and take out the money. He did so, making sure that no one espied what else was in the trunk. Dr. Wiseman handed the man one Pound bank note. The latter examined it with curious eyes, dwelling more particularly on the Queen's head on it.

"What is it?" he asked, after gazing upon it for some time.

"It is one Pound," replied Dr. Wiseman.

"What do you do with it?" he asked again.

"It is money. You buy things with it."

The man flung it contemptuously on the ground.

"Nonsense," he said. "Who will take this for a pair of stilts?"

"I will make it two," Dr. Wiseman offered.

"You can make it two thousand," snapped the man. "I will have none of it. Why, a million of it will not be worth one leaf from the tree over there. With one or two of those leaves I can at least wipe my bottom when I go to toilet. This your leaf, which you call money, cannot perform for me even that duty."

"What do you want then?" asked Dr. Wiseman, unable to comprehend the man's attitude.

"Gold, of course."

"What amount of gold?"

"Two small nuggets."

"You old rascal!" exclaimed Dr. Wiseman. "Do you think I do not know the value of gold? These stilts are not worth a hundredth of a small nugget of gold."

The man laughed, displaying a row of scattered teeth.

"They are not worth a hundredth of a small nugget of gold, did you say?" he asked.

"They are not, and you know it."

"Then go and get one for your useless leaves which you say can be used for buying things," he said. And with that he turned and went away.

Dr. Wiseman saw another man with about three pairs of stilts. He called to him and asked how much was a pair of stilts. The man stretched out one pair to him. It was exactly like the one the old man had refused to sell.

"Five small nuggets of gold," he replied.

Dr. Wiseman could hardly believe his ears.

"How much did you say?" he asked again.

"Five small nuggets of gold," he repeated.

"I will give you two pounds," Dr. Wiseman offered.

"What is two Pounds?"

The Doctor took and stretched out to him two bank notes. Without so much as looking at them the man flung them away.

"What do you mean by offering me ordinary leaves for my stilts?" he asked angrily.

"They are not leaves," replied Dr. Wiseman.

"What are they?"

"Money."

"What is money?"

"Something you buy things with."

"Gold is the only thing you buy things with, so don't tell me these are gold"

"They are not gold; but they are worth as much as gold."

"That is a lie" the man said fiercely. "If you think that you can defraud me of my stilts, you are much mistaken, my dear fellow."

"He is not lying," confirmed Kotokro, who had hitherto been merely interpreting. "In his country these are used for buying things."

"Which country?"

"The white man's country. You can see that he is a white man."

"They are fools! Why, if someone refuses to accept them in payment what can you do with them? They are absolutely useless."

"No one can refuse to accept them in payment. If he does he will be punished."

"By whom?"

"By the Government."

"Who is the Government?"

"The group of men who rule the land."

"Including the chief?"

"Yes including the chief."

The man laughed.

"The people must be cowards then," he said. "Why should they allow the chief and his elders to force them to accept these useless leaves in exchange for their goods?"

"I agree with you," said Kotokro. "I really don't know why they put up with it."

"Well, I am not ready to put up with it. His Government can do nothing to me."

And with that he turned to go away.

"Wait!" said Dr. Wiseman. "I shall give you gold. But five is far too much. I shall give you one small nugget."

"I shall not accept even two. If you really mean to buy them then take them for three. That is my last offer."

Dr. Wiseman said he could not pay that much, so the man went away. He and Kotokro approached seller after seller, but the least anyone would take was four small nuggets. Then the Doctor said to Kotokro:

"Let's look for the old man. He was prepared to sell his for three."

They searched for him for a long time without finding him. At last, just as they were about to give up the search, they espied him haggling with one of the men who was trying to buy a pair of long stilts. Approaching him Kotokro said:

"We are prepared to buy the short stilts for three small nuggets of gold."

The man smiled.

"I knew you would come back," he said. "My prices are the most moderate. How many pairs do you want?"

"Make it two." replied Dr. Wiseman. "I want one for myself and one for my young friend."

The man handed him two pairs. Dr. Wiseman reluctantly took out six small nuggets of gold from his brief-case and gave them to him.

"All of them are rascals and cheats," he remarked as soon as the old man had gone away. "Fancy his selling two pairs of common stilt, made of wood, for six small nuggets of gold."

"But you sold only a single cutlass and a pen-knife to Yamogi for four big nuggets of gold plus five small ones," remarked Kotokro. "Were they worth that amount of gold"?

"Whether they were worth that amount of gold or not, is neither here nor there," replied Dr. Wiseman. "Yamogi was glad to have the cutlass and the pen-knife for that amount of gold; and I too was satisfied with the amount of gold he paid to me. That is all that is important in matters of trade. As long as both sides are satisfied the deal is fair and reasonable. But in this case the old man is obviously satisfied while I am not. It is not fair. He has cheated me."

"Is that why the white traders who first came to Gamberia purchased people with only a small bag of salt?"

"Who told you that?"

"Old Rakito. That was why he asked you whether you had come to revive the Slave Trade in another guise when you and Jimfa came to Kantoma to take away a boy of my age."

"Did he really ask that?"

"He did. But I believe Jimfa did not interpret it to you. He must have been afraid you would take offence."

"Oh, I see. Is that why the crowd laughed?"

"Yes."

"Well, I don't think it was unfair to buy a person with a small bag of salt if the seller was satisfied with the deal. If he was not, no one compelled him to agree to it."

"But if you are not satisfied who compels you to agree to this deal?"

"Necessity."

"Then you should blame necessity, not the seller. I am sure he will be prepared to return your gold and get his stilts back if you are not satisfied."

"If I return the stilts how can I cross the territory of scorpions?"

"True, you cannot. So you need the stilts, and the deal is fair."

While all this was going on the other men were also looking for stilts to buy. At last everyone had had a pair and they all assembled together to resume the journey.

Kotokro helped Dr. Wiseman to put on his stilts. But the Doctor only managed to stand erect and take a few steps forward when he came crashing to the ground. Fortunately he did not hurt himself. He tried again and again but with the same result. It was evident that those few weeks without practice had made the learned Doctor forget all that he had learnt.

"It is no use," he said at last to Kotokro. "I cannot walk on stilts. Even if I succeed in going some distance I run the risks of falling among the scorpions before I can travel out of their territory."

"What is to be done then, Doctor"? asked Kotokro. "Having come this far, are you going to remain here or turn back because you cannot learn to walk on stilts?"

"I don't know. Maybe I can stay here and practise until I master it."

"But these men will not wait for us. And after they have gone we may not be able to find our way."

"That is true," conceded Dr. Wiseman ruefully. "I am in a hopeless situation. I cannot see any way out." And with that he sat down and propped his head on his knees in utter dejection.

Just at this moment Securri noticed what was happening.

"Is your white friend still unable to walk on stilts?" he asked Kotokro.

"He has forgotten how to walk on them," he replied.

"Never mind," said Securri. "He can hire some of these men to carry him across in a hammock."

Kotokro told Dr. Wiseman. He was greatly relieved to hear this. He sprang to his feet at once.

"I wonder if they will take bank notes" he remarked.

"No one will accept your bank notes on this journey until you arrive on Gamberian territory," replied Securri. "They will be of no use to anyone."

"What will they ask for, then?"

"Gold, of course."

The information dampened the Doctor's spirits once more.

"I wonder how much gold they will ask for?"

"Not much," Securri assured him.

"All right. Call them then."

Securri went away and was soon back with two hefty men carrying a hammock.

"Here they are" said Securri. "I have bargained with them and they say they will charge six small nuggets of gold."

"What! Six nuggets?" exclaimed Dr. Wiseman. "Do they know how much that is worth? About two million Pounds Sterling."

"How much then will you give?" asked Securri.

"Not more than one small nugget." replied Dr. Wiseman.

"But you agreed to pay three for the stilts which, by themselves, cannot carry you across without your expending your energy in operating them, even assuming that you could walk on them?"

"Quite; because I could sell them afterwards and get back some of my money," replied Dr. Wiseman. But I cannot sell these rascally fellows when they deposit me at the other side. I shall lose my money without any gain."

"True, Doctor," Kotokro agreed. "You cannot sell anyone these days. I suggest you give them three small nuggets then, for I am sure they will not accept one."

"All right tell them three, the Doctor yielded at last, Kotokro told the men. They laughed.

"This man is really funny," they said.

"How much will you take then?" asked Kotokro.

"We have already told your friend. We said six."

"Wont you take four?"

The men were so angry that without replying they turned round and went away. Securri had to go round again looking for others carriers. He found two who said they would take eight small nuggets. After hard bargain they agreed to take six. He brought them to the Doctor.

"Won't they take four?" Dr. Wiseman asked when Securri told him how much they had agreed to charge.

"Don't ask them, Doctor," advised Kotokro who was interpreting. "They may get angry and go away like the others did."

Dr. Wiseman would have continued to haggle about the charge, but by now the men who had been waiting for him, were getting impatient. They threatened to go and leave him behind if he delayed their departure further. So the Doctor very reluctantly agreed to pay the carriers six small nuggets.

"But what am I to do with this pair of stilts which I have already bought," he asked. "will the seller take them back?"

"He will, and there he is," replied Securri, pointing to the old man.

The man readily took them back and returned Dr. Wiseman his three nuggets of gold. Then the carriers brought a hammock and put the Doctor in, and the journey began.

They waded across the river and were soon in the territory of scorpions.

All the other men were in front, followed by the men carrying Dr. Wiseman, with Kotokro and Securri bringing up the rear.

Never before had Dr. Wiseman seen any sight so frightful. Huge scorpions, each about three feet long from head to tail, were swarming all over the ground.

As the men passed through them they raised up their tails to sting, burying them in the stilts. It was obvious that no man could have advanced a single yard through them on his own feet, for they would instantly have stung him to death.

They had covered a distance of some four miles, which was about half the distance across the territory, when the carriers suddenly stopped. They were sweating profusely.

"This man is too heavy," they complained. "We are tired. We cannot carry him for six small nugget of gold. He must make it eight, as we originally demanded."

"What are they saying?" asked Dr. Wiseman.

"They say you are too heavy, so they cannot carry you for six small nuggets of gold. You must make it eight," Kotokro interpreted.

"Didn't I tell you that these primitive people are unreliable and dishonest? " said Dr. Wiseman. "After they have bargained with me to carry me across for six small nuggets of gold they are now demanding eight"

"What do you intend to do then?" asked Kotokro.

"I will not add a sou," replied the Doctor angrily.

Kotokro interpreted it to the men.

"In that case we shall either leave him here or take him back to whence we brought him," they threatened.

"They cannot do either," said Dr. Wiseman when Kotokro told him what they had said. "A bargain is a bargain. They have to fulfil their part of it."

Kotokro told them.

"Fair enough," they agreed. "Since we undertook to carry him across for six small nuggets of gold we shall do so without extra charge. But right now we are tired. So we shall deposit him on the ground while we rest."

So saying they began to lower the hammock. Immediately a swarm of scorpions gathered round and raised up their tails to receive the arguing Doctor.

"Hey! Hey!" shouted Dr. Wiseman. "What are they up to?"

"They say that since you insist on your rights they will carry you for the six nuggets agreed upon," explained Kotokro. "But right now they are tired and want to rest, so they are depositing you on the ground first."

"Nonsense! If they want to rest they must do so without putting me down."

Kotokro told the men.

"We did not bargain with him to rest in that way," they replied. "So down he will go." With that they continued to lower him down.

"All right, all right" the Doctor said quickly. "Let them carry me across without resting. I agree to pay them eight nuggets."

Kotokro told the men that the Doctor had agreed to pay them the extra two nuggets.

"That's more sensible," they said. And with that they raised up the hammock once more, just as the Doctor was about to come into contact with the waiting scorpions, and resumed the journey.

At last they came to another river which was as wide and shallow as the one they had crossed. It marked the boundary of the land of scorpions. They waded across it and were soon on the other side. The carriers let down Dr. Wiseman and demanded their pay.

"I have a good mind not to pay you anything" said the Doctor. "You blackmailed me into agreeing to give you eight nuggets instead of the six originally agreed upon."

"Doctor, I think it will be better to pay them their eight nuggets of gold and let them go away. They may be black, but they did not carry you as a mail," advised Kotokro, whose English vocabulary was rather incomplete despite his generally good command of the language.

"Nonsense! when I say they blackmailed me, I mean they forced me, like the blackguards they are, to agree, against my will, to pay them eight nuggets instead of the six originally agreed upon."

"Black-guards, did you say?," asked Kotokro, feeling more puzzled than enlightened by the Doctor's explanation. "They are of course black. But I don't think they are guards."

"Nonsense!" shouted Dr. Wiseman impatiently. "When I say blackmail, blackguard, black-leg, black sheep or black anything at all, all I mean is that it is bad. In the English language we use the word black to connote an undesirable quality. Anything said to be black is no good."

"I see. Only white things are good?"

"Of course."

"But coal, ebony and many other black things are also good, aren't they?"

"They are."

"What about black men?"

"Some are good. But others, like these two rascals, are no good at all."

"What about white men? Are not some good and others bad?"

"Yes, of course. Among men there are good and bad ones. However, there are more good white men than there are good black men."

"Are you sure of that?" asked Kotokro.

"Sure"

"What is the explanation then?"

"We don't know as yet. It is one of the things I aim to discover in my research."

"I see. And there are more bad white men than there are bad black men?"

"How? Does that make sense, my boy?"

"It does" Old Rakito says that there are more white men than there are black men."

"Hey mister," cried the two carriers, growing impatient at the delay in paying them, "pay us at once and do not waste our time with babbling in a language we do not understand."

Dr. Wiseman opened his brief-case and took out eight small nuggets of gold which he grudgingly gave to the two men. He would have added his curses, but something told him it was not Christian. Besides they wouldn't have understood. And what is the use of cursing a person who does not understand what you are saying? You might as well do it behind his back; so he kept quiet. The men took it and went away.

By now all their fellow travellers had descended from their stilts. Many traders came round, wanting to buy them. Securri sold his, a long pair, for eight small nuggets, thus making one hundred percent profit; for he had bought them for four. Kotokro was also able to sell his stilts for four small nuggets. He too thus made a profit of hundred per cent. He gave it to Dr. Wiseman, saying: "You can have it; for you bought the stilts for me with your gold."

"Are you sure you don't need it?" asked Dr. Wiseman.

"No, I have no use for it," replied Kotokro.

"Thank you, my boy," said Dr. Wiseman, putting it into his brief-case.

All the others were able to sell their stilts for twice the amount for which they bought them. Seeing everyone thus making so much profit Dr. Wiseman began to regret not having come on stilts. If only he had been able to come on them, instead of being carried in a hammock, he too would have been able to make hundred per cent profit. Having bought the stilts for two nuggets of gold he would have been able to sell them for four, as Kotokro had done, so that not only would he have saved his eight nuggets but he would have gained an extra two, making ten. He felt very sorry.

"Cheer up, Doctor," encouraged Kotokro, observing his mood. "It is a lesson that will serve you well in the future."

"What lesson?"

"That it sometimes pays to be able to do things which only the unintelligent, such as black men and acrobats, do."

Dr. Wiseman made no reply. The loss he had incurred weighed too heavily upon his mind for him to be able to say anything.

After they had finished selling their stilts the men decided to spend the night there and resume their journey the next day, for it was already getting late. They had no difficulty in getting somewhere to sleep and food to eat. The inhabitants of the town vied with one another in providing them hospitality.

One man, an albino, came and offered to take Dr. Wiseman and Kotokro to his house for the night.

"How much will he charge?" asked Dr. Wiseman.

"Nothing," replied the man. "It is always a pleasure for me to entertain strangers free of charge."

Dr. Wiseman's suspicion was immediately aroused. He had never before heard of anyone wanting to entertain strangers free of charge.

"Are you sure he will not steal my gold when we are asleep?" he asked Kotokro. "I don't trust any black."

"He will not" Kotokro assured him. "Anyhow he is not black. He is a white man like yourself."

"He is not a whiteman" Dr. Wiseman disagreed. "He is a black man like you. In intelligence and general character he is like all other blacks."

"I don't understand, Doctor," said Kotokro. "What makes a white man white?"

"It is the absence of pigment or colouring matter in his skin."

"And is there pigment or colouring matter in the skin of this man?"

"Of course not. That is why he looks white."

"Why, then, do you say that he is not a white man like yourself, but rather a black man like me?"

"Because his features are not those of a white man. His hair is woolly, his nose is flat and his mouth is big."

"I see. So it is the features that make a man black or white?"

"It is both the features and the absence of pigment in his skin. This man possesses only one of the distinguishing characteristics of a white man."

"So if his hair had been straight, his nose pointed and his mouth small then he would have been a white man, even if one or both of his parents were black?"

"No, he would still have been a black man."

"I don't understand," said Kotokro.

"To be a white man his parents, right down to his remotest ancestors, must all have been white."

"Does it mean, then, that even if he had only a single drop of Negro blood in him he would still be regarded as a black man, even though he may look whiter than a white man?"

"Exactly. That is why many white-looking people in America and elsewhere are classified as black."

"But you once said that all men came from Adam and Eve?"

"When? I don't remember."

"When we were discussing about nakedness after the piece of cloth was washed away from your loins while we were crossing the river. You said that Adam and Eve were the first man and woman created by God, which means that they were the first ancestors of all men, black and white."

"My boy, that doesn't follow. They were the first ancestors of white men only."

"I still don't understand, Doctor...." said Kotokro.

"Of course you don't, because of your lack of intelligence," replied Doctor Wiseman, cutting him short.

The albino had been waiting for their reply to his offer of hospitality and was getting rather impatient with their long conversation, of which he could make neither head nor tail.

"Do you want to come with me or not?" he asked.

"Do you see that?" said Dr. Wiseman "You can see from his eyes that he has an eye to my gold. Otherwise why should he insist upon offering us free hospitality?"

"He is not insisting upon anything, and he will not steal your gold," replied Kotokro, "so let us accept his kind offer."

"All right, provided you are sure he will not steal my gold." Dr. Wiseman yielded at last.

Kotokro told the man that they accepted his offer and were ready to go with him. The man led the way and they followed. As they went along, Dr. Wiseman kept asking Kotokro if he was quite sure the man would not steal his gold while they slept.

"We can take steps to ensure that he does not steal your gold, if you have any doubt about his honesty." Kotokro assured him.

"What steps?" he asked.

"We will take turns in keeping watch."

Dr. Wiseman thought this to be a good idea. So he held his peace and followed the man quietly. It was not long before they arrived at his house, where he provided them with a sumptuous dinner. Although Dr. Wiseman was very hungry he ate very little, for fear he might sleep deep and wake up to find his gold gone, in spite of Kotokro's promise to keep watch.

That night Kotokro kept on waking up from sleep again and again to take turns in keeping watch as he had suggested, but there was no need for him to have thus inconvenienced himself. Dr. Wiseman never slept a wink. The fear of losing his gold kept him awake throughout the night, so that he rose up next morning feeling more tired than before he went to bed.

CHAPTER TWENTY-ONE
THE PASS WORD

Immediately after breakfast the next morning all the men gathered together and resumed their journey. After paying the eight nuggets of gold to the carriers Dr. Wiseman's brief-case had become lighter and so he was now able to carry it himself, although he still did so with some difficulty.

They travelled for another four days and at last arrived at a place called Dondolu, a straggling town of about four hundred inhabitants. It stood at the foot of a mountain that rose thousands of feet high. Houses were dotted here and there with inter-connecting paths and patches of bushy grounds. There was a market quite close to the main path leading into the town, where all sorts of merchandise were on sale. Everyone here wore clothes. It was the first time Dr. Wiseman and Kotokro were seeing people wearing clothes ever since they arrived in Wapito-land and they felt greatly embarrassed over their own nakedness, particularly the Doctor.

"This is the last town before we arrive on Gamberian territory," Securri informed them.

"Are we going to cross this mountain to get there?" Kotokro asked.

"Yes, but not over it." replied Securri. "There is a tunnel under it a short distance from here. It is the tunnel I spoke to you about. We shall have to go through it to get to the other side."

Securri added that all the men were going to rest there briefly before resuming their journey, as the passage through the tunnel was long and difficult. As soon as you entered you could not stop to rest until you found yourself on the other side.

The other men had sat down under the shade of a tree as Securri spoke. And now they began to take out dresses from their bags. Everyone of them had brought something to wear for the rest of the journey, except Dr. Wiseman and Kotokro. This made the Doctor feel even more embarrassed.

"From where can we get something to wear too?" Kotokro asked Securri when he saw him donning a pair of shorts, the same which he had worn when he was going to Blohim.

"Go into the shop over there," he replied. "They sell all sorts of clothes there. But be back soon, for we shall not remain here for long."

Dr. Wiseman and Kotokro proceeded to the shop indicated. They found dresses of all sizes and fashions on sale as Securri had said. The Doctor saw a suit which looked quite elegant and he asked the price.

"Two large nuggets of gold," replied the seller, an important-looking young man of about thirty, neatly dressed in a suit with a tie to match and wearing a bowler hat even though he was indoors.

"What! two large nuggets of gold?" exclaimed Dr. Wiseman "Do you know how much that is worth?"

"What do you mean?" asked the young man aggressively.

"I mean do you know how much that is worth in Pounds Sterling?" the Doctor repeated.

"I don't know and don't care to know!" the other replied testily.

"It will be at least ten million Pounds Sterling!" the Doctor informed him.

"And so what?"

"And so your price is inordinately exorbitant. Why, it is absolute robbery!"

The young man flew into a rage.

"Do you charge me with robbery? You stupid, naked albino. Get out of my shop at once!" And with that he rushed forward to throw him out.

Neither Dr. Wiseman nor Kotokro was prepared for a fight, so they beat a judicious retreat. It was the first time Dr. Wiseman had been described as "stupid" by any man, and he was highly piqued, particularly as such an insult came from a black man. As for the man calling him an albino he did not mind much, for it only showed his ignorance and lack of intelligence.

"I am sorry, Doctor," said Kotokro, observing his mood. "That man has no manners. But it is not surprising, considering that he is dressed up from head to toe."

"How? I do not see the connection" said Dr. Wiseman.

"When a man is completely covered with clothes he thinks that he is important, because he is then unable to see himself as he really is. That is why that man was rude to you, particularly as you did not have any clothes on."

"You mean the wearing of clothes influences people's estimation of themselves?"

"Of course, don't you know that? It makes people feel self-important and haughty and arrogant and pompous and contemptuous of other people. Have you not seen that throughout our journey? In point of manners they are the opposite of naked people."

Dr. Wiseman said nothing. It seemed to him, however, that Kotokro's words contained a certain amount of truth. He wondered whether great monarchs and formidable generals and saintly bishops and awesome judges and ponderous professors would feel important or impress anyone with their position or learning if they went naked. Who said "the cowl did not make the monk?" he asked himself. Only those who could not afford the money for clothes or would not look impressive in any garb, would think there was some truth in that saying. No wonder "The Emperor's Beautiful Clothes" was such a popular story.

They continued to go from shop to shop, still looking for some clothes to buy. All the prices were very high. Dr. Wiseman decided to buy just a shirt and a pair of shorts for himself, but even these would have cost not less than five small nuggets of gold, and he could not afford it.

At last they came to a second-hand clothes shop. There were all sorts of dresses, from the most faded to what appeared completely new. Hardly any of them showed much sign of wear and tear.

"Where are they from?" Dr. Wiseman asked the owner of the shop.

"They are from the white man's country," he replied. "They are what we call "dead whitemen's clothes."

"Are they clothes left by dead white men?"

"Yes. They were brought from Gamberia by traders who said that they bought them from Blaft, the capital of Gamberia."

"And who brought them to Blaft?" asked Dr. Wiseman.

"They were brought there by Gamberians who went to the white man's country, as I learn."

Dr. Wiseman examined them. He saw one suit that looked exactly like a suit which he had given away to charity. An organisation called "Friends of Africa" had appealed for discarded clothes which they said they were taking to Africa for distribution to naked people. But most of them had found their way to the open markets of towns and villages of people who valued the wearing of clothes. Dr. Wiseman wondered if these were some of those clothes. He asked the man.

"I don't know," he replied. "All I know is that they come from the white man's country."

Dr. Wiseman took the suit which looked like the one he had given away and examined it more closely. Yes, there was no doubt about it. It was his discarded lounge-suit. It was light-grey with brown stripes. The coat's middle button was still missing and a slight ink-stain on the trousers was also visible. He had given it away because the trousers was becoming a bit too tight for his stomach which had begun to bulge with good living. Now that his stomach had gone back to its normal size, in response to the enforced reduction in his daily intake, he had no doubt but that it would fit him fine. He asked the price.

"Four small nuggets of gold," replied the seller.

"What!" exclaimed Dr. Wiseman. "Four small nuggets of gold for a second-hand suit, and one that I myself gave away?"

"What are you talking about, mister," asked the man angrily. "Do you mean to tell me that you gave your suit away to go about naked like that, and that you now want it back for nothing?"

"No, no, never mind," he replied quickly, fearing that he would have to make a long explanation which the man was not likely to believe in the end. "I shall look for something more within my means."

"You had better do that!" barked the other.

Dr. Wiseman would have left that shop at once, but he realised that he was not likely to get cheaper clothes anywhere else, for it was the only second-hand clothes shop in the town. So he kept his temper and went on to inspect other clothes. The man too did not want to lose a customer, so he suffered him to continue with his examination of the clothes. The Doctor found all the suits there expensive, so he decided to settle for a shirt and a pair of shorts. These were not cheap either. In the end he purchased only two pairs of shorts, one for himself and the other for Kotokro. Both cost two small nuggets of gold.

"We shall be able to buy more decent clothes for something much less when we arrive in Gamberia," he said to Kotokro as they left the shop.

When they rejoined the men they found all of them dressed and ready to resume the journey. A more motley assortment of costumes you never saw even at a pantomime. Some wore only shorts or trousers, some wore shorts and shirts, some were clad in loin cloths and tail coats, while one or two appeared only in rain-coats. Securri wore the pair of shorts which he had worn to go to Blohim.

They set out and soon came to the entrance to the tunnel. A man stood there repeating some words to himself again and again.

Approaching him the man who was leading greeted him and said;

"We are men from Wapito-land and are on our way to Gamberia. Please tell us: What is the pass-word for today?"

"The pass-word for today is "Wate patapra de yu," he replied.

"And what is the question to which this is the answer?" Kotokro asked.

"The question is "Mante kaka kato ka?"; he replied, adding, "But that should not concern you. You should only remember the answer: Wate patapra de yu.."

They thanked him and began to enter the tunnel in a single file, each repeating the pass-word to himself as he went along. The first man in the line was a young man called Krabito, a first cousin of Securri. He was followed by the brother of Dankida, whose name was Frokosi. Seven others followed; then came Securri and Dr. Wiseman, with Kotokro bringing up the rear.

The tunnel was even darker than Dr. Wiseman and Kotokro had imagined. It was so dark that they could not see one another as they groped their way forward. It was also so narrow and tortuous that they kept on bumping against the sides. As one had to stretch one's hand forward in order to feel any obstacles in the way, Kotokro found the going very difficult by reason of the fact that he was carrying the iron trunk on his head and had to brace it with both hands. However, if this retarded his progress it also protected his head from injury.

At first the air was fresh and cool inside the tunnel. But as they advanced further and further it became more and more rarefied, and the heat more and more oppressive. Everyone began to sweat, but Dr. Wiseman much more profusely. The sweat ran down from his body like water pouring from a sieve. It was a lucky thing that he had drank plenty of water just before entering the tunnel, or he would have been severely dehydrated.

On and on they went. It seemed as if the tunnel would never end. They must have covered a distance of about ten miles when suddenly they began to feel the heat gradually reducing.

"We have passed the middle of the tunnel and are not very far from the exit now," Securri informed Dr. Wiseman and Kotokro.

Both Dr. Wiseman and Kotokro were very happy to hear this, the former more so, for he had begun to feel that he would never come out of that oven alive. The tunnel become cooler and cooler, and the air fresher and fresher as they advanced. At last they saw a ray of light penetrating through the darkness from the other end.

"What is it?" asked Kotokro.

"We are about to arrive at the exit," explained Securri. "It is closed by a door which is opened for you to pass out only if you give the pass-word correctly. What you see is the light from outside coming through a chink in the door."

They quickened their pace, for it was now easier to see one's way forward, due to the light. It was not long before they arrived at the exit. Krabito who was leading, as has already been said, knocked at the door.

"Mante kaka kato ka?" came a voice from outside.

"Wate patapra de yu?" he answered.

The door was immediately opened for him arid he passed through. It was quickly closed again. The second man, Frokosi, was the next to knock.

"Mante kaka kato ka?" came the voice again.

"Wate patapra de yu?" was his reply.

Again the door was opened and he also passed through. All the others repeated the pass-word correctly and went through the door until only Dr. Wiseman and Kotokro remained in the tunnel. Then Dr. Wiseman advanced forward and knocked at the door, just as the others had done.

"Mante kaka kato ka?" he was asked.

"What's the matter with you?" he replied.

"Return to the beginning of the tunnel and learn the correct pass-word and come back" came an order from outside.

Panic seized Dr. Wiseman. If he were to go back to the beginning of the tunnel and return he would certainly die. He could not even return to the beginning alive, not to talk of coming back. Already he had very little life left in him.

"There is no need for you to go back, Doctor," Kotokro whispered into his ear. "You must learn the pass-word again here and now. It is 'Wate patapra de yu?' Remember: 'Wate patapra de yu?"

"What's the patapra to you?" he repeated.

"No, no," said Kotokro. "It's 'Wate patapra de yu?' Can you remember?"

"Yes, I can," replied Dr. Wiseman.

"Good. Go then and knock at the door once more."

Dr. Wiseman obeyed and knocked at the door for the second time.

"Mante kaka kato ka?" came the question.

"What's the patapra de yu?" he answered.

"Return to the beginning of the tunnel and learn the correct pass-word and come back," came the voice again from outside.

Kotokro repeated the pass-word to Dr. Wiseman again and again, but he always returned the wrong response when asked. At last he decided that there was no need to try to teach the Doctor. He would never be able to repeat it correctly. He thought of a better plan.

"Doctor, I see that you will never be able to repeat the pass-word correctly," he said.

258

"How can I?" he replied. "It is quite a meaningless jargon to me, not resembling any sentence I know in English."

"All right. Never mind. I have thought of a way out."

"What is it?" Dr. Wiseman asked eagerly.

"I am going to knock at the door," he explained. "When the question is put to me I shall, of course, return the correct response. You will immediately go past me and stand behind the door. You can then go out in place of me as soon as it is opened."

"Excellent!" replied Dr. Wiseman with great joy. "Then you can later knock and give the correct response again, and so come out too?"

"Exactly."

"How clever of you, my boy!" Dr. Wiseman remarked with delight.

Kotokro said nothing, but went past him and knocked at the door.

"Mante kaka kato ka?" came the question as before.

"Wate patapra de yu?" he replied. And with that he immediately gave way to Dr. Wiseman to stand behind the door. He had hardly taken his position when the door was thrown open. He rushed out of the tunnel with such speed that he stumbled and fell prostrate on the other side. He made no haste to get up. He was so happy at his arrival on Gamberian soil.

There was some interval before Kotokro knocked at the door again. "Mante kaka kato ka?" the question was asked as usual.

"Wate patapra de yu?" he replied.

The door was immediately thrown open and he passed through. He found Securri and all the other men waiting for him. Dr. Wiseman had also risen up to his feet by now and was beaming with joy. The men were happy to see both Dr. Wiseman and Kotokro come out of the tunnel, for when the two did not follow long after Securri had issued out they concluded that they had both failed the test and had gone back to the beginning of the tunnel. No one was happier, however, than Dr. Wiseman and Kotokro. They had at long last, after all their ordeals and adventures, arrived in the Republic of Gamberia!

After resting for some time they resumed their journey and arrived, towards noon, at the town of Hoba on the shores of River Dimpo. This was the men's final destination. It was a market town of about two thousand inhabitants. People from all parts of the hinterland and from Blaft and other coastal towns and cities came here to buy and sell. Some traders even came from neighbouring countries, such as Muccaso to the West and Blohim to the east. It was by far the biggest trading centre in the whole of Gamberia.

There were all sorts of merchandise on sale, including agricultural produce, local manufactures and goods imported from abroad. There were two mediums of exchange, namely the Cupra (one thousand of which was equivalent to One Pound Sterling) and gold.

Kotokro had told Securri that the Doctor would first take him back to Kantoma, which could be reached through the village of Tonko at the confluence of River Mamba and River Dimpo.

"Tonko is only half-a day's journey further down the river," Securri informed them. "You can get there either by land through bush-paths, or by canoe. If I were you I would go by canoe, as it is quicker and less tiring. But, of course, it will cost you some gold."

Dr. Wiseman was not worried now at the prospect of having to pay gold in order to arrive back at Kantoma and eventually home in London. He reckoned that it would not be much anyhow; for the people of Gamberia were more enlightened and knew the value of gold.

"Where can we get a canoe to hire?" he asked Securri.

"Just go down to the river bank. You will see lots of canoes there for hire."

Having shaken hands with all the men and said good-bye Dr. Wiseman and Kotokro made their way to the river bank. There they found scores of canoes, all ready for hire. Approaching one they asked the owner how much he would charge to take them to Tonko.

"It's ten thousand Cupras or ten small nuggets of gold," he replied.

Dr. Wiseman thought he had not heard the man correctly. He asked him to repeat what he had said. The man did so at the top of his voice, thinking the Doctor must be deaf. Dr. Wiseman was greatly puzzled.

"Do you mean to tell me that ten thousand Cupras is the equivalent of ten small nuggets of gold in this town?" he asked.

"Yes, didn't you know that?" replied the man.

"I didn't know."

"Well you know now. So what are you prepared to pay - gold or Cupras?"

"Cupras, of course, if you will accept the equivalent in Sterling."

"I will," the man replied gladly. "It works out at Ten Pounds Sterling."

"Let's get going then. I shall pay you at the end of the journey!" said Dr. Wiseman.

"No, mister," the man objected. "You don't step into this canoe until you have paid the fare."

Dr. Wiseman counted out to him Ten Pounds in bank notes, and soon they were sailing down the river, with the canoe-man rowing vigorously and whistling happily to himself!

"Why is gold so cheap here?" Dr. Wiseman asked him as they glided down the river.

"Cheap? Who said it is cheap?" replied the man.

"It is incredibly cheap - only ten thousand Cupras or Ten Pounds Sterling for ten small nuggets of gold!"

"It would be incredibly cheap if it were true gold" the man replied. "But you see, what looks like gold is, in nine-hundred and ninety-nine cases out of a thousand, not gold at all but base brass."

"What exactly do you mean?" asked Dr. Wiseman anxiously.

"What happens is this"; the man explained. "This so-called gold, or base brass as we call it, is brought down here by Wapitis, who in turn buy it from the Republic of Blohim. It is quite abundant in Blohim, where it is dug from the ground or collected from river beds. As I have said, it is base brass; but occasionally some turn out to be pure gold. The people have no means of telling one from the other, as both look exactly alike, so they sell all very cheaply to the Wapiti traders, who in turn bring it here to buy salt, cutlasses, hoes and other manufactured goods. Since in nearly all cases, it is only base brass, you can understand why it is valued so little... Were it always pure gold the people of Gamberia would have flocked here to buy it."

Dr. Wiseman's heart sank when the man had finished explaining. His dream of becoming a millionaire vanished as rapidly as it had done when he discovered to be mere ant-hills what he had taken to be the remains of an ancient city. He felt even worse now, for whereas in the case of the ant-hills he had had some niggling doubt about the authenticity of his find, he had been hundred per cent certain that what he was now carrying in his brief case was pure gold. His disappointment on this occasion, then, was in direct proportion to the degree of certainty he had entertained. He felt like opening his brief-case there and then and emptying its contents into the river.

"Keep it all the same, Doctor," advised Kotokro, anticipating his intention. "It is better than nothing. You may be able to sell it for a few Cupras on arrival at Blaft, which may come in handy."

The Doctor heeded the boy's advice, but remained very morose throughout the voyage.

On arrival at Tonko they found a man going to Tumuru, the next village after Kantoma, so Dr. Wiseman implored him to take Kotokro with him and hand him over to Chief Brongo on arrival at Kantoma, who in turn would restore the boy to his parents.

"I promised to return him personally, when I was taking him to London; but I am too tired to be able to make the journey" he explained. "So kindly help me."

"But why do you trust me to deliver the boy safely to his parents when you don't even know who I am?" asked the man.

"My instinct tells me that you are an honest person." replied Dr. Wiseman.

"And is your instinct always right in what it tells you?" asked Kotokro.

"Yes, of course."

"So it was right in telling you about my dishonesty and stupidity and laziness and utter lack of any virtue?"

"No, no, my boy. Don't say such things" replied Dr. Wiseman shamefacedly. "You are by far the brightest, cleverest, most honest and most intelligent of all the boys I have ever met."

"Are you sure of that?"

"I am as sure as my name is Wiseman."

Kotokro was delighted.

"Does that extend to my race too?" he next enquired.

"Yes, by and large. They are like any other race of men."

"Thank you, Doctor" replied Kotokro. "I shall always remember that. But do you know what I too think of you?"

"No, tell me."

"I think you are the most deceived man I have ever met in my life."

"What! What do you mean?"

"I mean you are woefully deceived by appearances."

"How? I still don't understand."

"You are used to seeing things only at the surface and to attach great importance to what you see... Very sane and wise people appear to you to be either cranks and faddists or the unspoiled children of nature because they see advantage in going naked; those harmful fruits appeared to you to be edible because they were nice and tasty; people appear to you to be ignorant of the existence of God because they bow to woods and stones; blacks seem to you to be uncivilised because they live simple lives; you think whites are superior because they have invented many wonderful things. These are random examples to illustrate what I mean. Altogether you attach too much importance to appearances because you are incapable of seeing reality."

"Well, my boy," said Dr. Wiseman, after some reflection. "That is a hard thing to say; but I guess you are right; see how I was deceived by appearances into thinking that a group of ant-hills were the remains of an ancient city; and see how even now I am deceived into thinking that this base brass which I carry is gold because of its appearance. In future I shall examine things critically and think about them deeply before coming to a conclusion."

"Do, Doctor; and you will be a happier man." said Kotokro.

Before they parted Kotokro gave Dr. Wiseman the two animal skins, saying that the Doctor would have more use for them. Then they embraced and shook hands for the first and last time. As Kotokro set out for Kantoma Dr. Wiseman also resumed his journey down the river, having agreed with the canoe man to take him to Blaft for an extra charge of six Pounds Sterling which was all the money that he now had on him.

On their way to Kantoma Kotokro told the man, Mobari by name, all about his travel to the white man's country and subsequent adventures with Dr. Wiseman in Wapito-land. The latter listened to him with great interest, and when he had finished he said:

"Not only the people of Kantoma but also the inhabitants of all the surrounding villages, including Tumuru, heard of the news of your death in a plane crash. It is said that up to this day your parents still mourn for you, particularly your mother. I am glad to be the one to take you to them. There will be great rejoicing in Kantoma today. Let us hurry then to arrive there before nightfall." And with that he quickened his pace. Kotokro followed with joyful anticipation.

It was late in the evening when Mobari and Kotokro arrived at Kantoma. The sun had plunged into the western horizon leaving the early moon to dilute the darkness with its feeble light. Most of the people of Kantoma had just finished eating their evening meals and sat either dozing or telling stories before going to bed. Little boys and girls were playing hide-and-seek in the centre of the village, but none noticed the two new arrivals as they made their way to the house of Chief Brongo.

Kotokro would have liked to run to his parents at once, but Mobari advised against it, saying that he had promised the white man to take him to the chief first and he must fulfil his promise.

"Besides," he added, "if you burst upon your parents like that, after they have presumed you dead all these years, it will be too much for them. They may suffer heart attack. So let us first go to the chief who will get them prepared before you reveal your presence."

Kotokro saw some sense in what the man had said. He did not want anything to happen to his parents just at the moment when they should all be rejoicing, so he cheerfully accompanied Mobari to the chief's palace.

Chief Brongo had just finished eating his supper and was relaxing in his lazy chair while his wives sat telling stories, when they arrived. He failed to recognise Kotokro, not only because of the dim light and his failing sight, but also because the boy had grown much taller than before.

"Good evening, Chief Brongo," the stranger greeted. "My name is Mobari and I come from Tumuru."

"Good evening," Chief Brongo responded. "Please sit down," and he motioned him to a seat close beside him.

After he had sat down Chief Brongo's junior wife brought water for him and Kotokro, which the latter drank with great satisfaction. No water tasted as nice as the water from the stream at Kantoma.

"Well, with us, all is well. We have no complaint to lay before our Maker" said Chief Brongo when they had finished drinking. "But we don't know what has brought you here."

"I bring no bad news," replied Mobari. "In fact I should say I bring good news - very good news." And he deliberately paused to see what effect his words would have on Chief Brongo.

"And what is the good news?" the chief asked without much enthusiasm.

"I bring the son of Papa Asuboni and Mamma Alimana who is said to have died about three years ago."

"What?" shouted Chief Brongo, jumping out of his chair. "What did you say?"

Mobari repeated what he had said.

"Where is he?" Chief Brongo asked incredulously.

"Here; right before you."

Chief Brongo stared at Kotokro.

"Are you Kotokro?" he asked with disbelief.

"Of course I am," replied Kotokro. "Can't you see? I was taken away by the white man to his country three years ago and now I am back."

Chief Brongo could hardly believe it. But when Kotokro narrated all that happened to him and Dr. Wiseman since he left home, Chief Brongo had no doubt at all that the boy was, indeed, Kotokro.

"We must send for his parents at once," he said to Mobari. "But I must find a way of breaking the news to them. It would be too much for them to see the boy abruptly like that."

It was arranged that Kotokro should hide in one of the rooms in the palace and not show himself when his parents came, until he was told to do so.

"All right, I shall do as you say," Kotokro agreed to the plan. And with that he went and hid in one of the rooms in the palace.

CHAPTER TWENTY-TWO
JOY AT KANTOMA

It was more than three years now since Kotokro's parents and, indeed, the whole of Kantoma were thrown into mourning by the news of Kotokro's death. It came one evening with the arrival of Fiko Jimfa.

Papa Asuboni and Mamma Alimana, the parents of Kotokro, had just returned from the farm when a messenger came from Chief Brongo, saying that the chief wanted to see them in his palace. Very much wondering what could be the matter they followed him to the Chief's house.

On arrival there they were surprised to see Jimfa whom they at once recognised as the young man who had come with the white man to take away their son. It was more than one year since their son went away and they had not heard any news of him, although the white man had promised to return him within that period of time. Their hearts began to beat fast.

"Please sit down," Chief Brongo said to them after they had greeted, motioning them to two stools that stood facing him.

They sat down. Then Chief Brongo turned to Jimfa and said gravely:

"The parents are here. Please tell them what you have just told me."

"First of all," began Jimfa, clearing his throat, "the British High Commissioner in Blaft sends you greetings."

"We thank him" they replied, wondering what was to follow.

"He has asked me to bring you this parcel," he continued, handing to Papa Asuboni a large parcel in brown paper. It contained six pieces of Dumas cloths and the sum of Twenty thousand Cupras.

"We thank him very much." replied Papa Asuboni, accepting it.

"And how is he?"

"He is fine."

"And how is our son, Kotokro?" asked Mamma Alimana anxiously. That was what was uppermost in her mind.

"I was just coming to that." replied Jimfa with a solemn face. "The High Commissioner has also asked me to inform you, with deep regret..."

"H-o-o-o! h-o-o-o! My son!" yelled Mamma Alimana anticipating a tragic announcement even before Jimfa could finish the sentence.

"He has also asked me to inform you, with deep regret, that your son Kotokro is dead" continued Jimfa after a pause. He died together with the white man three months ago in a plane crash while returning to Gamberia."

Papa Asuboni was struck dumb with the news. The parcel dropped from his hand as his knees began to shake. As for Mamma Alimana whatever followed made no difference to her. She had already guessed correctly. She screamed and yelled and beat her breast in the most piteous manner. Soon her wailing brought almost the whole village to the palace. Many broke down in sympathy when they heard the news.

"And after killing our son the High Commissioner sends us six pieces of cloth and the sum of Twenty Thousand Cupras?" asked Papa Asuboni, recovering himself.

"Yes," replied Jimfa. "But remember he is not the one who killed your son. Kotokro died in a plane crash, and not even Dr. Wiseman, who took him away, can be blamed for that."

"We don't want his cloths and money." said Papa Asuboni, handing the parcel back to Jimfa. "Return it to him and tell him that nothing he gives us can make up for the loss of our son - no, not all the cloths and all the Cupras in Gamberia."

Both Chief Brongo and Jimfa pleaded with Papa Asuboni and his wife to accept the gift, but they would not hear of it. Mamma Alimana left the Palace still in tears. She was followed by a large crowd into her house, where more and more people gathered to mourn with her.

After she had left, Papa Asuboni also rose up to go away. Again Chief Brongo and Jimfa pleaded with him to accept the present.

"I don't want it," he said to Chief Brongo. "If you want it you can keep it."

"All right," replied Chief Brongo, who thought that Papa Asuboni and his wife ought not to lose such a handsome present in addition to the loss of their son. "I shall keep it until you change your mind."

"I shall never change my mind until my son comes back from the grave" he replied. And with that he too went away.

All this had happened three years before, but the loss of their son was still fresh in the minds of Papa Asuboni and his wife. She in particular bore it so ill.

Kotokro had been her only child and besides the pain which she naturally felt for his loss, she also dreaded the effect which this would have on her marriage. That affect had already begun to show in the way Papa Asuboni now treated her. He was no longer so tolerant of her ways and took offence at every little mistake she made. It seemed as if he was looking for an excuse to divorce her.

On this particular evening of Kotokro's return, Papa Asuboni and his wife were engaged in one of their quarrels, which had by now become very frequent, when a messenger came to say that Chief Brongo wanted to see them in his palace.

"What does he want with us?" asked Papa Asuboni with some irritation.

"I don't know !" replied the messenger.

Thinking that his wife had gone to complain about him to the chief, Papa Asuboni put on his cloth and followed the messenger. His wife also followed.

On arrival at the palace they found a stranger sitting beside the chief. They wondered who he was. He was certainly not Jimfa, the man who always brought bad news, for they had by now come to regard even his first arrival in their village with the white man as a tragic occasion.

"Please sit down," Chief Brongo said to them after they had greeted. They sat down.

"I have called you here to plead with you once more to accept the present which the white man sent to you from Blaft" continued Chief Brongo "for I cannot keep it any longer."

Papa Asuboni felt his temper rising.

"Chief Brongo," he replied with some heat "you do us great injustice by summoning us here again with a view to rekindling in us the grief that has been smouldering in our hearts for the loss of our son. You have kept this parcel all these years, ever since we refused to accept it. What makes you think that we have now changed our minds and can be persuaded to relieve you of it? If you can no longer bear the burden of keeping it return it to the owner and never again attempt to stir up the dying embers of our sorrow."

"But you said that you would not accept it until your son returned from the grave" Chief Brongo reminded.

"That is exactly what I said, and I still say so."

"Well, then accept it now, for your son has returned from the grave. This stranger here can bear witness."

"What!" exclaimed Papa Asuboni, jumping from his seat. "What did you say?"

"Papa, papa! Mamma, Mamma!" shouted Kotokro, bursting out from his hiding place before Chief Brongo could repeat what he had said. He had been listening to the conversation from where he sat in the room and could no longer restrain himself and wait for the drama to unfold as had been planned.

Papa Asuboni's heart leapt high in his chest, his head swam and he tottered as if to fall. What Chief Brongo and Mobari had tried to prevent was about to happen. But before he could fall to the ground with heart-attack Kotokro rushed forward and threw his arms around him."

"It's me; papa, It's me Kotokrotintomaguri!" he shouted. "I am not dead. I never died but fell to the ground in a plane crash."

At this Mamma Alimana, who had been equally surprised but less stunned, rushed to Kotokro and began to hug him in her arms. She had never fully accepted that her son was dead. For no particular reason, her instinct had always told her that Kotokro would come back one day.

"Oh, my son, my son!" she cried with joy. "Is it you indeed that I see again in flesh and blood?" Oh, ye gods and ancestral spirits, I thank you for your tender mercy."

At the touch by Kotokro his father also had recovered from his incipient swoon. His joy knew no bounds when he discovered that it was his lost son indeed who stood before him in flesh and blood.

Soon the news went round that Kotokro had returned from the dead. All the villagers rushed to Chief Brongo's house to see the wonderful phenomenon. They were surprised to see Kotokro looking very much alive, if taller and more grown up.

Mobari told them how he had met the white man with Kotokro at Tonko and how he had entrusted the boy to him to be delivered to his parents through Chief Brongo.

Then Kotokro also briefly told them of his journey with the white man to his country; how after staying there for one year they were returning to Gamberia when they suffered a plane crash; how they dwelt in the jungle for about two years before they eventually fell in with the people of Fomaki in Wapito-land and how they remained in Wapito-land for another one year before setting out for Gamberia. They listened to him attentively, and when he had finished there was great rejoicing.

"Well, I have done my duty and must beg permission to leave now" said Mobari when Kotokro had finished his account.

Before he departed Papa Asuboni thanked him and offered him one of the cloths which the High Commissioner had sent and which he had refused. He had now accepted it from Chief Brongo with great joy.

"No, no, I cannot accept anything from you" he refused. "It is payment enough for me to have had the opportunity of bringing you good news."

After he had left, Papa Asuboni and Mamma Alimana thanked Chief Brongo and departed with Kotokro, followed by the crowd. That evening and for several days after-wards the people of Kantoma talked of nothing but the return of Kotokro from the white man's country through the land of the dead.

CHAPTER TWENTY-THREE
DR. WISEMAN'S HOME-COMING

Meanwhile Dr. Wiseman had also arrived at Blaft. Feeling very tired and hungry he made straight for the residence of the British High Commissioner. After paying the canoe man he had absolutely nothing left on him and he needed His Excellency's help. Arrived there he rang the bell. He waited for a long time before the door was opened and a hungry looking janitor appeared. He was black.

"I am Dr. Wiseman" he introduced himself. "Is the High Commissioner in?"

"I am not sure. I shall go and find out," replied the janitor. And with that he shut the door in Dr. Wiseman's face and disappeared.

The Doctor was taken aback by the man's attitude. He should at least have invited him in to sit down in the waiting room while he went to find out whether the High Commissioner was in or not. The man's reply did not even make sense. What kind of a janitor was he that did not know whether or not the master of the house was in? Well, he must wait patiently. He had no choice.

The janitor, however, Daniel Globa by name, knew what he was about. Although he claimed to be a Doctor, far from looking like one, Dr. Wiseman rather presented the spectacle of a man whose head seemed to call for examination by a physician. His tattered pair of shorts, unkempt hair and bushy beard certainly gave him the appearance of one who had taken leave of his senses. Globa therefore thought that he would be putting the High Commissioner's life at risk by conducting such a man into his presence without first putting His Excellency on his guard.

The High Commissioner, His Excellency Mr Hugh Blickhead, had arrived in Blaft only some three months before, after the transfer of his predecessor, Mr Alexander Cowfoot, back to headquarters. He was serving in Pakistan when the news of Dr. Wiseman's death in a plane crash came. He first heard it from the B.B.C. news broadcast and later read it from one of the British newspapers that were sent to his mission every week. It was some three years before and he had long forgotten about the incident.

He sat in his study looking through some newspapers this afternoon when Daniel Globa entered.

"Good afternoon, Sir," Daniel saluted.

"Yes," replied the High Commissioner, raising up his head.

"There is a man at the gate, Sir, wanting to see you."

"What sort of man is he- black or white?" asked the High Commissioner.

"White, Sir. And if you ask me he is like Lazarus at the door of Dives, with the hair of Sampson and the beard of Nebukednezzer," replied Daniel, who was fond of analogies derived from the Bible.

"How?" asked His Excellency.

"Because, Sir, not even in these days of independence when many white men walk the streets of Africa in wretched conditions, forgetful of their past glory, have I seen any member of your race so indifferent to his physical appearance. He is barefooted and half naked, being clad only in a dirty pair of shorts, with a bow and arrows slung over his shoulders. If you will excuse my saying so, Sir, he is more like a mad man than anything else."

"Did he tell you his name?"

"Yes, Sir, he said he is called Dr. Whiteman."

"Dr. Whiteman?"

"Yes Sir, that is how he called himself. He is white all right, but if he is truly a Doctor, anyone would be taking a big risk in submitting himself to his medical care."

"All right, bring him in here," said the High Commissioner after a pause, bracing himself for the encounter.

Daniel went back and opened the door again just as Dr. Wiseman was getting impatient and was thinking of ringing the bell a second time.

"The High Commissioner is in and says you can come." He informed him. And with that he began to lead the way.

Dr. Wiseman followed him through doors and corridors until they arrived at the study. Globa knocked at the door and they were bidden to enter. They did so.

"Dr. Whiteman, Sir," Daniel introduced him with a chuckle.

His Excellency rose up to greet him, keeping his gaze fixed upon the bow and arrows all the time and wondering whether it would be safe to shake hands with him.

"Wiseman, Dr. Wiseman is the name," the Doctor corrected, putting down the parcel at the same time and stretching out his right hand.

The High Commissioner recalled the name at once, but he was as yet uncertain if this was really the man. He had never before met him in person, although he had heard much of the famous anthropologist long before his reported death in a plane crash. Dr. Wiseman noticed his hesitation and immediately pulled out his passport from his pocket.

"Here is my Passport," he continued, stretching it out to him. "I guess I have changed a bit."

The High Commissioner glanced at the photograph and the name in the passport. He had no doubt now about the identity of the man standing before him. He grabbed his hand in both of his and shook it warmly.

"I am glad to meet you, Doctor," he said. "Why? What happened? You were reported dead in a plane crash more than three years ago!"

"That is partly correct," replied Dr. Wiseman. "I suffered a plane crash but did not die, as you can see."

Having sat down at the invitation of the High Commissioner, Dr. Wiseman briefly narrated what had happened to him since he had the accident. His Excellency listened with rapt attention, and when he had finished he congratulated him warmly on his lucky escape.

"The reason why I came to you," continued Dr. Wiseman "is that I have not a penny in my pocket at the moment. I paid all the money I had on me to the canoe-man who brought me from Hoba on River Dimpo. I have therefore come to borrow some money to buy me a decent dress and pay my fare back to London. I also need something for paying my hotel bills pending my departure from here."

"That's no problem at all" said His Excellency "I shall give you money to buy yourself a decent dress, for you really need one. And as for your hotel bills and fare to London I shall take care of both. A plane leaves here for London just the day after tomorrow. I shall book you a seat on it. And since you are going to be here for only two days you may stay in my guest house."

Dr. Wiseman thanked him and was taken to the guest house where he was provided with a blade and toilet articles. He shaved his beard clean and washed his body and hair.

Food was brought to him and, after he had eaten, the High Commissioner also sent him Fifty Thousand Cupras, the equivalent of Fifty Pounds Sterling.

He was taken in the High Commissioner's car to the shops where he bought himself a suit, together with a shirt a pair of shoes and a neck-tie. He then went into a barber's shop and had a hair cut. When he returned to the house and dressed up, he looked little different from his former self. Only his reduced stomach and slightly lean face betrayed the ordeal he had gone through.

The next morning he accompanied the High Commissioner to his office. There he met Jimfa, who could hardly believe his eyes when he saw the Doctor.

"Is it you indeed in flesh and blood, Doctor!" he exclaimed. "This is the first time that I have seen anyone return from the dead."

Dr. Wiseman assured him that he never died when his plane crashed. He then went on to narrate briefly what happened, just as he had told it to the High Commissioner. Then Jimfa also told him how they had heard the news of the crash from the B.B.C.; how the previous High Commissioner had received an official confirmation of the tragedy the next day; how His Excellency had subsequently sent him with cloths and money to Kotokro's parents; how he had told them of the boy's death and how he had left the gift there with Chief Brongo when they refused to accept it.

The next day both the High Commissioner and Jimfa went to see Dr. Wiseman off at the airport. As the plane took off and ascended into the sky Dr. Wiseman recalled the last occasion when he found himself in the air and its tragic sequel. He prayed hard in his heart that he might arrive safely to see his wife and child once more.

The plane had not been in the air for more than two hours when Dr. Wiseman began to feel drowsy. He tried to keep awake, but it was difficult. At last, having surrendered himself to the irresistible force of slumber he found himself in the world of consistent inconsistencies and reasonable contradictions, where the impossible is always possible and the abnormal normal. He dreamt that he had arrived in London. It was now a big sprawling village of thousands of inhabitants, all white. There were no motorable roads, the houses being interconnected by narrow foot-paths. A big river ran through a ravine in the centre of it.

He had difficulty in finding his way to his house, which was now a small thatched hovel of three rooms. He knocked at the door and Mrs. Casely, now a very thin old woman, opened it. She did not recognise him. And even when he introduced himself she shook her head and said that he must be an impostor, since he bore no resemblance whatsoever to Dr. Wiseman, who had died about thirty years before in a plane crash. The Doctor was a short black man who always went naked, not like the clothed tall gentleman that stood before her.

"Where is my wife? I must see her at once," he asked in exasperation.

"Do you mean Mrs. Wiseman?"

"Yes, of course. Take me to her immediately.

"I am sorry she is not here. She left here long ago with her son," she replied.

"Where has she gone to?"

"I hear Mrs. Wiseman is married to the Maharaja of Tundarabad and has gone to live in India with her son. If you want to see her you will have to take a boat to Tundarabad. But if I were you I wouldn't go there, because if the Maharaja sees you he will have you arrested and incarcerated in the Black Hole of Calcutta."

Dr. Wiseman's heart felt as heavy as lead. He almost wanted to cry; whereupon snatching a broom Mrs. Casely struck him on the shoulder, saying:

"Stop that, you fool!"

At the touch of the broom Dr. Wiseman woke up to find the air hostess tapping him on the shoulder and saying:

"Fasten your seat belt, please. We are about to land in London."

Greatly relieved to find that he had only been dreaming Dr. Wiseman did as he was told and looked anxiously down through the window to see if London was already in sight. To his delight there it was, spread out endlessly beneath a radiant sky as far as the eyes could see. Toy planes and Lilliputian automobiles were plying up and down tiny rail-lines and streets that were hardly more than a foot wide. There also was the shining surface of River Thames, meandering between buildings that seemed to stand in close proximity to one another.

Then everything began to grow rapidly in size as the earth shot up to meet them. Soon they were racing at a terrific speed over the tarmac.

The plane gradually slowed down, turned round and eventually came to a dead stop. A ladder was let down and the passengers began to disembark.

Dr. Wiseman picked up his luggage, which consisted of his brief-case, the two skins done up into a parcel and the bow and arrows in a quiver. Hanging the last two over his shoulder he picked up the brief-case and followed the other passengers out. It was not long before he had gone through customs and found himself outside the airport.

And now for the first time the dream that Dr. Wiseman had dreamt on the plane began to give him cause for concern. He had no cash on him when he was boarding the plane and he had not asked the High Commissioner for any. He had reckoned that upon arrival in London he would take a taxi straight to his house where Mrs. Wiseman would pay the fare. But now, suppose his dream turned out to be partly true, and he arrived to find Mrs. Wiseman no longer in that house, how would he be able to pay off the taxi driver? He decided not to take a taxi until he was able to obtain some cash. There was a curiosity shop only a few yards away from the airport. He would walk to the place and sell either the bow and arrows or the two skins. That would give him enough money for his taxi fare and other immediate needs.

Having thus made up his mind he trudged to the shop. When he arrived there he saw a bespectacled old man of about seventy standing behind a counter with all sorts of odd objects behind him on shelves.

"Good afternoon," Dr. Wiseman greeted.

"Good afternoon," the old man answered. "What can I do for you?"

Dr. Wiseman deposited the bow and arrows on the counter.

"I wish to sell these," he said, pushing them towards the old man. The man took the bow and examined it carefully. Then he put it down and, taking out the arrows one by one from the quiver, he examined them also. Then he raised up his head and asked:

"From where did you get these?"

"I brought them from Gamberia" replied Dr. Wiseman.

"Did you say you brought them or bought them?"

"I made them myself while I was there," he explained.

The man nodded his head and smiled.

"Ah, exactly as I thought," he said.

"How much will you give for them?" asked Dr. Wiseman hopefully.

"They are not worth a farthing," he replied.

"What!" exclaimed Dr. Wiseman with great surprise. "Surely they are much finer than any I could have bought from Gamberia?"

"Quite right," agreed the man. "They are too fine and too well finished. They are quite unlike the ones made by the natives. They exhibit no artistic talent whatsoever."

Dr. Wiseman felt very disheartened. He had originally not meant to sell them at all but to keep them as souvenirs of his adventures. However, finding himself in financial difficulties, he had expected to be able to fall back on them. But now, here he was, being told that they were absolutely worthless. Well, he would keep them all the same as he had originally intended to. Meantime he was desperately in need of cash, so he must sell or pledge the skins. As for the gold he dared not offer it for sale as yet. He was almost certain that it was just base brass, as the canoe-man had said, and it might therefore lead to his arrest if he offered it for sale as gold. He must first see his wife and son before attempting to dispose of it. Then if he was sent to jail, they would at least have known that he was still alive.

Having come to this decision he quietly removed the bow and arrows from the counter and deposited, in their place, the parcel of skins. As the old man looked on, he slowly and deliberately unwrapped the paper that covered them and took out the two skins.

"What about these then?" he asked, pushing them towards the man.

The other took out his spectacles, cleaned the lenses and put them on again. Then he proceeded to examine the skins minutely, feeling the hair on them with his fingers.

"These are very good skins," he said, raising up his head. "They have been properly cured and the lace holes in them have been artistically cut. However, they have one serious defect. The removal of the heads makes them unfit for the purpose of taxidermy."

Dr. Wiseman's heart sank very low. It seemed he was not going to get any money for the skins either.

"Are they therefore absolutely valueless?" he asked despondently.

"No, no, I have not said that," the old man replied quickly. They are certainly worth something. All I mean is that they would have been much more valuable if the heads had been left on."

Dr. Wiseman's sinking spirit began to revive.

"How much will you offer then?" he asked hopefully.

"Well, the two together would have been worth at least six hundred Pounds. But with the heads off I can only offer you two hundred Pounds for both."

"Can't you make it three hundred Pounds? I am sure the skins on the bodies are more important than those on the heads and should account for at least half the price you would have been prepared to pay."

"No, no, you don't understand," said the old man. "It's like you and your head. Without your head the rest of your body is useless, just as without the rest of your body your head is useless. You see, both must be connected together for either to have much value."

"I understand," said Dr. Wiseman. "In that case just give me one hundred pounds and keep them as a pawn. I shall bring back the amount within three days and either redeem them or collect the remaining one hundred pounds if I decide to sell at your price."

"Fair enough," agreed the other. "I give you three weeks. If at the end of three weeks you do not come for them I shall be at liberty to dispose of them and give you the remaining one hundred pounds at any time you choose to come."

"Agreed."

The old man counted one hundred pounds to Dr. Wiseman and took the skins away. With money now in his pocket Dr. Wiseman stepped out of the shop into the street in high spirits. He hailed a taxi and told the driver to take him to No. 13 Baron street.

As the taxi wound its way with him towards his destination the Doctor began to imagine the joyful welcome that awaited him from his wife and son, and even Mrs. Casely and the others. At first they would refuse to believe their eyes when they saw him, thinking he was either an impostor or he had risen from the dead. Then when they realised that it was he in flesh and blood their joy would know no bounds.

His heart beat faster and faster as the taxi approached his destination. At last it arrived and pulled up in front of No. 13. He got down and paid off the driver. It was seventy-five pence.

Going up to the door he rang the bell. He waited for a long time without anyone coming to answer. He rang again, rather impatiently. Still no one came to open the door. Then he remembered his dream on the plane. His heart began to beat faster. Did it mean there was no one in the house?

"Who are you and what do you want?" came a voice from behind him.

He wheeled round and saw an old woman of about seventy holding a basket of provisions. His heart gave a jump. Was this Mrs. Casely so changed in three years? No, she could not be. For one thing, Mrs. Casely was tall and stout, with blonde hair. This woman had black hair with some greys; and although she was almost as tall as Mrs. Casely she was extremely thin. He knew of no sickness, apart from AIDS, that could have wrought any such bodily transformation in Mrs. Casely in three years. But Mrs. Casely was not the sort of woman that was likely to contract AIDS.

"I am Dr. Wiseman," he replied. "This is where I live."

The old woman stared hard at him.

"No, mister," she said. "You don't live here. I live here with my son."

Dr. Wiseman received the information with astonishment and disbelief.

"And who is your son, may I ask?"

"He is Dr. Woseman" she replied.

Dr. Wiseman thought he was dreaming again. His head reeled and he had difficulty in remaining on his feet.

"What! Did you say Dr. Wiseman?"

"No, mister." replied the old woman shaking her head. "I said Dr. Woseman. Don't think I don't know the difference between Woseman and Wiseman?"

"Where is my wife - Mrs. Wiseman?"

The old woman looked him in front from head to foot. Then she went round and surveyed him again from the back.

"Do you mean to tell me that you are Mrs. Wiseman's husband, Dr. Wiseman, who died three years ago in a plane crash?"

"Yes, yes, I am," he replied eagerly.

"You are?" she asked again incredulously.

"Yes, yes."

"Then tell me, Mister, how is it that you who died three years ago now stand before me in flesh and blood to ask after your wife?"

"No, no, I did not die. I suffered a plane crash but I did not die," he corrected hurriedly.

"Then where were you hiding all these years, that you now choose to come out?"

"I was not hiding anywhere. I survived the crash and got lost in the African jungle. It is only three days ago that I found my way back to Blaft, the capital of Gamberia. And now I am here."

The old woman looked at him askance.

"Is that a true story or an invention?" she asked.

"I tell you, it is true. Look at my Passport." And he removed it from his pocket and stretched it out to her. She opened it and peered hard at the name and photograph.

"My eyes are dim. I cannot see properly," she said, handing it back to him. "But if your story is true then I dare say it must be very interesting."

"Where is my wife then?" Dr. Wiseman asked again impatiently.

"She no longer lives here," she replied. "She left here with her son two years ago."

"Where did she go, and why?"

"She could not pay the rent. So the landlord, Mr. Nuggart, evicted her and sold the house to my son, who now uses it as a warehouse. He is an importer of Brazilian coffee. He is a bachelor, and I live with him at the top floor."

"So you have no idea where my wife has gone?"

"I have no idea, but my son may know."

"Where is your son? Is he in?"

"No, he has gone out to clear some goods from the customs. But I expect him to be back soon. You may come in and wait for him if you like."

Dr. Wiseman hesitated to accept her invitation, thinking it would be better to go and come back later. But before he could decide, a car pulled up near him. A well dressed gentleman in his forties alighted. At the sight of him the old lady turned round to meet him and held his hand.

"John, meet Dr. Wiseman, the dead husband of Mrs. Wiseman who left this house two years ago."

Dr. Woseman thought he had not heard correctly.

"What did you say, mother?" he asked. "Did you say that this is Dr. Wiseman who died three years ago?"

"Yes, yes, I am he." replied Dr. Wiseman, interrupting and stretching out his hand to him.

Dr. Woseman held back his hand. He shuddered at the thought of shaking a ghost's hand. Dr. Wiseman noticed his hesitation and smiled.

"I am not a ghost, you know. I suffered a plane crash but survived," he explained.

Dr. Woseman was soon put at his ease, as Dr. Wiseman went on to explain briefly what happened. Then he repeated his enquiry after his wife.

"She left a forwarding address," replied Dr. Woseman. "I have it in my notebook in my car." And with that he went to his car and brought out the notebook. He scrutinised it from page to page and at last said:

"It is No. 14, Flint land Road, N.W. 16."

Thanking him Dr. Wiseman took a taxi and made for the address. It was to a little old dilapidated house in a remote suburb of London that the taxi brought him. He alighted, paid off the driver and looked around him. There was a pile of rubbish in front of the house and dogs' mess all around. He could not imagine that his wife would be reduced to such a strait as to come and dwell in this kind of house and in such surroundings. He looked at the number of the house which was painted above the doorway. Yes, it was the number Dr. Woseman had given him. Well, what did it matter, as long as he could really find his wife here?

Stepping up to the door he rang the bell. It was immediately opened by a middle-aged woman of about fifty. She was exactly the size and build of Mrs. Casely, but she was definitely not Mrs. Casely.

"Good afternoon," Dr. Wiseman greeted.

"Good afternoon," she responded. "What can I do for you?"

"Does Mrs. Wiseman live here?" he asked without introducing himself. He did not want to cause surprise and find himself having to explain.

"No," replied the lady. "She used to live here, but she was thrown out by the landlord, Mr. Bluebutton, about a year ago when she fell into arrears with the rent."

"Where did she go? I mean do you know her forwarding address?"

"I am afraid I don't know. She did not leave any forwarding address. You are not the only one who has come to ask after her since she left. A certain lady, calling herself Mrs. Casely, came to enquire after her about six months ago and I told her the same thing. I have no idea where she has gone."

"And did this lady - Mrs. Casely - say where she herself stays?"

"No, she didn't."

"All right. Thank you," said Dr. Wiseman, and turned to go away, his heart heavy with disappointment bordering on grief.

"But who are you?" asked the lady.

"Never mind," he replied. "The name does not matter."

And with that he turned round to look at a taxi that was coming along the street. He raised up his hand and it stopped. He got in and sat at the back.

"Where shall I take you?" asked the driver.

"Anywhere," he replied mechanically.

"What do you mean by anywhere?" asked the driver impatiently. "Do you mean you are a tourist and want me to take you round the city on sight-seeing?"

"No, no," he replied hurriedly, realising his mistake. "I mean you can take me to any inexpensive hotel close to the centre of the city."

"All right. That is Whitfont Hotel, near Marble Arch. It is one of the best and cheapest in that area - Fifteen Pounds a night for bed and breakfast."

"Fifteen Pound!" exclaimed Dr. Wiseman "London must be very expensive these days."

"Telling me, mister!" replied the man. "Everything is incredibly expensive these days. Why, only a few years ago that would have been the charge for one week in a first class hotel."

"Is there no cheaper hotel anywhere around central London?" he asked.

"No, no, not within a radius of ten miles from Marble Arch. And even then the cheapest is fourteen pounds per night."

"All right. Take me to Whitfont Hotel then," he said with resignation.

Neither Dr. Wiseman nor the driver said anything again as the taxi sped towards central London. After a long delay caused by heavy traffic they at last arrived at the hotel.

"How much is it?" asked Dr. Wiseman as he stepped down from the vehicle.

"One Pound Fifty Pence," replied the driver.

Dr. Wiseman counted out the money to him and he drove away. With the bow and arrows slung over his shoulder and his brief-case in his hand, Dr. Wiseman entered the hotel. Approaching the receptionist he asked if there was a vacant room.

"Yes, you can have room No. 213 on the second floor. It's Fifteen Pounds per night, bed and breakfast." he replied.

"I'll take it," said Dr. Wiseman.

"What's your name?" asked the receptionist.

"Dr. Wiseman."

The receptionist wrote it down in the register. Then he took a key from the rack.

"How long are you going to stay?" he asked as he stretched it out to him.

"Well, three nights at least. I might stay a day or two longer."

Forty-five Pounds is payable in advance," he said as he handed the key to him.

He counted and gave the amount to him. He now had exactly thirty pounds left out of the one hundred pounds for which he had pledged the skins. This would be sufficient for only two extra nights if he decided to stay for five nights, and this did not even include meals. He decided that unless he unexpectedly came by some funds by the third day he would have to return to the curiosity shop and dispose of the skins for the balance of one hundred pounds.

Dr. Wiseman ascended the second floor and had no difficulty in finding room 213. He entered it and found himself in a spacious bedroom daintily furnished with expensive curtains, well-polished chest of drawers, Victorian chairs and centre table and beautiful mahogany bed with a cosy mattress and soft pillows. A costly Chinese carpet stretched from wall to wall. He had never before stayed in a room so beautiful, and he was sadly reminded of what money could do. Then his mind went to his wife and child who, for all he knew, might at this very moment be living in poverty and squalor if her last place of residence was anything to go by.

He deposited his bow and arrows in the ward-robe and locked it. Then he placed his brief-case on the centre table and, taking off his coat and shoes, lay on the bed to rest.

He had not meant to sleep; but what with the journey, his walk to the curiosity shop and his vain search for his wife, he was by now so tired that he had not stretched himself for more than ten minutes when he fell into a deep slumber.

He must have slept for about two hours, when he was suddenly awakened by the sharp ringing of the bell at his door. He sprang to his feet and opened it.

"I have come to make your bed," said the intruder, a middle-aged woman of about fifty-four, exactly the size and build of Mrs. Casely, except that she stooped a little at the shoulders. It was obvious that she was the charwoman.

Dr. Wiseman stared at her without a word. She thought he would invite her in and step aside for her to pass, but he did nothing of the sort. Instead, he continued to gaze at her in silence, still holding the door. The woman also surveyed him from head to foot with an expression of deep horror in her eyes. Suddenly she turned round and, without saying a word to him, ran precipitately downstairs. Dr. Wiseman did not close the door but still stood holding it open. The reason for this was that the woman resembled Mrs. Casely so closely that he thought it must be she. He was soon confirmed in this conclusion.

"What's the matter with you, Mrs. Casely?" he heard the receptionist say immediately the woman arrived downstairs.

"A ghost ! I have seen a ghost !" she replied in a voice of extreme terror.

"Where?"

"In room 213 upstairs."

"But that's the room of the gentleman who came in some two hours ago," said the receptionist.

"And what name did he give?" asked Mrs. Casely, still trembling.

"Let me see," said the receptionist, opening the register.

He ran his finger through the pages until he came to No. 213.

"The name is Dr. Wiseman," he said.

Mrs. Casely raised her eyes to the ceiling and made a sign of the cross.

"Holy Mary deliver me from the power of Satan!" she said, now convinced that she had indeed seen a ghost.

"What is it?" asked the receptionist, still unable to comprehend her strange behaviour.

"He is a ghost – a real, real ghost. Dr. Wiseman died three years ago in a plane crash."

"And you think it is his ghost that is in that room?"

"It is not a matter of thinking. It is his ghost, I tell you."

"Ah, Mrs Casely, calm yourself. There is no such thing as a ghost." said the receptionist. "I am sure the man you saw is no more a ghost than you and me. He must be a twin brother of the Doctor or someone with the same name and a close resemblance."

This suggested possibility had some effect upon the mind of the frightened woman.

"All right. Then let us go up and find out," she said more calmly.

"Follow me then," said the receptionist, taking the lead.

Dr. Wiseman was still standing at the opened door when they arrived upstairs. He was smiling broadly, having heard all that was being said downstairs.

"Oh, Mrs. Casely, don't get frightened. It is me indeed, Dr. Wiseman, who suffered a plane crash three years ago while taking Kotokro back to Gamberia." he said as soon as he saw them coming.

"Are you a ghost then?" asked the receptionist.

"No, of course not. I am the same Dr. Wiseman in flesh and blood," he replied. "I suffered a plane crash but survived."

"There you are. Didn't I tell you that there is no such thing as a ghost?" said the receptionist turning to Mrs. Casely.

"Oh, Doctor, is it you indeed in flesh and blood?" exclaimed Mrs. Casely, flying into his arms with utmost joy, now convinced that this was indeed the Doctor.

The receptionist left them and returned to his desk. Then Mrs. Casely sat down. Closing the door Dr. Wiseman narrated, without the details, all that had happened to him from the time his plane crashed, up to the time he came into the hotel.

Then Mrs. Casely also told him everything that had happened ever since he left London with Kotokro up to the time she last set eyes on Mrs. Wiseman and Master Wiseman. She said that the very next day after Dr. Wiseman's departure it was reported that his plane had crashed somewhere in the jungles of Africa and that it was believed there were no survivors. A search, however, had been mounted. A month later Mrs. Wiseman was officially informed of the tragedy by the Airways Authorities, which added that it had not been possible to locate the scene of the crash and that the search had had to be abandoned, as it was now certain that there had been no survivors. Mrs. Wiseman deeply grieved over the news and wept bitterly. She was sick for several weeks. When she sufficiently recovered she applied to several places for employment, but all in vain. Meantime she had been living on the traveller's cheques which Dr. Wiseman had inadvertently left behind. This lasted her only six months, when she fell into penury. As there was no one to carry on Dr. Wiseman's researches the Trustees decided to close down the Centre. Dr. Springfield and the other Research Assistants left to find employment elsewhere. The former went to Australia where he was now lecturing at the University of Melbourne, Mr. Balmer and Mr. Suppercot had also gone to teach in India and Iraq respectively, and all the others had found employment in various establishments in Britain and Northern Ireland. By now she herself had been able to secure a place in the present hotel as a charwoman, so that she was able to assist Mrs. Wiseman as far as food was concerned; for she would often take to her some surplus food which she obtained from the hotel. For her personal needs Mrs. Wiseman had to sell her clothes and jewellery one by one, until she had nothing left to sell.

"One morning, about a year after you had been gone," continued Mrs. Casely, "the landlord, Mr. Nuggart, came and said that the rents had not been paid for eight months. She must either pay all the arrears at once or else quit the house immediately. As she did not have even a penny to buy food she decided to quit. Mr. Nuggart then took legal action for recovery of the rents and had all the articles in the museum and library, plus all your personal possessions, sold by public auction."

Continuing her account Mrs. Casely said Mrs. Wiseman went looking for a place until she secured a room at No. 14 Flint- land Road, her last known address. She continued to send to her food from the hotel and to assist her occasionally with the payment of the rents which was only ten Pounds a month. Then she herself fell sick and was not able to visit her again for a period of six weeks. When she was well again and went to look for her she was told that Mrs. Wiseman had left the house, having been ejected by the landlord, Mr. Bluebutton, for non-payment of rents.

"That was about a year ago," concluded Mrs. Casely. "The new tenant in the house could not tell me where Mrs. Wiseman had gone, as she did not leave a forwarding address."

Dr. Wiseman was greatly troubled on learning of his wife's difficulties since he left her and that she could no longer be traced. He decided not to rest until he had found her.

He spent the next four days looking for her. But he might as well have looked for a needle in a hay stack. He went to railway stations and shops and gardens and cinema houses and theatres and all the other places where crowds gather, but all in vain.

At last he had spent almost all the money he had on transport, leaving him with the sum of one Pound only. Then he was seized with panic, as he did not have the money even for paying his hotel bill. He decided to go to the curiosity shop and ask for the remaining one hundred pounds for the skins.

On arrival at the shop he found, to his utter dismay, that it had been closed, with a notice saying that it would be reopened in a week's time. What was he to do? By now he had only sixty pence left in his pocket, just enough to take him back to the hotel in a taxi. He decided to walk.

It was quite a long distance from the shop to the hotel and he arrived there very tired just before 2 p.m. Then he sat down in a chair to rest and to plan his next move.

He had already spent four nights in the hotel and the money now left in his pocket would not be enough to pay his bills even if he decided to leave today. He could wait until the curiosity shop re-opened in a week's time, when he would go for the remaining one hundred Pounds. But by that time his hotel bill would have increased by almost twice as much, so that was no solution. What was he to do then? Must he ask Mrs. Casely for a loan? No, he would find that very embarrassing. Mrs. Casely had supported his wife on her meagre earnings while he was away. How could he then ask her for further monetary assistance for himself? In the end he felt that he was in a dilemma for which he would find no easy solution.

Then he began to think again of the things he had brought from Gamberia, namely the skins, bow and arrows and the base brass. The bow and arrows were useless, as he had been told, but he had been able to get something for the skins. Perhaps he could also get something for the base brass. If it fetched him another two hundred Pounds he might be able to survive until he found some employment. He must therefore take it to Messrs Copper brass & Co. Ltd, the Fine Metal Buyers, just across the street.

Having thus made up his mind Dr. Wiseman picked up his brief-case with its heavy contents and descended downstairs. Going out of the hotel he crossed the street and soon found himself at his destination. He pushed the door open and entered, closing it behind him. A middle-aged man of about forty was standing behind a counter. Going up to him he greeted.

"Good afternoon."

"Good afternoon," responded the man. And he looked askant at the Doctor.

Without any explanation Dr. Wiseman placed his brief-case on the counter and took out its contents. The man's eyes popped out with astonishment as he arranged them on the counter.

"I wish to sell these," he said when he had finished arranging them. "Please examine them and tell me how much you will offer."

"All right, just a moment," said the man. And with that he collected and quickly disappeared with them in a room behind the counter.

He was there for a long time. Meanwhile Dr. Wiseman's heart had begun to beat faster and faster as he awaited with deep anxiety the verdict which the man would bring after examining them. He prayed hard in his heart that they might at least be worth something. The canoe man who brought him from Hoba to Blaft had said that ten small nuggets of gold (by which he meant the base brass) were equivalent to ten thousand Cupras or ten Pounds Sterling. He had brought four large nuggets of gold and nine small ones. By calculation he might at least have got 50,000 Cupras, the equivalent of £50:00 in Hoba and £60:00 or £70:00 in Blaft. Here in London he was likely to get at least twice as much. Thus if he was lucky he might re-emerge from the shop with about £150.00 in his pocket. It was not much, but it might enable him to stay at the hotel for another week at least, when he could then go for the £100:00 for the skins. He waited and waited. How he wished the man would come out and let him know his fate.

At last the gentleman re-appeared with a smile on his face, bringing back the metals. Without any explanation he poured them on the counter and counted them one by one. Then he pushed them towards Dr. Wiseman who had been looking anxiously on and said:

"I am sorry, Sir.........."

The blood seemed to dry up from Dr. Wiseman's head. His eyes swam, his heart missed a beat, his throat became parched, and he felt as if he would choke to death. Noticing his condition the man cut short his sentence and looked at him with deep concern.

"What's wrong with you, Sir?" he asked.

"Water. Please water. Quick," the Doctor gasped.

The gentleman disappeared quickly into the room behind the counter and soon returned with a glass of water, which he handed to Dr. Wiseman. He gulped it down and asked for more. The man poured him another glassful. The Doctor drank a second time and heaved a sigh.

"I am sorry" he apologised as he handed the empty glass back to the man. I am all right now. It is an attack from which I suffer from time to time. Please proceed."

"As I was saying," continued the man. "I am sorry. . . . "

Dr. Wiseman's sight went blank and his head reeled again. The man noticed him and paused once more.

"Shall I get you another glass of water?" he asked.

"No, no, I am all right," he replied quickly. "Please continue."

"As I was saying, I am sorry……."

"For Heaven's sake, stop being sorry and tell me whether or not you want them!" shouted Dr. Wiseman.

"I am sorry, we don't want them" replied the man "Or rather, we can't afford them. You see, they are all pure gold - 24 carats. Even the small ones would be worth about ten million Pounds each. We don't have that kind of money. What I would suggest, therefore, is that you take them to Messrs Johnson Thomas & Sons Ltd, the famous jewellers. I am sure they will have enough money to purchase all."

Dr. Wiseman could hardly believe his ears. He thought he was dreaming.

"What did you say?" he asked, straining his ears.

"I said that they are all pure gold - 24 carats. We don't have the money to buy even one of the small ones. You may therefore take them to Messrs Johnson Thomas & Sons Ltd. I am sure they will have enough money to buy all." he repeated.

Dr. Wiseman staggered towards the counter, collected the gold back into his brief-case and, without saying good-bye to the man, went out of the shop. As he stepped outside again he felt so light in mind and body that he thought the slightest puff of wind would topple him over. Was he really awake or dreaming one of his usual dreams? he asked himself.

He pinched his nose. It hurt. He pulled his hair. That too hurt. He took to his heels. He ran only a short distance; then he halted and began to hop on the same spot. At first those who saw him run thought that he was hurrying to catch a bus in circumstances of extreme urgency. But when they subsequently saw him hopping on the same spot they came to the conclusion that these gymnastic exercises were not directed towards the attainment of any particular objective, but were merely the activities of a man not entirely in possession of his senses.

Dr. Wiseman, however, did all this just for the purpose of assuring himself that he was not dreaming, but that all that he was seeing, hearing and feeling were real.

He was re-assured when he saw people staring at him in utter disbelief; for he knew that in a dream no one would have considered his behaviour in any way abnormal.

Having thus satisfied himself that he was not dreaming he hailed a taxi and told the driver to take him to Messrs. Johnson Thomas & Sons Ltd, the famous jewellers, at No. 24 Helton Street, S.W.2.

As he approached his destination his fears and anxiety began to revive. Suppose the man at Messrs Copper brass & C0 Ltd had been wrong in concluding that what he had brought were gold, or knew that they were not gold but he was only pulling his legs? he asked himself. The more he thought of it the more he became convinced that the man had been deceiving him. If they were real gold he would not have asked him to take them elsewhere, but would at least have offered to buy one. How would a reputable company like Copper brass & Co. Ltd lack a mere sum of ten million Pounds? Cold despondency seized his heart and mind. He had only been dreaming after all, on a more physical plane, he concluded.

It was not long before he arrived at Messrs Johnson Thomas & Sons Ltd. He paid off the taxi driver and entered the shop. By now he was left with only twenty pence in his pocket. He found an elderly gentleman with spectacles perched at the tip of his nose. He was examining with a magnifying glass a diamond necklace that lay in a silver tray placed upon a table behind the counter. The gentleman stopped what he was doing and raised up his head to look at him as he entered. Dr. Wiseman greeted and he answered back.

"What can I do for you?" he asked.

"I have brought some nuggets of gold for sale;" he replied, placing the brief-case upon the counter and taking them out.

"Please have a look at them and tell me how much you are prepared   to pay."

"All right. Just a moment," said the gentleman. And with that he collected the metals into a tray.

"What's your name?" he asked.

"Dr. Wiseman," replied the Doctor.

"All right, Doctor, I shall be back soon," he said.

He took the gold into his office. Dr. Wiseman waited and waited until he was getting tired of waiting. He began to wonder why the man had delayed so long. Whether they were real gold or not it should not take more than a few minutes to find out, so why the delay? No, the man must have discovered that they were only base brass and had accordingly telephoned the Police. He was waiting for them to come and grab him for attempting to defraud. Dr. Wiseman began to regret that he has said that it was gold. He should have left it to the gentleman to discover for himself whatever they were. He couldn't then have accused him of attempting to defraud him by false pretences. He concluded that his best course of action was to disappear while he yet had the chance. If the Police arrived to find him gone they would not bother to look for him even though he had rather unwisely given his correct name to the gentleman.

Just as Dr. Wiseman was on the point of putting his decision into effect the man suddenly re-emerged. He had not brought back the gold. Dr. Wiseman's heart began to beat very fast.

"Congratulations, Doctor," said the gentleman, with a happy smile. "Yours is the purest gold that has ever been brought to this Company - 24 carats. We can offer Two Hundred Million Pounds for each of the four large nuggets and Twenty Million Pounds for each of the 9 small ones, making a total of Nine Hundred and Eighty Million Pounds. If you accept our offer I shall issue you with a cheque right away."

Dr. Wiseman was so flabbergasted that he did not know what to say. His head swam once more and his heart fluttered in his chest. He had difficulty in remaining on his feet. He did not know whether to jump or cry for joy. It was a long time before he could control his emotions.

"I accept your offer" he said in a quivering voice.

"Must I issue you with a cheque then?"

"Yes, yes," he replied quickly. Then he added as an after thought: "But at the moment I don't even have the money to take a taxi back to my hotel. So I need some ready cash."

"That is easily taken care of" replied the man, with a smile. "We offer our good customers special bonuses by way of extra cash. In your case we can give you ten thousand Pounds cash. That should take care of your immediate needs."

"Thank you," said Dr. Wiseman. "That is very kind of you."

Dr. Wiseman was soon out of the building with ten thousand Pounds in his brief-case. As he stepped into the street he felt as happy as a cricket. All his worries and anxieties had evaporated, leaving him as free as a bird in mind and body. He hailed a taxi and was soon back in his hotel in quite a different frame of mind from that in which he had left in the morning.

Having already planned for many years what he would do with money, he had no difficulty at all in deciding on his next move. He immediately bought a newspaper and began to study the advertisement columns, looking for a house to buy. Two caught his attention. One was the house of the Nizam of Huntarabad in Surrey, popularly known as the "Diamond Mansion." The other was also in the same vicinity and belonged to Lord Montville, the former leader of the House of Lords. Both were on sale.

Dr. Wiseman at once took a taxi and went to inspect both properties. He found the former the most magnificent building he had ever dreamt of. It stood in about ten acres of ground, amid orchards and parks and landscape gardens, with a private airfield and a landing place for helicopter. The entire edifice was constructed of polished Parian marbles and was of the most executive design and finish. It was being sold for five million Pounds. It was exactly Dr. Wiseman's dream house and he immediately paid for it.

That evening when Mrs.Casely came into his room to find out how he was getting on, she found him in the most jubilant mood.

"Guess what I have done," he said to her immediately after returning her greeting.

"What have you done?" she asked. "I can't guess."

"I have bought a house in Surrey," he informed her.

"Have you, indeed?" she asked with surprise and delight.

"Yes. And I want you to resign in a week's time and go with me to be my house-keeper."

Mrs. Casely hesitated.

"Doctor" she said, "I had a difficult time finding this job. And although the pay is not much - only ten Pounds a week - it is enough to enable me to contribute to my upkeep. Besides I shall be obliged to pay forty Pounds to the management in lieu of four weeks' notice."

Dr. Wiseman smiled.

"Is that all?" he asked. "Well, I am prepared to pay you ten times as much as you are receiving here. As for the forty Pounds which you have to pay in lieu of notice, here it is. You can pay now and give them a week's notice." And with that he counted the amount to her.

Mrs. Casely received the money and the offer with great surprise and delight. She took the money downstairs at once and was soon back.

"I have tended my resignation as from next week and paid the money," she said.

"Good", said Dr. Wiseman. "We shall go there in a week's time. "It will take that long to get the place ready. And, by the way, take this amount also as a gift to buy yourself a decent dress." And with that he handed her an extra four thousand Pounds.

Mrs. Casely's joy knew no bounds. She could hardly believe that the Doctor was now so rich and could be so generous.

A week later Dr. Wiseman settled his hotel bill and went to the curiosity shop to redeem his two skins. He found the shop open. Not only did he refund the one hundred Pounds which he had borrowed, but he also added another fifty Pounds as interest, all to the surprise and joy of the shop owner. Returning to the hotel he found Mrs. Casely ready for their departure. Soon they were on their way to "Diamond Mansion." Mrs. Casely's joy and astonishment can better be imagined than described when they arrived there.

"Oh, if only Mrs. Wiseman were here to see this!" she exclaimed again and again as they went round inspecting the premises. I hope you will hire a detective at once to look for her."

"There is no need for that," replied Dr. Wiseman. I have already put an advertisement in the newspapers. If she is still alive I am sure she will turn up soon."

Dr. Wiseman was not disappointed in his expectation. A week after he and Mrs. Casely had settled down in the house, with cars and servants, the latter was cutting some flowers along the drive when the gateman, Julius Welcock by name, came up to her and said that a woman and a boy of about seven were behind the gate asking to be let in.

"Did she give her name?" she asked.

"Yes, she said she was Mrs. Vitamin." replied Julius.

"What sort of a person is she?" asked Mrs. Casely.

"What sort of a person?"

"Yes. I mean what does she look like?"

"If you ask me, Madam," replied Julius, "she looks like one who is badly in need of that necessary food constituent by which she calls herself. She is extremely malnourished, like one who has not had a bite for the past one month - both she and her boy."

"Let her come in at once," said Mrs. Casely, unable to tell from Julius' description who she might be.

The gateman went back to the gate and opened it. A woman in a seedy old frock and tattered shoes entered, followed by a young boy whose appearance was even less prepossessing. He was clad in a torn and dirty pair of trousers and a dingy coat. His toes were peeping through his shoes, which were covered with dust and looked as if the soles were half-gone. Mrs. Casely was unable to recognise who they were, but the boy immediately ran and threw his arms around her.

"Oh Mrs. Casely, Mrs. Casely," he cried.

Mrs. Casely looked again. She recognised him at once. It was master Wiseman. She soon recognised Mrs. Wiseman also. She embraced her again and again.

"Oh Mrs. Wiseman, I am so happy to see you once more," she cried.

"I read an advertisement in the newspapers asking me to call at the "Diamond Mansion", she explained even before Mrs. Casely could ask. "That's why I am here. Are you employed here, and why do you want to see me?"

"Yes, I am," replied Mrs. Casely. "I have news of your husband."

"How? News of my dead husband?" asked Mrs. Wiseman incredulously.

"Yes. It was the master of this house who told me. Come with me and hear it from the horse's own mouth."

Mrs. Wiseman followed her into a spacious and luxuriously furnished waiting room.

"Wait for me here," she said. "I shall bring the master." And with that she disappeared into another room.

Mrs. Wiseman and Master Wiseman sat casting glances round the wonderful room. They had never seen anything like it in all their lives. The ceiling had all sorts of figures depicting historical scenes, all done in gold. The walls were of white marble polished to a shining brilliance and were hung with expensive pictures and tapestries, as well as a gorilla's and a lion's skin and a bow and a quiver of arrows. The floor was also of polished marble inlaid with gold. Beautiful Victorian furniture, all inlaid with gold and silver, stood here and there on most expensive Persian and Chinese carpets.

Mrs. Wiseman felt completely out of place. Her mean and tattered dress contrasted sadly with the splendour of the place in which she found herself. She felt so embarrassed that she wished she had never come. And yet she felt so happy at seeing Mrs. Casely once more looking so gay and prosperous. She wondered what news the master of the house had about her husband. He was probably going to tell her that his remains had been discovered somewhere in the African jungle. Of what use would that be to her?

She was thus speculating when the door by which Mrs. Casely had disappeared suddenly opened again and she re-emerged, followed by a tall handsome gentleman, exquisitely clad in a very expensive suit. At the sight of him Mrs. Wiseman hung her head down in embarrassment. She could not look him in the face. But to her great surprise and subsequent joy, the gentleman at once ran to her and embraced her tightly in his arms.

"Oh, Mary, Mary!" he cried, kissing her all over. "It's me your husband, John. Aren't you happy to see me?"

Mrs. Wiseman looked again and could hardly believe her eyes. She thought she was dreaming. But when she saw Mrs. Casely looking on with incredible joy in her eyes, she knew at once that this was indeed her dead husband. At the same time Master Wiseman ran and grabbed his father by the trousers. Dr. Wiseman lifted him up, kissed him again and again and deposited him in an arm-chair, dirty as he was.

That day there was great rejoicing at "Diamond Mansion" such as had never before been witnessed there when the place's original master owned it.

Dr. Wiseman told his story from the beginning to the end and, when he had finished, Mrs. Wiseman also told him all that had happened to her ever since he went away. She said that after leaving No. 14 Flint-land Road she found employment with an old couple, Mr. and Mrs. Redapple, in a little three-roomed house in Hammersmith. The pay was only two Pounds a week plus boarding and lodging. She did not have enough money to send Master Wiseman to school, so she decided to teach him in the house.

"We have been with the Redapples for only seven months now," she continued, "then only yesterday I read an advertisement in the papers asking me to call at this address. You know the rest."

"And where are Jacko and Robin-hood?" Dr. Wiseman asked after his eloquent parrot and faithful dog when she had finished.

"Life was so difficult for me that I sold them to the Zoo," replied Mrs. Wiseman. "I believe they are still there by now, and are providing entertainment to visitors, particularly Jacko."

Dr.Wiseman was sorry to hear that his two favourite pets had thus fallen casualty to his wife's indigence, but he did not worry much. He would be able to buy them back, even if he had to pay for them ten times the amount for which his wife had disposed of them. Both were easy to identify - Jacko by his incessant repetition of St. Matthew Chapter one, and Robin-hood by the white patches around his eyes. In fact, as far as Robin-hood was concerned there would be no problem of identification at all. He was sure the dog would be the first to recognise him immediately he appeared before him in the Zoo.

CHAPTER TWENTY-FOUR
DR. WISEMAN'S INVITATION

Six months had passed since Dr. Wiseman came to own "Diamond Mansion". He had fulfilled almost all his dreams. He had purchased an expensive private plane, a helicopter, a luxurious yacht and a fleet of expensive cars. He had also acquired a mansion at the Riviera, another at the Miami Beach and a third in Malta. After paying for all these he still had more than six hundred million Pounds left, which he invested in Government bonds and other high interest yielding enterprises, from all of which he received an annual income of more than thirty million Pounds. He had engaged a private tutor for Master Wiseman and settled an annual allowance of four million Pounds on Mrs. Wiseman for the purchase of dresses and other personal requirements. He had purchased back from the zoo his two favourite pets, Jacko and Robin-hood, both of whom were undoubtedly happy to see their master once more. His fame had spread far and wide as one of the richest men in all Europe, eclipsing his reputation as an eminent anthropologist. In fact, he had been no longer interested in anthropological research, which he now considered as a pursuit worthy only of impecunious academics, certainly not of a multi-millionaire.

He always liked to recount his unique experiences with Kotokro in the African jungle, to the attentive hearing of his family and Mrs. Casely. They liked his constant repetition, because in so doing he always remembered some new and more interesting details. After one of these interesting recitals one evening Mrs. Casely said:

"Doctor, when this boy, Kotokro, was here you always said that he had no intelligence. I, on the contrary, thought that he was not altogether as stupid as he appeared to be. It is true that he was always asking what seemed silly questions and making remarks and observation that, on the surface, seemed absurd. Yet to me these questions, remarks and observations appeared to contain a great deal of sense on deeper reflection. Such were his actions and remarks about boxing, about penalty scores in the game of ball, and about many other aspects of our so-called civilised life. But from what you tell us concerning the way he conducted himself during his period of enforced stay in the jungle with you, I can only come to the conclusion that he is knowledgeable, resourceful, skilful, generous, brave, honest and gifted with a good memory and a keen power of observation. If all these qualities and many more which he exhibited do not amount to intelligence, then tell us, what constitutes intelligence?"

"Mrs. Casely is right to ask this question, John," interposed Mrs. Wiseman before her husband could reply. "It seems to me, to be frank, that the boy displayed even more mental alertness than you in all the difficult situations that confronted you both, and that without him you would never have come out of that jungle with your life, much less with so much gold. Tell us then, once and for all, whether or not this boy possesses intelligence in your scientific understanding of the word."

Dr. Wiseman smiled.

My dear Mrs. Casely," he said. "I entirely agree with what you and Mrs. Wiseman have said, although three years ago I would have said that neither of you knew what she was talking about. But a man grows in knowledge and wisdom as his experience enlarges. Previously I had no experience of the ways of the African, all that I knew of him being derived from accounts brought back by white travellers who only saw superficially and had personal interest in making sensation out of what they saw. Now I have seen and known for myself what the African really is below the surface, and I confess that I was entirely wrong in my conclusions - conclusions that were supposed to rest on scientific basis, but which in reality sprung from prejudices and pre-conceived ideas. Kotokro has been my eye opener.

"You cannot measure incommensurables by the same standard or have a common denominator for things disparate. The different races have different environments and different experiences which would account for their performances in any indiscriminate intelligence test. To be able to obtain any reliable result, therefore, in measuring their comparative intelligence you need to ensure, first of all, that they have gone through the same experiences. That is to say that, first of all, the representatives to be tested must have been born on the same day and in the same place. This would give them an equal start in the absorption of knowledge. Secondly, they must also have lived and grown up in the same place up to the time of being tested. Thirdly they must have been brought up by a person belonging to a neutral race. That is to say, the person nurturing them must be neither white, yellow, brown or black, or of any colour approximating to any of these. This is essential, because a child's attitude to the colour of the one who nurtures him influences the quality of his experience. Since such a neutral person cannot be found, therefore, a way must be devised to eliminate this influence. In the fourth place, the person conducting the tests must also be neutral in point of race, since the examinee's attitude to the examiner's race (and vice versa) is also bound to influence the result. And lastly the language in which they are tested should be common to the examinees."

"It is only when the above conditions have been fully satisfied and the tests repeated a number of times, that any reliable result can emerge. Since these conditions cannot easily be met, however, the only other reliable way of assessing the comparative intelligence of the different races is to see how each performs under his natural environments. Going by this criterion, therefore, it is quite obvious that Kotokro showed a very high degree of intelligence. I am not sure if any of the other boys could have performed half as well in his native setting."

"Kotokro's apparently silly questions generally concern things most people do not reason about, because they take their existence for granted."

"All in all, I pronounce Kotokro to be a very intelligent boy and a credit to his race. I am sorry for all the ridicule, insults, scorn and contumely which, with little regard for their feelings, I poured on the boy and his race, and which they bore with such dignified restraint. I was blind, conceited, and arrogant, knowing little yet boasting of much. I am glad that he has been my eye-opener, teaching a lesson that ought to be learnt by all who claim to be authorities on things of which they are ignorant."

"I have now discovered the important truth, which I failed to see before, that the scientific and technological achievements on which we pride ourselves and on account of which we consider ourselves superior, are not the true criteria of intelligence, since they are mostly based on research, which is characterised by trial and error, and not on systematic and sustained thinking, so that a historian, a lawyer, a philosopher or even a novelist, of whom Africans have their share, may be more intelligent than a scientist or a technologist. I am sure that if Africans seriously turn their attention to science and technology they may eventually surpass us, even as Japan may be said to have done."

"All the vices and shortcomings I associated with Kotokro and his race are also common to all other men in the same degree. As for intelligence it differs more among individuals than among the different races, so that a black man may be more intelligent than a white, and vice versa."

"I am very glad to hear this, Doctor," said Mrs. Casely when he had finished. "I do hope you will write to convey to him your apology."

"I have done so already," replied Dr. Wiseman. "I did so on the day of our parting and I have apologised to him again in a letter I wrote him on my arrival here."

"That is very noble of you, Doctor," pronounced Mrs. Casely; "And, if I may be permitted to say so, you would act even more nobly if you would take steps to let him share in your fortune and happiness; for, as I see it, he was instrumental in your getting so much gold."

"I quite agree with Mrs. Casely," said Mrs. Wiseman before her husband could reply. "The boy deserves to share in your good fortune and you must make sufficient provision for him and his parents."

Dr. Wiseman smiled again. "I agree with both of you again," he said. "And it will interest you to know that I have already taken care of that."

"What have you done?" they asked simultaneously.

"Do you see that mansion on the other side of the street?"

"Yes. And what of that?"

"I have purchased it from Lord Montville, the former Leader of the House of Lords. It cost three million Pounds. I have provided it with a very expensive set of furniture and a fleet of cars including Rolls Royce, Mercedes Benz 600, B.M.W. and Citroen. I have also engaged ten servants for the place. All these I have done for Kotokro. I have written to him and his parents to come and live with us, and there they will live when they come. I also intend to settle on him an annual allowance of three million Pounds, so that he will be one of the richest men in Britain."

"Capital!" exclaimed Mrs. Casely. "Oh, I am so glad; I really love that boy and will be happy to see him once more."

"Your wish will soon be granted," Dr. Wiseman assured her, "for by now I am sure he has received my letter."

Dr. Wiseman was right. At the very moment they were discussing the boy, Kotokro and his parents had received his letter. It was brought, as usual, by Jimfa. It was on a Thursday, the day on which the farmers of Kantoma permitted mother earth to rest by resting themselves. Kotokro was playing blind-man's buff with other children while his mother was cooking the afternoon meal and his father sat under the shady tree in the centre of the village with friends drinking palm-wine and cracking jokes. When not working on the land Papa Asuboni always preferred to prepare his stomach in this way for a hearty meal. All three were thus occupied when a message came from Chief Brongo saying that they were wanted in his palace. They stopped what they were doing and soon assembled there.

They were not surprised to see Jimfa, for they knew at once that he had brought a message from the white man. After the usual exchange of greetings Chief Brongo said:

"I summoned you here at Jimfa's request. He says that he has brought a message from the white man who came here to take Kotokro away to his country, Dogtar Whatman. So please listen to what he has to say."

"Chief Brongo," Jimfa began, clearing his throat. "The last time that I came here I was the bearer of sad news for Papa Asuboni and his wife, indeed for all the people of Kantoma; for I know that in this village, as in all other villages in our dear motherland, anything that touches one man touches all. Today, however, I am glad to say that the message I bring is one that should bring joy to everyone, for it is no other than an invitation from Dr. Wiseman to Kotokro and his parents to come to him in London. .   "

"To come to him in London!" exclaimed Mama Alimana, interrupting.

"Yes. This invitation is contained in a letter addressed to Kotokro through me, which I took the liberty of reading. I read it because I know that there is no one in this village to read and interpret it to him. Here is that letter." And he produced it from his pocket and stretched it out to Kotokro.

"What is the use?" interrupted Papa Asuboni. "You say that you have already read the letter. Why not just tell us what it says?"

"I was going to do that in any case," replied Jimfa. "I only wanted you to believe that I have really brought a letter from Dr. Wiseman as I say."

Mamma Alimana laughed.

"As if that would make any difference" she said. "It is like showing a picture to a blind man to confirm the truth of your story! Just tell us the message you bring."

"Just as I said, Dr. Wiseman has invited all three of you to come to him in London. Here is what he says;" And with that he opened the letter again and began to read and translate it sentence by sentence. The letter read:

"My dear Kotokro, I hope you have by now received the letter I wrote to you as soon as I arrived safely back in London. In that letter I told you how I returned to find my wife and Mrs. Casely gone from the house in which we lived; how I took residence in a hotel, where I happened to meet Mrs. Casely; how I was still looking for my wife and master Wiseman and the difficulties I was encountering financially.

"Now, however, I am happy to inform you that all my problems have been solved. I have found my wife and master Wiseman. Those pieces of yellow metal, which the canoe-man said were base brass, have turned out to be pure gold. I have sold them for a very large amount of money - an amount that makes me by far the richest man in all Europe, if not in the whole world. With some of the money I have purchased the most splendid building in London where I now live with my family and Mrs. Casely and a host of domestic servants. I have also bought a private aeroplane, a helicopter, a yacht, a fleet of cars, as well as several mansions in different parts of the world."

"Now, the purpose of my writing you this letter is to let you know that I greatly appreciate all that you did for me while we lived in the jungle. I have already told everyone about how you saved my life on several occasions and were responsible for my coming by so much wealth."

"But mere expression of appreciation is not enough in the case of one who has done so much for me. I have, therefore, taken steps to show my gratitude in a more concrete way. I have purchased for you a very magnificent mansion situated just opposite my own house. I want you to come with your parents and spend the rest of your lives in freedom from the poverty and squalor in which you now live. You will have a fleet of cars at your disposal and several domestic servants to minister to your needs. You will also have a yearly allowance of three million pounds to spend as you like, so that you will never lack anything.

"With greetings and best wishes."

Jimfa folded the letter again and put it back into the envelope and handed it to Kotokro. He and his parents had smiles on their faces.

"And now, what do you say," asked Jimfa.

"He says that he wrote me as soon as he arrived safely back in London," replied Kotokro before his parents could comment. "Where is that letter? Did you bring it?"

"No, I never received that letter, which I believe he must have sent through me," replied Jimfa. "It must have got lost in the post."

"How?"

"Someone at the Post Office must have taken and opened it, thinking it contained money; and when he discovered that it didn't he simply threw it away." Jimfa explained.

"Why should anyone do that?"

"Because many people in this country have now been woefully afflicted by the terrible disease originating from the white man's country, which we here refer to as "money-mania". It is this disease that makes them do that."

"What a terrible disease." commented Mamma Alimana.

"It is really terrible," agreed her husband.

"Well, to come back to my question to which you have not yet given an answer" said Jimfa. "What do you say to the Doctor's letter which I have just read to you?"

"It contains a good message," replied Papa Asuboni. "At least it does not announce death. There are a few things, however, that I would like to know. First of all, what sort of land is it? I mean is there sunshine throughout the year, with seasonal rains and dry Harmattan winds to round off one year and usher in another?"

"Well, as Kotokro must have told you ....." began Jimfa.

"Kotokro is only a child, and he did not stay there long enough to know much about the place," Papa Asuboni interrupted. "You lived there for many years at a more mature age. Your word would be more reliable."

"That's quite true," admitted Jimfa. "Well, the land and the climate there are unlike ours in many ways. First of all, it is cold for the greater part of the year. In fact, for about half the year it is so cold that you have to put on many thick dresses when you go out, and even when at home you have to light a fire to keep warm."

"It is true, Papa," confirmed Kotokro. "Even when fire is lighted in the room it is still so cold that you have to sit close to it before you can feel warm. See how my shins are burnt black with sitting by the fireside." And he displayed his blackened shins, something he always did whenever he described the climate in Britain.

"It is about only four months in the year that you can go out lightly clad and do not have to make fire in your room in order to keep warm," continued Jimfa.

"What about the land itself?" asked Papa Asuboni. "Is it endowed with thick virgin forest and fertile soil that yields abundant returns to the farmer?"

"It has no thick, virgin forests, and the soil is not naturally rich, so that you have to use manure in order to produce abundant crops" replied Jimfa.

"If there are no thick virgin forests, then it means that one cannot go gathering snails and mushrooms or catch crabs and fish from cool bubbling streams?" asked Mamma Alimana.

"That is so," agreed Jimfa "But if you accept the Doctor's offer you will be so rich that you wont care for any of those things."

"You mean we wont care to make a farm and have the pleasure of seeing our plants grow and yield abundant crops or experience the joy of harvest, when our depleted barn is once more replenished with golden grains?" asked Papa Asuboni.

"All that would not be necessary, because you could have everything else that money can buy."

"You admit then that money cannot buy any of those things?"

"Yes, but it can buy anything else that will make you very happy."

"I am happiest when I sit by the brook bubbling underneath the cool canopy of giant trees, watching the fishes frolicking in the gleaming waters, while the sweet breeze gently stirs the leaves around; or when I listen to the birds singing happily in the trees, or see a family of merry monkeys chattering volubly as they playfully swing from tree to tree," Kotokro put in. "All these are lacking in the white man's country."

"You are quite right," agreed Jimfa, "but again you wont have need for all that."

"Why not?" asked Kotokro.

"Because you would be so rich that you could have everything else that you want."

"But I don't want anything else."

"I am sure you will change your mind when you get there and begin to see all the joy that money can bring."

"Will that be like the joy of sitting underneath the cool shade of a tree in the hot afternoon, drinking fresh palm-wine with Jumo and Kafari and Tepasu while listening to the thrilling anecdotes of old Rakito or the funny jokes of facetious Jollifu, as I was doing today when I was summoned here?" asked Papa Asuboni.

"Yes. And you will have something more than palm-wine to drink" replied Jimfa. "There will be whisky and brandy and gin and schnapps and champagne and wine and all sorts of alcoholic and non-alcoholic drinks. If you want something that tastes like palm-wine there is apple cider also."

"Does it taste exactly the same as palm-wine?"

"Not quite; for one thing, it does not contain as much alcohol."

"Ah, that is not good enough for me then. There can be no substitute for cool frothy palm-wine freshly collected from the tree on a hot afternoon. It not only quenches the thirst but it also uplifts the spirits."

"And will there be singing, drumming and dancing on funeral or festive occasions, with all our neighbours taking part and cheering one another?" asked Mamma Alimana.

"No. But dances are organised from time to time in dance halls where you will make friends if you like. One pays, of course, to take part in them. But that should be no problem for you, since you would be so rich."

"One pays to take part in a dance?" asked Papa Asuboni in astonishment.

"Yes" replied Jimfa.

"Then it seems that in that country one must pay for everything one needs to make one happy?"

"Yes, papa" Kotokro confirmed before Jimfa could reply. "You pay for everything in that country - even to go to the toilet. Mrs. Casely had to pay for me before I could attend nature's call when I was hard-pressed during an outing!"

"Oh dear!" groaned Mamma Alimana. "If one pays even to take part in a dance then it means that those who cannot pay will be kept out, including even one's closest neighbours?"

"Of course," conceded Jimfa.

"Which means that there will hardly be anything to deepen affection or the spirit of friendship that should exist between us and our neighbours?"

"I agree. But why should you care about all that when you would be so wealthy?" asked Jimfa.

"If wealth will make us not to care about all those things, then I for one will have nothing to do with it," replied Mamma Alimana firmly.

"I am sure you will change your mind when you get to London and see the life of ease and splendour that will be yours," replied Jimfa.

"From what you have said it seems to me that the people are not friendly and do not show enough interest in one another's fortune and welfare. Am I right?" asked Papa Asuboni.

"Well, I can't say they are unfriendly. But they certainly do not show interest in one another's fortune and welfare. If one did one would be considered unwarrantably inquisitive."

"Dear me!" exclaimed Mamma Alimana. "So if you met a neighbour in the street you would not greet him and enquire after his health and well-being?"

"No, you are not expected to do that," replied Jimfa. "If you did, it would be highly resented."

"Why?"

"Because everyone is expected to mind his own business and not to poke his nose into other people's affairs."

"Do you mean when two people meet they do not greet each other at all?" asked Papa Asuboni.

"If they know each other they do. They also do when they are introduced to each other by a third party."

"I see. Then they can ask each other how they are faring in health and fortune, and thus provide an opportunity for communicating their troubles to each other?" asked Papa Asuboni.

"No, you are not supposed to tell each other what is troubling you." replied Jimfa. "If your neighbour asks you 'How do you do?' you also ask him 'How do you do?' and that is the end of the matter."

"Do you mean if, for example, I have a splitting head-ache and did not have a good night's rest I must not tell him even if he happens to be a medicine man who could diagnose my sickness and suggest to me a cure?" asked Mamma Alimana.

"No, he would not be pleased if you told him. If you are sick he would rather expect you to come to his medical home and pay him a fee before he tells you what is wrong with you and prescribes a cure. You cannot have his diagnosis and prescription for nothing."

"Dear me!" said Mamma Alimana again. "If so, why then do you say that they are not unfriendly? How can a man be friendly when he is not interested in his neighbour's welfare and happiness except for a fee?"

"Well, they are friendly in a negative way, by each being his own keeper, not his brother's"

"Strange!" pronounced Mamma Alimana.

"Very strange indeed," agreed her husband.

"My dear Jimfa," said Chief Brongo, speaking for the first time. "I have listened carefully to the questions that Kotokro and his parents have been asking about the white man's country, and your answers. There is one thing I want to know. Suppose one of them dies in that country who will bury him, and what opportunity will his spirit have of being with those of his ancestors?"

"He will be buried by an undertaker in a public cemetery...."

"Who is an undertaker?" asked Chief Brongo, cutting him short.

"He is a person who makes it his business to bury people for a fee."

"I see. In that country it's not the relatives of the deceased and their neighbours and friends who bury and make funeral for him but an outsider who only buries for a fee?"

"Exactly."

"So that he will not even shed a tear for those whom he deposits in the grave?"

"Not necessarily. In fact, he may only be thinking of his profit while seeing to it that you are buried deep in the ground with no chance of resurrection. And there will not be many people to mourn for you and comfort your survivors."

"Ah, how cruel!" exclaimed Mamma Alimana, beginning to shed tears.

"It is cruel indeed," agreed Chief Brongo. "And it is even more cruel for a person not to be buried among his ancestors but in a public cemetery, where one may forever lie in the company of strangers."

"But, Chief Brongo" protested Jimfa "when a person dies does it matter where he is buried? After all, his spirit is then free and can join those of his ancestors wherever they may happen to be?"

"That depends upon the distance, my son," disagreed Chief Brongo. "Remember the white man's country is at the other end of the world and can only be reached by flying through the air or by sailing on the great ocean for many days. How then can his spirit come all the way here to join those of his ancestors?"

"If Kotokro or either of his parents dies there I am sure his body can be flown by air and be buried here among his ancestors," replied Jimfa, "I am sure Dr. Wiseman would see to that. He has a private aeroplane which can easily bring the body here for burial."

"Yes, he may bring the body for burial here, but he is bound to leave the spirit behind." Chief Brongo pointed out.

"Well, the spirit will find its way here, somehow."

"Somehow, eh?"

"Yes, somehow."

"My dear Jimfa," said Papa Asuboni. "We shall not waste your time with any more questions. It is already past mid-day and I am sure you are anxious to return to Blaft today. From what you have told us, which confirms what we have already learnt from our own son, Kotokro, the white man's country is not the place for us.

"But before I say anything further, I want you to listen very carefully to what I am going to say, so that you convey it to your white friend, Dogtar Whatman, when you write to him. It will enable him to see more clearly the reason why we live the way we do. It is this: We believe that the ultimate aim of every human being, whether white, black or yellow, is to be happy either in this life or in another. Every human being likes to think that happiness awaits him somewhere. But every normal human adult's mind is charged with three compulsive Desires which govern all his thoughts and actions and tie him to this world. These are the Desire for <u>SURVIVAL</u>, the Desire for <u>SEX</u> and the Desire for <u>SIGNIFICANCE</u>. All other desires are but ancillary to these three in the final analysis. It is these THREE DESIRES that often defeat our aim and bring about UNHAPPINESS instead; for in seeking to satisfy them we often not only suffer pain but we also cause pain to others.

"The Desire for survival drives us to seek food and protection for our bodies and to do what we think will ensure our continued existence in another life even after death. The Desire for sex compels us to go after our sexual opposites: and the Desire for Significance urges us to try to equal or even surpass our neighbour.

"It is the strength of these three Desires in us and the way we seek to satisfy them that often bring us pain or cause pain to others.

"<u>The Desire for SIGNIFICANCE</u> (that is to say, for being noticed, for being important in our home, in our community or in our nation) <u>which is peculiar to human beings only, but not to other creatures, or even to the Great Creator of the Universe who is also free from the other two Desires, - wherefore all the adulation and worship, which your CIVILISED MAN would have treasured so much, can make no difference to Him</u> – is the main cause of human Unhappiness. And the more a society advances in material achievements the stronger grows this Desire in its members. It is therefore stronger in your CIVILISED MAN, with his greater material achievements, than it is in us who, with no apology to anyone, have little to show for our existence by way of material possessions. For this reason your CIVILISED MAN cannot be as happy as we are. From a simple desire to be NOTICED, which is common to all human beings, he yearns for prestige, for pre-eminence, for honour, for glory, even for worship, especially where the fulfilment of his first two Desires is assured. Then, propelled by fierce competition, he carries his desire for Significance to an absurd degree, making its fulfilment the more difficult.

"In fact, were these three Desires not implanted in human beings they could be supremely happy, barring sickness and misfortunes. That this is so, can be seen from the lives of little children. In them only the Desire for survival exists. They have no desire for Sex and no Desire for Significance, although the seeds of these are already sown in them. These two Desires grow in them only as they grow older. For the moment their only Desire, namely the desire for Survival, which is primary, is satisfied with the help of their parents, who minister to their needs. This is why they are happy, especially when not unduly restricted by adults in the name of training, unless they happen to be sick.

"Inferring from this your CIVILISED Man may say, rather contemptuously, that our minds are like those of little children. In one sense he is right, because we are almost as happy as little children. In another he is totally wrong, because we know something which neither he nor little children know. We know who and what we are, and live our lives in the light of our knowledge; whereas your CIVILISED MAN does not know, or has sadly forgotten, who and what he is, blinded as he is by the glamour of his material achievements, and therefore imagines that he can attain his desire for Happiness by still greater material achievements. Thus he pursues a mirage in his quest for Happiness, not knowing that even if he becomes the greatest on earth – if greatest is to be measured by earthly success – he cannot be the happiest, <u>as long as his desires remain untamed</u>.

"No, far from having the minds of little children we are rather like wise old men and women of every race. Because of their dying desire for Sex and Significance, and even sometimes for Survival, which allows them greater freedom for the exercise of their intelect, these are next to little children in their capacity for happiness, unless when plagued with poverty or the infirmities of old age. You can see that they are more relaxed and live under less tension and stress than younger adults; for they can joke and laugh more easily, even though they see their lives coming to an end. Like us, they are not overwhelmed by the strength of any of the Three Desires, from which only death can liberat us.

"And so, my dear Jimfa, when you write tell your white friend, Dogtar Whatman, that we thank him for his generous offer but cannot accept it. We do not need a mansion, a fleet of cars, many servants and three million Pounds a year in order to be happy. We are already happy as we are, or have attained the degree of happiness possible for any human being in the face of his three desires, and no amount of material advantage can make us happier.

"Our Desire for Survival is easily satisfied with the help of Mother Earth, who supplies us with all our needs, demanding only a little exertion from us – food, water, clothing, roof over our heads, medicine when we are sick, and much more besides. Our desire for Sex poses no problem, for our sexual partners are not squeamish or difficult, only making sure that they keep to our simple social norms. And as for our desire for Significance, being minimal, it is not at all difficult to attain. It is no more than a desire to be recognised as an equeal member of our community. We frown upon any attempt by any member to put himself above his neighbour. Chief Brongo here does not consider himself superior to any of us by reason of his position or wealth,...."

"God forbid that I should!" interrrupted Chief Brongo.

"After all we all sprang from Mother Earth, we are all nurtured by Mother Earth, and will all eventually return to Mother Earth without exception. And as for wealth, who among us can claim to be wealthier than his neighbour? We all cultivate the land for our survival and make our farms only as large as will give us enough food to eat. We also build our houses and do everything else to meet our need, not with an aim to surpass or even equal our neighbour."#

"Exactly," agreed Papa Asuboni. "Thus it can be seen that no social or material advantage plays any significant part in our human relationships. But, as we learn from old Rakito (who was told by Father Borringer, the white man of God who once came to dwell among us), this is not the case with your CIVILISED MAN. He says that in his case you have the High-born and the Low-born, the Higher and Lower classes, the Titled and the Non-titled, the Rich and the Poor, the Master and the Servant, the Learned and the Ignorant, the Beauty-Queen and the Beauty Non-Queen and many other relationships of superiority and inferiority – all created by the society through painful competition, not by the Great Creator of the Universe – and that each thus advantaged thinks it important to make his or her advantage conspicuous in order to win admiration and respect. Thus in their blind search for Happiness, they create for themselves conditions that breed Unhappiness; in as much as those advantaged not only went through pain to gain the advantage, but also bound to cause to the disadvantaged the pain of dissatisfaction with their lot which, in your Civilised Man's materially competitive society, often arises not so much from not having as from others having more.

"Thus if we were to accept his offer and come to live in London not only would we lose the peace and happiness which we now enjoy, but we would cause pain to many of his compatriots, when they see us, whom they consider uncivilised and therefore less deserving, wallow in wealth while they grovel in poverty. It would not be a gain to anyone but a loss to all concerned.

"No, we don't want to live in a society with social relationships which we consider to be an incarnation of human selfishness, equealled only by the selfishness of animals.

"This is all I have to say. Not that we do not appreciate his generous offer, but in refusing it, it is important to let him fully understand the reason why."

"I agree with everything Kotokro's father has said," said Mama Alimana when her husband had finished. "Besides, how can we leave the land and people we know and trust to live among strangers in a strange country? We would feel like trees transplanted from a fertile valley to the top of a clean but barren crag. We would hardly thrive or find joy in our new abode, particularly when we would be among people who do not take interest in one another's welfare except for a fee."

"I am so glad, Papa and Mamma," Kotokro joined in. "I was afraid that you would agree to go to the white man's country, taking me with you. Then I would not have the opportunity of roaming through the forest gathering fruits or swinging on a rope from the branch of a tree or playing hide-and-seek with my companions or doing any of those things that I love to do so much. No, we do not want Dr. Wiseman's mansion and fleet of cars and domestic servants and three million Pounds a year. If he has really provided all these things for me and my parents we thank him but cannot accept them as my father has said. Let him give them all to Mrs. Casely with my love and compliments."

"Well said, my son." his parents and Chief Brongo said simultaneously.

"And tell the Doctor we send him our highest regards and wish him such peace and contentment as will match our own to attain which he should not rely on his wealth alone but reflect deeply on all I have said, and also take good care not only of his body but also of his mind." added Papa Asuboni.

"Take good care of his mind?" asked Jimfa, perplexed. "How can one take good care of one's own mind?"

"In the same way as one can take good care of one's own body, by refraining from those things that harm it and doing those things that improve it," replied Papa Asuboni. "The things that harm the mind are anger, rancour, envy, jealousy, hatred, ill-will, worry, anxiety and all other thoughts and feelings that agitate it. And the things that improve it are charity, good-will, kindness, altruism, patience, forbearance, sympathy, compassion, hope, trust, fortitude and all other thoughts and feelings that calm it."

"Oh, I see" replied Jimfa. "I shall remember these for my own education too."

"You are welcome," replied Papa Asuboni.

CHAPTER TWENTY-FIVE
EPILOGUE

Both Dr. Wiseman und his wife, as well as Mrs. Casely, had been eagerly looking forward to hearing from Kotokro and his parents. They had been imagining the delight with which the boy and his parents would receive the wonderful offer contained in the Doctor's letter.

"I am sure when it reaches them they will run wild with joy," pronounced Mrs. Casely who was so happy for the boy.

"There will be a big celebration," agreed Mrs. Wiseman.

Dr. Wiseman, however, who now knew the boy better, was not quite so sure of that. The boy and his parents would undoubtedly be happy, but not to the extent of running wild with joy or making a big celebration. He knew that to them money, even if in millions, meant very little. Nevertheless he too was certain that they would gladly accept his offer. Even if they did not like the idea of coming to stay in Britain the boy would request him to transfer to him all or part of the amount he had offered to settle on him annually, so that they could live more comfortably in their own country.

Such then had been the expectation of Dr. Wiseman when Julius the janitor brought a letter addressed to him as he sat glancing through the day's newspapers one morning after breakfast, exactly six weeks after he had posted the letter to Kotokro in care of Jimfa. The Doctor looked at the back of the envelope before opening it. The postage stamp showed that it came from Blaft in Gamberia. The handwriting was not that of His Excellency Mr. Blickhead, the British High Commissioner, which he knew well from the correspondence he had with him since his arrival in London.

He tore the envelope open. Before reading it he glanced at the signature at the bottom. It came from Jimfa. It ran:

"Dear Dr. Wiseman,

This is to inform you that I took your letter to Kantoma and read it to Kotokro and his parents.

Before replying they asked me many questions about the life and climate in Britain, to which I answered to the best of my knowledge. Then Kotokro's father treated me to a long philosophical lecture on the causes of human unhappiness, which I daresay some people might find rather boring. But since he charged me to convey it to you, I shall briefly do so for what it is worth. He said the ultimate aim of every human being is to be happy. But there are three compulsive Desires implanted in the human mind which are the sources of human unhappiness. These are the Desire for Survival, the Desire for Sex and the Desire for Significance. It is in seeking to fulfil these Desires that we suffer pain or cause pain to others.

"The Desire for Survival drives us to seek food and protection for our bodies; the Desire for Sex compels us to go after our sexual opposites; and the Desire for Significance urges us to try to equal or even surpass our neighbour.

"The Desire for Significance (that is, for honour, for glory, for worship) is the strongest of all our three Desires and the chief cause of unhappiness. It is stronger in the Civilised Man who, because of his greater material achievements, has forgotten who and what he is, and therefore imagines that the greater his achievements the happier he will be, thus chasing a mirage in his quest for happiness.

"As for him and his people, they know who and what they are and therefore live their lives in the light of their knowledge; which is that it is only the absence of these three Desires, or at least their diminished intensity, that can bring some degree of happiness. Fortunately, like little children or old men and women of every race, their Desires are not strong and can, therefore, be easily satisfied. They are therefore already happy as they are, and cannot be happier with any amount of earthly advantage.

Indeed, if they were to accept your offer and come to live in London they would lose the peace and happiness which they now enjoy, and would also cause pain to many of your compatriots who, seeing them wallowing in wealth while they themselves lived in poverty, would be dissatisfied with their lot. They therefore thank you for your kind offer but cannot accept it.

"Kotokro's mother, Mama Alimana, endorsed all he had said and added that if they came to live in London they would feel like trees uprooted from a fertile valley and re-planted on a clean but barren crag. They could not thrive in their new abode.

"Master Kotokro agreed with both his father and mother and clinched their replies by saying that he thanked you, as his father had already said, but that if you had truly provided all those things for him and his parents, then he would rather like you to give all to Mrs. Casely with his love and compliments.

"Kotokro's father's final words were that they sent you their highest regards and wished you such peace and contentment as would match their own, which you can attain not by relying on your wealth alone, but by reflecting deeply on what he has said and by taking good care not only of your body but also of your mind."

At first Dr. Wiseman found the reply most astonishing. But when he had reflected upon it, it occurred to him that it was perfectly in consonance with the philosophy and out look of the boy and his parents and of all blacks still uncorrupted by the white man's civilisation.

He summoned his wife and Mrs. Casely and read the letter to them. Mrs. Casely's joy knew no bounds. She rose from her seat with the agility of a school girl and danced with joy.

"Oh, how I love the boy!" she cried again and again. "He is a very intelligent boy, as I have always thought; and so are his parents. I thank him immensely. I do not care much about his father's philosophy. I shall be happy with the mansion and three million Pounds a year. May God bless them all."

Mrs. Wiseman was equally pleased. She thought that Mrs.Casely deserved something too in addition to her handsome salary, if only for her long and devoted services and the fact that she proved herself to be such a friend in need when she fell into penury after her husband was presumed dead.

"Please call me Julius," said Dr. Wiseman to Mrs. Casely after her excitement had subsided. "I want to see him."

Mrs. Casely went at once to call Julius, the janitor, imagining that the Doctor was going to offer him a gift of money too. It was not long before Julius stood before him, wondering what the Doctor wanted to see him about.

"If someone offered you the gift of a mansion, a fleet of cars and a pension of three millions pounds a year what would you do?" asked the Doctor.

"I would be so happy that I would hardly know what to do," Julius replied at once.

"It means you would accept?"

"Yes, of course; who wouldn't?" replied Julius, greatly puzzled, for he did not know what the question was leading up to. "Why do you ask ?"

"I ask because that is precisely the offer I made to the boy with whom I lived in the jungle for three years after we suffered a plane crash, and he has refused it."

"Good Lord !" exclaimed Julius "what sort of boy is he?"

"He is an African boy, from the Republic of Gamberia. His refusal was endorsed by his parents whom I had also invited to come with him."

"Are they Negroes?" asked Julius.

"They are."

"Ah, I am not surprised then. Those niggers have no intelligence at all. Why, if I were offered even a tenth of that yearly pension, not only would I accept it with deep gratitude, but I would also be one of the happiest men on earth."

"Are you sure of that?" asked Dr. Wiseman.

"Very very sure."

"Even if a condition was attached?"

"Even if a condition was attached; unless the condition was such as would be physically impossible for me to perform."

"Well, here is a cheque for three million Pounds for you then," said Dr. Wiseman, stretching to him a cheque for the amount which he had already signed.

Julius' joy knew no bounds.

"Oh, thank you, thank you ever so much!" he said again and again. May God bless you. You have today made me the happiest man on earth."

"I shall make you happier still by offering to double your salary," said Dr. Wiseman. "As from today your salary, as a janitor, will be sixty instead of thirty Pounds a month."

Julius' face fell at once. All signs of joy vanished from his countenance, and he began to look like a man faced with a difficult choice.

"Why, are you not happy with my offer?" asked Dr. Wiseman, observing him.

"No, Doctor," he replied morosely. "I cannot be a millionaire and a janitor at the same time. If I did, all my neighbours would laugh at me, saying that I am either so miserly or so daft that even when I could live like a king I continue to do the job fit for a beggar."

Dr. Wiseman shook his head and laughed.

THE END